LUANSHYA
MUSINGS

A boyish peek at an earth traveller's Soul in full flight

Allan Taylor

ISBN: 1523280182
ISBN 13: 9781523280186

A boyish peek at an earth traveller's Soul in full flight

A timeless story that hovers between how it should have, would have, and could have been.
An imponderable story: How it ended, if it at all did, is of no importance in how everyone saw it in the 'Now' moment of their timeless sight.
It was a Soul in full flight, for everyone to observe as the all-encompassing testimony of their own Soul purpose.

CONTENTS

PREFACE

Writing a story about your childhood is a complex balance of the real, the non-real and the surreal: It is where memory and imagination both vie for an elevated place in the pages of the book.

The musings of a young boy, which is what my writing could be described as being, is exactly that: realistically unreal. Somewhat odd you might say. You could also say that life can be odd: It is not a linear trajectory of logical events that can be read like a book – especially not in Africa.

Luanshya is an unfamiliar African name to most, and the art of musing has, on the whole, been replaced with computer games and social media.

While this is a somewhat convoluted story of my colonial African past, which I have gently sutured with the fine catgut of a personal philosophy, it is your story too. None of us are really unique. Every one of us carries a bit of the other in a gestalt that philosophers call mankind.

We have all, at one time or another, thrown an exasperated backward glance at our life to question its recorded moments. In my case, life, which I pretentiously call mine, seems to have recklessly danced this way and that. When I was a child, it seemed I was teetering on the brink of an ever-changing rhythm whose cadence was one moment invitingly familiar, and the next, almost perverse in its personal discordance. It was as if there was a whirligig within the conscious awareness of a small white boy in Africa that defied reason. I swayed to the hearty beat of a Congolese rhumba, all the while fearfully captivated by a witchdoctor's shuffle. On reflection, in spite of its eclectic tendencies, there does seem, however, to have been a common decency of purpose in my life.

Luanshya Musings: I like the verb 'muse.' Dictionary definitions hint at it having a meaning of both befuddled and meditative thinking. The word is derived from Greek mythology. The Muses were the nine divine daughters of Zeus, King of the Gods, and Mnemosyne, the goddess of memory. The Muses spent their Halcyon days whimsically weaving the threads of their fine arts through the lives of men in expressions of tragedy, sadness, joy, beauty and love.

Outside the boundaries of Greek mythology, musings could be seen as wistful searches for the half-forgotten source of our longings. As a small boy, I had deep longings for things that were unknown and yet were conversant parts of my being. These longings were effused with strong feelings of commonality, a hidden familiarity that captivated me into wanting to know more. Of what, I didn't know.

Musings stir the senses: They add extra 'out of the material moment' value to our conscious awareness as they gently drift in and out of the darkness of our psyche: They are not sugary sweet, nor are they bitter; otherwise they would be wants and dis-wants. Musings leave a faint after-taste of eternal remembrance that awakens the taste buds of our senses into curious inquiry. I have often wondered if musings are not self-fulfilling doodlings of the Soul.

My musings were not whimsical thought patterns. They had the energy of opportunist cockroaches on kitchen surfaces in the dark; scurrying from here to there, they picked up tasty societal and cultural titbits as I searched for answers to my veiled longings.

Because I have the tendency not to want to distinguish between the philosophical, sensual and the spiritual, it is unavoidable that personal philosophies surface within my story: It also seems that emotions and their sensual and supernatural origins are easier for me to recall than the salient facts of my past. In writing this story, my memories hardly seemed to settle before drifting off again, leaving a smudge of philosophical mention between the lines as proof of their brief visit. They did, however, leave a common clue; they were always drawn to the familiar unknown: an enigmatic force which pulled at my awareness of *things*.

I am also fascinated by the words ether and aether, which are often interchanged in meaning. Ether was once thought to be an inert substance that filled all space and offered no resistance to matter or energy. Whereas Aether was an ancient Greek name for the pure air of heaven, which became synonymous with the sky, the light of day and divine light.

I use the word aether to denote a meaningful world that sits in-between the mystical and the real, the body and the Soul.

Surround time – where the then time is the now time

In order to write this book I am attempting to create an open-ended piece of prose about the past. In doing so, I hope to shed some light on my inner clearing, which has endured the encroachments of time. To do this I have decided to intuitively look at things from afresh – from the 'Now' perspective of their current existence.

The 'Now' is a vibrant state of being. It is an incredible condensation of feeling, thinking, and doing right at this precise moment in time; it is an accumulation of everything that has ever happened to me; it is an intensely intricate energy pattern that I find myself in; it is my potential to meet my next experiential moment in full preparedness; it tells me that it is the 'everything' that I have, and that the more consciously aware I am of it, the more successful I will be. The thought of its unique role in my life makes my heart miss a beat. I am writing in the now.

I have taken the past, and cast it into the present moment of my current musings, which I like to call the present moment – the 'Now.' I have turned 'now' from being an adverb into a proper noun. For me the 'Now' has a note of energetic urgency and importance that the word the 'present' doesn't have. The present sounds like a casually unsolicited gift that is thrust into my lap whether I care for it or not. Whereas the 'Now' has so much more charisma. That is why I have chosen it to be a *surround time* reality show host; the 'Now' will artfully introduce a liberated past to a virginal present moment – all in the anticipation of an excitingly unknown outcome that is about to crystallise out of the folds of present moment spontaneity. I am bringing my past and present together to view them within a three hundred and sixty degree panorama where they have equal temporal importance in what I call *surround time*. *Surround time* is my vaudeville theatre where everything is viewed with spatial equanimity. Where all things of the past appear as fresh and free as the present when beheld outside of history's linear-thinking line of fire. There is no beginning and no end; things turn a full circle of equal importance in an uncanny synchronised manner.

Even though it was my past that laid the building blocks for my present, it is the present that wants to tell the past's story. I wish to stop any such notions of superiority. Both are of equal importance. I am not reviewing the shrapnel of my time gone by as a chronological documentary. Instead I am subjecting myself to raw imagery from all sides of the clearing; from the past, the present and the in-between. In *surround time,* I am looking at the freshly scripted events of a combined 'now' and 'then' reality show. A well-worn past, my child's 'then', is being invited along to take part in a brand new production. Any fame it is likely to receive will be dished out along with and because of its current co-star, the present moment. I don't know what is going to happen; that is the great attraction of a reality show. Together my past and present make up the gestalt, the total picture that is unfolding on the set in front of me. I am excited. Past events of the 'then' are likely to be seen in the fresh new light of the 'Now'.

My writing is living in a timeless world where my past child's events are free to spill their truth. Without the measure of time and consequence, it is my candid opinion that the 'on the ground' shenanigans of a white boy in Africa will point to more than straightforward adventure.

They say that the only creative moment of our lives is in the Now. The Now is a timeless place – it is as yet unscripted in time. It is where magic and miracles have power over, and above, measured real time. Sometimes we mistakenly call our timeline our life. This is not true. Life is our awareness. Time is only one facet of our awareness; and the miracles that we are searching for emanate from the source of our awareness – not from time.

Using s*urround time*, I wish to create a sense of all-time 'Now', which will give my past a rebirth. I want to catch a glimpse of my all-time inner being. If you join me in this creative experiment, our boundaries will shift and the colours of our vistas might change in hue. I honestly believe, however, that like every after-the-storm sunsetted horizon, it won't be a chaotic affair; in fact it will be serenely beautiful. In writing this book, a strangely striking inner structure has unfolded within me – meant for me; and I am sure it will unfold within you – and equally meant for you. This is because I believe that magic is an osmosis of evolving perception between people. You are the reader and this is my story: we share a permeable membrane of common expression, the fruits of which will unfold in units of our own often-mused self-worth.

A book without a reader is not a book. It is a long line of words without the punctuation marks of shared emotional and spiritual self-worth. My worth, which is about to unfold within the magic of my written word, and be consecrated by your reading, is going to synergise into the miraculously simple story of a small child finding its way in the world.

Refractions of inner light – surround time

The African snake eagle drops its tortoise prey from a dizzy height to crack open its tough carapace and scatter its warm innards.

Surround time dashes my singular time-crafted past individuality, my life's assumed self-importance, be it of self-pity or pride, upon the rocks of a timeless eternity.

It ejects my inner being out of its time capsule of claustrophobic conformity and severs the linear regressions of the past: Its sole intention being to re-shuffle the cause and effect sequences of my life events.

It is an ambitious attempt to return to the nirvana of timelessness, where everything can be seen clearly: as one miraculous whole within the sanctity of timelessness.

In writing this book I acknowledge the importance of two particular writers in my life. Deepak Chopra and Eckhart Tolle, both of whom have introduced me to my own conscious awareness – a heightened awareness of my role as an integral part of the Universe. Thank you.

PROLOGUE

Luanshya

*She was a living swell of the universal aether that
had its own mind as it eddied through my boyhood.*

This is a book about my life as a young white child in a small
mining town called Luanshya. Luanshya was on the border of
then Northern Rhodesia and the Belgian Congo in Central
Africa: the time, the fifties and sixties; the period, 'the winds of
change' for colonial Africa.

They said Luanshya meant the Valley of Death in the local language. Before the European greed for minerals dealt
with the carriers of death, it was a swampy area infested with
malaria-bearing mosquitoes and tsetse flies with their quirky
fairytale gift of sleeping sickness. In time, civilisation replaced
these African 'nasties' with its own evil; DDT, which killed the
nasties and a lot more. A hunter at the turn of the century
had shot a fine specimen of a roan antelope. Its thick cyan-red

blood, deoxygenated from the chase, stained a green rock. This was the discovery of a seam of copper ore and the violent birth of the Roan Antelope Copper Mine; and the growth of the Luanshya bush clearing. The Europeans quickly got on with mining Copper for valuable ammunition to fight wars in far-flung lands, and what was a colonial administrative post, a *boma,* became a mining industry that lured my particular white tribe to Africa.

These were the energies that swirled around my conception as a white boy in Africa. They were not the cause; they merely provided the spiritual terra firma for my Soul's journey.

This is an intuitive piece of work that delves into how I saw and felt about things as a child. Why I did certain things that, to the curious onlooker, might have seemed odd. It is, however, very unlikely that my actions were noticed – nobody cared. If anyone did notice, it was their fleeting opinion that I was nothing more than 'that child', that spoilt and sulky only child.

I did: I noticed my oddness, and even as a small child, I cared about what I saw in myself. I always had a constant niggling awareness that my behaviour was unaccountable; never unacceptable, simply unaccountable. Different, because no one else felt what I felt, or did what I did – of that I was certain. Otherwise I would have been one of a large cast of performers, each conscious of one another following well-rehearsed lines; as if they were performing one of many minor roles in the Roan Antelope Dramatic Society's Christmas Pantomime. There were many times when I felt that I was the only Soul on stage – without an apparent supporting cast or legible script.

There were many incidences when life should have told me that I had no leading role to play, and yet as you will see from my story, there hardly ever was another player under the spotlight. I was singularly different. Being different was like owning an empty space, a kind of internal bush clearing that defined me, that separated me from the common forest pulse. Being a child in that lonely metaphorical bush clearing of obscurity and self-assumed alienation, I was forced to find my own drum to beat. In a strange way, I was happy – in the end familiarity breeds comfortability.

Children carry a lot of the adult burden: rules, restrictions, societal likes and dislikes; all shifting cargoes that tax their free-spirited little shoulders, and for which they are given little credit or respect. I know this: Acclaim was not given for my great mythological battles singlehandedly lost and won.

This book is as a result of a swelling urge within me to question the realness of that bush clearing within me, and my never-ending awareness of it throughout my childhood. It was my quirk, my tic; a pang of hidden knowingness; an urgency of spaced being within me.

Akin to this yoked feeling of inner searching, there was also a feeling that I was being watched: Watched by a silent observer who seemed to stand at the edge of my inner clearing. Too young to take spiritual solace from his presence, I valued his silent support in my emotionally messy world instead.

So Hum

My little boy status often showed cracks out of which leaked a protoplasm that exuded further realms of heightened self-awareness from somewhere within me. Layers of feeling upon feeling, pain pressing upon pain, love calling love. Every sensation of perception layered in thumping resonance with my cupidities. As a small boy, my emotional squalls needed a bit of explaining. I believe in our lifetime, our emotions change their attachment to things. I also believe that is a part of our spiritual growth. As we mature, we increase our conscious awareness of what is important in life, and in so doing, we refine our affinities. We move from expressions of our crudest wants towards an increasingly finer state of inner knowingness. It is as if, in a lifetime, we experience a full rainbow of coloured emotions; from heated reds through to heavenly blues and beyond. True emotions – love, joy and peace, are the refracted light of our Soul.

I have created a metaphor for this journey of our inner being: it is the life story of So Hum.

I start each section of this book with a short piece about So Hum. So Hum was the first African chameleon; he was also the first living creature to change the colour of his skin according to his emotions.

So Hum lived inside Ah Hum, the first man. He was borne out of perfect black nothingness with an ingrained intention of climbing up an imaginary rain tree of emotional colours inside of Ah Hum. So Hum had a premonition that, if he climbed high enough, he would eventually see the light. Curled up like a prehistoric clock spring in the dark, with nothing else to stimulate his senses, So Hum had a single reoccurring dream. His dream was about silica crystal rains which showered him with their bejewelled light as he climbed his rain tree. He couldn't see their magical colours – he could only feel them – so much so that the colour of his skin waxed in accordance with their imaginary hues. His fantastic dreams weighed more than his reality; they certainly had more feeling, colour and texture than the sombre terrain he stalked, if he stalked it at all.

In an uncanny way, So Hum's imaginary colour changes mirrored stirrings both within him and in Ah Hum, his host. They shared each other's inner and outer worlds. It seemed that Ah Hum and So Hum needed each other. Eventually Ah Hum would also see the light – the light of God consciousness.

1

I AM...
OUT OF NOTHING MORE THAN
THE FEAR OF MY SURVIVAL

GARNET RAIN

GARNET RAIN

In the beginning So Hum was a frightened crude creature. Curled in a jet black world, he could not see any part of himself and there was no one, nor anything to confirm his physical existence – he just was; and yet he always felt as if there was someone watching him. This state of intangible being evoked within him a soft feeling of dark curiosity which confirmed his being.

So Hum

*I*n those hungry survival days silica coloured dreams were scant as So Hum lay in a foetal coil of fear in the dank pelvic girdle of the first man.

The colours of the sparse early crystal showers at the base of his rain tree did not excite him much – they were of cold blacks, dry dark browns and stale blood reds – but they were still the comfort food that filled his belly, that gave him security, and a sense of being; not yet wellbeing – but being.

They mirrored the metamorphic stirrings from under the earth's crust: if nothing more they symbolised the reality of his creation and mortality. In spite of their dark hues they had a softly incandescent latent energy which he slowly slurped up like golden syrup. This glow might have been his imagination, but whatever it was, it gave him his life force.

In those days his heart was a lump of obsidian; glassy, black and brittle. It was not an evil heart – it had purity of intent – but at that time it was nothing more than a primeval expression of the mere organic existence of 'I am'.

He could have been an inanimate rock himself. Maybe his rain cloud dreams, his fears and his glow were the only things that made him different from the metaphorical cold rocks of his darkness.

Ah Hum's Roots – I am

On a particular African day of no real importance, heavenly aether condensed onto and around a speck of cosmic non-dust to create a matter hitherto unbeknown to this world; it was Ah Hum.

First Ah Hum's Soul, and then Ah Hum's mind and body, were born out of this coalescence of universal aether, which housed the all knowingness of everything that ever was. Birth, survival, procreation and death, all housed in a single speck in a coherent moment of time. Out of this conglomeration of aethereal existence walked the human footprint of his Soul. A Soul that birthed its own physical being out of a conscious awareness of its own reality.

In time, Ah Hum became a sensualist. He sought to find answers to the truth of things through the rubbings of nature against his senses. It was also his secret wish to find magical answers and witness miracles every now and then, even if it was only in simple musings. It was these penchants that inevitably caused him to rub up against his soul every now and then.

Inner magic on a material plane

On turning inwards and looking back on himself, Ah Hum, as an herbalist and geomancer, would have chosen the following stones and herbs to describe his needy reasons for being:

Smokey quartz and its herbal accomplice vetiver roots: *to symbolise his earthy connection to the nature of all things.*

Melanite garnet: *to signify his metamorphic origins.*

Black tourmaline and juniper berry oil: *to dispel any chance of evil and stagnation.*

Obsidian and the leaves of hyssop: *for support on his earth journey.*

A white boy in Africa: my Soul had already left its footprint on every stepping stone of my life's path.

> Dark forests and night robbers
> The footprint of my Soul
> Nubian Soul mates and cross-border traders
> Fire on a tinder-dry vlei
> My life is not straight, my time not linear
> Colonial quirks and African roots
> Deities of the dark forest
> Puku on the vlei
> Emotional rubbings of the Soul
> Signatures of colour and smell
> Red: Congolese coppered blood

Dark forests and night robbers

I didn't trust them. Tall Msasa trees limbered over the road to Luanshya. They slyly flaunted their lichened grey arms out of the verdigris gloom that made up the miombo forests of Central Africa. I knew their mottled grey sloughed boughs were an indecent camouflage for the witchdoctors hut – like a hammerkop's nest – a sinister gathering of taboos in a mix and match of sagging mildewed grass, tatters of red cloth, and shiny trappings from the 'this side of the clearing'.

Evening going-homes as a small and only child, on the back seat of a fifties British Austin car, were frightening.

The *n'anga's*, witchdoctor's, drums were calling, they were always calling … I couldn't hear them … they tapped a call of anxious urgency in my veins and on my mind. Happily relaxed after sundowners at the club, my parents couldn't hear them: they weren't meant to hear them…only I was. Hugging my knees on the back seat, I tackled them alone in the colour-faded dusk, which turned forest shadows into canyons of fear. My thin frame, in high-waisted grey shorts, black lace-up shoes and three quarter socks pulled up to my little knees was a poor defence against the overbearing spread of spiritual dark that crept up on me on those vulnerable journeys home. 'No we can't drive with the interior light on,' said my father with a slight beer slur of words. When we got home I went straight to bed. I had been fed soggy snacks of tinned Vienna sausages, disgusting capers and marmite on no-longer cracking crackers, all served up on a green and red cocktail onion stained floppy paper plate at the club. To limit my anxious awareness of the dark side I would ponder on things like: how did they grow onions the size of peas, and what did the factory that dyed onions and sausages in bright colours look like?

It was not only the dark beats of witchcraft, but also the terrifying hyena calls and crushing elephant feet that would disturb my sweet dreams later that night. Was it that the pulse in my ear was in resonance with these awful faraway African night sounds, or was it that I was pressing too hard against my pillow in fear? Comforting pillow warmth and cold-toes fear were often my odd couple bedfellows.

The night was like a close-fitting black velvet glove and I sweated in its tight fit. I was in awe of this primeval power that crept out of Africa and its people. These were my early experiences in conscious awareness. My small mind and body were being exposed to an overwhelming power that would change my subconscious thinking forever; internally, externally, permanently, and beyond: it was unavoidable. Soon in that little warm bed of mine, self-love and preservation would force me to turn my fear-fettered awe into a spirit-governed respect and a sensual addiction to the power of the earth and its people wherever, and whoever, they may be: an addiction from which I would never escape, and never want to.

After a Sunday outing at the local boating and picnic spot, Makoma Dam, and exposure to a high sun that ripped the energy out of my child spirit, we were back in our suburban English car heading home again in the dark. I was fixated with the way the car's wily headlights pierced the roadside night, to transform sinister demons back into trees, road signs and posts. They also, however, pointed out the tall elephant grass that leaned over to gobble up the dirt road and its contents – our Austin, my parents and me. Their Rasta heads were heavy from evening rain; but our valiant British car bashed through them all as they spat venom on its windscreen. I huddled in the tea-stained tartan picnic blanket in fear. 'Please don't let the car breakdown, please don't stop Dad – oh please!'

We reached the English safe haven – Sam's pie shop in the town. Sam had waxy pale skin with the texture of suet, and a mole on his chin – as all English pie men on the way to the Fayre do. I restored my civilized values with flaky-pastry crumbs everywhere, and gravy dripping down my arms and staining my pants – 'piping hot!' my North of England father would remind me, as I puffed steam out of the gravy-congealed crust.

That night, soft rain muffled the different sounds that I might've, should've heard – but didn't. My doting mother woke me with a gasp. Her gentleness punctured my sleep bubble and dragged me into her anguish. Look there! Fine floral print curtains were ripped back from a defenceless window. The darkness, which was normally veiled with the ochre brown of a mosquito screen, was not as it should have been that night– a black scar gutted its centre and muddy footprints circled my bed. An intruder had been and gone!

They said that African thieves were naked so that they wouldn't be seen on a moonless night; that they shaved their body and covered it with civet fat to slip back into the dark if grabbed; that they had a scrap of red cloth or the tufts of a genet's tail somewhere on their intangible body as a talisman of protection; that they used hypnotic herbs to alloy their vile being to the recumbent victim in a gag of fear.

Why had this man gone through all of this for little me? As to whether this night robber had taken something precious was of no importance to me; it was how his presence of purpose weighed on my awareness that changed me. At worst, he could have taken my Soul, but he didn't; instead, he gave me oneness with the dark side of Africa. It was as if I had lost my virginal naivety. I no longer had reason to feel fear from the outside unknown.

That night, in a rare act of spiritual catharsis, my psyche was pierced and the dark fear of my child's mind was altered forever. Until that night, my fear was a shadow ever lurking in the background of my being. The night robber, as he hovered over my sleeping body, took nothing. Instead he graced my presence with a gift of 'knowingness'. He was the personification of the very fear I was shying away from in the recesses of my mind. Without any preconditions, at spirit level, he formally introduced himself; he was fear and my repugnance fell away. His strange gift was now inside me like a lode stone of black haematite; it pointed to both the creative and positive aspects of owning one's fear. I was compelled to accept its black light, and I felt very child-happy that it had all happened to me.

The 'this side' of the clearing civilised white policeman and his 'other side' of the clearing black cohort, with borrowed civilisation on his sleeve, didn't seem to be interested in my story. My childish facts were contrary to their trained way of logical thought about a crime. In their linear-thinking minds I must have lost something – but the fact that they were ignoring, was that I had gained something important. He didn't steal my fishing rod, nor did he steal my breath – in fact he strengthened it. I wanted to tell them the whole truth, and nothing but the truth, but they weren't listening, nor were my parents. I kept it to myself until later on in my youth, when I took it to my anthill on the Luanshya vlei for dissection. My anthill, a small hillock, was to become the testing grounds of my self-awareness. A vlei is a Southern African grassy, usually treeless, wet land that leads down to a river or a seep. Vleis were to become endearments to my Soul.

If then was now, and now was then, I might have wanted to tell them that this robber was not a thief; that he was simply obeying a particular set of footprints that were leading him back to the dark side of the clearing, from where he had first emerged. His crime was *un crime passionnel*. He had innocently crossed over to the civilised 'this side' of the Luanshya clearing to find work, but his strong tribal values wouldn't relinquish their hold on his Soul: He would never make a good domestic worker, nor a hardworking rock breaker, and the claustrophobic white shadow of Luanshya was making it hard for him to breath. I would surmise that a witchdoctor had put him up to this dead of night deed to break the chains of the white man's civilised juju, to bring him back to the 'safety' of the dark side of the clearing.

Through my child's emotional eyes I understood this earth being's dilemma – tow the colonial white line or rebel – I had a similar problem. I had nothing more to say. After the police had departed with their clipboards and forms in triplicate, and the door to my bedroom was safely locked, I was tucked up between my parents in their bed for the rest of the night. I was, however, unable to fall asleep. I couldn't stop thinking about him; I wished I could have met him in person. I regretted not still being in my room with a gashed gauze window that was now open to the African night with its accompanying bombardments of flying ants and beetles. There was an off chance – a real chance, that he might have come back to talk to me that night. I really wanted to hear his story, probably in the language of the Soul. The next morning, dozy-headed and pale, I got dressed in my Luanshya Primary School khaki uniform in a lifeless room with nothing to show of the spiritual awakening of the night gone by – except for a crunchy litter of suicidal beetle bodies. It crossed my mind that the room would have felt different if he had come back to talk to me about *things*. 'Stop dawdling,' my mother shouted in a kind way, and packed me off to school with soon-to-be-warm marmite sandwiches, Ribena black current juice, and an already brown banana.

I trotted off, but my truant Soul didn't go to school that day; it wasn't sick, it just mooched around my bedroom all day. Perhaps it was loathe to let go of an event of such intertwined and universal proportions.

The footprint of my Soul

From when I was in a carrycot in my parents Morris Minor station wagon, to my thirteenth birthday at Makoma Dam, into adolescence and on to boarding school, something impressed its prior-to print upon me. A déjà vu print indelibly tattooed into the emotional skin of my body. It was a hankering for something that was unknown and yet familiar. Its pull on my small persona was as delicate and yet as empirically important to my world, as the fleeting shadow of a noon cloud on open ground. It was as if it was the creator of my being. It was the 'I am' of who I was.

I was oddly different, and it seemed that neither I, nor my parents, could do anything about it. I was a bush loving cloud-chaser attracted to things different. I chased mythological shadows across an African vlei, half-knowing that their world of shapes and colours meant something important to me.

My allurement was like a footprint on my being to which I was seemingly entrained to follow with a passion that rippled across my persona; that coaxed and cajoled the cognitive me; that prodded and stroked the physical me as it introduced me to its penchants – I couldn't help myself.

My passions were strangers to me but their familiar design drummed a realistic beat on my child's mind. I was uncontrollably spirit-driven: obstinately single-minded, some grown-ups would have said.

This is a story of my affinities: the penchants of my Soul that played with my senses; that soaked the new bones of my being in a warm broth of familiarity: strange footprints in the sands of my conscious awareness.

Nothing could have been more familiar and yet unfamiliar to me than the foetal 'I am' that pushed and kicked within me.

Nubian Soul mates and Congolese cross-border traders
Our house, owned by the mining company, was a basic square of rough fired brick. It had a porched veranda with a waist high

wall and one long copper gauzed window. Except for the veranda windows which didn't have glass, the windows were small, and let in very little light. The kitchen, bathroom, small lounge and two bedrooms made up the other sides, which left an awkward windowless space in the middle of our house for a dining room. God how I hated that dark room which was devoid of natural light. To my distaste, it was used day in, day out. We ate all our meals in the oppressive darkness of that room, the dim 60 watt light bulb hanging by a cable with an enamelled metal conical shade, always switched on. Christmas feasts, birthday dinners, and Sunday lunches were all seasoned with dank condiments that cloyed the taste buds of my Soul. Spring onions gave me an unpleasant peppery sharp sensation in my adenoids, the evocation of which even today hurls me back to that room. It was very colonial to have a beer glass of water with celery sticks and spring onions on the table, and next to it, a small saucer of salt in which you dipped your wet *crudités*. I dislike spring onions, and celery should be confined to minestrone soup – all because of that horrible room.

I could blame some of my peevish frustrations on the fact that I was literally force-fed in that dark soulless room that hosted all our important events, turning them into ugly non-events. I hated that room for its depressing presence in my life. I refused to cross its space during daytime thunderstorms, the bruised light of which turned the room into an ulcerous void. I always pondered as to why electric light bulbs seemed so ineffective in the daytime darkness of storms. I would go out the back door, and run around to the front door, risking a tropical pelting of leaded raindrops, rather than run the gauntlet of that room's torment.

In that airless stifling room there was an unused fireplace, the folly of a colonial builder with misguided British values.

It was guarded by two black sentinels: stone hard, highly polished ebony head carvings. My father had bought them from Congolese street peddlers before my mother's arrival from England in 1947. They had considerable family significance as they were the first adornments to my parents' initially Spartan life in Africa. The carvings had a Nubian beauty to them, so different to the grimaced carvings that street peddlers usually touted on the streets. They were a regal male and female pair, both wearing a skullcap over their aesthetically pleasing Egyptian Pharaoh heads. They had travelled the paths of Africa to stand witness to our plain English culinary gatherings; cold to touch, never seeing the light of day, exiled from the ethnic throb of the wood chopper's forest and the village carver who birthed them. There they were, watching me as I ate my every breakfast, Sunday lunch roast, or Saturday night fish and chips – all in the dark breathless room that enveloped my being with its malignancy. There they stood – the positive terminals of my spiritual battery in a room of negativity, I was naturally drawn to them: I couldn't help it.

I took great comfort in their purity of presence because they were of the fearful dark, and yet they were hauntingly beautiful. They had the power to point to the flip side of the dark and in an uncanny way, their African wisdom comforted me. It was good to have friends on the other side – I touched them a lot.

We didn't have fences or gates, so Congolese curio sellers would appear at the back door – what a sight: indigo skins, keloid tribal face scars, strong teeth, salivated lips with mottled pink inners and enflamed tongues. The veins on their temples followed a strong beat, which I attributed to their gruelling nomadic life style. Most white madams and their children, *muzungu picanins*, were frightened of them, whereas I was enchanted by them. Perhaps my night robber had already introduced me to them with his secret handshake of fear. I was very lucky to know living nomads; they were so much more real than the Mongolian ones we read about in class. These lean buccaneers of the Congo cross-border trade were hardy. They walked across borders, avoiding both their own gendarmerie and our English-styled coppers – so as to charm us with a smattering of Belgian French *joie de vivre* and expert bargaining powers. Every now and then, they took a fancy to the odd item off the washing line should the white madam not be at home, and if the gardener was smoking a self-rolled *fodja,* tobacco, sometimes *mbanje,* marijuana, cigarette behind the servant's quarters. For me they were the ultimate in mystery and magic – but they weren't! They were hardened traders, rogues selling anything from kitsch Belgian rugs and wall hangings – to beaten copper pictures of long limbed Rwandan dancers, Sudanese leather poufs that reeked of tannin, and kiwi shoe-polished wood carvings. Casting reality aside, these ebony apparitions surely came from the dark side of Africa, the source of black magic. I had utmost respect for them.

The Congo and its un-British-tamed people became an uncomfortable fascination for me, like an itch under my skin that I desperately wanted to scratch; that was blissfully exciting when I did scratch; that consequently erupted into unrewarded longings. It took many years to realise that there was no effective balm to soothe this African malady because it was a Soul-driven affinity.

These traders were great showmen. They always had a final flourish, a *pièce de résistance* that came out last from their bottomless Mary Poppins bag. With a tongue rolling *eh voilà*, malachite stone eggs were cajoled out of their creased Belgian newspaper wrappings with a fine display of facial and vocal drama; these men had surprisingly shrill voices that hooked on to your attention. Malachite is a beautiful green mineral form of copper found in huge deposits of verdigris layered rock in the Katanga province of the Congo. To me, these semiprecious stone eggs were the crystal ball of every African sorcerer. You could see countless worlds in their swirls of green: from the serene undulations of far-off fresh-rained horizons to billowing clouds of broccoli-shaped storms, all in one pleasing-to-hold egg shape. They were warmer to the touch than my Nubians.

I would keep these itinerant treasure-bearing magi squatting on the *stoep*, step in Afrikaans, to our kitchen door for as long as my bum could take the burning heat of the concrete steps. In reality it was only until they could see that Madam had no intention of buying, or that the garden boy, as native gardeners were called then, had chased them away with a bantu clicking of the tongue, and some choice Chilapalapa. '*Voetsak, ena lo Sikelem – ena lo Naya*', roughly translated: 'Get lost, you rotter, you're trouble.'

Chilapalapa was the pidgin *lingua franca* of the mines in South Africa, the Rhodesias, and the Congo, it was a mix of Zulu, Bantu, Afrikaans and English. It was a necessary language in an industry that employed so many different groups of people.

These earthy traders who appeared at our back door silently spoke to me of another world beyond my childhood limitations. The English colonials always spoke cautiously of the Congo as if it were a treacherous Eldorado, rich in minerals, but wild and untamed: a place of tropical jungles, gorillas, pygmies, okapis and fearful tribes of cannibals. I interpreted their stories of the Congo into Africa's Wild West. Oh I wanted to see it so much. It seemed so much more exciting than the tepid English colonial duck pond on which I felt I was adrift. I would tune our wooden Pye Radiogram into the BBC French service and imagine French and Belgian colonials joining me as we listened to the world news *en français*, I from Jemimah Puddle Duck Lane Luanshya not understanding a single word, and they from Leopoldville, on the steamy banks of the mighty Congo River, offering guttural agreement. I made an entry in the notebook of my heart – learn French, live in the Congo – and in linear time I did! Or did I already know that I would?! A pre-emption of the footprint of my Soul perhaps.

Fire on a tinder-dry vlei

Another fire on the vlei; I see it all before me. October and November are the bushfire months. Six months without rain has turned the bush of the vlei into a *prêt-à-porter* bonfire heap which wearily whispers to the hot wind to speed up the arrival of the wild fires. Only then will the exhausted vegetation be absolved from further responsibility: free to muse over their rebirth at the first drop of November rain, leaving their ashen roots to plan the mortal details of their rebirth.

Our street is one of the last streets of the town before the irrigated-green golf course; before the October-brown bush; before the parched vlei, my vlei and my anthill. I can see bushfires brewing from our veranda. Their billows of black-ash-speckled smoke blot out the sun, giving a copper hue to the choked-up daylight. Like the hungry, insectivorous birds that stalk burnt-out vleis, I too am there for the picking. It is an unrivalled experience of furious destruction that sends all forms of life into a whizzing whirlybird of fleeing hysteria. Our macabre intent is clear, as is our planned journey towards, and not away from the holocaust; as is our methodic gate on arrival: ovarian insect-eaters and I are captivated by bushfires.

The forceful pace of the bushfire as it marches to a warring drum through my vlei drags my prickled senses with it as it sucks past me on my perch on the tree line at the edge of the vlei. Seed heads pop, grass stalks crack, and pods and fruits scream their regretful hiss of death – their seed being deprived of the chance to procreate. Locusts under enemy fire make hurried attempts to regroup into airborne squadrons of retreat. Weaver birds shriek obscenities as flames wrap their fingers around nests. Drongos swoop through rings of fire to spear half-toasted insects in flight. I am sure I can also hear the hisses and pops of snakes and cane rats.

As the blast furnace of heat broadsides the edge of the vlei, the Msasa trees behind me panic, recoil and tremble. My breath is taken away from me with no replacement offered – there is no air in the deathly vacuum that shadows a firestorm. Without breath comes fear and failure as the promise of death spreads its wings. The soft skin of my eyelids feels the abrasive heat and recoils foolishly to expose my eyeballs to a maelstrom of red-hot needles that fill the air in an attempt to set fire to the forest floor behind me. It is a voracious burning of brittle brown; a melting of red; a rude brashness of orange; and a viciously insensitive yellow – all incendiary colours that shoot out of a devil's rainbow that gallops across the vlei. An inferno cloaked in a villain's cape of choking billows of black and grey. The smoke is spiked with ashen copies of long, black grass leaves that are hurled up high in heat thermals. The cracking, spitting roar of it all pounds against my eardrums, sending my logic backtracking into the forgotten chambers and tunnels of my head. My diaphragm struggles to evoke exhalation and my inhalation is fated. In my heart, I die a thousand incinerator deaths with the fauna and flora on fearful days like this.

As if the spectacle of an October bushfire isn't enough; as if by magic, and likely because of short breath, the cataclysmic scene before me starts to shimmer and fade into an illusion: as if the brown fullness and the furnace red of the vlei had never existed. Edges soften, colours collapse, details are smudged over with soot, and my charred emotions grapple with what is left. The final cinder curtain has dropped. Metallic heat waves and silver smoke create the final screen, which does little to cover up the execution. Before I know it, the fire has goose stepped down the Luanshya valley, leaping from one innocent tinder bush to the next, eager to annex the next person's vlei, and the next, until it is a distant line of fire glowing in the night. Secretly I know that there is no overlord of the next vlei, nor the next – no one to see what I have just seen. No one else has exposed their being to such an omnipotent fiery onslaught with the spiritual grace and sensual knowingness that is thrown upon me by the Gods. I have witnessed a fire's brief ownership of an African vlei.

A spiritual voice whispers hoarse words into my being: 'it was meant to be.' I am so proud that Africa has picked me to represent my tribe at such an important event. There are tears in my eyes; it is the smoke isn't it?

I am emotionally exhausted. My skin feels too tight. A soft ache drips between my sinews, into my muscles, over my joints and down to my feet. I realise that my singed blood has retreated. Every thread of protein in my body has been drawn to snapping tautness; every nerve ending has had its synaptic neck broken in leaping resonance with the energetic spectacle before me. It is now over. I am humbled, lost for personal expression. I am part of the audible sigh of completion that rises out of the burnt ground of the vlei. A rustled relief from Msasa trees on a tree line that has escaped the fire, soothes my senses in a strangely comforting way.

Black ash, bruised light, broken sound in a shocked stillness – was there anything good left behind? Yes: black is the charcoaled colour of purification. There is a surreal snowstorm of twirling black leaf forms returning to the vlei: an uncanny backdrop for the cattle egrets, undertakers dressed in white, with bowed heads and feathered hands clasped behind their backs. They stoically perform high-stepped funeral marches across the carpets of ash, collecting all the dead bodies: crisp grasshoppers, heat-bloated ticks, and toasted centipedes. They leave the shrivelled remains of baby toads, field mice and weaver chicks for the ever-watchful hawks that hover above this *al fresco* open grill. Is that the marabou stork, the ignominious king of carrion? With his naked head, puce air sac, cracked and peeling beak, and long ashen legs, he looks as if he has been scorched himself; but it is his funeral finery. He is in fine fettle to carry away the larger mammalian, and reptilian carcasses. If they aren't quite dead, they soon will be – a sharp beak protrudes from below his rapacious eyes.

The earth of the vlei has what looks like a three day stubble of elephant grass stumps, too robust to have been flattened by the fire's scythe. Pointed and sharp, they mimic clumps of porcupine quills in their black and tan erectness. I am gingerly weaving my way around them, as if they will shoot their spines out at me. At bath time, Dettol time, it will look as if they had. A post-bushfire inspection is going to take the best part of today. I have learnt to bring marmite sandwiches, and a bottle of Ribena black currant juice.

I am too overawed to be sad: I tramp the vlei with curiosity. The smell is dark in colour, metallic in taste, and the sight is acridly organic, not unlike the marmite smeared on warm sandwiches. There is a lingering heat on exposed rocks, small termite mounds, discarded bits of metal refuse, and the odd broken Coca-Cola bottle. Glowing embers peer out from under fallen branches like crocodile eyes under the scrutiny of a night hunter's torch. Mother Nature is still popping and hissing in clucks and sighs of dismayed cynicism: 'Yes I knew this was going to happen. I told you so. The sun was far too hot for a normal September, then that wind blew up; then there were people, then suddenly there was fire … and very soon it was out of control … and the rest speaks for itself …. Oh well, let's pray for an early rain to start the new season.' I worry that she thinks I am the arsonist. I wonder how bushfires start when there are no humans to be seen.

Stripped of her thick vegetative mane, my glorious vlei is stark naked. I am captivated by her sudden vulnerability, which she expresses so willingly, and in such an honest way – she really is powerful in her humility. I pore over her earthen body and explore her every blemish: mounds, gullies and ridges – everything is exposed for my eyes only. Bush paths that were previously hidden by the long grass, snake across her undulations. Free of foliage, they are like snail traces across her black African flesh. The Luanshya River, now visible in its length down her belly, accentuates her torso with a gentle bend here, and a wide curve there. Her soil is dark, moist and rich, and bamboo reed beds grow prudently out of her riverine folds. Up from her withers, her soil is cracked and pockmarked with the imprints of Bemba poacher's feet and antelope hooves. High up on her hairline, where miombo woodlands stand like a head of matted Rasta hair, her soil is leached, leaving bald patches of sand where nothing grows bar a few wizened sedge grasses, which are too leathery and unpalatable to be gobbled up by even the hungriest of wild bushfires.

The Luanshya vlei reveals her adornment too, which she wears with feminine abandon across her entirety. Sun bleached snail shells, small skeletons of bush hares and snakes, a bizarre half-a-horn skull of a duiker and the ivory carapace of an ancient tortoise with its outer nacre finesse long gone. Precious ant bear and porcupine holes are exotic body piercings that added to the excitement of getting to know her better.

Like a house emptied of its furniture, a fresh open perspective gives the vlei the gift of the vast freedom of new beginnings, which takes my eager mind with it. An empty house begs for the new, a promise of regrowth. A feeling of absolute liberation reloads my spirit with adventurous hope on this vlei, which has survived the false bravado of yet another October bushfire.

My stretched senses are talking the language of my Soul as they recklessly flow with the moment. These feelings are immediately translated to my psyche. I feel there is meaning and purpose to my being – the vlei is teaching me to accept fear, frustration and adversity as integral parts of my being. This is my freedom from all that dogs me. I fully believe in my vlei and her silent cathartic message rings true in my heart – she makes me happy. I am an earth being and as such, my connection to her presence can never be severed.

I have tromped the vlei and reached the edge of the town. I am smeared from head to foot in black ash. I find an open spot on the river, where the water is flowing fast – to avoid bilharzia infection – and avoiding the leeches, I strip off and wash, dress still wet and run home. The raw cuts and scratches are stinging as my skin shrinks: a breeze chases me as I flee from the fast approaching evening chill of the vlei. My mother looks askance at my filthy shorts and shirt, and at my clean, puckered skin tinged with purple welts. She can't fathom out the blackened Jockey Y-fronts sitting on top of the closed lid of the tribal weave wash basket – but I say nothing. I never figure out how to remove white underwear from a blackened body without covering them in telltale soot. Maybe that's why some of the South African boys never wear underpants. Tonight I will take great delight in blowing blackened dried snot out of my nose and into my clean, Persil lemon scented, white hankie. It rekindles the fire – the smells and visions of the day. It furthers the pure intentions of my Soul.

My life is not straight, my time not linear

Whether it be bohemian Congolese men and their magic stone eggs; or envisioned Soul conversations with night thieves; piping hot pies from Sam's pie shop, or October bushfires, I see more than a straight forward timeline in my story. It is not straight like a spiritless flat length of string, with the knots of birth and death at opposite ends. Instead, my Luanshya life has the rounded shape of a soft rubber ball with a seeming *nothingness* inside. As I write, I am joining all time events like dots onto a seamless circumference measured in connected units of Luanshya round time.

I recognise a unified familiarity. It is like joining the dots to uncover a pre-described reality, and when I join this dot to the next dot, I start to get a rounded picture. I have a comfortable feeling that *things* in my life have a common purpose. My reality is a never-ending, ever-connected circle of all is one and one is all, its rounded shape forever warping, but always maintaining its cohesion. My story is a hologram where each part contains a connection to the whole; where the known and the unknown have a lot to say about me, and about each other.

Each event in my life is an amalgam of fathomless vectors radiating from the centre of my time ball, which is my inner being. There is a commonality to each and every moment in my rounded timeline, which alters the quality of my perception. I am operating from a centre of all-knowing awareness somewhere inside of me – through which all my life events pass on a well synchronised and prescribed algebraic journey of symbolic meaning.

Blaise Pascal, the seventeenth century mathematician, once said: 'Nature is an infinite sphere of which the centre is everywhere and the circumference nowhere.'

Round time is endless: A moment in my time, in fact my whole lifeline, is nothing more than a single shutter shot of the infinite wholeness of all time.

Refractions of inner light – self-expression

I am a single speck of falling rain, whose thistledown impact momentarily sends soft ripples radiating out on the surface of an aethereal expanse of time that we call the Universe.

I am a fleeting occurrence of kinetic round perfection, a small droplet of self-expression.

My childhood story is a simple gathering of archetypal events within the wide arena of circumferential time. They are as fragile, obscured and painfully purposeful as a cloud of damsel flies that collects above the meniscal waters of a forest pond; if for no other reason than to unconsciously reveal their tender purpose. Each seemingly frivolous creature performs the dance of its fellows: a fleeting reflection of each other on the water. How sweet and full is this damsel fly's short life? It glows with the common purpose of its kind: not unlike the seemingly random events of my child's world that tells my one all-time story.

Colonial quirks and African roots

Most mine houses were sparsely furnished, with second hand or pseudo Cape colonial furniture and rudimentary trimmings: Morris chairs; ball and claw tables with matching coffee tables and sideboards; usually a simple, dark-stained wooden dining room suite; freestanding bedroom wardrobes; clumsy dressing tables with hinged mirrors; tubular iron-framed beds; a white enamel-painted, metal-topped kitchen table; Formica-backed kitchen chairs; a paraffin fridge; and simple electric stoves. Our house still had a vegetable and meat safe – a wooden-framed box cupboard on long legs, with copper gauze sides, which stood in the cool depths of the house. It kept our fresh provisions aired, dry and free from flies. Later we acquired a paraffin fridge, which gave the kitchen a permanent 'on safari' wick-burning smell.

Red floors were polished on Mondays and Fridays, and buffed to a shine on the other days according to need. Our domestic – house boy as we called him – Wilson, knelt on old bits of my father's miner's overalls, and slid on his knees. After letting it dry a bit, he buffed it up with my old underwear and T vests, which my mother said I wore out far too quickly. I hated polish days. The house reeked of paraffin, and I always needed to get into rooms that were no-go areas of smeared polish. No one had fitted carpets – 'they house all sorts of insects' people said. I saw my first fitted carpets on a trip to England when I was six. Till then a carpet was something that the Congolese cross-border traders sold – the silky pictures of exotic scenery and animals with shiny artificial silk red and black tassels.

Luanshya life was straight forward. You went to Werner's butchery to place your order for meat, and a little later, a bleeding brown paper parcel tied up with butcher's string was delivered to your back door by the butcher's boy on his bicycle. If I was around it was my job to unpack it. Steak, liver, kidneys, mince and 'boys' meat', shin beef, for the domestic staff. This meaty medley gave off a smell, which, combined with the stale sweat smell of onions and earthy potatoes, was an olfactory signature of my early childhood. Rudimentary vegetables arrived at our back doorstep in the same delivery boy bicycle manner. Free-lance vendors would strike deals with the white madams over combinations of pumpkin and tomatoes or beans and carrots in steamed-up clear plastic bags. One of these vegetable vendors, not a Nyanja but a Makishi, would become a great friend of mine. Beer and spirits were bought at the Mine club off-sales, and dry commodities from an Indian wholesaler who had taken over from the European general dealers in the early sixties. If anything was needed after hours or in a weekend emergency, Jimmy the Greek had everything one could think of in his cafeteria, Theo's Corner Lounge, which welcomed all races and pockets, as well as all flies and bees. Flies for the *biltong* and *boerewors*, Afrikaans for jerky and dried sausage, hanging above the serving counter on simple wire hooks; and bees for the sticky buns, *baklava* and South African crystallised fruit; which when all combined, gave his jam-packed café a strange coriander, rancid animal fat, and honey-sweet aroma, which was edged with the rosewater perfume of Greek biscuits made by his mother-in-law.

When it rained, it rained hard. The corrugated iron roof amplified the fury of the black and blue bruised clouds that lashed us with their lead-tipped whips of rain, all accompanied by damning peals of titanic thunder. Rain storms fell upon our houses with such a certitude of conviction, it was as if we were the transgressors – we needed to be severely punished for our audacity to live where we did. At times it was as if all the rain in the heavy sky was falling on our one small tin roof. At other times it was the clatter of fiendish wild horses' hooves, as waves of heavy rain crossed from one side of the house to the other as the storm cloud galloped from A to Z Avenue. On those storm-driven nights, when the lightening had severed our electricity, and the rain had blocked out all other sounds with its deafening din, my urgent calls for comfort were inaudible. I was too frightened to run the gauntlet of galvanised bullet shots to my parents' room: that's when the Luanshya night had me entirely to herself. I was captive. I knew she was possessed about having me in her clutches.

The gardener, Long One, said that the storms were bad in Luanshya because the tribal spirits were displeased with the way the white men were pulling copper out of the ground. White men said that the intensity of minerals in some areas acted as conductors, attracting the overburdened tropical clouds to discharge their static build-ups – particularly upon those mining towns which had seams of ore running close to the surface. White men also pointed their tall metal hoists and water towers to the heavens, which acted as conductors for electric storms. We had two large and very tall metallic water towers in our street; they looked like a silver salt and pepper set on stilts. During nighttime thunderstorms, I pondered over these and many other things in my foetal position between the sheets, too wide-eyed to sleep. Intense fear and fascination both had the same effect on my body as it curled up tighter and tighter – until I was like a dried-out acacia pod, ready to spit out its innards.

As a white child on an African border between English and Belgian colonies, I was like a suicidal moth to a naked flame. I was attracted to opposites, which made my life surreal. My spirit was an energetic spark that repeatedly arced out of the gap between the soft fear of the present unknown and the past bliss of a half-familiar known. Like the ever-circling Abdim's storks that returned on summer thermals to the same open vlei every year, I too resonated with Africa in a vaguely reincarnate way. As if my roots lay well hidden there.

My parents' roots were English – I should have been safe and sound under their tribal protection. In Africa, the British Colonial Government made the most of an all-too trite carbon copy of an English utopia brimming with post-war placidity. My parents were happy to dip their toes into the seemingly easy colonial lifestyle, and that's how I should have been brought up; a carefree English child of the Colonies – but I wasn't.

It seemed to me that every white person felt that life was good. They had their feet firmly planted on the civilised side of the clearing. I alone was being drawn by a land and its people whose print upon my life seemed to come from the fearful far side. It called to me in a strangely familiar way.

An old water diviner told me that, in Africa and off the beaten track, away from the influences of civilisation and deep in the forest, clearings are meticulously swept by the women folk bent double and holding handleless brooms often made of vlei grasses, but sometimes of medicinal herbs to repel evil spirits from the dark side. Every morning the area around the huts and up to the forest edge, is swept to dusty smooth perfection. A strange footprint, or worse, the side-winding slurry of a snake in the sand, could be a harbinger of evil, whose presence needed to be exposed as a *satan nyoka* – a devil snake announcing no good. He also said that snakes don't like swept sandy surfaces, for it gives their malevolent purpose away, and that hyenas who steal the Souls of dying people in the night, and Makishi dancers who abduct young boys for ritual circumcision, also don't leave their footprints in forest clearings. I could understand the villager's concerns of callings from the familiar unknown.

Every open bush clearing has a darker side: the side you are not on, but look across to from your point of arrival, from your side. In time, the far side becomes the familiar unknown. I continuously felt the pull of the other side, the dark side. I had a small European 'this side' spiritual footprint, and the disparity in size, and draw of Africa's large footprint from the other side made me feel uncomfortable. My feeble English roots offered me no protection – only the night robber did, but even then, I never escaped a niggling angst from within. It was a fear of the unknown: that it was partially familiar, made me irresistibly attracted to it.

Refractions of inner light – Unconditional fear

Unconditional: the state of effect or cause whereby a happening is neither affected by the past nor the future. It has escaped the threads of time-bound reason for its being. Anything unconditional is in the state of the 'Now', a fancy-free zone in time, the only place where magic and miracles take place.

Unconditional fear is fear for the miraculous sake of it – it just is. This type of fear is greater than magic because it is an uncanny perception from within that warns us of things out of balance. It is miraculous because it is outside the boundaries of time and space. It is part of our 6th sense. It is an accomplice to truth, and like love, it cannot be explained, cannot be planned or feigned; it just is.

My fear was not an emotion. It was an unconditional state of being that coloured my five senses of perception and heightened my sensual awareness. It made me more aware of *things* around me. I saw this same state of aware-being in every animal and bird on the vlei. It gave them surround vision, in which they could scrutinise their stalking grounds, while at the same time having an acute awareness of immediate danger.

This amorphous feeling of alert unease stoked an adrenal response within me. It fired up the spunk of an unstoppable bonfire of self-discovery, which eventually freed me from both sides of the clearing. In time, neither side could lay claim to my Soul. Both were ineffective in establishing African pegging rights as I took possession of the centre of my clearing myself – or did I?

Deities of the dark forest

That my time and place was Colonial Africa was useful. It abounded in raw imagery that was possibly of great graphic value to my swashbuckling spirit – but the venue was not essential for my inner adventure. I could have attempted to do that as a 60s rock singer on a Woodstock podium. Instead I was a white child conceived in Africa, and that's where my Soul found its quest. I wanted to find meaning to my life. My physicality was playing with the raw emotions of an origin unknown as its navigational brief: It was left impoverished of fact, but richly possessive of cryptically embossed emotional maps of nostalgia. It was left to me alone, to navigate my awareness out of my current territory and into the open Soul-deep waters of spiritual reality.

My childhood was thus continually thrown into an eclectic menagerie of untamed images and ideas from 'here and there' and 'now and then,' which prowled around my inner corridors like hungry predators. I knew I had a Soul. I imagined that it had walked many bush paths, had entered many clearings before me, and had fought off phyla of metaphorical wild beasts;

the emotional snapshots of which were pinned to the walls of my subconscious psyche. I also knew of the sentimental and real value of my Soul and I wanted to honour it; but I only had a half-hidden footprint as spiritual solace and as a compass bearing on my journey. For this reason, the story of my life is more than its known parts, more than flat chronological fact.

One day, riding up and down the tree-lined avenues on my bicycle to kill a Saturday afternoon, I passed a small church hall. It was modern and not English. It belonged to an evangelical American church. There was a poster of a squat wooden carving at the door announcing an upcoming exhibition of ethnic art from the Congo. My stomach wanted to throw out the Coke and milk brown cow I had just drunk at the mine club; and for a while it seemed that breathing wasn't an option. They say that the body shunts blood away from physiological systems that are not needed in times of great stress. My body was shunting all its blood and energy resources to somewhere else – possibly to my Soul.

Carvings from the Congo; this was the biggest happening since the Boswell and Wilkes Circus arrived by train from South Africa the year before. I couldn't believe my good fortune. I would be able to see a bit of the Congo without even going there. British colonials hardly ever visited the Congo, though it was not fifty miles away. I put it down to the fact that they were spiritually scared and emotionally inept. The truth was that they felt 'put-out' by anyone who spoke a language they couldn't understand. They weren't intimidated by the black people of Southern Africa: They had quickly taught these keen folk enough English to get by. It was an anathema, however, to conceive of meeting white and black people who spoke French when they didn't.

In what seemed centuries of colonial time, the exhibition opened the following week. The hall was small, the artefacts many, the smell a delicious ragout of aromas: herbal raffia, rancid hardwoods, blood-caked totems, and the erogenous odours of civet and monkey scent glands – the juices of which had been rubbed into some of the carvings. The exhibition stroked my eager senses: geometric Congolese chairs, triangular headrests, corroded Katanga crosses, ceremonial axes, thick copper and brass slave bangles – with deep notches where I imagined the limbs of the deceased, and not so deceased slaves had been hacked off – and carvings, wooden carvings from across the vast regions of the Congo.

The forest people carvings were the *pièce de résistance*, and took prime place, also because of their size. There were two of them, a male and a female. Enormous – taller than me and four times as wide – they were carved out of whole tree trunks. I spent a good bit of time measuring them with my body. They were squatting, which made them grotesquely imposing. Their elephantine calves were cramped, and their short wristless arms and large spreading thighs stuck out in a lewd, wanting way. They were totally naked except that she had a string of real beads around her wide hips. Large circumcised male genitals rested heavily on the ground at his stubby, almost clubbed feet. Pendulous full breasts with large conical shaped nipples and deep tribal scars rested on her large extended belly, out of which her navel protruded like a third breast with its own tattooed nipple. The fully rounded buttocks of their posteriors provided ample proportional balance for their swollen frontal appendages.

At first these gross effigies were sexually shocking to my European child's eye, and it took time for my senses to settle. Goodness knows what the SOE, the Sons of England, ladies would say. Eventually my colonial child sensitivities bowed down to the power of presence that this pair gave to the exhibition, which outstripped their blatant nudity. My spiritual eye started to pick up the threads of their story. 'They are Pygmy forest Gods,' said the American missionary lady who saw me gawking. She had a white plastic name badge that I never read, a white short-sleeved blouse, a navy blue skirt and white patent leather shoes on navy stockinged feet. 'Oh,' I said.

I went back to the exhibition every day after school and missed cricket practices to see the forest deities. It took a long time for their story to sink into my psyche. I understood what some of the grown-ups were saying about them being so grossly out of proportion. They both had fearful grimaces of distorted noses and lips that seemed to merge into one writhing plate of fat grubs and worms dotted with nostrils and eyes. Their eyes and ears were small and hippo like, and tight springs of hair zigzagged across the amorphous boundaries of their immense foreheads and bloated cheeks.

These Quasimodos belonged to the gothic arches of a Congolese forest canopy where their omnipotence reached far beyond the earth, the forest, and the sky. They certainly did not belong in a church hall with an evangelical little American lady explaining the pastoral forest-gatherer life of forest pygmies. 'Pastoral?' I asked. The sweet old lady explained to me what pastoral meant with a condescending smile. Rubbish, I thought, there was nothing meek and mild about these Gods. They were ruthless dictators of a violent jungle world where there were no limits when it came to dishing out witchcraft, negativity, torture and death to their club-limbed people of the forest. They ruled their kingdom by an overpowering black fear, which in a night robber way, I was no stranger to: I could feel it as I stood before them every day.

How did these American church people get these carved statues? I thought. How many pygmies did they kill to prize these giants out of the short arms and chubby fingers of their rightful owners – for them to be able to tell us civilised folk of the 'this side' of the clearing about the peaceful family life of the Pygmies of the Congo? I asked the lady if these Gods had been displayed first in New York, London and Lusaka, the capital of Northern Rhodesia – grown-ups always said that Luanshya always got to see the popular movies after everyone else. She didn't know, which I found quite strange – surely everyone in her congregation should know the itinerary of such an important exhibition.

As I stood before them, these arboreal monoliths reaffirmed to me that fear was not a temporal emotion, but an enduring part of my being. These forest deities carried their fear with them – as physically present as the tropical wood out of which they were hewn. I could feel it and share it as if it were my own. It was as if they had gently handed it to me in their stubby hands. I did not consciously know of the culture or the rituals that had created the fear that they bore. The lady had only talked about nice Pygmy things – the fear that I had taken on inside me was not intellectually acquired. They did not frighten me like some of the other carvings on display, so my fear was not emotionally self-instigated either. It was my own state of familiar angst that had been pointed out to me by these homeless African forest Gods who dealt in fear every day of their lives.

Neither the night robber nor the forest deities frightened me out of violent circumstance; they introduced me to my own state of fearful being. They helped me close the gap between my immature conscious awareness and my fear; the gap where irrational negative thoughts can find emotional roots. My fear was not an emotion. It was a state of being, and as such was part of my Soul, where things are seamlessly one. When you distance yourself from your fear, spineless feelings will move into the gap – hyenas will feed off your Soul. I would not be one with my fear unless I fully acknowledged this strange Janet and John pair of the Congo jungle. I fully embraced them as long-lost friends.

The missionary lady who, in my mind, was an extension of these remarkable carvings, had taught me something. It all depended on where you were viewing things from; from which side of the clearing you were on, and wanted to be on. Here were two carved pieces of wood: The truth about them was simply a matter of spiritual perception. She saw pastoral purity, I saw earthed fear, and grown-ups saw crudity. The mechanics of perception were so simple. What we saw in the Congolese forest deities, we embraced from within ourselves. The spiritual truth was beyond our subjective opinions: that was the omnipotence of my newly acquired friends – their truth was theirs alone.

The forest deities were not the only carvings in the exhibition to leave a deep impression on me. The wood carvings from the Congolese border with Rwanda and Burundi, also Belgian colonies, were long-limbed dancers whittled out of black ebony. They frightened the emotional me with a fear that I didn't want to recognise. I didn't stay long to look at them. Their agitated poses unnerved me, their arched, high-kneed legs and snaking torsos made out as if these frenetic whisking Rwandans were shunning the good earth they danced on; they were demented. The wild animal hair used to depict their whisks and head-dresses gave off a strong base smell of animal fear. These sur-real gyrators were playing with the earth spirit. They were the antipathy of my earth bound forest Gods who told me about the ownership of fear. These demonic dancers were spinning in the gap between my conscious being and my personal state of fear. They lashed out fear as a threat to me.

Puku on the vlei

Mr Harrison, the headmaster of Luanshya Primary School, told me that in the African bush it was survival of the fittest. Only the lion could afford to be fearless – they called him King of the Jungle because he feared no one – until the hunter came along with his gun. The rest of the animals, including the elephant, had to be instinctively fearful to survive. The lion, however, was not fearless – he was simply in control of his fear, so much so that he was able to dish it out at will. That was why he was con-sidered to be the possessor of royal largesse. I was not at all convinced about the omnipotence of the lion. On a spiritual level I believed that the leopard was far superior.

I once watched a herd of puku antelope loose total control of their fear to a leopard on the hunt. To begin with, the cap-tivating flick of their ears and the beauty of their form bore proof of an awareness of their own fear, a fear that although under their control, had to be constantly safeguarded. They still had the upper hand as the singular leopard began stalking the perimeter of their vlei. They showed no apparent concern, but as the leopard worked on transferring his deathly fear into the inner space of the puku, so the palpable nervousness of the herd increased. They were rapidly losing control of their fear.

When one of their members foolishly gave its strange whistle of danger, a death was predestined. The tension rose like winds of an afternoon thunderstorm. Things speeded up. A bolt of feline intention struck. One antelope's fear toppled, and in a flash, a puku had submitted – first, its inner space, then its innards to the fearful leopard. In a dash the herd returned to their ungulate grass-chewing ear-flicking calm as if nothing had happened – they were once again in control of their own fear. The leopard had climaxed his fear. He was now spent, quietly eating his meal in a tree like a docile domestic cat. The night safari had been a spectacular display of the mercurial transcendence of fear, from its metaphysical origins into manifested reality and back into a metaphysical prized possession – the ownership of fear.

Without the tides of fear that wash our inner space, be they real, imaginary or metaphysical, we would be a cancerous form of life with no boundaries, no aspirations, no caution, no inspiration, and no Soul purpose. We would be non-creation.

Emotional rubbings of the Soul

> *'Maybe his bejewelled rain cloud dreams, his fears and his emotional glow were the only things that made him different from the rocks of his darkness...'*

In time, short time, consequence popped my baby bliss bubble with its butcher's knife and I began to serve real time: A life sentence of forced resonance with time's linear beat of cans and cannots; what colonial English parents would call a child's routine: bath at 5, dinner at 6, bed at 7; no hat – no going in the sun, no afternoon nap, no playing with the kids next door, no mosquito cream – no wandering around under the mango trees at dusk to spot fruit bats foraging. There were consequences to everything I wanted or didn't want to do. It seemed at times that my life was an oppressively ordered beat of parent pleasing with lead-lined gaps of Luanshya boredom in-between: empty caverns of spiritual inertia and lifeless staged societal events that were not of my own making nor of any Soul importance – they seemed totally devoid of positive future consequence.

The same old water diviner told me about a swampy area 'not a 100 miles from here as the crow flies'. It was called the Kasankas. Every year thousands of fruit bats arrived from as far away as Central Congo and Tanganyika to feed off wild fruits that grew there. Large crocodiles lay under wild fruit trees fertilised for centuries by drips of stinking bat guano. Spattered with dung, they took advantage of causalities, as the young, old, injured, dead and bickering fell out of the trees. A soft nerve impulse in a membranous wing in another land had caused these debauched reptilian monsters to haul themselves from their riverine habitats to become forest creatures during bat feeding frenzies. The bats came for the fruit, and the crocs came for the bats. Life and death were welcomed to the same dinner table: both invited by Lady Consequence, their gracious host.

An early conscious recognition of drawn out 'can't haves' and staccato 'can haves', and their consequences was the birth of my emotional being. In my early childhood it seemed Luanshya time wanted to plan both my outside and inside worlds for me. Forced afternoon naps in the hot air of my bedroom were painful beyond boring. Going to the Mine Club with my mother for afternoon tea, togged up to the nines, was tedious, at times for both of us. I wanted all things to be exciting: that's when the Luanshya bush started to call me.

Force of circumstance made me align my sense of being to that which I felt I wanted the most – oddly the things that caused me the most effort, emotional pain and confusion. In the afternoons, after a sweaty nap on my candlewick counterpane, I would sometimes lie on the front lawn and stare up at the sky. It was in the clouds that I found clues as to what I wanted the most. Different shapes and colours, depending on the weather, would evoke deep-rooted emotions that were so strong and yet frustratingly unclear. Cloud chasing gave me the most hurtful longings. Longings for what? I didn't know. Fantastic cloud shapes became the precursors of my deepest desires, and deeply sensitive they were: too emotionally deep for a child many a Luanshya grown-up would have said if they could have read my mind. At that early stage of my inner explorations, my searchings were translated into mythological characters. My godmother had bought me a book on Greek mythology and I could see just about every character of that book in the Luanshya skies. In the spirit of circumferential time, it was logical that these mythological figures of ancient Greece should embed themselves as archetypal resonances somewhere within the reality of my being: to resurface later as my passions and affinities for the African bush and its people. Just as I could see Greek heroes, villains and glorious realms of the Gods in the clouds; so I could see the same marvellous miscellanies in the people, places and events of my Luanshya clearings. It didn't matter if I fantasised over a Pygmy god or a Grecian god; their energies were of the same universal source of one-stuff.

My outer clearing was the sensual truth, the only reality that my five senses of perception could grab hold of. It was governed by the boundaries of my Luanshya world and was the manna of my child-hungry curiosity.

My inner clearing was a world governed by spiritual boundaries: where my purpose was a throb of instruction issued to me in a biochemical Morse code between the cells and tissues of my being. It defined the size and purpose of my Soul journey.

As a small boy I had passions, the intertwining of my two clearings. They were my affinities.

I became my affinities personified. Whether I could understand and control them, or whether they were hurtful and awkward, had no relevance. Because they excited me so much I swore allegiance to my affinities, and in so doing, I gave free expression to them and their accompanying emotions, as well as to my spirit of adventure, all heady resonances of my same one Soul.

My white subtribe and the world via the BBC paled in importance to the raw energies that I was exposed to on my vlei in the African bush. Deafening boredom and the emotional pain of my exiled existence had stripped me of the thin veneer of societal protection. I had shown my vulnerability for the sensual. I would no longer be innocent – maybe not even decent. I was attempting to wholeheartedly resonate with whatever excited me the most: and there seemed no half measures in my choice making. The Anglican Rector might have said I had profligated my Soul. I would have said, 'I am following my Soul, for it knows best.'

As I exposed my vulnerable cognitive self to more and more of what was going on around me and in me, it was inevitable that I would end up rubbing against my Soul. My emotional status was as a result of those eager rubbings, an energetic portrait of what I thought was a reality in keeping with my affinities.

Every child is a vesicle for the expansive Soul of the universe. Grown-ups often don't see this because they use intellectual and physical stature as a measure of a child's importance. They fail to acknowledge a child's miraculous position in that aethereal place between things: Where cause and effect have not yet yoked them with the shallow consequences of linear time and logical thinking. In describing a child's simplicity grownups call them innocent, which implies a lack of knowledge coupled with naivety; when, in fact, children are at the centre of all knowingness. They still have the freedom to live with their affinities, within their bubbles of timelessness, where all knowledge is one.

Signatures of colour and smell

The smell of everything: from the heavy November nights that awaited rain, to the stagnant reed beds of the Luanshya River; chewed cedar wood pencils, to worm encrusted fishing hooks on Makoma dam. They all created profound emotional signatures within me that were continually cross-referenced and researched in the annals of my inner and outer beings. My cognitive being needed to measure and record everything it came across using its olfactory lexicon of odours.

So well-worn were my olfactory pathways that smells spontaneously stirred-up submerged memories from the muds of my subconscious awareness. They were so excitingly demanding that it didn't matter where they came from: I simply had to follow them.

Differentiation of colour, smell, taste and texture was lost. I tasted the smell of black earth, touched the amber of moist forest litter and felt the pungent aroma of ripped grass. I tasted the pink copper of mosquito screens and felt the acrid smell of Lifebuoy soap. My cognitive being had amassed a collection of interchangeable sensual images that on spontaneous recall

sent urgent ripples of emotional knowledge through my facul-
ties. These reflexes were not intellectually acquired over time.
They were too powerful and unrehearsed for that. They were
amalgams of two aethereal worlds: the subconscious awareness
of the strangely sensual veiled worlds of my Soul, and an emotionally surreal Luanshya landscape recreated by my hungry
senses of perception. My senses were shackled into slavery by my
affinities, which needed them for a definite purpose.

My boyish sensuality was one with my organic spirituality.
I would only ever see God through my senses of perception.
There would be not a trace found in my intellect, religious practice or moral integrity. The Anglican rector would say that this
was pagan blasphemy. I would say 'God given.' My sensuality
was sanctioned by my Soul. Without it my mind and body would
have withered away.

The colours of black and red had the most to say about the sensuality of my perceptions.

Black people were of various shades from Bourneville dark,
to milk chocolate light and on to liquorice. My phantoms of
the Congolese cross-border trade were black, blacker than
black: their physicality fascinated me. They had gentian black
skin which contrasted dramatically with their whiter than white
teeth. The tight black hair on their heads looked like the burnt
ends of logs pulled from an extinguished fire – a fine fuzz of
charcoaled chalk that contrasted dramatically with their oily
high cheeks and foreheads.

Their tongues were slimy fuchsia reptiles that seemed to be
restrained against their will to the recesses of their sun-baked

mahogany heads. Every now and then their tongues would self-ignite into violent red flashes as their dental jail keepers released them to moisten the furrows of their large lips. I decided that these entrepreneurs had long broad tongues redder than ours, as a sort of cooling mechanism during their long treks through the bush. Leopards and lions cool themselves through their tongues; why shouldn't these awesome men of the wild Congo do the same?

Black is the African colour of acceptance. In African villages, the folk don't shun the black of night. They welcome its spiritually slow arrival as a family member of their tribe who creeps into their village clearing at an appointed time. The time when tree shadows spread like molten chocolate in a late afternoon sun that is rapidly losing its grip on its own reality.

Like all family members, blackness has its quirks. It makes itself first seen skulking in the forest, then starts to lurk at the edge of the bush clearing, before entering the clean swept spaces around the huts, and like the hyena, it leaves no footprint in the sand. In a hushed manner, it greets every village member who in turn, greets it in anxious awe. They know it harbours scorpions and night adders in its palms, and keeps strange company with ferocious and cowardly beasts: all creatures looking for an alibi, a thick cover in its blackness to absolve them from their deeds. 'Oh it happened in the black of the night,' as if the night was to blame for the disappearance of a goat. The crafty hyena goes so far as to carry the blackest night in its heart.

Night blackness also carries away dead bodies and sleeping Souls, but it means no harm: it is family, and only does what it does best. Unabashed, the black of night sits with all its extended family in a circle around the embers of every village fire across Africa. Every gathering is connected to the other in crouched contemplative union with the ancestral spirit of the night, who listens to the articulated stories of its Pan-African kith and kin. Eventually, towards the midnight of their dark vigil, the night has a universal story to tell, and it whispers its knowingness to the village elders through trails of smoke. It echoes its thoughts through the sounds of crumbling coals and the spits and pops of the last tinder. When the hyena's maniacal laugh is finally heard in the distance, the villagers retreat, leaving the darkness to tiptoe around the sleeping huts; to finally slip into the pre-dawn dampness of the forests: without leaving a footprint in the sand.

You can intuit the past visit of a dark night and imagine the stories it told by the fire through the smoky smell that it has left on its family's skin. I could always smell smoke on our servants, and I used to imagine what they had talked about, and what they had listened to for so long into the night. I could see their grouped ember-lit faces from my bedroom window. The dark had been invited to their fireside, but time never was; they always looked so sleepily satisfied the next morning.

Africans expressed themselves fully through blackest of nights and so did I.

Black was the feminine darkness that caressed me every night. She could be voluptuous, velvet, and soft; that's when I could smell her jasmine pepper-sweet body. But she could also be black ice, cold and sharp and unsympathetic to my whimpers and muffled groans on those close nights that choked me. She carried this distrustful sting of ambivalence even when she was running her long fingers of sweat through my tangled hair. I could have feared and hated her – but I didn't: I loved her, and always would. She was my black spirit of sensual addiction. Her nightcaps were of sequins embroidered on rich velvets of dark plum, burnt caramel, and indigo. Colours dependent on the time of night, dust in the air, fires on the horizon, phases of the moon, lurking storm clouds – or simply the midnight closeness.

She was a Mephistopheles who kept strange company: arguing parents, barking dogs, the ghosts of distant hyenas, unknown owl calls, or the unsettling shriek of a bush baby in distress. Her smell then, was a fetid waft from a swamp – or was it that our septic tank was blocked? I used to ponder as to why our septic tank always belched at night, and never during the day.

I ended every day with my ebony queen of the night. Over baked beans on toast, or liver and onions with mash and tinned peas, I would ponder as to how loving or unkind she would be to me later that night. I never could read her mind prior to being tucked in.

I sucked up her dark energies as a circadian healing balm against the harsh sun of the day gone by. Hot days could also mislead you into a complacency where idle lassitude could suddenly turn into unexpected cold fear. I needed her embrace then to restore the connection to my Soul.

On good nights her night colours were also the echoes of the African people I came across in my dreams: all the people that I met on my way to the vlei, on the street, and in the shallow water's edge of Makoma Dam.

On bad hyena nights, those same people became dark colourless people from the other side of my inner bush clearing. They seemed not to reflect any light at all. Their faces were pocked with dark holes, and they had no seeing eyes for my Soul to converse with. There was not even a glow from their inner space for my love to catch a glimpse of. I could not measure them other than with my own repulsed fear. I knew that it was these demons that spilt Congolese blood and caste the bones of death in witchdoctors' huts across Africa. Luckily my allknowing night robber had pulled me away from these dreadful creatures of the African night.

Red: Congolese coppered blood

Red was a repetitive and yet jolting colour in my childhood. Its ambivalence never ceased to befuddle my sense of values: Just when I thought I knew it – I didn't.

My world was, on the surface, dead ordinary red. The mine management put red iron oxide into the screed of the floors in our houses, recreation facilities, hospitals and schools. Servants polished these floors with red wax polish that reeked of paraffin – I was told it deterred beetles, scorpions, house snakes, red ants and centipedes. On rainy days the seat of my pants took on a red sheen as I slid around the floor on my bum instead of playing outside on the lawn. Everything I owned, including the seats of my pants, had red scuffs.

I was told that the lifebuoy soap that I hated, that stained the basin, that stung my eyes and sent peppery popping sensations up my nose and into my sinuses, that stung my body and its sensitive bits if I didn't wash it off properly, was good for me because it was designed to disinfect part of a mucky colonial child's body.

I drank red juice, had red dyed pumpkin, instead of fruit, jam on my sandwiches, ate red Vienna sausages, and was served cokes and sausage rolls by waiters wearing red fezzes who shuffled across the red veranda floors of the mine club. Even the mine swimming pool had a red copper fountain at the shallow end and red wall edgings and red floored changing cubicles. I hated going to the toilets at both the club and the swimming pool because the urinals had red blocks of carbolic naphthalene that only made the stench of urine and paraffin stronger. Red had a metallic chemical taste that dragged my senses down to base ordinariness. But the ultimate and unpleasant picture of red came to me when I placed my nimble tongue on copper.

Roughly smelted copper was maroon with colour hues of orange, pink, purple and cobalt blue. I could smell its colour and feel its smell. When I placed the flat of my tongue over a piece of smelted copper it would tingle and tremble. My nose would crinkle up, and the area by my tonsils and adenoids would pulsate uncomfortably. I would half gag and the reflex would shoot down my throat into my innards and my stomach would turn. Spreading my tongue on copper made me emotionally sick. Sucking a Northern Rhodesian copper penny, and sticking the tip of my tongue into the hole between the two elephants standing on their back legs, did the same, and yet for some quirky reason, I did it fairly often. In my mind, copper smelt and tasted of dead animal blood and guts. Its colour hues were a sinister metallic impression of ripped flesh with sheens of skin pinks and intestinal blues, of sinew greens and puce veins. Oxidised copper had the same putrid organic smell as decomposing flesh, as if a metal could rot like bush meat. Copper carried the colours and smells that bluebottle flies found irresistible in rotting carrion. Everything repulsive that I could think and feel, came to me when I placed my tongue on copper.

Neither the deep shadows of late afternoon that showed up the miombo forest's darker side, nor the witchdoctor's hut frighten me as much as the image of putrid flesh and blood that copper evoked in me.

It had something to do with a rebellion not a hundred miles from Luanshya in the Katanga Province of the Belgian Congo. We awoke on my mother's birthday to a rude banging on our door. It was a Sunday dawn. 'Get anything you can spare – blankets, food, clothes – and come to the MOTH club – there's been a rebellion, we are expecting refugees from the Congo, many of them – come quick with anything you can spare – you will be needed there all day.'

We went, we saw, we stayed: I saw more than I could ever have imagined, and my psyche remained for far longer and travelled far further than the temporal boundaries of that fateful event. My parent's good friends from the Congo were there – they had just arrived. They were shocked and broken. I saw a thick pool of congealed blood on the floor of their car. There were bullet holes in a door and the back window was shattered. I didn't dare ask what had happened and whose blood it was: they seemed physically unharmed. These early arrivals of well-off families had paid heavily in hard currency to the gendarmerie to get out of a mini Brussels turned de-mented, and be permitted to cross the border into Northern Rhodesia. Others, who came later in the day, had followed bush tracks across the border, probably the same bush routes that my Congolese magi used. Every white Congolese family that arrived told of an atrocity. Until then, I didn't know much about spilt human blood and violence, let alone had I heard stories of machete-hacked bodies of women and children. An old Irish Catholic priest seemed to have lost his mind as he raved on about dismembered genitals stuffed in the mouths of black and white priests; of tongues and penises pinned to rebel uniforms as medals. Our embarrassed grown-ups struggled to keep him quiet. The perversity of it all was far beyond the furthest dark boundaries of my inner clearing. By the end of the morning it was all too much for me. My sensitivities had been violated, but no one had the time for me. There were distraught white Congolese family members who had been separated, wailing women and fretting children to console, and all our parents were English stiff-upper-lipped busy.

I staggered around as useless as the birthday card I had wanted to give my mother on that special day. I could not escape the continuing avalanche of horror stories that came in endless pounding waves. No, I could not say why I did not want to go and play on the swings and roundabouts outside with a coke and a packet of chips like the other Luanshya MOTH Club kids. Had they not seen or heard what I had witnessed? How could they play their stupid games? Did the grown-ups that encouraged them to go and play put blinkers on them? Did they think that could sever a child's emotional feelers so easily?

In broken English these Belgian copper miners, shopkeepers and factory owners were verbose in telling their story. They had to get it out, again and again and again with their Franco-Flemish guttural accents. Faint echoes of past Nazi-occupied Belgium were thrown in for embellishment and depth of meaning. Raped Congolese nuns; butchered priests; murdered civilians, black and white; looted homes and shops; slaughtered pets, dairy cows and prize show jumping horses. The Congo didn't have a British colonial police force to uphold common decency, never mind restore it: Law and order had been turned on its head. I had never heard so much negativity in my life. By afternoon time I could accurately describe the taste of violence, perversity and destruction, not on my physical tongue, but on the tongue of my Soul. My outer sensitivities had been peeled away, my being stripped to its core, my senses of perception laid to rest. I was no longer capable of cognitively patronising the grief and rightful indignation of those distraught Belgians who never seemed to stop arriving in our town. I stood in their midst, and stood, and stood, staring, not really staring, just standing, not coldly, but not sympathising either. I was now a fellow victim. My Soul had been raped, my mind pillaged.

I was silently screaming and sobbing from within, all the while my outer appeared indifferent: I suppose that's why the busy adults there didn't feel or see the need to comfort me. My immature cognitive being was incapable of applying any logical explanation as to why this had happened, or what I could do to save myself, never mind the distraught Congolese. It was then that my Soul made a stand. I felt its silent instruction as a pressure against my breastbone. If I was to survive this emotional onslaught that had arrived unexpectedly in my life on that birthday morning in early July, I had to remind myself of my night robber. The dark Soul with whom I had wanted to have a meaningful discourse with on fear, and for whom, in my sleep, I had been prepared. The one who had combed alien fear out of my sweaty hair. If he had been there that day, I would have thanked him for his earlier gift, but I would have told him that the civilised edge, the fearless side of my clearing, was not where I had thought it was. Things had changed. A fearful unknown was moving in to occupy the near side of my psyche. *Things* were no longer under my control. Alien fear was pulling at my Soul and flipping my senses to make me feel nauseous. What should I do? The thought of his possible presence in that wretched hall lent some courage to my child's presence.

What if the sweet American lady who had sown a Christian frill around my Congolese deities was there? After all she did live and work in the Congo, and more than likely lived in the shared fear of others. She would have seen fear many times and had likely conquered it through God. What would she have said to me? Suddenly my situation was no longer of importance as panic gripped the nape of my neck – what if she was caught up in the 'bloodbath' as some insensitive grown-ups called it – what a shocking word, 'bloodbath' – what an appalling thought. Then I thought back to her passive, almost angelic demeanour among the sexually explicit forest carvings and the evil high-steppers, and I felt reassured that she had miraculously repelled evil in this moment in time.

The sun that streamed into the hall that day seemed so callous and bright. Even in broad daylight it spot-lighted the 'Now' reality in the harshest of lights. I had always believed that evil things happened in the convenience of the darkness of the night, where I could quickly cover my head with the blankets, and yet this evil anarchy happened in full light. Murder in broad daylight, its debris now being highlighted by an insensitive sun as a postmortem for all to see. This overturning of cognitive values caused an uncomfortable imbalance in my child's psyche. I hated that sunny Sunday, and for a few years after, when hot Sunday suns pointed out my lassitude, I felt they were tainted with the slow blood of all-day violence.

I can't say if either the Soul of my night robber or of the little old missionary lady had whispered in my ear in that hall of broken dreams, broken families and shattered values. The aethereal discordance of it all had scrambled my senses. Something did happen however. Both of them might have told me something that caused me to see things from another side of the forest clearing, not this side or the far side, just another side.

My overwrought inner feelings and accompanying emotions took a tumble and collapsed in a surprisingly lucid heap in front of me. Frazzled emotions can only vibrate with their devilish intensity for so long before suddenly, and unavoidably, they collapse into the collected state of being called survival. Confused emotional steam can, in a split second, turn into a frigid clarity of presence. These Belgians' tragedy was not mine to judge; their emotions were not mine to share, nor was their fear. Their situation was theirs. It was real: spilt blood was real; death was real; it was all terribly real to these Belgians. Their suffering was a consequence of where they stood in their clearing, not from where I stood. There was nothing else to think about, nothing more to be said. Perhaps their collective psyche had unwittingly allowed their Belgian Congo world to drift too far from its Soul purpose. Perhaps their awareness of *things* had slipped and unexpectedly their umbilical cord attached to the good life had been slit, and it was now spewing blood.

There were no longer complicated false emotions of angst and regret to uphold between us, be they my inadequate, embarrassed sorrow or their exaggerated expressions of real horror. I read their situation – overnight their life had become a ravaged vlei, but it was still their vlei, their story, and it would always be their story; just as my vlei would always be my vlei, my story. These Belgians had to take ownership and control of their own fear, not beg for mine to be released in resonance from my child's inner being. In fact, all they needed was a roof over their heads and a meal in their tummies for an approaching night of reflection and consolidation. I was always told the Belgian Congolese were tough.

I went to bed that night with quietly weeping Belgians camped out in our blankets on our red polished veranda floor. I could taste blood and death in the air that I was breathing, but it no longer asked for my emotional attachment. I had shared a sombre dinner table with these Belgians; all our dining room chairs had been used so there was no place left at the table for emotional explanations, consolations or regrets. Things were under quiet reconciliation: None of the people at the table had lost family members in the massacre. Throughout the meal all I could taste was copper, a cold and indifferent metallic taste on my tongue.

Ownership of our individual lives was more important than all the messy emotions flying both ways on that day. If I had remained an opportunistic voyeur, gobbling each horrid story up with relish, I would have resonated with secondhand grief and anger until I was the grieving angered one. My life force would have gushed out of my every tissue, leaving me more destitute than those poor Belgians because it would have been a pretentious state of being. I would have been crying foolishly over something lost that wasn't even mine. I stood there all afternoon, and I can't say if my seemingly indifferent presence helped or not. In a way it was a bit like a stiff British upper lip. After all, when you are verging on falling to pieces, it is helpful if the person next to you is not doing the same. I believe I did help in some childish way.

I watched homely English colonial women clucking in disbelief, and homeless Belgian colonial women crying. Two sides of a flipped coin that could have fallen either way on that fateful day on our common border in the bush. Without the darkness of depravity, one cannot measure the light of hope: That was that and that was all there was.

From that day on, the Northern Rhodesian colonials took cognisance of their own African fear, even if it was only subconsciously. Perhaps this Congolese happening had serendipitously prevented a bloodbath of our own. The Belgian dominos had fallen for all to see.

In time, the Belgians went back to their ransacked Congolese homes, shops and factories to start again, and in African time, they suffered more rebellions, more spilt blood and turmoil – it seemed to be the way of the Congo. They appeared to openly accept it – did that mean they knew their fear? These foolhardy Congolese whites had sold their Souls to the fear of the Congo long before they first arrived in the MOTH Club hall on my mother's birthday.

Some months later, our white Congolese friends from Elizabethville, who had previously swam in on that human wave of tragedy, came across the border to visit us. They brought us presents: for my parents, a beautiful Lalique crystal statue of a dancer, the likes of which could only be found in a fancy gift shop in Elizabethville, one that had probably been ransacked not a year before. They were so grateful for our help, and my parents were delighted with their expensive gift. What had happened to our common African fear, I wondered. It might have been temporarily forgotten by my parents and conveniently camouflaged by the Belgians, but it was still lurking somewhere at the edge of the clearing like a cunning hyena, I was sure of that.

They gave me a Katanga cross, a copper ingot the size of a fishplate. Katanga crosses were the ancient currency of the Luba people of Congo, who used them to buy and sell commodities such as slaves, wives and ngoni cattle. It was old, and was burnished with the same dark brown hue that seems to cover all African artefacts, from ceremonial wooden masks to well-used *pangas*, knives. The cross was pitted with blisters and cracks that harboured a greasy blackness of long usage. Underneath its sombre jacket, however, there were the tell-tale blood and guts colours of maroon, pink and iridescent bluey green – the colour hues of my fear. I did not want to press my tongue against it at all – not out of microbial caution, but spiritual rejection. Fateful stories sat in the layers of its history, all waiting to engulf the beholder.

In spite of my spiritual hesitancy I treasured my gift from darkest Africa for its antique significance, but it was also the last rivet in my lead balloon – it pinned my psyche to the permanence of indiscriminate fear in Africa. A fear of spilt blood and death that went far beyond witchdoctors, hyenas, Congolese rebel soldiers, and even beyond the boundaries of my inner clearing. Like a strangler fig this hideous fear was trying to staple itself to one of the steep cliff faces that lined the vulnerable gap between my Soul and the cognitive me. It had nothing to do with my own fear – it was a noxious weed to be rejected. It was the antagonist of my burglar and my Pygmy deities, both of whom encouraged me to make peace and close the gap between my innate fear and my Soul – but would I succeed? This alien fear wanted no parley: It was seeking domination and control.

I could see why the foolhardy white Congolese went back. They refused to let it have its way. Could I ever be as strong as them? It seemed not.

This well-meaning gift birthed afresh my mistrust for what I assumed was my healthy state of fear, which was once again faltering. Congolese spilt blood and death came back as a dull threatening force in my lower gut – close to my roots. Fearful images of bluebottles buzzing over murdered Congolese bodies, their spilt blood drying in the sand, began to haunt me again. I still didn't have as tight a control of my fear as I had thought I had, and this frightened me. It was a particular type of fear that was announcing itself with a muffled echo from unknown depths. It was a Congolese Beelzebub, a lord of the flies, which proclaimed that my own fear, even though I had befriended it for life, would always be confronted and challenged by the spirit of Africa. Africa harboured a fear that relentlessly wormed its way into the inner space of everything that ever was. The Belgians accepted it – my English subtribe were oblivious to it – but for how long? What made these Congolese atrocities all the more terrifying, was the sad fact that the spilt blood that I had seen on the floor of a car, was not entirely as a revolt against Belgian colonial rule. The out-dated colonial regime was the tip of the iceberg. Underneath the *joie de vivre* and the kwasa dancing, there was deep-rooted ethnic hatred between the black folk of the Central African region. We all knew of the atrocities against the white Congolese via the BBC world news, but the atrocities between tribal groups was underplayed – 'it is an uncontrollable elephant in the room,' said my parents' friends from Elizabethville. 'The departure of us Belgians will not lessen the violence.' They were right. Fear continued its heavy stalk in the form of an ethnic cleansing induced by

ALLAN TAYLOR

witchdoctors – the most powerful people in Africa. Congolese blood, African fear and witchdoctors continued to haunt me at night. My night robber failed to console me, and the night lost a portion of her seductive appeal for a good while after.

In time, like the cripple with his gammy leg, I had to get used to African violence and fear. Even as a privileged little white boy, I had not been the cause of it, and it wasn't aimed at me – it just was – and like the Belgian colonialists, I just had to accept it. Confusion clogged my sweated brow on those dark nights when I spurned the night's loving care. What was I supposed to do? Perhaps, like the Belgians, like Long One, who never talked of these events, like all Africans – I should do nothing. One day truth would wander into the clearing, or would it be fear – were they not the same thing?

2

I FEEL...
FEELING GOOD FOR NO
PARTICULAR REASON, OTHER
THAN THAT 'I AM'

POMEGRANATE RAIN

POMEGRANATE RAIN

So Hum – Feeling rain

As So Hum climbed into the first sturdy branches, a new dream rain fell. It was warmer than So Hum's first dream rain, and it had an attractive colour. Hum could feel new stirrings in his being; a faint tear in his fear-lined coat; something warm and inviting rubbing against the inner walls of his bloodless veins and sloth intestines.

He started to feel good about himself for no particular reason other than there was nothing else to feel good about, that is beside his enriched dreams.

At times he felt he would explode as his good feelings tried to elbow their way out of him…

In spite of what seemed to be a blast furnace of feelings smelting his innards, So Hum survived. His persona grew, as did his strength, and his dreams and desires. Ah Hum his host, felt a stirring in his loins...

So Hum felt the need to share his feelings. Sharing implied oneness with another, but he didn't know if there was another.

His conscious awareness was prickled into desiring more – more of what – it didn't matter what: how should he know? All he knew was that it felt good and he was strong.

His imaginary feet left prints of self-satisfied empowerment, which if he had been born with an intellect, would have turned to vanity. If asked where he got his determination from; he might have said, if he could have spoken, that he got it from the new rain.

Ah Hum's Roots – I feel

Ah Hum's emotional roots grew out of the early feelings of So Hum, his inner-being partner. These early roots were like feelers of sensual joy that radiated out from the base of his spine; they heralded his vitality and his zest for living. They crept into the sinews between his flesh and bone, there to coalesce into his senses of perception, thus enabling him to feel the ambient colours of his new world, of warm reds and glowing oranges. From then on new roots never stopped growing, longer and longer, deeper and deeper, they penetrated his body. They were a never-ending sensual spread of hair-like feelers of emotional knowledge that snaked their way into an ever-changing world of hidden power. These roots were soon the biggest part of him, but they remained for the most part below the surface of his material world. When their tips were exposed they were his passions and his positive emotional ballast. When hidden below, they were his Soul purpose.

Inner magic on a material plane

On picking up on the need to further nurture his emotional roots, Ah Hum would have self-prescribed the following stones, herbs and spices:

Iron Pyrite (fool's gold) and black pepper: *symbolic of the Sun's role as the source of all energy.*

Blood stone and thyme: *to ensure his courage.*

Pyrope garnet and cardamom: *to ensure abundance and vitality.*

Ruby and patchouli: *to enhance his life energy.*

ALLAN TAYLOR

Feelings – emotional signposts

> The seat of my inner child
> African bush paths
> Cerberus, the custodian of the Luanshya River
> The Lady of the Night
> My anthill citadel on the vlei
> Soul mechanics

The seat of my inner child

I was spoilt and mollycoddled as an only child. I was my parents'
5th attempt at having a child. Three were lost, either during
pregnancy or at birth, and one died at one year old. Luanshya
was kind to me, but was not kind to my mother. I survived, I was
a miracle, and I was loved. I was the talk of the town, and Figov's
stuffed elephants and rubber monkeys were showered upon me.
Figov's was a small general dealer's shop run by a Jewish family.
It was on the opposite corner to Werner's butchery, which was
owned by Polish South African immigrants.

All the physical love and attention did not suffice however,
and by the time I was four or five, I had put down my rubber
monkey and instinctively took up my time-ball, and all it stood for.

That's when people started noticing that I was nothing more
than a moody, tempestuous, difficult to please, often peeved,
useless little sod – as someone from the North of England would
say. I did not like being yanked out of the mother comfort of my
time-ball of inner security – but these Luanshya folk didn't, and
wouldn't want to know that would they?

In situations that I didn't care for, Church of England fêtes
or birthday parties of my school 'friends', I would pull up my

long socks, lift my grey tailored shorts even higher above my navel, and stick my tummy out. Behind well-rehearsed rejection I would grab a meringue or a Marie biscuit clown face and withdraw into my cuddly inner oneness. I liked to slowly force chocolate Smartie eyes out of their marshmallow faces with my tongue. My 'sulk' was as deliciously soothing as being tucked up in cool sheets on a rainy night after a sunburnt Sunday of fishing at Makoma Dam.

In those fecund colonial days expansive energies abounded; it was not difficult to make a good life for parents and children alike. I simply chose to join the dots in a different order to the other kids. They got Mecano sets, Scale-Electrix cars and talking dolls, and I got beckoning bush paths and rivers. We used the same free-floating dots but we got different designs. The Luanshyaites said I was odd, I was becoming a loner – and an ungrateful one at that. It was true – I was moody – I was too young to heed whatever it was that was calling me under my skin. It was as if I didn't belong to where I was – as if I belonged to somewhere else.

Every small town has its sulky boy who behaves oddly for a short time, gets over it, and moves on, all under the watchful eye of those who know better and care. I didn't. My introvert behaviour, which was an expression of my inner sensibilities, was becoming an addiction. It was a hidden world where the conventions of pushy people and the forced events of my physical life would have increasingly less of an impact on me. I did not have to exercise my boy-child ego to pin the tail on the donkey, please the teacher, or be smiley polite to adults – I didn't need asinine approval if one and all were an extension of the wonderful world of the inner me.

I was far from being independently hard-headed and strong. I was soft: I simply used my child's softness to slowly permeate the breadth and depth of my world. These were the early creative workings of my conscious awareness. Every soft child has access to it before their ego takes over – I was nothing special.

With my small town situation often demoted to the background of my pointed awareness, I had timelessness on my hands with which to kick up the spiritual dust. Most kids dived into the fantasy worlds of kings and queens, cowboys and Indians; copy-catting the imagery in comics and on the cinema screen. Egos flared, tears spilled, boredom set in, and plastic guns, arrows, axes and crowns were demoted to the back of the smelly shoe cupboard. A bath, a burger, and a quick snuggle in bed were the noble conquests for a child knight of the 'early dinner' table. That was not for me.

I had the propensity to make quantum leaps away from the popular symbols of the 50s and 60s that espoused a return to civil prosperity after the Second World War. Instead, my Soul threw half-submerged worlds at me; exciting worlds partially embedded in the archetypal annals of all men and women around me, black and white; half floating like crocodiles below the emotional surface of my conscious awareness. I took the Greek Mythology book that my godmother had given to me to Theo's Corner Café to show my Greek classmate Dimitri. I thought he would be *interested*; I liked people who were interested; but he wasn't, and I found that quite strange. He said, 'What good is a book like that to you if you only like going fishing?' He worked with his dad every weekend in the delicatessen so he never went anywhere interesting. I wanted to tell him that actually it came in handy when you wanted to give names to describe and explain things, especially when no one else could help you – but I didn't. His father, who was looking over my shoulder, said, 'Look at me. I have never read a book in my life.' He was proud of this strange fact, and even more proud of his workaholic world – which would prevent him from ever reading a book in the future.

'Oh,' I said, and Dimitri nodded. All the kids at school knew that Dimitri would be rich one day, but like his dad, he wouldn't have any free time to spend his money, nor read a book.

Roll on the good times. My parents were caught up in a never-ending chain of English socials and dances, and in keeping with the jolly atmosphere, dragged me along to as many birthday parties, swimming parties, church fêtes and children's events as they could. I went, I saw, I left, and I can't say I was always unhappy, but my Soul, wrapped in the swaddling clothes of a zealous spirit, had other leanings.

African bush paths

My fearful awe of dark nights had metamorphosed into a creative impulse: a constant state of eagerness fuelled by the worry of not meeting my passions full on. I was being steered down a bush path of sensual delight that defied colonial reason, and white adult logic. It was not of my conscious making. Stepping onto an African bush path tapped into a Soul-driven urgency that inflamed every facet of my being.

My sensuality was my spirituality; they were one and the same aethereal footprint on my being. My child's mind never balked at the perverse things that my soft sensuality encouraged me to do – it was steered by winds of youthful spontaneity. I was not an immature off-shoot of the hedonist Western hippies; I was a small white boy in sensual union with the African bush through the kind introduction of my Soul. I was one single iota of a common universal Soul as it vibrated in harmony with the freedom of the times. In my case on a watery seep in Southern Africa.

African bush paths have earth bound creative magic. They are never perfunctory, but always heavy with spiritual purpose. They are the pulsating vascular system of the African continent. The intent that they carry is a cargo of both good and evil, as they shunt the cultural lifeblood of an entire continent from here to there and back again in Afro-rhumba slow time. I could feel the energy of every bush path that I trod – sometimes my body bristled in powerful resonance; at other times I recoiled in damp fear – was this path leading to an unseen vlei or a witchdoctor's hut?

Every path mesmerised my child's mind because of their different characters. Not half a meter wide during the rains, their sides of grass heads whipped my thighs and abdomen, soaked my socks and shorts, and caused welts on my skin, which stung and itched in the hot sun. After the rains, and in the early dry season, their flanks of elephant grass towered above me as impenetrable tinder walls, alive with locusts, dormice and elephant shrews, nesting birds and grass snakes; all awaiting consummation by fire and reduced to sandy meanderings through a charcoal-moon landscape. Some paths were so old that they had become hollowed-out depressions, polished smooth and shiny like snail traces through the landscape. Others were dust trails of footprints, bicycle tracks and maize cob husks, discarded bark string, peanut shells and wild fruit pips. I stayed away from those paths, for they were going to other settlements, and I was only looking for the empty, open bush.

Sometimes, on a path with high grass channelling your surround vision, another path, a less worn path, would suddenly jump out and lead off. At the junction of that rude split, a clump of long grass would be tied in a loose and heavy knot that weighted the grass, making it bend and sway ominously over the path – as if it had a life of its own. Sometimes there was a piece of red cloth tied into the knot. I never ever went down those paths. There were sure to be cloak-and-dagger goings on down there; ritual camps or days-long funeral rites on the go, and in my simple mind, death and the brewing of beer were complicated affairs best to stay away from. I would take a deep breath, and march straight past the dreaded knot in hopeful anticipation of another vlei; a vlei unknown to me; another clearing, an open and free clearing in the bush. Nothing could excite me more.

Cerberus, the custodian of the Luanshya River

My relationship with the Luanshya vlei was on its way to becoming a full-blown addiction for my awakening senses. We moved from 109 Casurina Avenue, next to the primary school, to 2 Poinsettia Avenue, next to the golf course, a rise in Luanshya social ranking. The area was considered to be housing for middle management; it was assumed that only middle management and above needed to play golf. The golf course was carved out of the banks of the Luanshya River as it snaked its lazy way through the town. The white folk, and especially the focused golfers, were oblivious to this wily African river's charms.

'I am taking Kerry for a walk on the golf course Mum,' I would call out from the back door, as she kneaded the pastry for yet another meat pie for dinner; and as usual, my softly spoken, softly thinking, softly loving mother believed me. Why shouldn't she? I always took Kerry, my fox terrier, with me but he would go as far as the furthest green and no further; from where he would await my return.

For me, the safe, sculptured and clipped lushness of the golf course was a ploy, a decoy for the foolish – it was a superficial taming of the African bush that still lurked on the far side of the furthest green. To the sharpened eye that could not be hoodwinked, there was proof of Africa's reality show just a scratch below the orderly surface of spirit-level greens, open fairways and tractor-mowed rough.

Leeches with razor-sharp mandibles writhed in the water that separated fairways. Back-fanged snakes with large eyes and slit pupils hung in the reed beds, where frenetic yellow weaverbirds nested; their floppy-necked chicks to be consumed year after year by one of the writhing locks of a green medusa. The *boomslang* family, Afrikaans for tree snake, and her competitor, the Angolan green snake, both ruled over this African waterway.

Refractions of inner light – Medusa

Perseus, the son of Jupiter, was sent to kill Medusa who was terrorising the people of Greece. She was a vain woman who was in love with her beautiful locks of hair, which she, in arrogance said were more beautiful than those of the Goddess Minerva: who in her anger, turned Medusa's soft curls into writhing snakes that curled about her face in venomous hate.

So horrible was her appearance that anyone who looked into her face turned immediately to stone. Perseus, protected by Minerva's invincible shield, and assisted by Mercury's magic winged shoes, killed Medusa by cutting off her head, which he carried off to present to King Polydectes as a gift. As he flew over Libya, the first drop of blood that fell onto the open sands of the African continent turned into Pegasus, a magic horse with beautiful wings. The countless drops of blood that fell thereafter all turned into snakes, which filled the whole of Africa.

I reckoned that leguaans, jealous about the importance of snakes in this famous story, got into many fights with pythons over it; I had seen quite a few myself on Makoma dam. Pythons always won because they were progeny of a hideous serpent that hid in a cave beneath Mount Parnassus, the home of the Muses. The only person to finally conquer Python was Apollo the Sun God himself, who for some odd reason never supported the leguaans of Makoma Dam in their wars against pythons.

The golf course at the edge of the town, and bordered by bush, was a throb of animal abundance – that was the reason for my initial attraction to the area. Because golf was not my game, nor my aim, and my errant dog and I were getting in the way of the golf *fundi,* we were soon enough shoved into the edges of the far bush. Before long, the golf course was nothing but a lead-up to the pearly gates of my heaven beyond; the delicious safe-haven for my Soul that was the Luanshya bush.

My heart would beat on the strained chords of my voice box and a constriction of energy would press against my pubic bone. I had reached the golf course edge. Although I was far from being a teen, I knew that this was what I had to do. For reasons of manhood, to be issued to me later: I had to sensually lay claim to the psyche of the African bush. I went beyond the furthest green, not to conquer the bush, but to consummate our relationship.

This particular African path, at the edge of the 7th green, professed utility – a means of getting from here to there. In my reality, it offered me power and freedom. It ranked in importance almost as high as the first rains of late October, which washed away the dust of hot days. Both these rains and this path made me feel good; that's when the meniscal boundaries of my timeless bubble of conscious awareness widened of their own accord, and I felt spiritually wise enough to further my inner journey.

The bush path started its life as a stomped, clay track through a reed bed along the river. I was oblivious to the sharp leaf points of reeds that pricked my bare legs, and to the leaded mud that weighted my shoes. Very soon the river lost its controlled form and direction; a rebuff against its earlier life as a tamed and decorative watercourse. It pooled and swirled slowly in heavy folds of grey, its banks greased with malignant bubbles of scum. It opened up in slow, still surfaces and withdrew again, choked by armies of reeds. I would come across an open area. This was no riverside colonial picnic spot – narrow rivulets in the reeds between the pools of stagnant waters were the work of a Luba fisherman. There he was, knee-deep in the water, setting his traps. Naked and squat, except for colonial shorts now turned into a loincloth, there he sat on his muscular haunches. He stunk of fermented mud and rotting barbel guts. I was sure he had webbed feet, for I had once seen him out of the water. Others would have said he had mud caked between toes swollen from constant standing in the water. Only I knew that he had webbed feet with skin that was as rough as a leguaan's back. He had a drum-tight paunch and a protruding belly button. His facial features were flat and wide and his eyes were pushed back into his head by the grimace of a sweating sun. Mud and dry snot caked his wide nostrils, sweat pressed against his greasy cheeks, and grass stalks pierced dirty slits in his earlobes. I always tried to see his teeth but failed – his malevolent lips would never allow the truth to be revealed. They said that in the 20s and 30s, some tribes on the Congo border filed their teeth as part of a cannibal ritual – I thought maybe they still did in some areas – like my vlei. The barbel my Luba fisherman caught would wriggle in a pouch woven from Msasa bark dangling between his legs. Although he didn't have three heads – not that I could see anyway – he was the Cerberus who guarded my river Styx. I received a grunt, never more, as I watched him for a while, and then passed by him and his stench, to follow the path out of the reed beds and up the gradual bank to the hallowed ground that edged my vlei.

My Cerberus was the custodian of the dark side of Africa. He was so repulsive that decent white folk never crossed his threshold, nor ever wanted to. He was necessary in order to keep the Luanshya commonalities at bay, which made the vlei so special.

The only shadow that did cross my child's mind was that of a faint longing to share this Eden, my vlei, with someone special. That never happened. Instead the 'someone' watching on the edge of the clearing was the closest I would get to having a playmate on the vlei; and in fact he was the best company I could ever have hoped for in my Luanshya world, except that I did have someone who visited my little bed at night.

The lady of the Night

While I did not feel a part of the grown-up and children goings-on, Luanshya herself was precious to me. Daily routines and school interfered with my relationship with her, but when I was confined to barracks, and absent from the vlei because of colds or rainy days, or on dark nights when I was in my bed, I would sample her quirks, of which she had many. I had a strong affinity to her ways.

Nyx was the goddess of the night, the night robber introduced me to her, and I called her Luanshya. She was a secretive all-encompassing female creature of an African mother earth, and I loved her out of bonded respectful love. She was a living swell of the universal aether, which had its own mind as it eddied through my boyhood. For my senses, she was a Carmen, Bizet's ultimate steamy lover. As I lay in my metal-framed bed at night, my mind and body well spent, she would hover over my deepest sleeps, picking out the shards of broken dreams and desires from my punctured flesh. It was not a humble act of love and devotion; she was too powerful for that. It was out of an almost connubial respect of each other's needs. Because of my infatuation for her, I convinced myself that she must need me as much as I needed her. That was the only security I had that she would never leave me.

It was not the mine conveyor belts, refineries and smelters that I heard every night; the uncanny drone of her wings back-dropped my night reveries and fanned my desires for a bright new morning. She was like a benevolent tropical mosquito that gently pierced my skin with her proboscis to inject a sweet strain of delirium into my veins: an antidote to a colonial-induced child tedium.

In the dead of night her subcutaneous elixir would take possession of me. My slight frame would be racked with a reflex that would start at my toes and end with a pop at the back of my nose. My spine would curl up like freshly peeled Msasa bark and my knees would involuntarily spring up to my chest. I would stay in this rigid foetal position with my arms wrapped around my knees, holding on for dear life. I could feel my equilibrium shift from one side of my narrow bed to the other. My doting mother would have thought I was racked with fever, but I knew it was no malaria: it was Luanshya's injected passion, advancing like a heatwave towards my Soul. I had to gag the odd squeak to avoid alerting my parents in the next-door bedroom. Her energetic serum would catapult me out of my schoolboy reality and deposit me into another information bank with its own time and space: it would winkle-hook my curiosity, and temper my need for urgent resolutions. That is when I had my 'eureka' moments, my quantum leaps into universal knowledge. There was nothing special about me. Most kids have these experiences; it is just that no one listens to a child long enough to hear about them, and on top of that, children are apt to forget such *things*: nice dreams, eureka moments are hastily dragged back into our subconscious. Sadly our parents don't encourage us to see magic and miracles beyond bedtime stories, never mind gather them in real life, and definitely not upon waking when school is calling.

On some days I would wake up with so much energy that I didn't know what to do with it, I didn't know where to start, and I would spend the rest of the day frustrated and moody;

her powerful elixir misspent and abused and grown-ups not amused.

Luanshya allowed me to see beyond her props and back-drops. She allowed me to sneak into her backstage, where every theatrical script in the Universe was to be found. She pushed me into believing that I was the chosen one, a singular player on her stage, where everyone else was a repainted, ever-changing hardboard prop. I loved her for treating me like this. Perhaps that was the reason for my oddness and my lonely isola-tion from other Luanshya folk. True love is not a group thing: I wanted her alone. I was obsessed by her, and still am, although her time and space forms have since changed.

As her novitiate in theatrical love, my feeble senses were put to the test as she stretched my perceptions to ever-increasing limits. Her shimmering midday heats, brought in from across the far vleis, and heated further by her iron roofs and black tarmac roads, slapped me in the face and ripped at my breath to test my emotional metal. She teased me with the repulsive cool darkness of our dining room, which almost seemed attrac-tive in light of her heated onslaughts. The heavy shadows of her darkness that chased me all the way from the vlei to home were always edging to be one step ahead of me. She further flaunted their billowing forms in the recesses of the mango trees in our garden. She forced fruit bats to crash out of their leafed safety in panic and flung darkness at me just as my toes took hold of the warm *stoep*. All this should have frightened the life out of me and it did; but I still loved her in my breathless state.

When a heat fraught summer's day was all said and done, with a dollop of black humour, she forced our overburdened senses to do a flick flack. She replaced the unbearable burn-ing colours of our daytime world with frenetic night sounds – a maddening cacophony of frazzled beetles that buzzed and pinged on the gauze of our windows. She was brewing up a storm.

Her violent thunderstorms were edged with the rattle of her corrugated iron roofs. Her lightening was as sharp as an old hag's tongue as it flicked and forked the town apart, always rending a soft-wood tree apart. The gardening white folk, not my white subtribe, would lament, 'Oh, what a shame. It was planted by old Mr 'so and so' in 1939. It had such beautiful flowers,' and Luanshya's retort would be: 'No place for Brazilian exotics in my life. Have you not seen my Msasas in their spring foliage of copper and ruby? Well haven't you, speak up! Has a colonial cat bit your tongue? Speak up.' She could be so insensitive at times. During her most violent night storms she replaced every bright coloured flower in our gardens with an achromatic blitz of silver and white ash as she hammered on her steel kettle drum for further battalions of thunder and lightning.

Some nights Luanshya withheld the cooling rain to enforce the oppressive heat of sleepless nights. These nights, heavy with a false expectation of rain, were like clammy sponges that should have burst their waters – but didn't, their bolshie presence pierced only by the whine of acrobatic mosquitoes. She was always testing the steel of my senses. As a brave lover I had to see through her ploy. I had no option. There was no escape; she had me pinned to my little bed. I never gave in; unlike grown-ups, I never wished for highland retreats, cool nights, or trips back to England. Instead, I would come out of the sheets, take my wet towel and place it over my bed. I would lie motionless in its invisible cooling mists and absorb her dramatic presence through all my senses.

She cast her personality over me as a symphonic poem of night sounds. Early in the evening her nightjar was calling – called the litany bird, it seemed to say 'Good Lord, deliver us' in prophetic desperation. Late in the night the eagle owls called each other in baritone duets of vooo-hoo, vooo-hoo. All her African night calls were backdropped by the popping sound of a million reed frogs down by the Luanshya River; and in the foreground of my senses was the swish of the maracas – the soft flip-flop sound of emperor moth's wings against the copper mosquito gauze. Then arrived the insensitive gate crashers of the night: her squadrons of hard-bodied sausage flies, rose beetles and the occasional rhino beetle, all captives of an obscure and cruel Soul purpose that hurled them against my gauzed-in windows without any plausible meaning. The grand finale, which I always tried to stay awake for, was when, in a most uncanny way; there was a hiatus in sound. In the deafening silence that followed, the warm night air seemed so taught that it could snap. The tension in the throats of silenced frogs, crickets, cicadas and night birds could be felt. It was as if they were all reading the same symphonic score. Then, from somewhere in the black folds of her velvet nightdress, a slow tapping of her long fingernails was heard. At first it was distant and regular, then it was close and irregular; then without time to ponder on its origin, it was upon me – on the corrugated iron roof above my head. An atmospheric drummer's solo that pummelled the iron, sending my emotions into a joyous spin. Luanshya, in her incorrigible way, had announced the arrival of her greatest gift: the rain. There was still tension in the air: Even after such a herald of certainty, she could withdraw her gift in an instant. A heavy drumming upon the steel of our high hopes; a false pitter-patter reveille of her forward artillery in mock advance;

then a complete withdrawal of her rear guard. There was thunder, lightning and heavy drops but no soaking rain, and that's when my emotions would plummet into the bottomless dark regions of my sleep for the rest of a steamy and uncomfortable night. That happened often, but when she did give us rain, what followed was a re-enactment of her daytime storms. This time the darkness introduced an echoing quality that seemed to bounce the thunder of her artillery to everywhere and back: around the garden, through the town, and even between the walls of my room. Her lightening was both the conductor and choreographer in this 1812 tympanic symphony. It was accompanied by a demon's shadow dance across the garden – thankfully, only a fraction of which was cast onto my curtains and reflected down onto the polished floor below my window: but it was more than enough to occupy my senses with rapt awe and fearful respect. During those sound and light shows I forgot to breath. I became drowsy and then left the room for a date with my tempestuous queen of the night in a state of deaf oblivion; deaf and dumb to her feigned anger, which she recklessly tossed around her. It was time for her to free herself from any form of intercourse with the fainthearted. It was not that I had a tougher heart than other kids: It was simply that I made my immature body suppliant and available to her rough wiles. Like a bamboo cane bending in the storm, I succumbed to her ways not by submission, but by swaying in complicity.

If it was October and Luanshya was still withholding her rain, I might have drifted into an unsettled sleep because of the seductive scent of jasmine perfume that she splashed on the nape of her long, curved neck. The quiet Afrikaans lady, Mrs. Gouws, who lived next door, had a large trellis of jasmine on the common border between our gardens. At night, the overpowering scent of jasmine would waft into my bedroom. I had read that jasmine was also the chosen aroma of Selene, the goddess of the moon. On a full moon I would peer out my window to see if it was true that jasmine flowers glowed with a white fluorescence in the moonlight – they certainly did, but so did everything else white, including my baboon skull, which I had mounted on a rock right outside my bedroom window.

In December, tea-scented drifts of hot air would hint of new moon flowers unfolding, the thought of which would carry me into the comforting arms of deep sleep; then as midnight approached, and when the large petaled corollas of these haunting flowers were fully extended, I would be further drawn by their soporific scent into my curiously familiar dreams. The Luanshya night pollinated these plate-sized trumpet flowers with moths and bats. By morning these fragile beauties were limp afterthoughts of her post-midnight magic. Whereupon she would gently press the residues of their lily and orange perfume into her pre-dawn wrists in a mood of quiet acquiescence and spent nights. Her night reveries were forced to bow down before the heated arrogance of yet another day to come.

My anthill citadel on the vlei

I firmly believed that Luanshya created her surrounding bush especially for me and my senses. In my small boy mind, no other Copperbelt town had bush quite like hers, and I more than loved her for it.

Out of the reed beds and the clodding mud, and with a prising of clumps of clay off my shoes, I would make my way up to the tree line. Once there I would stop and look back onto the vlei, the marshy seep that breast-fed the Luanshya river, now free from her quaggy Luba fisherman's shackles, and more importantly, from the golf course, which had failed to bridle her any further. I did this with a sort of pride that only comes from intimate love. Further down, the Luanshya River did not carry the same stagnant negative energy that Cerberus' reed beds so freely offered; her fresh purpose was as pure as the subterranean waters that were percolating down from the surrounding forests into her riverbed. If the murky, bilharzia-infested waters of the reed beds were the large gut of effluence and elimination; then the vlei and its pure underground water were its cardiovascular system which oozed renewed African life force down from its forest lungs. For reasons familiar and connected, this vlei with its riverine heart, and breathing forest edges, and all vleis beyond my youth and into my young adulthood, would evoke an overbearing feeling of physical and emotional oneness. A warm intimate male-female sharing in my heart, which would radiate into all my extremities. Vleis provided me with more than just wholesome enjoyment. They were the tangibly 'felt' emotional evidence of creation – the truth of mankind in a perfect universe.

Eternally bathed in the African sun and rain, the Luanshya vlei willingly shared its energy with me. Every visit was a micro-percolation into my being of energy, which I stored in the reservoir of my heart. Energy that initially precipitated out in the form of adventurous inquiry and silly boy shenanigans; but in time crystallised into an inspirational love of life. It happened every time I came across a piece of open bush, and still does.

This vlei, my vlei, was peppered with termite mounds like liver spots and moles on a weather-beaten back. In some parts it was drowned in tall elephant grass that swayed above me on a hot wind, and in other parts the grass was knee-high, flexible, almost evergreen and shiny; this grass was soft and was ideal for lying on when I was in my cloud-chasing moods. The sky above my vlei was always wide open and free, no matter what clouds the brewing storms would drag over its horizon in the rainy season. Vleis keep the daunting forests at bay, no tree daring to cross the line of their leeched soil boundaries. No gatherings of trees, no dark shadows. That was one of the reasons why I felt safe there, comfortable in myself: I felt I had both my mortal, and spiritual backs covered.

I discovered a termite castle of grandiose proportions, and immediately proclaimed it as mine: an island mountain jutting out of a grassy sea which rolled its dusty breakers across the vlei. It bore its own dense riparian forest of half a dozen evergreen trees: wild fig, pod mahogany and water berry among them. The soil was of ant-refined clay, and of such a superior building quality. The termites had crafted and moulded it into amazing gothic cathedral arches, turrets and spires; out of which arose a thick canopy of shade and camouflage. Not a mere arbour, nor innocent bower, but a panoply of protection; a grandiose pavilion with wild clematis creepers flying my ensign on a hot Luanshya wind. My anthill castle would have been the envy of every knight of Camelot.

I called it an anthill – we colonials understatedly called them anthills, but in truth, they were termite mounds. But the word mound didn't do justice to them. They were small hills, and they didn't house ants – they housed termites: white ants we called them. I had claimed ownership of this castled kingdom, and I suppose that also meant matrimonial possession of its queen in residence; but to be honest, I didn't think of that at the time.

This clandestine copse on a termitine hillock became my citadel of warm retreat: somewhere I could withdraw to let my soft inner forces work *things* out.

Something, someone – animal or human, I was never quite sure – had been there before me. It had gouged out a haunch-shaped lookout area on its pinnacle that looked out across the vlei. A depression where I could place my own bum, or squat in African style, with armpits cupped over my raised knees, my body in a semi-foetal pose just watching; barely thinking, just waiting… waiting for something or nothing to happen on the vlei. After meeting Mr Kumar, the Indian tailor, I alternated this pose with squatting like a yogi to see if it gave any better results in achieving nothingness: I think it did.

Because it was natural and comfortable in my heart to position myself like this on hot afternoons when the air was slow to enter my lungs; insights about my life and needy solutions to my childish, and not so childish, problems would pop out of my subconscious awareness. I attributed this inner happening as part of the magic of the Luanshya vlei, who seemed to want to push my boundaries, if not beyond hers, to at least on a par with hers.

If I wasn't on my throne of quiet contemplation, I was busy experimenting halfway down in an exposed well of roots and termite convolutions that was my alchemist's laboratory; the place where I scrutinised and dissected objects of my current attention and fascination. Lizard eggs, 'iffy' school reports, old family photos, bird's nests and grown-up paraphernalia were studied to hopefully explain and appease the emotional intensities that made up my childish world of wants and dis-wants. It was a den where I could also muse over my desires to fly, hatch chameleons; catch newborn rivers and other *things*.

Shenanigans – boyish peeks at life

Wall geckos and house lizards lost their tails as an escape mechanism every time I tried to catch one – to then grow a new one – which I found fascinating. Their tails would wriggle and squirm for a long time after they had been cut off from their supply of oxygenated blood. I liked to tickle my nose, eyelids and ears with their seemingly immortal flick flacking dismemberments. I brought both types of tails to the anthill on the vlei to experiment with. They had the same texture and taste on my tongue. Although the geckos' tails were a bit rougher because their scales were more like thorny warts. They both had a metallic Brasso taste. Brasso was the chemical our domestics used to polish the window brasses and taps. The tails both dried without giving off a rotten smell. The lizard tails smelled of *kapenta*, sun-dried water sardines from Lake Tanganyika, while dried gecko tails smelled of mummified reed frogs that got trapped in window frames at the end of the rainy season. When burnt, the lizard tails smelled of dead pythons; whereas the gecko tails smelled of the singed hair. I never had success fishing for bream with reptile tails for worms – maybe it was tiger fish bait and

anyway, they were too bony to thread onto a
small bream hook.

I was certain that I shared this termite bastion with others; silent and sly others, who always arrived in my absence... night
visitors, when-I-was-at-school visitors, and when-I-was-on-
Makoma-Dam visitors. There would be trampled foliage, scuf-
fles and drag marks in the dirt, and sometimes even a lingering
organic smell. I could always tell if a python had been there –
they have a distinctive bird's feather smell, and their poo stinks!
They said that besides pythons; cobras, ant bears, porcupines
and pangolins; aardvarks and aardwolves all frequent anthills.
Like me, they make them bastions of secure camouflage and
defence. We all took shifts in command of this special termite
mound: sometimes I felt some of the other commandants
hadn't quite knocked off duty as I retook control at the helm.
As Quasimodos, of the same earth spirit as the Congolese forest
gods, they were still skulking in the vaults of our gothic fortress.
If they weren't physically present, they were present in spirit,
and at times I felt they oversaw my experimentations, possibly
even influencing the results. Always being a loner on my anthill
on the vlei, and seemingly the only person in this expanse of
bush – besides my trusted mythological acquaintances and the
observer on the edge of the clearing – I was given the honour
of creating my own world. I was entirely in command of my own
thoughts and intentions; I had no one to answer to, and abso-
lutely no one person, or no one thing to follow or please. What
I felt and imagined reality to be, was exactly what reality was
showing me. How lucky I was to come across such a wonderful
Camelot.

I felt I was the benevolent dictator of my termite kingdom – unlike the aardwolf, ant bear and the pangolin, I didn't have the penchant for eating my termitine vassals. One day I spotted a column of Matabele ants approaching the anthill. These creatures were named after Lobengulas's *impis*, the warrior descendants of Shaka the Zulu king's reign. While I liked the name 'Matabele ant,' I also called these insect warriors the Myrmidons. The Myrmidons were fierce ants that were turned by the Gods into the warrior soldiers of Achilles in the Trojan War. Matabele ants march in columns many feet long, and up to two inches wide. Their arthropod goose step is heard as the ghost click of an executioners death march. The most stoic of men and beasts become unnerved by the sight and sound of the sheer collective intent of these singular-minded marauders whose Soul purpose was to annihilate termite colonies, or so they said – how bizarre, how wicked, I used to think. I didn't get chance to see how the Myrmidons made their attack on my defenceless minions because Perseus had to go home for an early bath: there was a birthday dinner, and we were getting together with friends for our favourite North of England dish – potato pie served piping hot with pickled red cabbage, fresh sliced onion and tinned peas. The next day the anthill appeared as if it had escaped a genocide, and the Matabele ants were gone. It seemed that the termite's motto of safety in numbers, and the sheer grandeur of their secret catacombs, was their success story. Then again I wasn't at all sure of what the tell-tale signs of a Matabele massacre would be. In my heart however, I knew that the marauding ants had done what had to be done: mass slaughter was the footprint of their one Matabele Soul.

The foundations of large anthills are a groundswell of weather-beaten clay and exposed roots that twist and turn in perpetual termitine slow motion. They said that the local people, under the orders of witchdoctors, carried out funeral rituals on anthills. Bodies, especially of deceased children and the senile, could have be buried in my anthill long before. In a child's moment of musing, I thought that perhaps they needed the expert services of the ant undertakers, who could dissolve a timber structure in a matter of days. In reality, I knew this couldn't be true – termites only ate plant cellulose – but I rather fancied the thought that termites could be so helpful.

The *hammerkop* is the Afrikaans name for a bird with a hammer-shaped head. The perverse doings of hammerkops in nest building in the air were akin to the doings of witch-crafted earth beings in the anthills of Africa. These strange birds build large, flat communal nests, not unlike like the roof of an African hut of clay, sticks and dry grass, and not far short in size. They uncannily adorn their nests with human trimmings of old bits of plastic, wire, tin cans, old shoes, domestic animal hair, skin and bones; and cloth – especially red cloth. African folklore says that this hankering for human artefacts points to the fact that they are possessed by the spirits of the dead. Anthills seemed not to be much different.

Each rainy season the subterranean earthen seas of anthills would throw up an African jetsam – sloughed snake skins, parched bones and teeth, buried animal horns stuffed with desiccated animal body parts, shattered clay beer pots, beads and strips of red cloth – artefacts for the dead on their journey. I once found a bicycle bell. They were all the totems and tools of gothic visitors – the *n'angas* of bygone nights and their ardent followers. A macabre bric-a-brac of juju unceremoniously exposed by intrusive rains which whittled away at my anthill's human and not so human secrets year after year.

I firmly believed that my night robber, the same night, after having visited my room, had also visited my anthill. His Soul had conversed with the termitine Soul of the anthill: he had been under obligation to do so. On the anthill he had said that he was sorry for the disturbance that he had caused in my room – but he did what he had to do, and that made him feel good about himself. The thought of this made me feel glad. With all the colonial policeman hullabaloo going on around me that night, I had no way of knowing or surmising that this might happen, until later on in my anthill musings.

I was, and will always remain, in immeasurable awe of all anthills, and of all people and animals who used them on all vleis, in all of Africa. The millions and millions of termites that created them had knowingly erected beacons of the African spirit from Cape Town to Cairo: in close communication with each other, as I later found out.

These clay monoliths were also vast ant worlds of hierarchy: colonising armies, vassalage, forced slavery and fungal horticulture to breakdown cellulose for food, all silently orchestrated by an omnipotent queen. They say that anthills are like icebergs – seven eighths of their size lies below the surface – with ventilation pipes designed to aerate and cool their subterranean kingdoms. In the 18th century, an Afrikaans biologist, Eugene Maris, wrote *The Soul of the White Ant*, such was his fascination for the complex life of termites. Small, seemingly simple creatures that masterminded intricate divisions of labour, and built earthen empires beyond the comprehension of men of that time. Termites are a million times larger in creative spirit than what we give them credit for.

Refractions of inner light – The Soul of the white ant

'You must consider a termitary as a single animal, whose organs have not yet been fused together as in a human being. Some of the termites form the mouth and digestive system others take place of weapons of defense like claws and horns; others form generative organs. ... You understand now what the psychologist means when he says that the instinctive psyche cannot deviate from the inherited formula of behavior, and that no individual can acquire a causal memory – in other words he cannot learn by his own experience. I also said that the psyche of inherited memories is a force which cannot be turned aside even by death if escape means behavior.'

The Soul of the White Ant. 1937 translation from the Afrikaans *Die Siel van die Mier,* published in 1925.

Although I could not voice it as a child, I could feel it: Anthills are a microcosm, a holographic icon of the connected and creative spirit of Africa, which incorporates all its people, plants and animals. As such, anthills bestow upon all living creatures, an unspoken sacred duty of common respect and a reverent knowingness of every living thing that has gone before. There is not a single unfolding event that goes unnoticed by these overseers of the African bush. The fearful death of an animal; the erection of a primitive human structure; the defecation of a pile of dung: all is recorded – and a reconnaissance mission is sent out to substantiate and deal with the real situation at hand.

Termite colonies are an ever-moving expression of life force and causal energy. Their divisions of labour refine the crude earth of the deepest vleis into the finest of grits, which they endlessly pile up high above the surrounding land in honour of the highest Gods. My anthill in particular, became my North Star which pointed to the validity and reason for my present moment being. Of the finest aethereal 'stuff', it was the best gift that the Luanshya vlei could have bestowed upon me. It enabled me to polish my self-awareness in better sentience of my important role as a small white boy in Africa. It was synchrodestiny, when years later, my boarding school biology teacher, and housemaster, who was a fiercely proud Huguenot from the Cape, introduced me, without the slightest prompt, to a book written by a relative of his: *The Soul of the White Ant.* This fine teacher, with a passion for scientific inquiry in the field of bushcraft, was to further my own passion for the African bush during my high school years. The serendipity of it all brings a wry smile to what feels like a slightly upbeat Soul as I write these words.

The anthill on the vlei was the home dock for my journey of the Soul. The timeless spiritual goings-on below the surface of my anthill world were not machinations of ill intent that some might have wanted to believe. They were African bush happenings imbued with the spiritual perfection and honest goodness that ruled all nature. By some quirk, by placing my bony little bum on that anthill, which possibly still housed pythons, other reptiles and vile mythological beasts, I had access to a spiritual treasure trove. My shenanigans above the surface of the anthill were sanctioned and blessed by a trillion little gods of knowingness below the ground, which in turn, along with strange Quasimodos, made up the one thinking African spirit, the Soul of Africa.

That no one else made use of this gift, I was sure. The base and lower reaches of my anthill, and most African anthills, have fierce mythological sentries that repel all intruders without a scaly or hard skin like the python and the leguaan – or without a course pelt like the honey badger. Trained, well-disciplined, and emotionless sentries were on a 24 hour guard outside all entrances. They were stinging nettles and worse – buffalo beans, a plant that bore pods covered in minute barbed hairs, which caused an excruciating itch under the skin. I officially named these guardian plants after The Symplegades, the open and closing rock faces that prevented ancient sailors from reaching the Black Sea, the Gateway to the East. Jason and the Argonauts conquered them with a small white dove – I with a bush duiker. After Jason had managed to pass through The Symplegades, these horrific cliffs froze in an open position, thus allowing the Ancient Greeks free passage to the East forever. In a similar way I was able to slip past my Symplegades time and time again. Heavy rains had hollowed out a hidden tunnel under the buttress roots of my largest fig tree. It was wide enough for little me to creep up until I had passed the ferocious herbal sentry line. How I found this secret path was fortuitous. The tunnel was leading to the home of a duiker antelope, also thick-pelted, who had worn a sentry free path up to its entrance, and even higher. I often wondered if it also climbed up to put its rump in the well-worn saddle throne to ruminate on *things*. On an early reconnaissance mission, when I first stood in awe of the anthill, I was almost upon the duiker before it bolted out of its den in fear. Curious to see what a duiker home would look like inside, I crept in, and as Mother Nature would say, the rest was history. The duiker didn't seem to mind my frequent visits. It would see me coming, retreat to the long grass on the tree line, and watch me. Solitary duikers have an insatiable curiosity, and so every time I was there, it was, along with my silent observer, following my crazy antics. I named her Pegasus after Perseus's winged horse. Pegasus, after nobly helping Perseus, flew up to the celestial home of the Gods, where she was tamed by the Goddess Minerva, and presented to the Muses for their divine enjoyment.

The anthill island was my lofty platform from where I planned my break away from the pathetic role of an only child in a colonial slow-town. I could have remained a daydreaming boy wistfully looking out of a veranda window with pop songs from the Monkeys and the Beatles buzzing in my head. I would have not heard the call of the other side as it beckoned to me from somewhere beyond my ken. Instead my conscious awareness was given wings on an anthill, my anthill on the vlei.

Soul mechanics

Some would say that our Soul is an intrinsic and confusing lesser part of us, something vague that loosely tags along behind us. Something to be used as a spiritual CPR kit in matters of life and death, prayer and devotion. Others say, with a hushed voice, that it is our connection to God, and as such it must be revered and never misused.

Just as I can describe the relativity of my time as a hollow rubber ball, so can I describe my Soul as being the sole owner of my gawky mind and body.

Inside my time ball there is an apparent nothingness which defines the outside circumference of my outer oneness. My life, like a rubbery skin, passionately wraps itself around this mysterious rounding force of nothingness; which in turn defines my physical wholeness, my rounded permanence, which in turn is my creative potential for being. I call this inner space of 'nothingness' my Soul.

A pot is a pot, and not a useless hollowed out lump of clay precisely because of its inner emptiness. The outer shape of the pot doesn't matter – its usefulness is inside, which in turn, defines its potential worth to hold, encompass and carry things. A hollow ball is a little different in that its nothingness is meant to hold nothing inside but instead defines everything on the outside of its inner roundness – therein lies the usefulness of its inside nothingness. In the same way this seemingly useful round nothingness defines the existence of my inner purpose, my 'who I am' – my validity. No matter how colourful, dull, intricate or simple my outer might appear to be, I am my inner nothingness – I am my Soul.

Roundness demands an inner force of universal cohesiveness, which is defined mathematically by the connected unity of every material point from its circumference to its centre. Therein lies my inner time ball's immeasurable power of spiritual oneness. My Soul is a rounded force of cohesion and attraction. Whereas physical laws govern gravity to ensure my material presence on earth, it would seem that spiritual laws of inner cohesion govern my Soul. My inner nothingness, which is my Soul, is my limitless potential for being: It would also be timeless if it weren't for my enforced physical addiction to time – which defines my physical mortality.

My Soul will probably fly even further and faster when I am physically gone and free from my timeline. For now it is content to nestle in the heart of the temporal me: to whisper in my ear every now and then; possibly having quiet chats with my observer at the edge of my inner clearing beyond.

The events of my life do not delineate who I am. They are mere chaff in the wind compared to this inner presence that continually redefines the physical thinking me.

The centre of my time ball is not really filled with nothingness – its substance is aether. Aether is the magic non-stuff that permeates the entire universe with its subtle presence, which it does without discrimination or time-bound relevance.

On the inside, it sensually creeps between the sheets of my body. It enfolds all my organs and tissues, fills my mouth, lungs and gut. It is my inner space, and I can feel it; it is dark red, warm and supportive. It defines my physical self-awareness, my sensual joy and my eternal desire for loving oneness. It houses my cognition, my love, my resolve and my emotional intelligence – my 'everything'. It is my conscious awareness, and because of that, it is my self-empowerment, and because of that, it defines the role of my physicality.

Refractions of inner light – Aether

Aether was the son of Erebus, the god of darkness, and Nyx the goddess of the night, my Luanshya night. Aether was the personification of the rarefied air that the Gods breathed. This was as opposed to the air that mortals breathed, which was called Chaos.

The aether's 'here, there and everywhere' character makes it an accomplice in the endless transmission of electromagnetic and bio-chemical messages of warmth, light, knowledge, truth and love. Without the aether there would be no conscious awareness. Everyone on earth would be a sightless, feelingless, meaningless, loveless blob of nothingness unaware of their own or any other's existence. Life would be a senseless black hole.

This unfathomable stuff of nothingness is my inner awareness, a force of spiritual cohesion that endlessly defines my wholeness – my oneness with everything that is, which is the ultimate expression of my love of life.

I am subservient to my Soul because I am of the aether. I am a whisper-faint physical echo of the primordial formulae that make up an aether-based informational universe of perfection – a thinking universe with a structured intelligence that safeguards my Soul.

3

I WANT...
I AM, I FEEL, THEREFORE I WANT

CITRINE RAIN

CITRINE RAIN

So Hum – wanting rain

So Ham took time to move among the broad branches of his imaginary rain tree. In time his gait changed. It was still a hesitant rock – back and forth, a slow rhumba; but when his front foot lifted, and the back foot landed, they did so with an added permanence of 'I want', which was followed by, 'I want more'.

So Hum partook in pleasurable things for a good while; in fact, beyond the boundaries of time, but then a citrine bejewelled rain was carried in. It was one of those timeless soft rains that carried a promise of consolidated growth, and yet So Hum could swear that this time it was edged with foreboding.

His wobbly bobbly eyes had lost most of their malignant fear during the good times, but now they were cataracting over with avarice and a mistrust of perhaps not getting enough of everything that he really wanted.

He foolishly interpreted its offer of quiet restraint and fortitude as a spartan choice, and rejected it because he saw it as a punishing onslaught against his greedy senses. This vagary would cost him much emotional pain.

In So Hum's small delusional mind, if you could call it a mind, the citrine rain came in a cutting slant of slivers of bright yellow crystals that stung his defenceless protruding eyes, whipped his hunched back, and brought him to his first tears of confused disappointment.

Why were his dreams changing? What was wrong with him? Was he weak? Why was he being punished? He needed a second opinion. What was the point of feeling good and strong about yourself if you couldn't see your reflection in others? He wanted somebody out there to measure his self-worth against, someone to help correct his shortfalls, if he had any: a 'someone else' to put his dreams back on track and get the good old rains back forever. And if there was nobody, then he must at least find himself. So Hum felt threatened.

Yellow is a callous and uncompromising colour. It is overly generous and bright, but it does not hand its hues over with grace, nor does it know its boundaries. At best it is brash, and more often than not, hurtful. So Hum needed to take control of the situation because no one else would.

After centuries of mulling over inclement rains, he began to see things clearer. Without eyes and a proper mind, this was not easy, so he relied heavily on his emotions.

The truth was there was never anything wrong with the citrine rain. Nothing of importance had changed, except for a small part of So Hum. It was as if his blind eyes could 'see' a bit further than before. He felt optimism drifting in and out of him like those half-formed cloud banks that escape the greed of a violent storm. Cloud banks that eventually condense into soft rain over a grateful savannah, rain that washes a blameless blue sky with primrose yellow, the colour of encouragement and hope.

Was it that So Hum was now seeing the truth behind the citrine rains? With hope and perseverance, he would get everything he wanted. He had to keep climbing.

Ah Hum's Roots – I want

Because of the secretive, dark wanting nature of his emotional roots, it was not unnatural for Ah Hum's senses to be ill at ease. They brought dull pain and anxiety to his mind whenever he felt he wasn't getting enough; enough of what? It was a sense of foreboding, which he found strangely comforting at times – a sense of feeling sorry for himself, a perverse kind of self-love that reinforced his wanting need for love and change. It was as if he needed to suffer if he was to get anywhere. His gut palpated in sluggish resonance with these earthed feelings, and he felt strangely grounded. Grounded enough to want to take the next step forward into the fearful but irresistible wanting of the unknown.

At times his sensitivity picked up on the sharp grits of his reality and he felt the need to gird his loins. This gave his urgent needs the power they deserved, but with this strident sensuality came a propensity for irritation, anger and frustration. It was in this heated defiance of the unknown, which he seemed to want so badly, that the worst side of his overbearing ego came out – it could have been his best. He was determined to get what he wanted.

Inner magic on a material plane

How could So Hum deal with such powerful swells in his body? He turned to the materials of his soothsaying trade for help:

> Citrine and lemon grass: *to further self-control through the Soul and not the ego.*
> Golden topaz and rosemary: *to solidify good intentions and accomplish resolute action.*

Chrysoberyl and lemon oil: *to sharpen his focus and rid him of small-mindedness and confusion.*

Moonstone and jasmine: *to help him understand the natural cycles of change, of hot and cold, good and bad, joy and fear, male and female.*

Needy desires as affirmations of self-worth

A child ripped from its roots
Janet and John
A hand in the Libyan Desert
Offbeat evangelism
Dug up, refined and smelted
Makoma Dam blues
Landlocked stargazer
Canoes and Bemba fishermen
Truth on the water
Tribal wars – culture clashes
Hyenas and termite mounds
An odd rain
Pandora's Box

A child ripped from its roots

Mine houses didn't have built-in cupboards. Everyone had a freestanding cupboard in their bedroom, cheap imitations of Cape Dutch cottage furniture made by Johannesburg factories to meet the demands of the steady flow of immigrants to the Colonies. Ours were stained dark and were plain, whereas some of the wealthier South African families, whose fathers were management, had beautiful fruitwood and oak carved cupboards. The top of any parent's cupboard is a secret place, where parents stored things like Christmas presents, or things... other things. I got up there; I have a mental block as to how – maybe I coerced Paul the then house servant into the dastardly deed.

There it was... in a hatbox was this thing... a scuffed Bakelite trumpet-shaped thing with a perished red rubber bladder. Something told me it wasn't a child's toy, not a hooter horn...

it was something to do with sex. A boy in my class brought condoms to school that he had found on top of a cupboard. The sight of this grotesque toy that I found had a serious effect on me. After having pulled it down with effort, I held it in my hands. I could immediately smell alienation. Scrutiny turned to rejection and my body lost balance and reason – this thing was obviously used in times of my exclusion and I felt betrayed.

Few of us want to acknowledge the pain that stabs at the fragile Soul of a young person upon their first sexual imagery, especially when it is to do with their parents, and especially if they have been wrapped in cotton wool. Intense fascination skewered by betrayal, anger fanned by lost love, and the pain of rejection. Things fly out of our control. Nothing is ever as it was before. Parental hugs and kisses become tell-tale signs of adult collusion. I took that breast pump, as I later discovered, to the anthill for a serious mental dissection.

I took this object to be a harbinger of my confused origins. I already had a strong feeling that I did not belong to my particular white tribe and now it would appear that I did not belong to my parents either. My mother, so soft and gentle, was a perfect image of feminine spirit and unconditional love. Why did she have to suffer so much over lost children? This weird contraption with sexual connotations substantiated all the stories of the difficulties my poor mother had with giving birth. This thing, this off-limits thing, was hidden on top of the cupboard because it was meant to have been used to produce healthy babies. It was held from view because it had never worked. I was surely adopted. The fact that I looked so much like my father – curly dark hair, deep set eyes and expressive lips, pouting, some would have said – was of no relevance.

Now I really was a lost child, an only adopted child without material lineage and without a tribe. This brought a wrench to both my solar plexus and my ego. All the parental love I had been given was false. I was a fraud: once a fraud always a fraud. Why did I have to climb up and get this horrible thing? Things were going reasonably well until then.

On the anthill I came to the ruthless conclusion that I had to find my own open waters in a spiritual battle for my own identity for the good or the bad. I could sort of forgive my parents and those that were loving and kind to a genealogical misfit like me, but I couldn't forget, at least not for a hurtful while.

It was the good life of the sixties. Trini Lopez singing, 'Lemon tree very pretty and the lemon flower is sweet – but the fruit of the poor lemon is impossible to eat.' SOE fetes, tombola at the club, and the grand opening of *The Sound of Music* at the mine cinema made life easy. While I enjoyed parts of them all, especially the naughty nuns in *The Sound of Music*, everyone was in cahoots, hiding the shocking truth: nuns, rectors, scout guides, teachers, grown-ups, and even our domestics. Oh, the utter shame of it all.

Times were good but things were also becoming turbulent. Miners, black and white, went on strike without pay. The Vietnam War and the Cold War were being talked about on the BBC broadcasting from London, and I felt their heavy edge on our small-town events. They made my bedtimes complicated.

As a child of spirit, I came to the simple conclusion that good and evil were both visitors to my Luanshya clearing, whether it was via the BBC or in person, but this didn't mean that my world had become their world – the Belgian Congolese showed me that. I was helped here a bit by Mr Harrison, who noticed I was more introverted than usual. He told me that good and evil should not be measured separately. I took his words, in true African spirit, to mean that if you did not know what was right or wrong in a given situation, you simply waited long enough for the problem to resolve itself on its own. Good and evil were identical twins. They would happily step into the limelight on behalf of the other if the situation so warranted it. No one would be any the wiser as to who was who until it was too late and change had done its job – but good or evil would still be there. Africans did not like to push good and bad against the wall of inquiry, whereas my white subtribe preferred resolute action. They saw everything in opposite tracks of good and evil, of black and white. Send more troops to Vietnam they said, and they condemned the Russians to even colder winters. Why were Russia and the USA and her friends fighting over the cold anyway? Contrary to all the black and white folk I knew, I felt I would only find the truth to *things* when my bum was firmly placed on my haunch-carved anthill. Maybe that's why the Africans went to the witchdoctor – I believed that witchdoctors and white ants had a lot in common.

The stories of good and evil were out there on the vlei; and it was true – it was difficult to tell them apart. Perhaps one of them spoke with a sly lisp! But I wasn't sure of that either.

In a vigorous 'like meets like' campaign I committed myself to getting to know my affinities better. I had to know what I wanted out of life, what made me tick, in order to prove my own self-worth. At that time, I was also reminded of what the naked robber of the night told me: I had to guard my own fear against an alien encroachment of African fear, which I attributed to the 'evil' in good and evil.

My spirit of solidarity and self defence were fuelled further by African political events just over the border only an hour or two away. The Congo massacres of blood-filled depravity were brewing up again, and Northern Rhodesian Africans were urgently demanding independence from their colonial master. I saw a burnt-out car on the Ndola road with political slogans in red paint on its charred frame, and I could feel the heat of impending fear on the vlei. I could smell fear in the bluebottle flies with the rotten meat colours of black, iridescent blue, and death-stained purple blazoned on their backs. They would buzz heavily on the stench of human faeces that were deposited on the sides of bush paths. Their Congolese kin were partaking in far more revolting meals than simple defecations: and Trini Lopez sang on.

Janet and John

I used to sing hymn 21, 'All Things Bright and Beautiful,' in morning assembly with gusto because it was my favourite.

'The Lord God made them all,' we sung.

I loved the stylised drawings of the smiling, laughing rabbits, birds and lambs that bordered the words of hymn 21. I felt that these little creatures of God knew the truth about everything, and because of that, they would be happy forever after. I wanted to be like them. I was also strangely intrigued by Janet and John, the characters of my early reader.

Janet looked pretty, and John handsome. They never seemed to be rushed or in a hurry, and yet everything worked for them. They were never in a bad mood. They had tea and cake, moist and delicious, always a wholesome fruit cake every day at four served by their beautiful mother. In the evening their fit and kindly-looking father would come home, take of his stylish fifties trilby hat, pull up the front creases of his Oxford bags, and settle into his armchair to read to his Aryan children. He didn't work down a mine, or have a glass of beer in his hand for a sundowner, and he didn't have a *beer bop*, Afrikaans for a beer tummy, and was never getting ready to go the MOTH Club. Janet and John would listen to his every word with such knowing attention; while their mother, neatly coiffured and trim-waisted, kindly looked on, tea cloth in hand, in control of a roast chicken and potatoes in the oven, and homegrown veg on the boil.

They fascinated me because they were able to run their whole lives from their timeless bubbles of inner contentment. There were many times when I wanted to be picture-perfect like them.

Strangely enough, Janet and John didn't have a surname – they must have been adopted worthless souls like me, and I began to mistrust them. Under their perfect smiles Janet and John were hurting – something stank.

There was a Johannesburg family in the next avenue called the Fouries. The father was a metallurgist, and the mother a high school teacher. They were obviously more sophisticated than us. They were also fashionably correct like my Janet and John. The Fourie children, two girls and a boy, were, however, frustrated and miserable. They were never allowed to get their pale bodies or their 'bought in Johannesburg' clothes dirty; they weren't allowed in the midday sun; they wore ridiculous floppy hats outdoors; they were made to lie on their beds or at least stay in their dark bedrooms between one and three-thirty in the afternoon; and at four on the dot, after playing briefly on the freshly mowed front lawn, they had *rooibos* herbal tea and ginger biscuits served in Tupperware cups in the shade of their garden rondavel. Their eyes were dull. Mr Kumar told me that gurus believed that the eyes reflected the Soul of a person. The Fouries' eyes told me that their beings were mortally trapped in a banal conformity that had well and truly cataracted their souls. They were not happy-go-lucky children. They were faking perfection, and badly; whereas Janet and John were very good at feigning the truth. I felt dreadfully sorry for the Fouries, and was beginning to really dislike Janet and John.

The fateful lot of the Congolese refugees on my mother's birth-day reminded me that there was simply nothing I could do for the Fouries. However, there was something that I could do about Janet and John, who I resented for having such tidy little lives.

What on earth was the message that these post-war child idols Janet and John were sending to the white children of Great Britain's colonial Dominions and Protectorates? Were they icons of a perfect civilised world that would systematically percolate common decency into our malleable psyches? Were they designed to rebuff infiltration from the primitive societies we were exposed to? They went far deeper than their stock phrases of 'Look, see Janet run. See John kick the ball.' Like in all good gossip magazines, you dislike the people they write about, but you still want to know everything about them. I really had to work on breaking my curiosity of the perfect pair of no-name frauds: It was becoming a bad habit.

I took a leap into difficult reading, skipping *The Hardy Boys* and going with *The Adventures of Huckleberry Finn*, *The Adventures of Tom Sawyer* and *The Jungle Book*. More than a few words went over my head, but Tom's, Huckleberry's and Mowgli's senti-ments of boy-freedom, as opposed to societal conformity, went straight to my core.

If inquiring adventure was a facet my soul, then I needed to embrace it with the experiences of other curious boys – that is if I ever wanted to know the whole truth about me. I knew my life was emotionally messy, but according to Huckleberry, it was well worth it in the end.

A hand in the Libyan Desert

When going to England for our two-month holidays, we finally abandoned taking the boat train from Ndola to Cape Town – a 1000-mile journey to catch a Union Castle passenger boat to South Hampton on the English coast. Instead we flew to London from Ndola via Entebbe, Wadi Halfa, and Benghazi. The Vickers Viscount plane flew high enough to be a professional airliner, but not so high that I couldn't make out things on the ground below. It also had large oval windows designed for little boys to look out of. Remote clearings in an otherwise seamless mat of thick forest below ripped at my curiosity, and I had a longing passion to visit every one of them right across Central Africa. Who had cleared this small piece of ground below me? Who was down there? If there was a vlei, what secrets did it hold? If there was a clearing, who lived in it and what were they doing? The burning intrigue, which hijacked my stiff body from pressing against the double glaze of the window, was only reigned in when the long shadows stretching all the way from faraway Angola and the Congo finally put my landscape into obscurity, and when the hostess interrupted my reveries.

The air hostess brought me a bag of Nyasaland roasted peanuts, the biggest peanuts I had ever seen, their rich oiliness coating my fingers and chin. I was happy, and she smiled graciously. Later she came and pulled the blind over the plane window, whose oval shape was as black as a night adder's pupil. I had been cupping my hands and peering out with neck-cranking determination. I could see bushfires in the blackness: With the perspective of distance gobbled up, they were jagged streamers of orange and red. Where were they? Who caused them? Was it hunters, gatherers, or witchdoctors – friends or foes of the African forests? Blind down and without my own planetarium and floorshow of the African night, my body put itself into a self-induced sulky comma.

Refractions of inner light – clearings

Clearings in the bush define the spirit of Africa. From the air they are isolation in the depths of a fearsome forest: from the forest floor they are a fragile attempt to define the tenuous existence of a small humanity within an expansive African Soul.

I awoke to the air hostess handing out tartan travel blankets. Goosebumps the size of warts covered my arms, the fine blond hair standing to attention. The calm manly voice of the captain, who definitely smoked Peter Stuyvesant cigarettes, announced we were flying over Lake Victoria, and we would be making our descent towards Entebbe in Uganda in half an hour. Uganda. I was shortly to be landing in the Kingdom of the Gorillas. Can you believe my despair, when the air hostess announced that passengers would not be disembarking, as it was only a short refuelling stop?

On the ground in Entebbe the oval door to the cabin was opened. I really felt I could smell the clammy bamboo air of gorilla forests and so wanted to have my feet touching the ground – I did my best to contain a sulk. That's when I remembered that

Mr Harrison told my class that the air we breathe is the same recycled elements of oxygen, carbon dioxide and nitrogen since the beginning of time. I was now breathing in the same air that countless gorillas in the deep forests had breathed, and that made me happy. My father and I were content; he supping Tusker beer on a London-bound plane in Uganda; I supping ape breath in a reverie of nearby gorillas in bamboo thickets. We shared the same core bliss, but on different coordinates.

The next fuel stop was Wadi Halfa in the Libyan Desert. The hostess announced we would be able to disembark as the ground staff would be spraying the plane with insecticides – probably DDT. Wow the desert – date palms and camels, Bedouins and mirages. I had to get off and investigate this world. To my horror my mother's ankles had become swollen, and she couldn't get her shoes on. She would have to sit there with a hankie over her nose while the Arab cleaning staff sprayed, and my father would stay with her – and me – surely not, surely not me too! Was I now being deprived of descending to the desert floor. That's when the air hostess changed her form; from being a glorified white nanny to Baudicia, the compassionate warrior and saviour of poor wretches like me. She took my oily hand and announced to my parents, in no uncertain terms, that I would be accompanying her down the steps of the aircraft, onto the tarmac and into the airport terminal where I could buy a postcard which she felt I might like. Gosh how I suddenly loved her dearly.

As I got to the oval doorway of the aircraft the hot air of the desert ripped the breath right out of my throat. The simoom pressed my clothes to my chest, tummy and thighs as we ventured across the oily tarmac, which had been on the turning point of softening in the aftermath of a very hot day. The night heat, whipped to an anger and peppered with flying sand, stung our English faces. My hostess held on tightly to her ridiculous pillbox hat with her free hand, the other firmly wrapped around my excited fingers. I was twenty foot tall as 'me and my gal' braved the resentful wind that was trying to push all infidels back into their British colonial flying machine. That is when I discovered my egotistical male streak. I was proud and very happy, and I squeezed the air hostess' hand tight. I think she knew it was out of sheer exhilaration, and not fear, and she gave an echoing double squeeze back. My affirmation of self-worth was complete; even if it was just to get a smelly postcard of the airport building. For a short moment in time I was Lawrence of Arabia and she was Jasmine, the most favoured concubine of the Arabian nights.

The rest of the journey has been forgotten: Benghazi was a refuelling stop, which I slept through, and the people and goings-on of London Gatwick must have not stimulated my senses in any memorable way.

Offbeat evangelism

As I progressed through childhood, I found it increasingly difficult to understand why my father was so often away from home. If the truth be known, my father spent his life in pubs not because he had bought a ticket to alcoholism, and was looking for the right bus station, but because he had such an uncontrollable love for all of mankind that he couldn't keep it contained in his heart for us alone. He loved everyone – that's why I never saw him cross or angry. That was the Joe that everyone knew. He was the life and Soul of every party – so people said.

Reflections of inner light – a dictionary for his birthday

Joe was my father's name, Annie my mother's. She bought him a dictionary for his birthday because too much alcohol each evening, along with horrific war memories, cut deep into his sleep. He would be awake at three in the morning doing the daily crossword while chain smoking in bed; an unfortunate habit that caused my mother to develop a chronic state of asthma over time. They say that asthma, in spiritual terms, is an inability to accept things as they are, whereas insomnia points to an inability to let go or surrender – a lack of trust in life.

Most people on earth have the farsighted intuition that their love is limited and cut the cloth of their lives accordingly. Whereas, some know that they have no love of their own and certainly none to give – they become avarice pirates, pillaging the Souls of others. Others have just enough love to always give a little. In my father's case, he had too much love to give, and he gave it blindly unaware of the negative consequences that it thrust upon his Soul purpose. My mother and I, like ejected flotsam, were tossed in the wake of his unstoppable need to please others.

My father's difficult war years had worn his being so thin that his Soul showed through the thin human parchment that should have been his normal protective skin and good sense. Love oozed out and he couldn't stop it, even though it was draining his Soul. Was this his way of compensating for the death and destruction that had blighted his life? My mother had seen his debilitated Soul through his translucent outer caul on first sight. He was a being in desperate need of deep nurturing, and on the spot she decided to marry him. While his skin did grow thicker through my mother's loving care, it was still thin. Without being in the service of a church with strict religious vows, or following a compassionate career as a missionary doctor, what options did my father have to pour out his altruistic love; other than to visit a bar to express his spirit in the name of a love for all mankind? A bar that had a perpetual flow of lost Souls knocking at its door. Spiritual love is oneness; an empathy for mankind, sharing the load of your neighbour, treating him as you would treat yourself, and giving all you've got.

There was a Catholic priest in Luanshya, Father Patrick. Everyone knew him, especially the men at the MOTH Club because he used to drink there, as well as in other bars around the town – he was a 'bloody good chap' and everyone wanted to buy him a beer. He was on a more ecumenical mission than my father. He too knew of the impoverished Souls that crossed the thresholds of the Luanshya bars, and he had taken his vows as a parish priest to help them; ironically he did so at the source of their fatal addiction – the bar counter.

Father Patrick relied on confusion of the spirit to find salvation in the Souls of his assumed brethren. Perhaps my father did the same, the only difference being that Father Patrick did not suffer from the same war afflictions of the lost Souls that he was aiming to heal, whereas my father did. I suppose Father Patrick never helped my father because after all, my father espoused brotherly love, and if he got hurt in the process, it was a spiritual hangover that was meant to be. Father Patrick probably had some hangovers too, more than likely of the sore head kind. In any case, my father was not a lost Soul – he was an abused one – all because of an overabundance of love. Obviously, Father Patrick had more hopeless cases to pull out of the gutter.

The reasons why my father chose bars to love mankind were clear. To love the women of the town was socially unacceptable, and anyway you needed a big ego for that and he didn't have one at all. To love his family – in all honesty, as a singular wife and child, we were not big enough a vesicle for his love. Perhaps he would have been kept busily happy if all my siblings had survived. Instead he chose the MOTH Club, and as his involvement grew, so his ways became more entrenched in male company, and the rules became more rigid. Being a home dad was socially unacceptable within his circle of bar friends. Drinking men had to be drinking men, whatever their familial commitments. So there it was, love the men of the town: that was the most obvious solution. After all, the war had brought men so close together that they knew each other inside out. He needed to find a group of men to bond with in spirit. Perhaps his long wars years had reinforced male bonding as a way of life. To give him fair due, on his arrival in Africa, he did attempt to go down different avenues to find camaraderie.

Joining the boxing fraternity was a likely option. It was an unusual fact that my father had been a champion boxer in pre-war China. He was so small, slight and nimbly quick, that he was the featherweight champion of South China. Which was fine in a country where most people were extra slight and short, but in Northern Rhodesia his level was ungraded. The 'Dutchmen', as the *rooi necks* – the English – called the Afrikaners, dominated the boxing scene. Because of their ancestral roots they were all big and tall, and approaching heavyweight. Getting involved in the boxing world, even as a trainer, was not an option – the tactics of a heavyweight boxer and a featherweight were very different. The only man who was his featherweight grade lived in Elizabethville in the Belgian Congo.

My father also took up cricket. He caught a high ball badly, ripping a fingernail back, and Sister Caruthers at the mine hospital causing more pain and damage than the ball did. Most South Africans had a war record, but some had kept the machinery of the Colonies going as part of the war effort, and by chance, a fair number of them were in the cricket team – he didn't have a lot in common with them. They worked mostly above ground in the mine offices. They were *office wallahs*, as members of my white tribe who served in India during the war would say, whereas my father worked below the ground. On his miner's license was the humble title 'Rock Breaker'. Cricket was not a game where men expressed themselves freely from the heart. That's probably why the more conservative English and South Africans liked it, and my father rejected it.

With options narrowing, and a heart bursting with love, he needed to find a community where he could express his love freely, without fear of ridicule – his skin would always be thin. He needed to be able to talk to people who understood pain. What about an ex-servicemen's club and bar? And so it was: his life changing choice.

To be a MOTH a man had to have served in the armed forces during the Second World War. There was a plaque in the MOTH Club which read:

MOTHS
(Memorable Oder of the Tin Hats)
When you go home
Remember this of them and say
They gave their tomorrows for our today.

It was a place that his war-torn Soul could call home. Where he could swear his full allegiance and absolute gratitude to those who fell in the war. Perhaps his Soul had made a promise in a jungle clearing in the presence of dead and dying fellow Chindits in Burma. There is no doubt that his Soul was finally able to open its floodgates of unconditional love on the MOTH members and their dependents. He did a commendable job, and everybody loved Joe in return. Maybe that caused some confusion in my mind, and caused a part of my peeved state of being. My mother and I should have demanded more from him – but we didn't. Instead I broodily disliked all those that took more of the pie than we did. My father had a unique Soul, but it was sadly peppered with other people's shrapnel.

Dug up, refined and smelted

In African mining towns there was no tradition, little cultural history of consequence and no pretensions. Instead there was a spirit of expansion that saw everything as raw, new and exploitable in an honest hard-working way. Paradoxically this would mould the spirits of the colonial perpetrators far more than their physical surroundings. Africa was hard to change. How could the spiritual energies of miners and their dependents – wives, children and domestic staff – not be smelted, stirred, purged of floating scum, refined, and alloyed along with the mineral that they worked? Eventually we would all come out of it as flat sheets of usefulness which could be manipulated and bent according to societal wants and rules. We would be without any individual markings, dare I even say free from spiritual flaws, which, in colonial society's opinion, might otherwise have tarnished our purpose on earth: which was to serve the Colonies well in the wholesome post-imperialist tradition.

After coming up the shaft, leaving the refineries or the smelters, adult friendships developed in men's bars and week-end socials and dances at the many clubs. In South Africa women were forbidden to enter bars, and that custom crept its way up north to the Copperbelt – something to do with Calvinism. Black men never entered bars either, other than waiters and cleaners. There was unofficial apartheid throughout the British colonies, which the administration called class distinction. The Mine Club had a cocktail bar for both sexes to socialize in – although the men's bars had magnetic preference for the average hard-working, hard-drinking mining man.

A strong white society was established out of a lighthearted banter between the English and the South African white folk over drinks. Colonial politics, hard-earned copper prices and the domestic services of a willing but uneducated subservient black population were the talk of the day. A unified mining society was being forged; work contracts could not be broken and free enterprise was a rare commodity. There was a spiritual cost to copper mining. As compensation for refined uniformity, the mine management funded the establishment of recreational clubs to meet the demands of their employees who wished to further their personal interest in sports and hobbies.

The MOTH Club did not further sport nor hobbies. It was a charitable club with a large hall for dances, a bar, and a children's playground. We children of the MOTHS – pupae or caterpillars – were dragged along to social evenings every Friday night and to lunchtime drinks every Sunday. On Sundays, if it was raining, and we couldn't go outside, we were allowed to play darts on a worn-out board using an old, discarded strip of rubber conveyor belting from the mine as a mat. The club had a very serious darts team that toured the Copperbelt wining many a trophy. We weren't allowed to play on their very serious dart-board or touch their professional darts which were imported from England. Out of sheer boredom, with not a grain of competitiveness or interest in my being, I used to watch these men play. It was a cult. One of the men who had worked in a UK coal mine before coming out to Africa, had coal dust still embedded in the large pores that polka dotted his pallid down-the-mine complexion, and because of this, his face always looked dirty. A crooked nose, and a broken front tooth, made him look like a street fighter – he had probably been that too. Coming straight from the mineshaft shower room to the MOTH Club bar on every weekday, and propping up the same bar counter on weekends, left no time for him to enjoy the outdoors, the bush, or the African sun, and as a consequence, nor did his family. His deep-water squid skin bore testimony to this sad misfortune of a personal choice, and I disliked him for it. His, 'in the navy', muscular arms bore tattoos of semi-naked women, eagles, anchors and arrow-pierced hearts. His provenance was the Gorbals – a poor working class area of Glasgow in Scotland. The long hair of the crown of his head hung in greasy dollops over his almost shaven, Hitler styled, short back and sides. He was such a good darts player that he could hold his cigarette and a pint glass of beer in one hand, and accurately throw a dart with the other without spilling a drop, and without missing the desired shot. He talked with stale beer breath, and had a permanently lit cigarette dangling from his parsimonious lips, the acrid smoke of which curled up into his narrow slit eyes, maintaining a permanent scowl over his face. He defended his total lack of self-worth with an arsenal of foul language, and sought male approval with dirty navy songs and ditties. Worst of all he looked down on all women and children, and always left his own brood sitting at home with nothing to do. They didn't even have black and white television to help them pass the long evenings. He was one of those ex-servicemen friends of my father who added no joy to my mother's or my life.

This man totally abused my father's goodwill and generous understanding. On some weeknights, at about nine, jovial, well-meaning and a bit tipsy, my father would roll up home from the club with this despicable centaur of a man in tow. It was a well-known fact that my father often picked up this man's drink tab because he claimed poverty. My gullible father was now wanting his too-long-in-the-warming-drawer, dried-out dinner. In a belligerent manner, cursing his own wife for never keeping him dinner, this evil man wanted my father's dinner too. He had 'after bloody all' come straight from the mine to the club and was now starving. He shared my father's plate of food – a cremated plate of bangers and mash or potato pie with extra slices of white bread – all the while making threats of reprimanding his poor wife when he got home. His wife was a thin, meek woman with five children to feed and look after while he spent other people's money, a little of his money and all his time in the bar. It was rumoured that he stashed his money elsewhere, and the rumours were substantiated when he left his wife and children for another, obviously more attractive, childless woman, with whom he lived the life of O'Reilly, as the grown-ups put it. They also said this new woman could only have gone with him for his money. His poor wife packed her and her five children's bags and returned to bonny Scotland, none the richer for her sad African sojourn.

I would lie in my bed listening to his awful voice that was tense with an anger of his own making. His strange accent and the soft sounds of my mother's and father's voices added to the

horror of these evenings. It was as if an armed robber was holding our Souls at gunpoint. I heard confused disappointment in
my mother's voice, a sadness that she was to carry for the rest of
her life, and I heard poor excuses from my goodhearted father.
My senses would run wild like a witch's cat – I was frightened of
this Minotaur of a man who had entered our, my mother's and
my space, but I was also angry. He trashed my father's bonhomie and crushed our sense of values. He was despicable and I
could honestly say I hated him. There were other social leeches
in the town that sucked on my father's rare ability to believe,
and have unconditional faith, in every person who crossed his
path. I disliked them too, but I despised him the most.

It would be too simple and spiritually unrewarding to hate
the Glaswegian on a purely emotional level. Instead I sucked his
toxic persona into my gall bladder one night at the MOTH Club;
and the next morning I puked it up on the grit of the anthill
for a thorough dissection with my portable microscope. After an
educative study of the workings of his dark-spirited anatomy, I
gutted him and flung his stinking entrails into the long grass for
the jackals, the self-employed carrion collectors of the night, to
deal with as they saw fit. I butchered and skewered the ugly pale
muscles of his tattooed sailor's legs and arms with Msasa bark
string, and hung them to dry like poachers' bush-meat.

Bloated bluebottles took leave of their human dung pile
banquets along the many African bush paths, and congregated
over the remains of his dismembered body *en masse*. They kept
arriving until every space on his putrefying trunk had been
covered by a creeping carpet of body-fluid-sucking scumbags.
They carried out a dissection of their own. They entered his every orifice, wiping their excreta-soaked feet on his Soul as they
worked; only to be pushed aside by their disgusting progeny of

maggots – far more specialized in burrowing into all the physiological alleyways of their victim: his arteries, veins and between his connective tissues and bones. I dragged what remained of his body onto open ground, whereupon a writhing sea of pincered insects of all kinds and sizes sliced the unpalatable remnants of his hair, ligaments and tendons into the molecular dusts of oblivion. I submitted his tormented bones as macabre tinder for a witchdoctor's fire. I saw nothing good about him.

I sold his sun-dried meat to a secretive cannibal tribe from the darkest forests of the Congo. They ate the flesh of their opponents in bush wars as the only effective way of conquering the spirit of their enemy. With the proceeds, I sent his wife and children to Durban beach for a holiday.

His mind and body paid dearly for his conscious disregard for my father's Soul, his arrogant denial of the existence of my mother and me, his wife and children, and all the women and children of Luanshya as well as the African bush and its people – in short all the facets of life that he so blatantly abused.

Why a child should take on such spiritual witch hunting was strange. It did cause my immature being to suffer self-induced barbs of emotional pain – but I could not help myself.

I notched up more than a few spiritual murders on my termite mound on the vlei: The stuck-up librarian at the mine club, who refused me entry into most of sections of the library, including the travel section – she said it was for adults only. The mine dentist, who was specially trained to be nasty and hurtful to those children he didn't like. I was sure he didn't like me because once I left Cheapy, my pet chicken, in a box in his waiting room while I was having a check-up. Cheapy got out, took fright, made an awful squawking noise and pooped on the carpet of the waiting room.

These murders were probably childishly irresponsible, and mood-driven; but in the case of the Glaswegian Minotaur, it was Soul-driven witch hunting. The night robber would have agreed, and maybe even the sweet missionary lady would have turned a blind eye.

Makoma Dam blues

Makoma Dam had a role more important than Wadi Halfa airport and spiritual murders when it came to wanting to find my self-worth. It was a recreational dam created next to the mine dumps to keep the mining families entertained on the weekends. On alternating Sundays there were yachting regattas, powerboat racing events and fishing competitions, although personal fishing along the edges was permitted at any time. There was a bar that was open all day to meet the secondary needs of those that might like a refreshing cold beer at some stage in their activities. There were, however, those folk, like the men of my particular white subtribe, that went to Makoma Dam because they wanted a lot of bar, a little sun and no outdoor activity.

If we didn't go to Makoma Dam on a Sunday we went to the MOTH Club. It is not always possible to explain the dissonance between perception and reality with rational thinking. It is a dissonance that can manifest itself in intense waves of heated and sometimes confused emotions that can only be understood outside the time frame in which events take place: even then, they run the risk of being subverted by the intellect. *Surround time* is the best prophylactic to avoid a chronicler's bias. Makoma Dam and other scenarios in my story have all been thrown into the present moment of a live reality show where their emotional validity is not to be questioned, endorsed or nullified; but simply looked at in the synergist process of viewing something in the light of my childhood whole.

The light that filtered in through the long, narrow windows of the MOTH Club hall had that stilted luminescence which leads the senses to nowhere pleasant. Lethargy in the form of ill-defined shadows filled its dingy corners and boredom accentuated the mundanity of the military objects hanging on the walls – as if there was no worthwhile story to tell. Empty coke bottles, crumpled chip packets, tatty South African gossip magazines, and strewn playing cards on the floor: We, the children of the MOTH Club had expended all offers of appeasement from our parents. The Sunday afternoon social scene clawed at our Souls. Fading light hinted at a wasted day coming to a close, and forbade any form of strong breath. Tired air dragged itself in and out of lungs suffering from bronchial disinterest. Lengthening shadows crept across an empty hall to steal our pluck away – we couldn't even muster up the enthusiasm to play outside in what was left of the sun. We were prisoners of our own despair.

An adult litter of empty cigarette boxes, bottles, glasses and ashtrays cluttered ring-marked tables. Empty beer bottles had a flat yeast smell of a party gone wrong: of pointless arguments and women's tears. Overflowing ashtrays have a distasteful organic smell of burning and destruction, a smell that invokes memories so unpleasant you can only sense them with sadness. Beer dregs tipped into a full ashtray, like a drunk man's breath, was the vile olfactory summation of how a Sunday afternoon could be robbed of its glory. Cigarette butts flicked into the men's urinals, edged with the crude smell of disinfectant blocs, and embellished with hissing water cisterns, carved distaste upon my Soul and stirred hate in my spleen. I detested the MOTH Club, especially on sunny Sundays.

When we all finally left to go home in the failing light, we were drunk: adults with alcohol, children with lassitude. An ingrained uncomfortabilty would once again leave a rotten taste in my life, one that toothpaste could not lift. They say that depression is suppressed anger – I was a moody child. I went to bed with red eyes and a subdued Soul: I was ill-prepared for my rendezvous with the Luanshya night. My mother had washed her spirit with a bit of alcohol, and with weary eyes, said she had enjoyed the female company. I knew she wasn't telling the truth. She went because of my father.

Going to Makoma Dam on a Sunday saved my Soul, although not without a bit of effort, rejection and arrogance on my part; and empathy on my father's part.

On the Makoma Dam Sundays of my early youth, much to my embarrassment, we would arrive in a convoy of British cars. Was there not a self-determining bone in our family's body? If we went alone I would be able to plan all sorts of adventures with my dad, but this didn't happen. Out of need, I took a brave stance – I rejected my cheap tourist status, and started working on other alternatives. That was when I was labelled as being uncooperative and ungrateful.

The men expected the wives to set up a picnic spot on English rolling lawns that led down to the African water's edge. The lawns were dotted with Norfolk Island pines called monkey puzzle trees. All the indigenous trees had been felled. While the women buttered the bread and sorted out the over-excited kids under the shade of grass umbrellas, the men went up to the clubhouse to ostensibly get a singular beer for themselves and cold drinks for the women and children.

Forty minutes and three beers later they braved a sharp lemon sun to return to their now irked wives and kids, who gulped the drinks down. This gave the men the excuse to return to the bar for more. They would eventually arrive back half-inebriated and hankering for the picnic lunch to soak up the beer in their bellies. I would watch these adults, male and female, of our English subtribe, and take stock of the way they presented themselves. What the hell were they doing here, and more importantly, what were they dressed for – a Roan Antelope Mine Dramatic and Operatic Society (RADOS) Gilbert and Sullivan comic opera production? What an embarrassment. Then again no one saw what I saw.

The women were either in long cotton frocks in fine florals, or cheaply patterned crimplene one-piece dresses with long-sleeved cardigans, and always closed shoes. Seldom were tailored shorts or a short-sleeved cotton blouse worn. They supported Marylyn Munroe sunglasses and garish headscarves, which saved their coiffures from wind off the water. Their faces were powdered and rouged to accentuate their Englishness – it was protection from the sun, they said in defence of frequent trips to the powder room. They would sit on wooden folding chairs called deck chairs, which they obviously took a liking to as they surveyed the Atlantic on the Union Castle liner that brought them out to Africa. The men were in safari shorts – powder blue, olive green or mustard brown – with matching coloured polyester ribbed socks and safari jackets that trailed the bum with a vent! My portly father always wore a trilby and dark glasses, which his friends said made him look like King Farouk of Egypt. We children sat on heavy imitation tartan rugs that doubled up as lap warmers at outdoor movies in the chilly night months of June and July, and which still smelt of spilt hot chocolate throughout our hot November and December summers.

These British folk all had children who were supposed to play with me. I believed that they were just as frustrated as I was, but they were taught to say nothing and not do much more. Some of the older ones certainly got on with different activities: cigarettes and talk of sex, drugs and rock and roll behind the boathouses. When the picnic was served, we all sat on our tartan rugs and drank tea in tartan-patterned thermos flasks. We couldn't seem to leave the United Kingdom behind – I suppose it also didn't help that we all sang 'God Save the Queen' at every event of major and minor importance. The tea was good for the children, who had had too many cokes, refreshing for the women, and punctuation for the men in their beer drinking.

There was a nice swimming pool in front of the club, but most of the time we English kids were not allowed to swim. A sign said swimming was strictly under adult supervision. Our fathers were in the bar, and our mothers couldn't swim, and anyway it was dangerous to swim in the midday sun according to my subtribe rules. The South African kids would pull tongues at us as they swam without supervision throughout the day. It seemed that only my bovine subtribe followed rules. The South African kids all had great tans, but our parents said that was because of mixed blood, which gave them a skin that could take the sun; which was rubbish according to my South African classmates. I wanted to be like them, do like them. I hated my English whiteness, my English triteness. But in slow African time, which under the domination of colonial time dragged by even slower, I changed my state of affairs as part of 'Operation on the Water'.

The Mine management, in the interest of public health, had concreted the edges of the dam at the end of the lawns, raked the shallows free of reeds, and added chemicals to the water; all with the well-intended aim of keeping bilharzia, leeches and malaria breeding mosquitoes at bay. The oil slicks from speedboats did the rest. Our side of the watery clearing was civilised – it was stone-walled-dead civilised. What this meant for us English kids was that fishing was pointless. Swimming, even paddling, was also frowned up on: Our parents still didn't believe that bilharzia had been eradicated. With good reason I was a moody little sod on my early day trips to Makoma Dam.

Operation on the Water was further cemented when I was lucky enough to be invited on one occasion, by some South African kids, to go across to the other side in their father's boat. It was my idea of paradise. There were reed beds, submerged anthills, shallows, and all sorts of animal life: fish, birds and reptiles. My father noticed how taken I was with the other side, and made promises to make a slow move towards acquiring a canoe for me. Nothing happened fast in Luanshya, but his promise was enough to raise my sights. Without a boat to get to the other side we English kids were marooned on a lawned desert island.

Besides the serious motor boat and sailing fraternity, who were obsessed with courses, buoys and points aggregates, some South Africans preferred to rough it on the weekends. They trekked to places like the Kafue River, where it was wild. They would also come to the dam, whereupon they would look at us *rooi necks* askance. They had boats which they kept in boathouses that served as a base with fold up tables, chairs and a small

ion: They could have been on the shores of Lake Titicaca, and

paraffin fridge. They had *braai*, barbeque, facilities and they chargrilled delicious *boerwors*, beef sausage, and steaks. They also made *padkoes*, Afrikaans for a traveller's road meal – a meat and vegetable hotpot, cooked slowly in an African three-legged cast iron pot over a low fire. They had professional fishing rods, keep nets, and all the right fishing tackle to get good results. They made the most of the day, and even stayed overnight on a Saturday, sometimes taking their domestics with them. My white subtribe made the least of the day and fled to the bar at the first sign of receding light. Different folks, different strokes people would say. I would have said we were not worthy of the African experience – in my opinion, my subtribe were incapable of taking in the world around them. They were stagnant Souls incapable of extracting themselves out of a narrow culture. Africa had nothing to do with their jaded appetites for stimulation: They could have been on the shores of Lake Titicaca, and their response would have been the same.

Conversations on those dam excursions, surrounded by glorious bush, were centred on English trivia, drivel as I put it. English football results, a new couple from Yorkshire – 'a proper bonny face she has too' – the proposed Union-Castle liner trip home, or the new British Caledonian flights to London Gatwick from Ndola. Never mind about the wading birds on the water's edge – the jacanas, or the wattled plovers, the giant kingfisher or the fish eagle's call. They were not interested in the reed frogs, which gave a sonic chorus of beebs, like a million enemy submarines on the sonar screens of our subconscious awareness. If the members of my subtribe had any awareness, it was apparently left at home on days like these. They were unaware of the pythons that inhabited half-submerged anthills-turned-islands on the far side of dam. Ignorant to the stand offs between leguaans and pythons reliving their mythological differences by vying for possession of these kingdoms; where terrapins, catfish and mellies nested in the termite-refined mud.

At four o'clock the wives packed up the bomb-shelled picnic accessories, and the scattered children were collared to take the dry goods, rugs and deck chairs to the hot cars: the Morris Minors, Austin Cambridges and Vauxhall Vanguards, all sitting patiently in the car park with British aplomb. The mothers joined the men up at the clubhouse. Like the MOTH Club, there was a bar, toilets and a hall dotted with low Formica-topped tables and coloured tubular chairs The first port of call for the ladies was the powder room, where compacts, lipstick and hair spray were the reinforcements of their 'white lady in Africa' status. There was also a small kitchen and a serving hatch from where the management would serve teas at four o'clock onwards for a 'nominal' fee. Sundowners followed on the veranda overlooking the dam, with the menfolk skipping the tea bit. We 'only kids' were given some small change to go to a tuck shop where we bought a Coke or a Fanta, some potato crisps and either a stiff marshmallow banana, salted or pink sugared peanuts, or small, perfumed sweets called pink elephants. If you dropped a salted peanut into a bottle of Coke, it sank to the bottom, giving off bubbles. Depending on the amount of salt and fat on it, it would then rise up to the neck of the bottle propelled by its own bubbles – before dropping lifelessly to the bottom again. However, you could regulate the speed of its initial ascent by creating pressure in the bottle with your thumb on the neck. If you were well practiced, you could make the peanut rise and fall, and sometimes even keep it suspended in the middle. This never-boring trick made the coke flat but we soon got used to the taste.

In spite of my frustrations, my early Makoma days furthered my cautious investigation of my own self-worth. I knew what I wanted and I made a decision to push my boundaries beyond the confines of my white subtribe. I also accepted that it was up to me; no one could do it for me, although my empathetic father furthered my quest in a way greater than he would have ever realised. I started whetting my appetite for when I was considered old enough to have a canoe. I would make sure I was always at the slipway when South Africans and a few adventurous Englishmen returned from the day's fishing. They always had an interesting fish to show and a story to tell, stories of leguaans and cormorants, catfish and large mouthed bream. Sometimes snakes were seen swimming between sunken anthills which had become small thickets of water-marooned bush in the rainy season. One old fisherman told me he saw a snapper terrapin take a small bird that came down to drink.

Landlocked stargazer

I had grown out of the Cub Scouts and, even though I was an ardent follower of Mowgli, and still of the right age, I had had enough of Arkela, our leader, and some of the other senior wolves of the pack. Arkela was a bossy woman who failed me in the domestic proficiency test one too many times, so I joined the Sea Scouts – in the middle of Africa. The initiation into the Sea Scouts affected me profoundly.

The Sea Scouts met every Friday night from six-thirty to eight. That first night, my parents dropped me off and went by road across a small rivulet to the MOTH Club. The two buildings were separated by about 500 feet of sloping low-lying bush. Both were in shouting distance of each other across the small valley. There was a social at the club, and at one of the many dreadful moments of my Sea Scout ordeal that night, I could hear the music they were playing: 'Itsy Bitsy Teeny Weenie Yellow Polka Dot Bikini' being repeated over and again.

My dolly blued white uniform had been laboriously ironed by Wilson the house boy, who said he was proud to iron a sailor's uniform. It comprised of starched white shorts and a navy cut horizontal neck top with dark blue trimming; all topped with a round sailor's hat. I was told I had to keep the hat spotlessly white with 'takkie' cleaner, the same white paste we used to paint our cricket pads. I was proud but I was also shy, and felt totally inadequate in spite of my starched formality. The Scoutmaster was on scouting business elsewhere that night. The older boys with deeper voices were handsome, strong, and able-bodied seamen. They were doing knot-tying drills, studying a chart of the stars, raising and lowering different coloured flags and chanting their usual scouting DYB DOB DYB mantras. Do your best – do our best – do your best. Oh how I wanted to be like them. I naively mused as to whether this was where I would launch my ship. In these professional, but friendly waters I would discover a new world: the land of my male perfection and happiness. Was this where I would finally set my bearings? Had I caught sight of my northern star? Oh roll on puberty and manhood.

Then all mayhem broke loose! We, the lambs were sent to walk the initiation plank of utter embarrassment. A boy in my class and me both started together that night. We were dragged out into the dark bush and down to the rivulet. There, we were stripped of all our crisp uniforms, shoes, socks and underwear, and abandoned to make our way back, totally naked and barefoot to SS Cement Ship. At first I was unable to move. Shock had nailed me to the earth. Thin fingers of a ghoulish damp air crept up from the rivulet and started to paw at my naked flesh. I tasted the bitter gall of resentful fear. Anger and embarrassment were kindling and snuffing out what was left of my tenuous spirit, and all the while we could see the bobbing lights of Jolly Ship SS MOTH Club. We could hear the jovial sounds of parents having sundowners, their silhouettes dancing in the portholes. That edifice of grown-up fun in the safety of their ship had the terrifying energy of an ocean liner sailing nonchalantly away from a man overboard in the night. We were sinking. My heart screamed like a ship's siren at those adults hovering over their beers and G&T's. No one looked out into the darkness – no one heard – the music drowned my calls. In a pathetic 'Save our Souls' manner we began a sniffing stagger through the darkness of our vulnerability back to our now hostile ship. What else could we do? We were too embarrassed to go anywhere else. In the dark, every rock and stubble of grass seemed intent on slicing our soles, and scraggy shrubbery poked fun at, and into our raw flesh. Because of my intimacy with the African bush, I could cope with this part of the ordeal. However, being in the dark bush made my friend uneasy, and I could hear him whimpering behind me as we made our way back to the Sea Scout's pseudo ship. When we finally got there we found our trampled clothes and muddy hats tied to the yard-arm ropes and hoisted high in the middle of a room lit by stark neon lights.

There we were: back on board our brick and mortar ship with the brightness of the hall exposing our nakedness. We gazed at our clothes flying high above the waves of laughter and jocular abuse of a now extremely ugly-looking group of low class, scurvy-ridden sea louts, not even worthy of being deckhands. Eventually a kind Soul – I believe every pirate ship has one – the doctor's son, lowered our kit and the rest of his motley crew made a ring around us and laughed and pointed as we teetered and tripped on underpants that hooked onto our heels and toes. Without a gale warning, and on a still Luanshya night, a stormy Atlantic swell of male anger suddenly gripped my clavicle, launched itself from my sternum, and gave a great heave as it hurled itself out of my throat. It manifested itself as an unintelligible howling roar that lacerated my innards like bicycle grazes to the knees. It ripped at their shocked faces. Time stopped dead in its tracks. The room fell silent. The 'mature' young men stepped back, and we clothed ourselves in an eerie awkwardness for all concerned. In a state of emergency, I had momentarily retreated to my inner bubble of my spiritual oneness to find myself. My fear was not negotiable, neither were my wants – I wanted nothing of what was going on. A teenage crew were transfixed into Medussian stone – I did not need them or their 'do good' mantras. Clutching the rest of my uniform, I stormed out into the beckoning night and crossed the stretch of dark bush and the rivulet that separated me from my parents, with my dazed friend in tow.

Many creatures make a sound discordant with their intrinsic nature: Hyenas have an uncanny feminine, whooping call, which supports the myth that they are hermaphrodite. Reclusive bushbuck can bark like a watchdog. Ostriches give a lion's roar from a distance. My gale warning call for manhood did not fit my demeanour at all. The ship's junior officers were shocked – but not as much as I was. I had drawn energy from an unknown source, so powerful that it had vitriol to spare. I spewed magma onto my seafaring aggressors in spite of their manly voices and reef knot proficiency. I scorned them for the immaturity that plagued their Souls.

That night I abandoned ship; the Sea Scouts' ship and all other ships that had no worthwhile contribution to make to 'Operation on the Water' and other important plans in my life.

The next day I took that soiled Sea Scout uniform to my own ship, SS Anthill, wore it and commandeered the vlei to prove a point – I had seas, more important seas of my own to chart. I had to move on. Alien fear would always be nestled somewhere in the yardarm – I had to be more careful.

Canoes and Bemba fishermen

My greatest want arrived. It was a yellow canoe made out of fibreglass. It had two seats but I rarely shared it with anyone. Only out of forced generosity did anyone else ever sit in the second seat.

I would sit in my canoe, knees akimbo, until I got round a promontory of bush so as to be out of grown-up view – not that anyone was watching. I would then stand up and paddle like the African oarsmen did in their wooden dugouts, to glide over the waterweed beds that the European boats, with their engine propellers and keels couldn't traverse. I steered my craft towards the upper reaches of the dam, and on into freedom. Still standing, I would use the double paddle as a pole to punt my way through a shallow wilderness of lily pads, fish, birds and reptiles to meet the Bemba fishermen. If I went far enough, I even left the fishermen behind. I was completely alone. The sun beat on my body and I didn't care. I was of the age that I could strip naked without any pubic show of adulthood, jump in the shallow waters for a cool down, and wind-dry as I paddled onwards to the highest reaches of the dam. African black boys my age were on the water naked so why couldn't I do the same if I should feel so inclined? I would skim across the water, the breeze caressing me down to the bones of my being. I was Mowgli and the creatures of this water world were my friends and protectors; not my particular white tribe lolling on the lawns with the pretence of appreciating Africa.

Body dry and Soul massaged by a kind sun, I would don my trunks – a funny word I used to think, as if things down there needed to be locked away for safe keeping – and head along the shoreline looking for interesting *things*. We Colonials might unexpectedly catch an African naked at a river crossing in our English cars, and not think twice, for in fact it was his bathroom – but that they should ever see us naked was taboo: that should never happen. I envied adult black men and women naked or semi-naked, as at a distance, their overall dark colour acted as a wash of dark decency that hid their pubic hair, recesses and appendages should they abandon their clothes to fish in the muddy shallows, or when they soaped themselves at the water's edge. Nakedness seemed natural to these earth folk, and they had secure ownership of it. I felt that most of my subtribe didn't, and that troubled my adolescent mind.

The African folk that frequented the upper shores of the dam got used to my presence, and I felt an affiliation to them. The men were there to fish, and in the water their glistening black bodies were of muscular perfection. Their heads were shaven: Sometimes tattooed patterns of keloid scars split their breast bones and ribs into left and right. They made these raised tattoos by slitting the skin with a razor blade and rubbing ash into the wound. What a deep-rooted feeling of being human it was that had made them dig so deep within themselves to bring their self-expression to the surface. The thought gave a stinging sensation in my head – I was too weak to do that. Their keloid scarring was ribbed and bold in dark molasses and magenta colours, whereas I was pretty sure that if I had tribal scars, they would turn into a warty puce pink. Enough of a reason for me not to ever do it, I mused.

If there were young women fishing, or more commonly washing clothes – always separate from the men – they were only slightly more protective about their bodies. Like the men, their sexuality had a functional place in their daily lives, and they flaunted their freestanding breasts under wet cotton tops in an easy manner. Sometimes they were bare-chested. Their breasts were firm parts of their anatomy. They did not need to hide themselves behind frilly bras of feigned innocence and moral restraint. It appeared, so Long One told me during many chats at the bottom of our garden, that their sexual role had been clearly defined as to when and with whom. There would be no pretence there. The young African women were strong on the shores of Makoma Dam, and in fact they were far cheekier than the men. They always had a shrill whooping banter that showed their light-hearted independence. When they got to know me, although we never spoke – I never really spoke to anyone on the 'far side' of the dam – they would whoop and wave. Some would run onto dry land, and with one foot swivelling on the spot they would, with a repeated flick of the hips, use their swaying behinds to manoeuvre the other foot round in a circular movement. They would stop, look at me, continue the swivelling movement in feigned concentrative silence and then burst into an uproarious cackle, and clap and whoop before splashing back into the water. All of them would then be reduced to a gaggle of thigh-slapping mirth. I envied them and their sexually simple lives, especially when I got older and sexuality seemed so complicated and emotionally messy in small town Luanshya.

They all knew me by sight, the proud Bemba fishermen and the happy washerwomen. Our voiceless camaraderie was simply a spiritual placing of people and emotions in the bigger picture of the spirit of Africa. Their presence in my life did however influence my perception of things. My world would have spun on a different axis without them. Whereas I was pretty sure that my white shadow had absolutely no effect on them – they were who they were meant to be, they were happy, and that made me happy.

The juxtaposition of sensually proactive Africans on the water's edge and the forced English conviviality created a dichotomy of perception in my being which, as a young white boy, I sometimes struggled to hold together. But I needed them both. Without the English in me I wouldn't have seen the African in me. The one provided for my physicality as a tadpole in a still colonial pond, and the other provided for my spiritual expansion. This dichotomy released a synergistic latent energy of opposites, which was building up to further my Soul's intent. The black fishing folk had accepted my odd ways. I was not a touristic voyeur and they showed bonhomie. The white fishing folk in their motor boats, which I paddled past, were only interested in the weigh-in at the end of the day's fishing competition. The over-dressed white folk never seemed to notice my colouring from the sun, or even questioned what I did on the water for so long – supposedly in the next bay. In essence I was living in an idyllic limbo between two worlds, created by the watery gap between different cultures. Makoma Dam was more than a gap. It was open waters that raised a resonance within me: It echoed a generous African spirit that spanned across endless expanses of water, savannah and vlei. My love of it all was a faint reverberation of its omnipotence.

ALLAN TAYLOR

Although they thought I was a wanting child, as far as I can remember, all I ever really wanted was the excitement of the bush: The vlei, the Makoma Dam shoreline, beside a country road – any bush or river would satisfy my needs. Of course the Kasankas or the Kafue flood plains would be a dream come true – but the Luanshya bush never failed to excite me.

To the casual unconscious eye, the waters of Makoma were the artificial shallow waters of a dammed river course. To me they were the raw spirit I was born with: There was no darkness on this shimmering expanse of water – only freedom and excitement. I felt that these waters, where the light danced, counselled me on what I needed to know for the darker side of my spiritual battles on the anthill on the vlei. There seemed so much more clarity of intent on Makoma's waters, and less flies to interrupt my deeper musings. Wisdom was not given to me in words, but in a dimension of perception that was familiar to my Soul. I could say I 'felt' *things* but that is not the right word. If knowing is a sense of perception I would say the wisdom of these open waters was imparted upon my Soul in flashes – not unlike light reflected off the water. It was an unconditional all-time knowledge that was available to every person that has ever crossed the open waters of self-discovery – it was theirs to start with. My happy musings on the Makoma waters were merely the rippled residues of a seamless transfer of universal all-time knowledge.

Truth on the water
After Independence Northern Rhodesia became Zambia. My parents had friends in Kitwe some twenty miles away who were English expatriates. Expats came to work mainly on the mines on two year renewable work permits. No longer were Europeans

allowed to take up permanent residence. Any Europeans deemed to be unpatriotic of newly independent Zambia, expatriate or otherwise, did not have their contracts renewed, and in some cases, were deported. If British, they were given twenty-four hours to board a Caledonian plane bound for London, and if they were South African they had to pack their car for a hurried departure to the south the next day.

These friends of my parents had only been in Africa a few years and their son Peter, having stayed in England at a boarding school, was now a third year university student in the UK. Peter had only visited Africa once before during his university vacation, and was now revisiting his parents. They came to Luanshya for the day, and we all went to Makoma Dam because my kind father had told him that I would take him on a tour of the dam in my canoe. I was an expert on African rivers and waters he said. Used to being a loner, I found it difficult to share my world with anyone and Peter was a lot older than me; but I had no option but to spend the day with him. Deep down I resented being forced to introduce anyone to my secret world on the other side. To delay the inevitable I decided we would spend the morning fishing from the concreted bank. Fishing in dead water is tortoise slow and so he had loads of time to ask me questions, questions about me and my life in Africa. He didn't seem to be too interested in Africa, only me; maybe that's what proper Europeans were interested in – other humans. I had heard a grown-up complaining about the herd mentality of people back in England, and I decided that this is what they meant – they couldn't see the forests for all the people. Peter was studying psychology at university, which I had been told was the study of people's minds and their personalities. That must be difficult and messy, I thought to myself.

Because he was the first person to really ask me deep questions about myself and what I did, I let it slip out about my anthill on the vlei, which lead to talk about my canoe jaunts, and then back to the anthill. He was friendly and he listened, and because he seemed so kind and interested, I let out more than I should have. He was so pale that his skin looked like that of a young boy, and his sun-weak eyes made his face appear fragile. In spite of his soft skin, he was definitely an adult in the way he behaved. He had a deep, to my mind rough, and yet also soft spoken English voice. I was told later that it was a broad Yorkshire accent. He wore a heavy three o'clock shadow on his chin and the jowls of his square jaw and upper lip. His baritone presence carried on a thick frame which, contrasted with his gentle demeanour, disturbed my judgement. He appeared to be childishly unassuming, and yet he was also confident like a grown up. My mind, which warmed to his grown-up-child ambivalence, had dangerously let down its guard in front of this strange creature from 'Mud Island', a derogatory name given to the UK by long standing English Southern Africans. My mind abandoned its well-rehearsed stance of grown-up mistrust, and with false logic, I repeated two self-reaffirming thoughts: 'He isn't really a grown-up, is he?' and, 'He isn't a child, is he? I decided I liked him because he would fully understand things. Up till then I had allowed my secrets to calcify around me, now here was someone tapping on my shell. They did say that psychologists could crack the codes of people's minds. This was a novel situation for me, and in a self-centred way, I rather enjoyed it. I even felt proud that I could converse with a budding psychologist like him. It reminded me of my conversations with the sweet little missionary lady. I thus willingly opened myself up to his questioning.

He asked if in the afternoon we could go for the promised canoe ride, and that's when things changed. We had hardly paddled out of the concreted shallows, when a jagged reflection of sunlight bounced off the water and obstructed my rosy view of the way things were going. It carried with it an unexpected fear, which snuffed out my pride of ownership of the very waters that I was supposed to be showing him. What on earth were the waters trying to tell me? Well whatever it was, it was too late; there was no going back. A whirlwind crossed the waters in front of us on its whippy journey, not unusual for that time of the year. I enjoyed them because they broke the water up into minute waves that looked like a shoal of sardines caught in the sun. But I didn't appreciate this one. It was edged with a sharp chill. The permanent furrow on my forehead spasmed and told me that life was a constant battle. Something else told me I needed to be more cautious and less foolish. Cautious of what, I wondered. I felt uncomfortable on the waters of my African fantasies. Was there some sort of weird complicity between this unreadable Englishman who was sitting in my canoe and the strange messages I was picking up? I was pretty certain I wasn't imagining things.

He sat in the front, and I paddled from the back. When going over shallow waters it was better that way. He looked straight ahead. He seemed not to notice the wading birds, the malachite kingfisher, the shoals of baby bream, and the baby leguaan hiding in the lily pads from the fish eagle that was hovering over our heads. He seemed not to notice the Bemba fishermen with their thin bamboo rods and broad smiles. He seemed to be only interested in destinations: 'Where are we going next?' he would frequently ask.

ALLAN TAYLOR

I took him to the half-submerged anthill where a large python and a newcomer to the dam, a grizzly old leguaan, were
vying for supremacy. As I moored alongside the contested territory, in the proud hope of finding something exciting, he said
it was nearly teatime and shouldn't we be heading back. Time
to head back, huh, backwards – damn backwards, always backwards, I peevishly thought to myself. Like a grown-up, he was
looking at a wide open future within the gloom of backwards-
looking time. It was inconceivable to me that a young man
should turn his back on anything African, and I was getting
tired of being socially responsible for such an insensitive lout. It
is so much easier to be a loner. You do what you want to do when
you want to do it, and in fact you enjoy it more when you are
lonely. Self-inflicted isolation and sadness can be satisfying –
especially when you are in total control of it. In the situation
I now found myself, things were completely out of my control;
and when I was out of control, I became angry.

My enflamed emotions saw his indifference to my affinities
akin to a world war nerve gas: The heavy molecules of his casual
disdain were floating out of his body onto the floor of my canoe
and creeping out across the water to poison the whole of Africa.
I hated him for that.

We got back to an early, too early in my opinion, stewed tea
and ate drop scones with runny butter and warm honey. Again
we had time on our hands, and that's when he said, with honey
and butter emulsion dripping down the stubble of his soft chin,
'This all seems like fun, great fun. In fact one could become
easily addicted to it.'

'Really? You didn't show it,' I thought as a sharp lump of
crystallised honey scratched my gullet forcing me to turn away

and cough. Then he said, 'But it's not real. What do you want to be when you are older?'

'Be?' What a stupid question, I am what I am, what the hell do you mean, I thought and then, as if to turn my African world completely on its head he repeated; 'What do you want to do? Are you going to leave Africa and work or study in England?' And with a final twist of his Anglo-Saxon dagger, which had already lodged itself deep into my solar plexus, its icy blade sitting dangerously close to my heart, he said, 'There is nothing here in Africa for you – you need to go somewhere else.' If he had spoken a rare form of Tibetan Sanskrit I might have understood him better. What diabolic train of thought was running through his puerile English mind? It was the worst thing that had ever been said to me. Even my anger, which I could normally whip up at a drop of a hat, had retreated in cold shock of his executioner's words. In a few sentences my African world had been made worthless. I could feel my heart was still intact, but my blood had iced over and my mouth and throat were filled with the quicklime of dissolution. It was like asking Mowgli if his wolf pack were a performing poodle act in a Bombay circus. It was an attack on my values. Africa's worth was being trashed. I was too weak to respond. By under-valuing Africa, my own self-worth was about to be declared dead by a pale Englishman.

He ignored my gagged spiritual silence. He had been totally unaware of my world, the Bemba fisherman's world and the world of the leguaan and the python. Yet in spite of his narrow ignorance of *things*, his enquiring psychologist's mind had zoned in on me. My inner truth and its allegiance with the African bush and its people was under siege. As I saw it, his words were an accusatory finger pointing at the validity of everything that I loved and stood for. They were pointing at the futility of my thoughts and actions, and demanding that I be fully accountable for them. His words unequivocally demanded an answer – an answer as to what good was the African bush to me. He had dissected me like fresh road kill; a post-mortem result of which would have been his own foregone conclusion. I did not give him an answer. I couldn't; his words left a vacuous trail that deprived my hurt feelings of any possible toehold. For the rest of the afternoon I quietly withdrew, deciding that I now disliked him. I half-listened to him talk to others so as to try to find fault in his words. To my surprise, I found myself questioning my own feelings more than being able to find fault in his opinions.

Peter's words stung my ego badly, and that's what it needed. I had an ego that had always allowed me to do what I wanted to do. I loved my anthill on the vlei and my days on Makoma Dam and that was about all I thought about. His words made me question what this love was. Was there something faulty about it? Was it interfering with my future plans? Would it sap my self-expression and hamper my self-realisation – which he labelled as 'what do you want to be'?

Was this love for Africa nothing but an addiction? Was Peter saying I had no purpose? The next door gardener, Lameck, smoked *mbanje*, marijuana. He couldn't get through a working day without a few trips to the compost heap, where he would draw on a newspaper cigarette. Because of his addiction he was a hopeless worker, but his wife, who worked in the house, was a good nanny for the children, so his employers kept him on. They weren't keen gardeners so his dismal efforts went by largely unnoticed. Was that going to happen to me? Was Peter saying that I would be useless at what I did in later life – all because of a youthful addiction; a reckless affinity that had me well and truly in its embrace? If I failed in life would anyone even notice or care? I was a loner, and I liked *things* to be like that. I did not want to do what the other kids wanted to do. I took pride in expressing myself differently to every other child that I knew. Was there anything wrong in that?

If what Peter was trying to tell me about 'needing to get somewhere' was right, should I not join the Makoma Dam junior fishing competitions; try to get into the grade six cricket team, or join the Luanshya swimming club? Everything that I took part in would be for the good of my future life. Perhaps Peter found mucking around on African waters trivial and dirty, and thought of the primitive notion of secretive goings-on on anthills and vleis as perverse. He should know – he was a soon-to-be psychologist, and a good one at that. Hooking thoughts and words from out of other people's hidden worlds were the tools of his trade. Maybe Peter was right, not about perversity and filth, but about my moving on, moving on without big Mama Africa always holding my little white hand.

I was not like the gardener next door. I was not taking each day as it came without a single thought to my future. Those mesmerising little eddies and whirlpools that seemed to aimlessly muse themselves into oblivion in the temporal backwaters of the Luanshya River: they knew one day they would meet the great Zambezi, and eventually the grand shores of the Indian Ocean. Like them, I had to go with the flow. Our futures were not stagnant pools of mosquito larvae infested water in the vlei. Like mosquito larvae, life called for change.

The anthill on the Luanshya vlei was the material coalescence of a 'Now' moment in all-time, of which my time was one iota. If I kept it in a jar, I would destroy its magic. Sitting on a tartan rug with python and leguaan stand offs shoved to the back of my mind, my conscious awareness told me this.

Sitting on that tartan rug, Peter's cutting words also brought me to the door of a nightmare. I always had the same nightmare. It lurked in my sleep like a hollow-eyed hyena. Neither the seductive Luanshya night, nor my naked night robber could help me with it because it was the ill-seeded progeny of my own fear. It came from source; it was not alien. It came in the depths of the night to rob my Soul of its pleasant memories, and like a hyena at first light, it holed up in a foul-smelling den somewhere far deeper than where my conscious thoughts and feeling dared to go. There it waited for the next curtain fall of the night. Sometimes I would catch its rotten stench as I went about my daily schoolboy chores. That's when I would freeze up and crack, as if I were in fearful embarrassment of knowing too much. Of what, I didn't know, and that made me feel uncomfortable; just as I felt right then on that grass burred rug.

It was the same repetitive scene: a small girl sat on a bench in the Luanshya Primary School garden, the toes of her dainty shoes barely touching the ground. It wasn't Janet, who had no surname. It was a 'Shirley Temple' type girl with curly locks of hair. She wore a short frilly pinafore dress with pink-edged socks and white patent leather shoes with a silver buckle. In her hand she held a single daisy with white petals and a bright yellow centre. Happily kicking her feet, she was waiting for brothers and sisters that she never had, and yet she was excited at the thought of joining them next year at 'big school' to which she would never go. The sky was high, and the clouds had collapsed into nothingness. Suddenly something terrible happened, and she became engulfed in tons of earth and rock, which turned like the Christmas cake mix in my mother's hand mixer – a mass of bloated raisins, broken eggs, cinnamon, and ever-creeping Demerara sugar, cracked nuts and bitter candied peel. It was an ever turning, folding and pulping mass of shapes and textures. I would catch fleeting glimpses of a lock of her golden hair, the freshly painted park bench, her delicate salmon pink arm, a dainty shoe, the daisy. Images of happiness gobbled up and re-appearing in a rhythmic never-ending, ever-churning mass of brown rocks and crumbling earth: the repetitiveness of which made me frightened and sad. I desperately wanted to save her, care for her and make her happy again, but there was abso-lutely nothing I could do. Deep down, I knew that something about her had pre-determined her fate. It wasn't an accident; it was meant to be. The immensity of the ever-moving earth, and the terrible grinding and crashing sound that it all made, pre-vented me from getting close to her, or even calling her name. The shame of it all was that I couldn't remember her name, and yet she was so familiar to me. It was a sad collage of sweetness, horror and acute embarrassment.

The fear that this nightmare released was in a gabble of muted words that bemoaned my helplessness – I was not in con-trol. Its emotional residues were a muffle on my self-expression for days and grown-ups couldn't understand why.

Peter's words were the sharp knife that cut into that op-pressive Christmas cake of unresolved fears that were turning on their own axis of horrid purpose; that were waiting for me in a slow churn of sickly sweet confusion. Stagnation, uncer-tainty and false vanity were the breeding grounds for failure. Peter's words were insinuating that alien fear was waiting for when my addictive affinities would harness my body, weaken my intentions and crush my Soul. Fear would turn to spite; my childish frustrations would no longer be aimed at my white subtribe. They would turn on my inner worth: call it a Janet and John no-name fake with no hope of rescue or redemption. What a terrifying thought for Perseus, conqueror of all anthills.

By the time I crawled into my bed that night, I decided that I did still like Peter. Why did I ever think that the abundance that I saw around me was all there was – and that it was mine? Why did I think that the anthill on the vlei was in my personal possession? That I had discovered the Makoma backwaters and its Bemba fishermen? The truth was that they all found me. They had uncovered my inner truth: they had allowed my senses to resonate in their reflection in temporal shades of affinity and love. I had to be a sensual being to explore my world, but sensuality was only a particular facet of my spirit of adventure. It exposed me to my affinities. If I wanted to find my spiritual truth, my purpose in life, I had to follow these affinities with loving detachment – which called for trust in a love that I had always had.

If love and oneness were the same thing, was that not proof that chasing the bush world that I loved so dearly, was a pointless thing – I would be chasing my own tail.

The grey-water truth that Peter had pumped out of me was again brought to the surface a few days later on the Makoma waters.

Refractions of inner light – grey water truth

I could never be a personage of the likes of the black Bemba fisherman, who after breaking rocks down a mine all week, was fishing for small, bony fish for his Sunday dinner with *nshima*, sticky maize meal, to eat with his fingers.

A man who might have more than one wife, and more than a few children in the mine compound, and back home in the rural area, *kaya kamina*.

A man who had been saving up for more than a few years to buy a cheap bicycle, who was still paying of *lobola,* a dowry, for one of his wives, and who had no access to a bank to safeguard his savings.

A man who in spite of it all, was content. I could never be him, physically, cognitively nor spiritually.

I should invite him to my Hall of Fame, along with the night robber, the Congolese forest deities and their American au pair. All to be admired and respected but never emulated for I was not offered that spiritual right.

I was invited to come across them barefoot, and move on, as I followed the footsteps of my own Soul.

Tribal wars – culture clashes

Not all the white folk were the same, nor were their children. In fact my parent's subtribe were a minority, and I had the inkling that my parents had been unwittingly initiated into it. They had crossed into its territorial waters because of my father's joviality and from then on, they had to adhere to its banal working class rules. In fact, I should have shown my parents greater respect for their strength of character in such an awkward social situation. Unfortunately it put me behind the iron railings of my subtribe, and I missed out on friendships with the kids of the more outgoing South African and English families. There were many – I might have had loads of fun with them, but I was obstinately shy.

Makoma Dam offered an eclectic mix of people. There were the powerboat people: They added little to the aesthetics of Makoma Dam with the howling of their boats, which came in and out of earshot as they plained around marker buoys with a smack of water against their hulls. To be a speedboater you had to be more than a tinkerer of things nautical – motor mechanics was their game. I would wander along their jetty at the opposite side to the concreted-in fishing jetty – far from my secret Africa on the other side. Multi-coloured rainbows of hot oil eddied on the water and blue swirls of rich fuel smoke pierced my nose and eyes. Burly but patient hands carried out mechanical vivisections on non-performing engines, and there always seemed to be many of those. Conversations were of fuel pumps, throttles and the order of races, speeds and winners. Alcohol and bar stories had no role where self-worth and achievement was measured in piston pressures, speed and agility. It was an African alien world too. They never saw the timelessness of my wild, shallow waters, but I found some form of deep respect for their rejection of the superficial existence of my subtribe as well as for their timeless fascination for anything mechanical. I felt they disliked me and wanted me off their jetty, but they probably didn't even notice me in the ordered perfection of their mechanical world. The yachting folk had the same approach to planned perfection in their silent world of spinnakers and rudders, and they seemed not to notice me either.

There was an Italian family from Ndola who were in the Makoma motorboat world of tinkering and giving full throttle, but their penchant was not racing boats. They tinkered with fancy big boats for water skiing. Most Italians on the Copperbelt were naturally mechanically minded, and owned either garages, contracting companies, or engineering businesses. Some of the younger ones were the families of Italian prisoners of war captured in Abyssinia and North Africa, and incarcerated in prisoner of war camps in British Colonial Africa as artisans, to build the most difficult and yet best roads and dams of the colonies. Others came to the mines after the war of their own free will, because of their mechanical and building propensities. I was told that Italians had built the Kariba Dam on the Zambezi River, and that some of them had a terrible accident. They had fallen into the concrete as it was being poured, and their bodies were still in the dam wall, which had become a huge mausoleum for what were ostensibly simple artisans. Whether the story was true or not, I wasn't sure. It was told to me by one of my father's English friends, who had staggered out of the MOTH Club bar one Sunday afternoon complaining about being offered pizza as a bar snack, and got round to telling me the unfortunate Italians' story; almost as if they deserved an unfortunate death for belonging to a culture that invented pizza.

This Italian family from Ndola was made up of two young brothers in their thirties, their families, and their mother. I never asked what had happened to their father, and because they never mentioned going a couple of hundred miles to put flowers on Kariba Dam wall, I decided that his body was not entombed there. The mother was a warm, bubbly woman, who oozed love in her ample folds of healthy coloured flesh. The young wives were attractive in their Southern European way, emotively powerful, and voluptuously beautiful, with dark eyes, thick dark hair and olive skins. They wore Indian cheesecloth kaftans sheer enough to see their bikinis underneath. They both flaunted a gold chain around an ankle, and an exotic ring on a deliciously chubby finger. The one always carried an amazing snakeskin bag. The other often wore a crocodile skin belt over her kaftan. Both told me they had bought these exotic adornments off Congolese traders. I was sure it was from my very own magi – of course I would conceitedly think that. They didn't ever need the powder room. The sun was their beauty treatment, and their olive skin was pampered with expensive moisturizers, and open to sun, wind and air when it needed to be. God how I loved both these softly vivacious women.

If my father was the Dionysus of the Copperbelt, then their husbands were cousins to Adonis. They had chiseled visages, aquiline noses, strong brows, square jaw lines – the older one more so – and intense, dark eyes. The older one was more re-served, slightly arrogant and very proud of his family. He spoke in strong words that earned respect. The other was soft, and loving to all and sundry, but most of all to his family. He had dark curly hair and deep set eyes like my father. I admired them both for being so loving and kind to their perfect families. They were my Roman heroes. When they weren't attending to their speed boat they were water skiing, showing off their athletic skills and up to date fashion sense in men's bikinis. The women of my white tribe could not believe men would wear leopard-patterned swimming trunks so skimpy! Their women skied too, showing that their feminine folds and curves camouflaged strong flexible bodies that could jump across the waves with ease at great speed.

When I wasn't in my canoe I would wander away from my tribe whenever I could. I started hanging around the outskirts of the Italian family's boathouse. I was a runt of an English boy scavenging for cultural scraps. They openly accepted me into their alfresco world – a glorious bit of good fortune. A stupid tartan rug would not do for these continental ladies – they needed a solid table to make a sound meal for both their menfolk, who they adored, and for their bambinos, who had the rolling figures of cherubs from the roof of the Sistine Chapel. That was the first time I had ever smelt honest Italian food, seen people drink wine at a picnic, and heard a language that rolled off tongues in love with its own self-expression. Their bonvivance became an addiction that sprouted a pang of familiar neediness under my breastbone. A strange allure that had no time lined or cultural explanation. It was like falling in love. They were not unlike the indulgent Belgian Congolese that my parents knew. I was totally struck with an urgency of wanting, desperately wanting everything that they had for the immediate 'Now' and the eternal forever. My own European roots were long dis-eased and dying, but miraculously they were being given a rebirth in the rich volcanic loam of Southern European ways. I needed to know everything about their philosophy of life: I had to live in complete empathy with them if I was to survive the heart sore attraction that I had towards them.

Late one chilly July Sunday afternoon, when the wind had started to bite and my skin stripped of its oil by too much midday swimming in the shallows on the far side, I rushed up to the men's showers and changing rooms behind the bar at the main club house. I flew in, my thoughts preoccupied with bream, barbel and fishing hooks.

There they were, the two Italian brothers showering in a cloud of steam under a single dim 60 watt light bulb. They never used this changing area – not many people did. The speedboat people had built a far nicer one of their own. In fact 'my' Italians never came to the main club or the bar because it did not serve wine, only beer and spirits. Shocked at the full frontal assault of their nakedness, I started to step back towards the chilly late afternoon air. 'Hey there's room here. There are three showers,' the normally reserved one shouted, as he turned on the third shower with gusto. I was almost too embarrassed to get undressed, and so took my time dawdling over my towel and slipslops while they began to smother me with their warm familial banter about how my fishing had gone. They didn't stay long on the subject of the size of fishing hook or lead sinkers, but moved onto eating instead. This Italian cameo of mine were always eating, but never got fat. I used to wonder why. They liked bream fried in garlic and olive oil, served with farfalle pasta and sprinkled with fresh parsley, oregano and lemon juice. They explained this a few times so that I could memorise the preparation, and each time ended with a gathering of soapy fingers to the lips, and a loud exclamation of '*Squisito*'. I found this quite odd as the men of my white subtribe certainly did not cook, and thus knew no recipes whatsoever. While they were discussing the cooking rather than the catching of fish, my mind was spinning as to what my plan of action should be. I had picked up, and put down, my towel three times by now. Their sincere friendliness, however, overtook my inhibitions and I plucked up the courage not to dash under the shower with my costume on, and dash out of the shower block, as quickly as possible. I gingerly removed my colonial trunks, and stepped into the long rectangular shower trough as they turned and fiddled with the taps to get the water nice and warm for this slightly large bambino of theirs. A lot of things rushed through my mind: Well thank God my sun-filled antics on the water made me look as if I was at least a decent mix of skin colours, like them I hoped. I knew I did not have a stark costume line like white sugar icing on a deep fried donut – so far so good! Yes I was a bit like them. The next thing that went through my mind was – that's where the similarities stopped. Except for similar dark curly hair, that was it: I was not strong, not Italian and not proud of my roots, my cuisine or my culture. Although to be impartial, these fine young Italians would be just as disinterested in leguaans and pythons as were the folk of my white subtribe or the mechanical gurus of the powerboat section of the Makoma Dam. Leguaans and pythons were for my fascinated senses alone.

These Italian brothers were so friendly and accommodating, and I was trying to be the same, but it was so hard. A cocktail of embarrassment, jealousy and hero worship was blocking my throat, and stifling my every attempt of self-expression. I so wanted to be strong, friendly and handsome like them – and I wanted it right now! I couldn't wait for my own perfection to grow. I kind of knew that it would be hard work, and even after a hell of a lot of work I probably still wouldn't be like them. They chatted to each other, and to me, really taking their time in the warmth of the shower after hard play on the water. They were my first notable impression of the adult male that I would desperately want to become. I thanked the Gods, obviously Roman Gods; that this was how it happened. These two men displayed so much more than schoolboy laughed-at nakedness;

they showed warmth, love and beauty in their nude vulnerability. Both were muscular and fit, one burly and powerful, the other lean and defined. The burly one, who was the older, had a strong, hairy chest made for lifting two bambinos at a time, maybe even three. Because of his similar looks I imagined my father to have looked like the younger one in his Shanghai boxing heyday, when he too was lithe, good looking, and fit. Thank goodness for Jupiter and his godly gang, that this was my introduction to the male spirit – not some uninspiring, potbellied, tipsy member of my pink subtribe; some bland audio-visual experience of beer burps, *bops* and flab to be buried and forgotten on my anthill. Even my father, who was good looking in photos of the thirties, had let himself go. Too much alcohol, cigarettes and idle bar talk had sallowed his complexion and slightly distorted his facial features. He didn't carry the good life well, and his short five foot two stature now supported what the Southern Africans called a *beer bop*, a beer tummy, which to my embarrassment, he said he was proud of. It made me slightly sad because I desperately needed a hero in my life, and his rounded tummy was an indicator of his drinking habits. I loved him dearly, which made me even sadder.

Because of my two Italian soap suds heroes, I went home that night so optimistically happy about who I was and who I would become – a man, a lover, a bon vivant, and a good father like them. At that time, all the boys were wanting to be a Fred Flintstone or a Barney Rubble in their stone car in a carefree life that Bedrock gave them. Bedrock and Luanshya were quite similar, and the two tubby Stone Age non-heroes, and their yakkety yak wives, Norma and Wilma, were Luanshya familiar too. I was glad I had found Romulus and Remus of the Makoma Dam instead.

As the Gods would have it, this tableau of perfect manhood was complemented a month or so later. The Italians had had lunch, I included of course, proper Italian-style salami made by an Italian farmer near Ndola, white ciabatta bread, olives, fettuccine pasta in a basil leaf and tomato sauce, and wine. Afterwards the family tidied up and the men went for a ski. The wives lay on sun loungers at the back of their boathouse, a secluded spot that got the softer rays of the afternoon sun. I was playing with the children, who had the most amazing Italian toys, each piece a work of aesthetic and engineering art – Italian toys were a cult in those days. The grandmother was dozing, and the two wives were chatting in Italian. Unconsciously the one took her bikini top off to sunbathe, not taking any notice of my presence; after all I was a boy ... a boy of sorts. I had heard about topless sunbathing on a cheap British comedy show, which made it sound a risqué smutty joke – the 'nudge-nudge-say-no-more' humour of the terrible comedians on British television. This, however, was so spontaneously normal, and beautifully natural. The two young women fell into a sun silence and closed their eyes. I could not help but scrutinise the one's almost naked body on that lounger. Her flesh was light caramel, soft but firm. Her muscles were of the same symmetry as that of the menfolk, but with different turns and involutions. Her breasts were innocent mounds of flesh that spoke of intimacy, nurturing and confidence. Her nipples were of a henna colour that I had never seen before. She was beautiful: her perfection became permanently engraved on my mind. Her husband was the slender one, and I felt that her body and his body, her mind and his mind, her spirit and his spirit were one; and out of their perfect synergy, a new dimension grew of which their children were only a part. The combined memory of the Italian couple was first carried to the anthill for quiet rumination, and then close to my heart for the rest of my life as a template of love-filled perfection.

On those Makoma Sunday nights, after a hot pie from Sam's Bakery, I would bath, cover my sunburn with calamine lotion and jump into bed, where I would snuggle up between the white cotton sheets, wearing a tan that felt too tight on my cheeks, chest and shoulders. My toes would curl up and I would adopt a foetal position of supreme satisfaction. My Soul was happy. I felt I had intimately known all the characters of the day, who had now been gathered up into the last few pages of a fairy story. A day of warm imagery was being sucked deep into my being with not a drop wasted. I felt the loving embrace of an Italian lover, the pride of ownership and tradition of the black fisherman and his subservient washerwoman wife or wives; and in my jolly little English home, tucked up in bed, with no cheese and onion sandwiches in my belly to stoke nightmares, I wanted for nothing more. I did not want to be a Romulus or Remus nor an African fisherman on the waters. I was all of them in that present moment in my bed. I was a part of them from before my time, and would be a part of them after our linear time. We were half-recognized facets of a one Soul of humanity. We had each taken on a particular role. Without us and countless others, the theatre of the Universe would be a flop. We were the necessary vehicles of expansion for the continued spiritual coalescence of a material world. Without them, my spirit would have faded. Without me their uniqueness might have been overlooked – not that they would have noticed anything different. I noticed, and as the eyes of the Universe in that moment in time, their offering to our one humanity was given value – I loved them all. These thoughts didn't come to me in words. They came to me in a toe-curling all-time knowingness that reaffirmed my purpose in life. One didn't have to be an astronaut to touch the stars.

Was I ready to take on Mrs. Versaakie's nine times table, and a spelling test the next day? Well not quite! But I had caught a glimpse of my Soul.

Hyenas and termite mounds

As the Friday evening get-togethers at the MOTH Club progressed, and our parents became ensnared in conversations at the bar, we children slid out into the surrounding bush and anthills outside the fenced confines of the club. Did they honestly think we would sit outside the bar or play all night on the brightly painted swings, roundabout and seesaws made by the mine engineering department? We formed our own tribe. I was anti-tribal but this forced conspiracy of rebellion appealed to my sense of independence. We crept through the undergrowth of the surrounding bush and on to the rivulet, near to where my Soul had barely survived an attempted defilement by a band of sea scouts on the steroids of misguided adolescence. I was long past the stage of wanting to conform to the mantras of Lord Baden Powell chanted by the Cub Scouts or the silly seamen in the middle of Africa. Like the other MOTH club kids, I wanted freedom. The African night was more than willing to assist, and I loved her for it. I gloated in the fact that I knew her better than anyone else, of that I was sure – why? Because she told me so.

We skulked through the night like a pack of hyenas, oblivious to the possibility of coming across a night adder. We choose to be hyenas, not lions or leopards because we were led to believe that hyenas were the most despised and despicable of all African animals – they were always up to no good. It was the gruff-voiced leaders of our pupae pack that had decided that our underhand activities made us worthy of being called hyenas. Nothing could be more appropriate they said.

Sometimes we would cross the main Ndola road to reach the first line of houses at the edge of the far bush, the other side of town to my vlei; otherwise I might not have been so keen to get involved. As surreal hyenas, we would yelp and howl to scare the many white folk who didn't frequent the bars of the town. Choking with laughter, we would run back to the safety of the bush darkness. We were searching for our small identities, which we couldn't find sitting outside a bar, bored to tears.

There were powerful hierarchies in our pack, with status and position being measured on various attributes from pubic hair to boarding school attendance and the car our fathers drove; we weren't all boys either. My friend Alan and I – we were in the same class at school – were at the bottom of the dung pile when it came to hierarchical importance, which suited me fine. I had already fully accepted that I was not a leader of men or women, and I didn't want to be either. We tagged along at the back of the hyena pack where it was more exciting. We had the chance to stand alone in the dark with the safety net of being able to run and catch up with the rest of the pack should things get a bit scary; which they sometimes did. I would never have gone into the bush at night on my own. Not because of a worry that alien fear might attack me, but because in a darkness of melting perspective and shifting boundaries, my own fear would start to malfunction and set off a false alarm.

Some nights storms were brewing in the sky and we knew we wouldn't be out for long. When the heavy clouds hid the moon, and all was dark, the lightening was the switch that could turn our nighttime bush-world off and on. When it struck, it stripped us of our bush cover and our secrecy: it cast light and reality onto the individual forms of everything around us, 'off and on'. When the lightening was gone, collusion returned: darkness had joined everything in the bush together again as an inseparable oneness. Black and white, good and bad, separate and united. Everything was of the same essence; it was simply dependent on the colour of the light your eye took in, or the emotional colour your mind cast upon things in that particular moment in time.

Secretly, however, I had another reason for wanting to become a fully-fledged hyena on Friday nights at the club. Hyenas fascinated me. Something about them told me that their lives were not straightforward. They bore strange markings on their Soul. Every opportunity of going into the 'proper' bush far from the towns was an opportunity to see a hyena, or so I naively thought.

My father had a geologist friend who knew of my interest in crystals and attractive pieces of coloured ore. He was going on a day's journey into the bush with an old water diviner to site a new mine. My father asked if I could go with. I didn't like the geologist. I felt that he considered me a burden, but I wanted to go deep into the bush. I wanted to see wild animals and find wonderful crystals. Most of all I wanted to see a hyena. The start of the journey was exciting; it was my type of bush – thick forests and open *vleis* – but the dense forest soon petered out. Village charcoal burners had thinned the forests to make charcoal to sell across the border in the Congo. On the way there I was sitting straight, looking out for wildlife – but I saw nothing. The area had been hunted out long before. There were no crystals to be found either, and the geologist sarcastically said, 'elephants and crystals don't grow on trees sonny – anyway this bush is dead.'

Only a prig like you would say something like that, I thought. I had learnt the word 'prig' from a Somerset Maugham story about an arrogant rubber plantation manager in Malaya. I liked both the sound and meaning of it. I could name a few prigs in Luanshya. The geologist was added to my prig list. The day was tedious and uneventful. On the way back I was tired. We had been out nine hours. I flopped back in my seat on the point of dragging my musings into a funk hole – I was told I was very good at that. The old water diviner, an Afrikaner who had been raised in the Karoo desert, the driest part of South Africa, must have sensed my gloom for he started telling me stories.

He told me he was able to find water with two copper rods, but that he could also divine with two green sticks. The geologist, who was actually doing the groundwork for a modern hydrological survey, respected the water diviner and his methods. They often yield interesting results, and the geologist had brought him along 'out of interest.'

The diviner went on to tell me that, contrary to what you see and think you know, Africa does not always deliver what you would expect. Even if you had prior knowledge as to what should happen – it might not happen. He said he used this way of thinking when he was divining for water. Underground water was never a given – Africa had many dry rivers both above and below the ground. He then fell into a preoccupied silence as he groped for his tobacco in a canvas bag under his seat. What was this wizened old man with tobacco stains on his teeth and fingers telling me? I guessed it was going to be interesting. Then he looked at me, and cleared his tarred throat; it was as if he was about to give a wedding speech. His pupils were like glistening black diamonds as he spoke, and my curiosity took a strong hold.

Out of earshot of the prig steering his rattling Land Rover, the diviner told me that in Africa, physical things could suddenly appear and then just as quickly disappear. 'But they did nothing of the sort,' he said with a confident snort. 'It was the way we were looking at them that made these strange things happen.' Everything had an energy of its own which could never be lost – it merely altered its shape in time and space. Nodding in mused self-agreement, he then kept quiet for a good while. 'Energies are like hyenas,' he finally uttered. Wow! Now I really was all ears. I really wished I had a grandfather like him. With slow, forceful words he continued, 'An area could have no hyenas – then suddenly out of nowhere, one would appear.' If someone in a remote village had been cursed; that night, without a single pug mark on the floor of the village clearing, a hyena would appear at his door – even though hyenas had not been seen or heard of in the area for a very long time. 'This was because the hyena had always been there,' he said with a smug air of assurance.

True to form, the prig appeared oblivious to our important conversation, his mind doggedly fixed on the bumpy road that was pulling his vehicle to pieces. Once again, I was sitting upright looking for hyenas in what remained of once-thick miombo woodlands while the old diviner spoke. My ears were pricked, my eyes were peeled and my skin bristled – my bony little bum hardly made an indent on the green canvas of the backseat. Out there in the failing forest light I was hypersensitised to everything real and imaginary. I knew that hyenas were tribal omens for very important things in Africa; that's why the

Nyau and the Makishi only used effigies of hyenas in their most serious rituals. There was no logical reason for a hyena not to re-appear in the 'dead' bush, in the immediate 'here and now' of our homeward journey in the prig's rattle wagon.

The diviner continued: 'Hyenas are a mystery to their fellow beasts. They can eject an aardwolf, an aardvark, or even a bad-tempered honey badger from its burrow in an anthill, commandeer it, and with the collusion of the termites; do the strangest of things.' My mind ran wild, throwing my thoughts all over the back seat and floor of the vehicle as it trundled down that remote dirt road. The light was receding fast and Mr 'Cool' the geologist put his foot on the accelerator of his landy. The diviner fell into another one of his tobacco-chewing silences and I started to ruminate over *things* – I took as long as it took for him to suck on nicotine, spit spent tobacco, and pick his cracked lips free of the soggy shreds. Whatever it was that crept through his well-seasoned mind was worth waiting for.

'Lion, in particular,' he said, 'despise hyenas, and will hunt them down and kill them – sometimes killing hyena pups in the den so as to curb the number of hyenas in their territory.' When being chased by a lion, he explained, a hyena would disappear down a burrow in an anthill and never come out. The lion would give an eerie howl of frustrated annoyance, but no matter how long a lion waited; even if a pride of lions took turns to be on guard for a month, the hyena would never come out – this was because the hyena was no longer there.

'When a hyena takes over a burrow in an anthill,' he said, 'it is his intention that his mind and body be melted down by a sea of termites.' This was very different to a dead animal being eaten by red ants. It was the morphing of the hyena into an aethereal life force that parasitically attached itself to all members of the termite queendom. After an uncanny gulp of breath he explained further: The termite mind is a collective mind. It thinks as one mind, spreading and sharing its synaptic thought processes between queendoms right across subterranean Africa. Because the hyena had slyly embedded his spirit into this endless termitine mind, their 'everywhere' and their consequent awareness of all bush goings-on had become his for his own perverse machinations. By the same intent, he would then coalesce his virtual spirit-being out of the termite world and back into his physical reality: to resurface wherever he felt his presence was needed – or not needed, as in the case of the lion. And with that, the old diviner returned to his tobacco pouch, leaving me to digest his awesome words.

What could have been a tedious journey home, flew by. The long edges of evening shadows melted into a deep velvet of forest dark; there to be sown up for the night with thin threads of wood smoke from village charcoal burners along the roadside. Soon we would be back in Luanshya with its cheery windows and warm tarmacadam roads. Once home I asked my father to offer the old diviner a beer and a lift home, which he graciously accepted; luckily the prig was in a hurry to get back and write his report. For me it was a quick bath with Dettol, a fish finger and tomato sauce sandwich, and bed. I did not really object.

Hyenas danced a sly shuffle on the silver screen of my fading consciousness. I knew that they had been there in the bush; they were everywhere, even in my bedroom, but in reality, you just couldn't see them.

ALLAN TAYLOR

I often used to cycle alone around the town and scavenge for quirky things afoot. One hot Saturday afternoon, while my parents were taking an afternoon nap, I cycled past the bowling club, and there the old diviner sat: on a bench, in front of lady bowlers all dressed in white, wearing floppy sunhats. He saw me, and beckoned me to join him. He told me that if he was not out of town divining, he came every Saturday afternoon to watch his wife play bowls. He didn't care much for the game, and so he never played. How boring I thought. From then on, out of town jobs permitting, we had a permanent Saturday afternoon rendezvous. I think he enjoyed telling me his stories, and of course I loved hearing them – but he did go away a lot. Divining for water in remote areas was both difficult, lonely and time consuming, he said. I thought the same about cloud chasing: I was so glad that we had *things* in common.

The old diviner went over his incredible hyena story over quite a number of chats, as if he wanted me to fully understand the mechanics of it – after all, it was not just another MOTH Club bar story.

He told me that the one thinking mind of termites can pick up the slightest of vibrations in the soil. That they were aware of the movements, and thus the whereabouts, of all creatures everywhere and at all times. 'There is nothing they don't know about – they are a force to be reckoned with,' he told me. 'You know how damp tubes of red earth carrying termites can arrive on a doorframe, under a tarpaulin, or in the beams of a house in a single night. How in two nights, a man-sized termite mound can mushroom out of the earth; and in five nights, termites can dissolve any organic obstacle? Well the hyena certainly takes full advantage of this power,' he said, in a rare instance of old man's awe.

What really fascinated me, and took a fair bit of musings into my teens to fully comprehend, was this: The diviner had said that because one termite mind was seamlessly connected to many termites' minds, it was not unreasonable to assume that – with distance and space not being an issue for instant cognition – measured time was not of importance to the termite mind. It was cognitively busy in all-time, and knew of everything that ever was. Termites ruled a hidden underground African world that had no yesterday, today or tomorrow. Everything just was – a timeless world floating on the awareness of its own omniscience. Millions and millions of termites scurried across the boundaries of time in every moment of an African day. Termites were time travellers. That was the reason both hyenas and witchdoctors invested so much importance in anthills.

The old diviner went on to tell me that the hyena used the power of his intent to shift his shape. 'Intentions are like bush paths,' he explained. 'If the first set of footprints through the grass is followed by a second set, and then another, and another, there will eventually be a bush path. These paths are the wants of every person, creature, culture or herd that has stepped that particular way, no matter what the reason.' In the same way, a collective mind is a route map of well-worn thought patterns, he told me. Singular intentions when constantly repeated, become the blueprint for the infinite layering of thought processes and satisfied needs. They become trails of purposed intent that endlessly crisscross the psyche of the herd, swarm or colony – what biologists call instincts, he said. They help animals to find their food, water and safety, and their assured success becomes a habit over all-time. In the same way, the hyena consciously wills his intended body to be somewhere else, and he uses the collectively repetitive mind of white ants to do it. White ants don't play with black magic – he liked his little joke – the psyche of the white ant has long been dipping its collective toes into pure spirit – the hyena simply takes advantage of it.

Over chats about *things* with the old diviner, I decided that witchdoctors knew very well how powerful termites were, and fully endorsed the hyena's abuse of these intelligent little creatures. I felt certain that witchdoctors themselves used both termites and hyenas to be more effective in their predictions.

From what I understood from the old diviner: If the white ants should die, the hyenas would die, and the witchdoctor tradition would die, and Africa would die. Therein lay a clue to the surreal state of the Africa spirit; which seemed to inveigle its timeless Soul in and out of its creatures and its people. Africa was carried on the back of termites. Under the ground, and under the footprint of the African people, the termites had supremacy – the Colonial white shadow that limped behind was powerless in comparison.

Take Sean Brown's accident: now there was sure proof of what the old diviner was saying about the power of the white ant. In fact Sean's illogically tragic story made total sense.

Sean Brown was new to Luanshya. His father had been transferred from another copper mine twenty miles away, and he was now in my class at school. Until I met Sean, I thought the biggest anthill in Luanshya was on my vlei, and I was very proud of this secret possession which I had never shown, and hardly even talked about to any of my classmates. Sean lived in T Avenue (Tacoma), which ran parallel to the Luanshya River, a fair distance upstream from the golf course and Cerberus' gate. It was logical that before houses were built there, it was a vlei area with anthills.

I thought it strange that I had never before seen what was in his garden, the biggest anthill I had ever seen. My parents' first house in the late forties, shared with another couple, was in T Avenue, just a few doors from where Sean now lived. I had often ridden my bicycle down that street. Surely I would have noticed it before. It took up most of his front garden. Maybe it wasn't there before, maybe it was somewhere else, but it was certainly there now. Could anthills shift their shape? Maybe its arrival had coincided with Sean's arrival. It also had the largest pod mahogany tree that I had ever seen growing out of its crown. Were both the anthill and the pod mahogany apparitions in in-carnate form? Mr Kumar had reaffirmed the old diviner's story about the hyena – he told me that shape shifting happened a lot in India: objects, big and small, could appear and then suddenly disappear. In its pre-reincarnate state, outside the realms of measured people time, this anthill with its healthy pod mahogany canopy was no different. Now it was an inert clay shadow of its former reigning self – how could that be? Could dead anthills still shapeshift? Over the years, the DDT squad from the mine had a ruthless policy of white ant eradication. All anthills in the suburbs of the town were poisoned and then levelled. Levelling a dead anthill was not something that these fastidious men could have overlooked. Yet here was a 'dead' anthill – reincarnated. It was a mystery, and I was confused.

Was perhaps the mahogany the instigator of this reincarna-tion? The old diviner told me that pod mahoganies liked rich soils, which our area lacked, and were not likely to be seen on the Copperbelt because of the high altitude. This ruled out the mahogany as the mastermind behind the anthill's arrival. I thus deduced that because the termites had dug deep kingdoms below the surface, they had created a rich designer loam of which our two unique pod mahoganies took full advantage. I asked him, if these trees didn't normally grow in Luanshya, how could the original seed have arrived on the anthills? To which, for once, he had no answer. It was a mystery: mysteries are like naked night robbers; they have a reason attached somewhere to their slippery minds and bodies. I wanted to know the reason. At the time of Sean's arrival, the possibility of spiritual provenance was a pleasant musing that I kept to myself; but things were to change.

In my further musings, I worked out two possibilities of which I was very proud. The first was that the termites had, for symbiotic reasons, carried the life force of these magnificent trees all the way from a distant low altitude area called the Lowveld for a rebirth in the Luanshya bush.

My second postulation was that a pod mahogany seed had been brought to both anthills in a traditional necklace as part of a burial ritual. I had always felt lucky that I had a pod mahogany growing on my anthill, double lucky because the pod mahogany is also known as the *inkehli* lucky bean tree. It produces hard, black seeds with a bright red wattle like the ground hornbill. The Ndebele women of Matabeleland used lucky beans in tribal necklaces, especially for the unbetrothed. Maybe an Ndebele woman had died young, and had been buried in my anthill, whereupon a pod mahogany seed from her funeral adornment had grown in honour of her spirit. This would make this magnificent tree on my anthill all the more special, but surely this romantic story couldn't be applied to both our anthills and both our trees?

The old diviner had also told me that the buffalo beans that guarded the lower reaches of my anthill didn't grow on the Copperbelt either. As they would not lend themselves to being used decoratively, or funereally; my first postulation held the most water. Both the pod mahoganies and the buffalo bean plants on my anthill were transcendental migrations instigated by the most spiritually powerful creatures in Africa, the white ants of both termitaria. This explanation seemed a tidy one – but it didn't explain the reason for the arrival of Sean's anthill, which even in its sorry state, was bigger than mine – as was his pod mahogany. I was jealous. Without knowing the facts, my ego was striding out ahead of me in blind ignorance, and resentment was clouding my vision. Trouble was surely looming.

Sean's anthill became a *wag-'n-bietjie,* hook-thorn in my side. My perceptions of *things* continued to shift in an uncomfortable manner: That the biggest anthill in Luanshya belonged to a new boy in town had brought an emotional adversary for me to contend with. I also felt that he was showing off about it. I was incensed by this irritating state of affairs. Before Sean's arrival, an ever-increasing arsenal of mythological and bush craft allegiances on my anthill had been propping up my loner's life. I had been comfortable in my skin – but no longer. I had never encountered such an experience of personal displeasure before. It wriggle-niggled under my skin. It squirted its bitter bile into my sweat glands, which made my skin uncomfortable and clammy. It marinated my mind in sour anger.

The mind has a devious way of working: it teamed up with my ego, and sprung back with a notion of conceit. His anthill is dead. It has no magic, my ego announced. No Cerberus to keep intruders at bay, no Pegasus on guard, no secretive night visitors or strange rituals. Most of all, it had no African soul, no termites whose catalytic presence made it all happen. DDT had brought down this bull elephant of all vleis. In cheap superiority, I decided that nothing remained but a useless sun-dried carcass – it had no real purpose – even the mahogany would abandon it in time. I had sunk lower than a puff adder's belly in soft Kalahari sand.

There was quite a drop in height from the top of the 'dead' anthill to what remained of a once wild vlei behind Sean's house. His dad had erected a *foofie* slide, a zip line, from high in the pod mahogany tree, past their house, and down to the open ground of the vlei. A bar on a pulley could be pulled by a loose rope up to a platform high in the tree. Hanging onto the bar, you could whizz down to the bottom, where there was a pile of old tires to break your fall: you could also fall off and break something else! All the boys in my class wanted to visit Sean in the afternoons to go on the foofie slide. I often went along, but I could never do it. The fear of falling off at great speed was just too daunting. Different emotions were running around inside me – was resentment whipping up an alien fear of rejection – and I refused to make a fool of myself in front of my classmates by falling off. Or was my own fear warning me of a pending disaster – especially given the abnormality of *things* as they stood?

My classmates mocked me, they called me a yellow bellied coward. This hurt. I was a warrior of the African bush: none of them had single handedly penetrated the bush as deep as I had; sat alone in thunderstorms on a vlei; poled a canoe far across tangled reed beds and up rivers beyond the civilised white boating territory; seen so many snakes and wild bush pig spoor; or fought off the mythological monsters that frequented Luanshya night and day: and they called me a coward. Why did yellow signify cowardice I wanted to know? My hurt congealed into further resentment, and I shunned them for a while. Their parents didn't frequent the MOTH Club, so these boys weren't part of the hyena pack, and they never would be if I had my way.

I gave my ugly yellow belly a lot of thought on my anthill. Should I share my anthill with the boys in my class; show them the narrow path through nettles and buffalo beans; take them on Makoma Dam in search of leguaan and python stand-offs: should I really show them my true worth? I did not have a yellow belly at all. Every time I thought of their audacity, I saw red. Pegasus moved away to the safety of the miombo forest: she knew my moods better than most. I also knew she would move away permanently if I invited the boys to the vlei.

One day, half-squatting on my ant mound with its dank shadows and contorted roots, I began to feel particularly insecure: even the vlei showed little appeal. I made a move to wend my way home. Sick lethargy added to the weight of my mud-caked shoes. I felt unsafe, and I wasn't looking forward to seeing Cerberus's ugly features. I was alone in my self-pity as I staggered through the long grass of the vlei. Grave thoughts were clouding the sun. There was a strange chill in the air that nipped at my ears, making them numb, and my nose started to drip. I stopped on the tree line, and in a desperate attempt to settle things, I decided to invite the boys into my world. I felt a sudden wave of nausea creeping up my gullet, but walked on. Then reflection pulled me aside. What the hell was I doing? I had already lost a chunk of my self-worth with the foofie slide. Now I was about to subjugate my 'everything' to the scrutiny and ridicule of every Tom Dick and Harry in my class. Without further thought, I turned around to embrace the innocent riverine breeze for what it was, and stomped back to 'my' anthill.

I stayed on the anthill for the rest of the afternoon. Pegasus returned from the miombo forest to watch me. I sat on my termitine dais not thinking much about this or that – I needed to clear my head of whimpering notions. As often happened when my bum was in contact with the grit of the anthill, and when my head was empty – I began to sense a change in *things*. In spite of my heart labouring under a sluggish emotional hue, it gave a sharp convulsive turn. As was my habit on the anthill, I welcomed this tangible body change, and went with the aethereal swell that had caused it. I began to see things differently: Exposing my secret world to the boys was a complete sell out. What exactly was it that I really wanted, and for what reason was I wanting it? That was a very difficult question to answer. Africans had shown me that you did not always need answers to questions; it was quite acceptable to ask a question and go with its timeless flow without any expectations of a conclusion. In the light of this useful bit of advice, I started to feel better in myself.

Pegasus was facing me full on, and I honestly felt she winked at me – as if to say 'at it boy, that's the fighting spirit.' I had read that Pegasus, the winged horse with divine powers, had helped Bellerophon to slay the terrible Chimera, and win many other mythological battles. I also read that Bellerophon eventually abused Pegasus' solidarity by trying to fly up to the Sun, the seat of the Gods – so in love was he with his own misconceived self-importance. This was an affront to Jupiter, who sent a horse-fly, I reckoned it was a tsetse fly – they could bite really sore – to sting Pegasus in the rump. Pegasus bucked,

Bellerophon fell off, took an earth bound tumble, and ended up as a lonely, lame and blind subject of an impoverished Soul for the rest of his life. That mustn't happen to me, I thought. I must not expose Pegasus, the vlei, or the power of my termite queendom to the boys in my class for my own selfish importance. I would find a rightful place for myself without having to abuse everything that was special to me.

On hearing the first Hueglin's robin's crepuscular call, I left the anthill. I marched back through a gauntlet of spiky reeds and Cerberus' world of trenches and catfish guts without seeing him; he may have been there, but I wasn't looking for him. I was fired up for the battle of the anthills. In spite of having been emotionally wounded, I was now more than fit enough to defend my secret mythological and earthy alliances. I was ready to protect my bush world and all it stood for. Besides, I was having second thoughts about Sean's dead anthill, and I needed to investigate its origins further. I had more to do than mope around feeling sorry for myself.

As it happened, things were changing and I didn't have to do anything at all – other than wait in seemingly timeless African time. Below the surface, like the collective mind of the white ant, *things* were in constant flux. It was a spiritual world where change was not limiting – nor was it capable of choosing a particular outcome – as I was to find out.

Change, the aethereal wax and wane of events that affects all things, all of the time, is a composite of both positive and negative energies. On the spiritual plane things don't change for the good or the bad; they simply change. Things might look different; good and evil might swop places at our table, but they are still the same dinner guests. They are the unconditional states of universal being which are invited to partake in our lives. What will change, will be our response to the perceived good or bad of it all. Only then do the dominos fall on the playing board of our perceptions, and we start to point out good and evil. We will our own destiny upon ourselves: we see what we want to see, and we get what we want to get. The Africans that I knew all thought in this way – except that they wanted *n'angas*, the witchdoctors, to nudge the dominos for them. They allowed their beings to be buffeted by change, and in so doing, were open to magic: but it also made them vulnerable to alien fear, which in my mind, wasn't such a good thing.

In the African bush, good and evil were both visitors to the forest clearing. They slowly arrived in the darkest of nights, without any preconditions or planning on anyone's part. Africans didn't wish for their arrival; nor ask for their departure. If they wanted to know more about their night visitors, they would visit the witchdoctor. He was able to communicate outside the boundaries of time and space. He could see good and evil at face value, and in throwing the 'dominos', his bones, might even point to their footprints in the sand – even when there were none. But he would turn his back on their reason for being, leaving it up to the villager to unravel the damning threads of cause and blame from within. He would then consider his cathartic job done – he had picked up on the strange arrivals, and had formally introduced them. It was now up to the Soul of Africa to nudge things along the path of finality. Any potions, charms or incantations done for money, were theatrical incidentals to appease his clients' distress and line his pocket.

It was this African wisdom, where change for better or for worse was detached from its source and independent of its intended or wanted outcome; which lead me towards the slow unravelling of a tragic event – which for no reason, everyone and no one had full complicity in. It wasn't African collective fatalism; it was simple reality.

An odd rain

The first rain of the season was an unusual one – which in Africa, can be a portent of ill-boding. It was most out of keeping for late October rains, which were usually a few heated dollops carried in on a breathless sky at the end of a hot day. Those rains began hard, ended abruptly, and did nothing but accentuate the smell of dry dust in the air. At the most they gave a florid sunset the quick face wash it needed. If they had no permanence or weight of conviction, they could be forceful in their impetuous arrival – sometimes they were bold enough to carry six months of stick debris and leaf litter with them to gutters and drains on their way to the Luanshya River. Gardeners cursed them: they were never generous enough to give the soil a good soaking – but irresponsible enough to rob the earth of its mulch.

This one was different. It came in the middle of the night without thunder or lightning. It was soft January rain which continued well past morning tea time the next day. It had soaked the ground 'good and proper' as grown-ups from the North of England would say.

When Sean came home from school in the afternoon he wanted to go on the foofie slide, but his gardener, Boniface, was busy pulling something out of the anthill. His mother told him to stay away from the anthill if he had homework to do, and he

179

did. By afternoon tea, when the air had warmed up after the cooling downfall of the previous night and day, a steamy drizzle fell upon the town. By six o'clock flying ants, termites with un-realistic Icarian wings, were pouring out of the 'defunct' ant-hill by the thousand. House boys, garden boys, and maids from everywhere around were collecting these soft-bellied insects that fluttered out of the mound. Their wings were so ungainly fragile that they broke off almost as soon as the insects took flight, leaving these sorrowful little aviators to their unfortu-nate destiny – to fall to the ground and be gathered up for the frying pan. Flying ants are a delicacy in Africa.

The next day when Sean came home from school, it was no longer raining. He did not even enter the house for his lunch, where caution might have grasped him by the arm. He was more than eager to use the foofie slide, and he scrambled up to the summit to grab the bar. He slipped on a fine mush of mud and discarded flying ant wings, which blanketed the sodden anthill. He slid down sideways from the very top, breaking his fall on a pointed angle iron bar that was protruding halfway down. Sean hadn't seen it because it was covered with a reed mat.

The tip of an iron bar had appeared out of the anthill on the first morning of the long rain, and Boniface had uncovered it further, lifted it slightly, and propped it up where it was. It was next to a gaping tunnel as wide as a man's leg, which bore down into the anthill. He had returned it to its original use, a use that someone had started long before houses were ever built on the edge of that part of the vlei. He had taken an old reed sleeping mat and had draped it over the semi-erect iron bar to hinder the rapid departure of flying ants. On hitting the reed mat the flying ants would lose their wings and Boniface, and his wife and children would gather writhing handfuls of wingless ants and stuff them into old 2 gallon Nestlé's milk tins. It was his intention to sell the ants in the town.

When Sean fell the angle iron skewered his leg to the earth. The reed mat and iron bar became defunct. On that day there were no more flying ants to be seen. The anthill was once again dead.

How did I know all this? Because all gardeners were part of a communication system almost as sophisticated as that of the termites. Their information transfer network had a wide coverage. If I knew my gardener, Long One, which of course I did, I, informatically speaking, knew Sean's gardener, Boniface, too. Whatever Boniface saw, Long One knew about; and I got to hear about.

To maintain an unbroken information chain, in what turned out to be a long and drawn out African sequence of events, I asked my questions to Long One, who passed them on to Boniface, who via Long One gave me the answers I was looking for. Because I was more than interested, there was lively transfer between Boniface and Long One. In fact, it was a never-ending information chain that necessarily included other alphabetically placed gardeners between T Avenue and C Avenue, as the news travelled over the hedges, from garden to garden, and from one end of the road to the next. There was Amos in R (Riverside) Avenue, Aaron in M (Mimosa) avenue and Job in D (Datura) Avenue, to name a few. We did jump a few letters, and thankfully speeded the information transfer up because Long One's brother Lazarus, who worked in M avenue, had a sister-in-law called Rachel, whose husband was a house domestic in O Avenue, but she worked in E Avenue as a nanny. This human short circuit in information delivery was crucial when news was important. Added to this, because Lazarus was a curious sort – I was sure he belonged to a Nyau secret society – I often felt that his desire for fresh information was what kept the chain's momentum going.

This was the classic story of thwarted pride, mine; a mortally wounded ego, mine; and a possible case of revenge. The tragedy was his: he had done nothing wrong. In essence the story was about me, and so in more ways than one, it was all my doing – I had resented Sean's initial good fortune. Luckily my informants were as keen as I was to keep the inquiring town finger, mine, on the pulse. What a dreadful situation I had found myself in: he was an innocent victim of circumstance, and I was a victim of my own blooming suppositions and accusations. Luckily I had trusted friends in the information chain who, in the phlegmatic spirit of African unfolding, would moderate the damning truth with their ambivalence towards misfortune and outcomes. Members of my white subtribe would have reacted very differently, and to my detriment. The kind support of gardeners, maids and house boys did not however change the fact that I was the guilty one.

The sequence of events was almost too terrible for Boniface to tell: His initial shock was repeated with more than a few 'Aah too selious, ah! ah! Too too selious,' with Bantu clicks and tuts as it made its way down the line of gardeners and maids. I temporarily reverted to my white subtribe information source for the medical facts. The sharp point of the metal rod went straight through the back of Sean's thigh and he ended up in intensive care. He had lost a lot of blood, and had severed two muscles of his hamstring. We, as a class, visited him in the Luanshya mine hospital. We had drawn and painted a poster of us all with Sean having a *braai*, a barbeque. We hoped he could put it on the wall of the ward but he didn't stay long enough to appreciate our sentiment. There was a danger that his hamstring muscles were shrinking. He and his family would have to return to the UK for more professional, and up-to-date treatment. We were concerned about him, but, as if we were Dresden china dolls, we 'only kids' were put back into the cotton-wool-lined, stiff-upper-lipped box of colonial correctness and were never told anything more about Sean and his leg, and we never saw him again. This unnerved me. Long One felt equally uncomfortable – he didn't know anyone trustworthy in Ndola to say that Sean had even got on the *ndegi,* airplane; never mind a reliable information source in 'Ingrand', who could confirm that he had got off the *ndegi* at the other end. He seemed troubled by these weak links in his information chain – as if he had failed. Boniface, who stood abjectly in front of the anthill, as I paid another visit to the scene, looked down in silent shame, which could have easily been misconstrued as moroseness. Without saying anything to each other, we knew Sean's story was not yet complete.

Boniface saw it. He had not been in a hurry to see it – perhaps that's why he saw it. When it happened, he told Long One, Long One told me, and I immediately went to see it: I had to, otherwise I would never have believed it.

It was exactly one week after the terrible accident and the cessation of the flying ants. In the middle of the afternoon the flying ants resumed their mass evacuation. The sheer force of it was unsettling as countless insects rose on misshapen wings into an early afternoon air that was too hot for flight. There was a pointless feel to their projectile as they hovered in uncertainty above the anthill before collapsing back onto the ground still bearing their ineffective wings. It was uncanny. It was as if the anthill's latest ejected progeny were doomed – possibly rejected. Boniface said this was a very bad omen. Bad word spread, and no one came to gather up the white ant bodies into tins. Boniface said that there were no greedy toads or other small creatures like geckos visiting the anthill that evening either – but I wasn't sure if that was true; toads were never to be trusted. I believed him though, when he told me that the normal night visitors of bush babies and bats were replaced by strange creatures that he had never seen before. The anthill continued to spew these pathetically odd flying ants in stops and starts; and Boniface told Long One that local village elders had come one day to see the strange happening for themselves. I could imagine them squatting on their haunches, jawlines resting in cupped hands; clucking and 'ehh eh ing' in otherwise silent scrutiny. He also said that a witchdoctor came just before dark one evening, which I doubted very much. If he was a true witchdoctor, he wouldn't need to come. He would have known everything there was to know about this untoward happening from his mildewed grass hut in a secret bush clearing.

The gardener's information chain was still solid, and the irregular lava flows of aberrant flying ants and their odd visitors continued. I even got evening dispatches through my bedroom window after my parents had packed me off to bed. A python, not normally partial to such minuscule meals of insects, was seen on the anthill. It had an extra-large cloacal claw. One day an opportunist Zulu woman arrived with a wheelbarrow and spade to dig up the fine grit of the anthill. She said she had a market for it in Durban – *sangomas*, South African witchdoctors, would pay good money for it she said… and Boniface showed signs of withdrawing into himself.

A further week passed and the unaccountable flying ants became a permanent feature in our lives – so much so that we almost forgot about the permanence of change. But change was change, and it was still on the move – we had simply over-looked it. Overnight, or so it seemed, the anthill began to die; its earth appeared to crumble and the giant mahogany tree's leaves lost some of their waxy sheen. It seemed as if the ant-hill was collapsing before our information chain eyes. Were there secretive events going on inside the great mound that we were unaware of? Boniface was now the caretaker of an empty house and a dying anthill: He was not happy, and it showed on his countenance. His normally shiny facial skin had turned to a mat dull black; the whites of his eyes had turned to caramel; on top of that, he stopped talking. This was a serious drawback for further investigations – he was the key link in the knowledge chain. Boniface disappeared for a day, went to the witchdoctor, got some *muti*, medicine – roots dug out of a faraway '*kuchana*' anthill – a special anthill – and the next day he was back in charge of the local information network of words, clucks and eh ehs with an oil shiny face, and half a smile. I pondered as to what his witchdoctor really knew, and who he had pointed to on the edge of Boniface's inner clearing. This information might have been useful in understanding what had happened, and what was still going to happen deep inside the anthill.

Then it happened: At three o'clock in the afternoon, far too hot for a flying ant departure, the last wave of flying ants flopped out of the mound. Thwarted by the heat they fell to the ground; and at five there was a departure of flying ants, which Boniface said, looked much bigger, and darker than the rest. After that, no more flying ants took to the air. The flying ants – the white ants – the termites, whatever one might want to call them, were gone – gone for good, Boniface said.

I was in the bath all soaped up, when Long One knocked on the bathroom window to tell me all this. I was bathing early because I had been to cricket practice: otherwise I would have spent the afternoon in Tacoma Avenue. I had missed something important – what a terrible pity that I had not been there to witness it myself. With Lifebuoy soap behind my ears and in other sensitive places, dressed wet in my pyjamas, dressing gown and slippers, and against my mother's wishes, although she could see the urgency; I cycled as fast as I could over to T Avenue. When I got there I could smell finality in the still air. The flying ants had indeed made a final departure. I had missed the grand finale. A small group of domestics had quietly gathered in front of the anthill. It was six o clock and there was not one flying ant in the air – we all knew Boniface was right – it was the end. I had no option but to try and grill Boniface to get every detail out of him before he fell into one of his uncooperative moods, which I saw coming. He was a proud Lozi from the Zambezi flood plains in Western Northern Rhodesia, and he had an ancestral king to look up to – King Lewanika of Barotseland. He clammed up because he didn't like being pushed into corners – which I could understand – he would tell me everything in his own good time. I had no option but to accept his African ways and wait.

He later told me that the last flying ants were like airplanes. They were more determined in flight, and flew low with a heavy drone – more importantly, they did not lose their strong wings, *ena lo tsimba,* they were strong, he said. They headed of in a northerly direction in close formation; out across the vlei to the open bush, he explained in his hesitant way. Their departure, according to Boniface, and I totally believed him, was followed by absolute silence. When I got there, it was too quiet for that time of day, when rising thermals should have carried evening sounds across the vlei: The birds had stopped calling, and the locusts and cicadas had ceased their background drone – there was not even the usual riverine evening breeze. I could do nothing more than join the still silence. The flying ants had made a final departure, and as I was told later, they had taken their wingless queen with them, the old diviner didn't think so.

That evening, so Boniface told me, not a single opportunistic night raider turned up to be disappointed: the bats, night apes, mongooses, night adders and geckos all knew of the unusual late afternoon departure; it was an event already written into the history of the fauna and flora of the vleis and forests of all-time. The anthill was abandoned in a solidarity of knowledge and all oneness. Boniface said he could not sleep that night because of bad spirits. He had locked his wife and children in his quarters and had sat close to his fire with a blanket over his head. The next day he looked tired when I saw him, but he said he was fine. The bad spirits had gone and the sounds of the wind, birds and insects on the vlei were back. I asked him what he had thought about all night sitting on his own in the dark, but he didn't give me an answer. I later asked him again, but still he wouldn't say, and I wondered why.

What meaning did Sean's misfortune and the exodus of the white ants and their queen leave behind? What apocalyptic message was inscribed on the crumbling walls of a dying anthill? Perhaps there was a message reverberating in the void that these events had created: a spark of dark spirit that both Boniface, the birds, rodents, snakes, bats and the breeze had felt.

The fine January rain returned and the anthill became a broken-winged mush of fragile earthen walls whose filigrees were slowly collapsing into what seemed to be bottomless holes. Tunnels like necrotic limbs bored past the exposed roots of the unhealthy pod mahogany tree, its leaves hanging limp. Lucky for me, this event, in timeless African tradition, had overflowed into the Christmas holidays, so I could cycle over more than once a day to record events as they unfolded. I also had my sometimes sullen, otherwise witchdoctor healed, oily faced war correspondent who reported back to me on any major shift in events as they unfolded; be it night or day. He had time on his hands because he had nothing else to do.

The anthill was totally defunct inside and out and not one corporeal insect morsel remained, except for inert wings of cellophane. Two nights after the queen's departure, so Boniface said, two toads and a herald snake returned. I reckoned the toads were too thick-skinned to worry about bad spirits, and had come to inspect possible new lodgings, and the snake had come to eat the toads. Other than that, not one mammal, reptile, or bird returned to the anthill. Instead pests of another kind, the human kind, arrived on the scene. Much to Boniface's disdain, a mine amenities Bedford truck full of workers wearing gumboots and overalls trundled into the garden. They chopped down the pod mahogany tree, which I fully understood and agreed with – it was terminally ill. They exposed its red heart wood in watermelon slices and they filled and levelled the anthill with more than one two-ton truck of rocks and soil, and that was that – or was it?

As the workers got to work, I carried out a thorough inspection. I did it as best as a boy could with a white superintendent down my neck, and his black staff shooing me away in feigned annoyance. I added their white boss to my prig list. With the magnifying glass that my godmother had given me for Christmas, I studied the severed roots of that pod mahogany tree. Contrary to what the grown-ups said, the pod mahogany had not died because its roots had been eaten away by the white ants. Of course I knew that. The magnificent stand of trees on my anthill were healthy only because the white ants lovingly looked after them. They fed them with fine nutrients because the termites' fungus gardens were cultivated between their roots. Below the surface, termites and trees had a symbiotic relationship. Unlike humans, termites would never cut off their one collective nose, to spite their unified face.

After four-thirty, when the Mine amenities department workers had left, I lay on my tummy and snaked up to the crumbling edge, digging my toes, knees and elbows into the clay. I tried not to imagine what my mother would say about my mud-smeared clothes. Warning tape hadn't been invented yet – there was only one neatly painted 'Danger, men at work' sign erected at the base of the anthill. I saw it as a considerate warning to be careful – not as an announced prohibition – so I lay spread-eagled on the rim of a subterranean white ant world that had imploded within itself. I could see that the gaping passageways that snaked their way into Hades were spotless – this queendom had been tidied up before it had been forsaken. The walls were compacted from the continuous pressure of a trillion ants' feet over time and smoothed by the dragging sweep of well over a million wings. As I peered down to look into the nothingness below, my face was blasted with moist warm air that smelled fleshy and sweet. This richly organic smell came from the fungus gardens, which the termites cultivated as a cellulose food source, so the old diviner had once told me. What would happen to these gardens now that the white ants had departed? Could fungus gardens ever be overrun with subterranean weeds, or gobbled up by subterranean locusts, I wondered.

What had really happened to Sean, to the white ants, their queen and the mysterious giant anthill? Through Boniface, and Long One's eyes and a few ears and ideas between C Avenue and T Avenue, as well as my 'on the anthill' ruminations, an answer was to come; but for now, it was still brewing. It was an African answer that would take time. Like the body of a shot crocodile, it was taking a long time to float to the surface, and when it did, if it did, but it surely would, we might not like what we would see. While I was a bit nervous, my cohorts were patiently waiting, almost not waiting, for a slow answer. Their apparent disinterest frustrated me, so I repeatedly told the old diviner the whole saga to keep it alive. Luanshya gossip had informed him of the injured boy, but not about the African intrigue. I was very glad that I had told him the facts from where I saw them.

For quite a few Saturdays the old diviner sat emotionless on the bench at the bowling club while I regurgitated every morsel of the story; if I told it once, I told it ten times. He quietly listened to every add-on: about the mysterious arrival of the anthill in T avenue; my initial jealousy of Sean's good fortune and my uncomfortable reaction to his subsequent misfortune; about the uncanny goings-on in the anthill and its strange visitors; the final departure of the flying ants and the demise of the anthill and its pod mahogany. I included my thoughts on the synchronised timings of flying ant departures with the events of Sean's tragedy. He never interrupted me once. If I hadn't painstakingly put my story together for him, and he hadn't taken me so seriously; I would never have carried my musings to

beyond my idle daydreams and into a deeper conscious awareness of *things*...

I had two options when it came to understanding Sean's
accident and the revival and final departure of the white ants. I
firmly believed that the two events were connected.

Scene 1

The logical first scenario, was that Sean had an accident.
Weather patterns affect the life cycles and habits of many
creatures in Africa. The early rains had caused the apparent
'rebirth' of a white ant queendom. In so doing, they were attend-
ant to Sean slipping in fine mud and falling upon a piece of
sharp angle iron that had deeply penetrated his leg. Sean could
have had the accident at any time during the rainy season. The
accident could have happened to any one of his friends – it
could have happened to me.

The world of the white ants is a reflection of a greater
one thinking universe manifested in part through the spirit
of Africa. In that particular year, Africa had reacted to global
weather patterns, which were brewing over the Indian Ocean
from as far back as August. As a consequence we had January
guti, drizzle, thrown at us in a sweltering October. Africa had
mirrored this untoward weather pattern in more quirky ways
than one. Not only did she prompt an anthill of a bygone era to
flex its termitine muscle in a blitz of time-travelling flying ants,
she also cast her spell on other creatures. The old diviner told
me that the rain bird had acted strange well before the arrival
of unusual rain. It was as if Africa had had a premonition of
things to come. This busybody bird had been calling his 'du du
dudu' call of 'the rains are coming, the rains are coming, the

rains are here, the rains are here, the rains have been, the rains have been' from the beginning of September – which was not at all the norm. The rain bird's prophetic call was much to the surprise of seasoned colonialists like the old diviner, but had gone unnoticed by my white subtribe. The old diviner said you couldn't miss the rain bird's melodious song – it is like spring water glugging out of a carafe, he mused. This intriguing bird could have done a rain dance right down the centre of the Mine Club bar counter, nimbly skipping around glasses, beer mats and ashtrays, and my subtribe wouldn't have noticed it. I marvelled at the idea of a bird being so affected by a premonition of rain.

Rain spiders, what people thought were spiders, but were not, also started running through our houses earlier than they should have. These strange insects with an intense phobia for light, would normally start dashing across our lounge floor in the last two weeks of October. This year their evening streaking was in eerie synchrony with the early call of the rain bird. The old diviner had taken cognisance of this aethereal connection but I hadn't. People wrongly thought that these large hairy insects were ferocious spiders: If encountered, they rushed towards you as if on the attack – but they weren't; they were simply looking for a shadow – yours – to hide in. The old diviner, as if he was a clairvoyant, said, 'I know you saw the rain spiders early this year,' and the penny dropped. He also mentioned that the Mhonondos, a similar tree to the Msasas, had come into leaf early. It seemed nothing happened by solitary chance in a one thinking Africa where the weather had such power.

Global weather patterns had brought the bizarre rain and had likely caused the rebirth of an anthill. But could they have orchestrated the stop and start ejections of hapless flying ants, the death of a large pod mahogany, strange nighttime visitors and the final evacuation of a queendom? Could they have also have brought about all the negativity that came pouring down upon me?

Scene 2.

The second scenario was less realistic on the ground – but more encompassing of things out of control – and quite likely to have involved shape shifting and changing energy flows.

Sean and I were wrapped up in a spider web of aethereal connectedness. My almost obsessional jealousy of him was the first omen of an invisible bond between us. The uncanny involvement of white ants and their collective mind in both our lives, so secretive that Sean was probably not even conscious of it, was another indicator as to how our threads of existence were connected.

To look into that web for consequential connections of cause and effect would be a human error based on calculations made in time and space. There was no causal reason and yet there was every connection in the unfolding of events. Neither the early rain, the flying ants, Boniface, his reed mat, Sean's accident, nor my guilt were the cause, nor were they the effect. Each one of us was fulfilling our unconditional role as points radiating out from our common aetheric core of all time. We were existential facets of a one happening that unfolded through the spiritual law of all is one. This was the construct between Sean and I – fingers of blame and calls for pity could not be issued within the circumferential sequence of events. The spiritual truth was that there were no winners, no losers, only players.

Our individual stories were human threads loosely intertwined and then inadvertently snagged in the cogs of Africa's machinations. We were momentary facets of a much greater story of expansion and collapse. The same story would and could have happened precisely so without us. Props, lights and a stage are extras when the original script is in the player's hands.

My European mind still had an African lesson to learn. There was no real answer, only a fleeting glimpse of its mechanics. Madam Vlei would have said, 'you can't look for the same one thinking answer here and there: especially when it is likely to be found nowhere within the set boundaries of your time and space; especially so when it is from the everywhere of nowhere that the answer will come'. I took her words to mean that Sean's story had nothing to do with the personal me, nor the footprint of my Soul – and she didn't have to explain herself. It was not my destiny to be the guilty one. Why then was I so emotionally caught up in it? Even though it had a strong pull on me, I knew it wasn't an affinity. Why then was I both bothered and attracted by its perversity? There must have been a reason hidden somewhere on the body of our one story.

African answers will eventually arrive in the forest clearing of their own accord. To look for them, call out for them, or even worse, plan for them, would be absolute folly – European folly, a bemused African would have said.

As to which scenario was the most likely – it was easier for me to point to which was the least likely. The weather was not the catalyst of change in my life, and nor was it so for the termites. Our single mindedness, the termites and mine, was proof that our individual Soul purposes were not prone to damning rains – nor was Sean's.

Was it ever possible that my sensibilities had gotten tangled in what was nothing more than the grandiose musing, the wants of a million white ants? That what we saw, Boniface, all the domestics and I, was nothing more than the outer fringes of termitine shape shifting: and in so doing, we, Sean included, had got sucked up into the powerful slipstream of their aethereal intent. African events, as simple as these, needed no answers.

Pandora's Box

The MOTH Club was an eclectic gathering of ex-servicemen, who had survived the war, and had brought together the path-worn energies of war-torn places like Singapore, Normandy and Tripoli. Aside from strutting Johnny Walker whisky bottles, mellow South African brandies, and the beer in the fridges, it was a rough malt blend of human shortcomings. These men were lost Souls: they had misinterpreted the gift of emotional rehabilitation and a new beginning. They were turning their backs on a matrimonial offering of a colonial African virgin land, unfettered by memories of war, fecund with expectations, and brimming with surprising liberties and opportunity: sadly they couldn't see that.

On dull Friday nights of soaking rain we didn't scare good folk or devour night energies like hyenas in an attempt to find ourselves; instead we sneaked the keys from the MOTH Club offices for the storeroom that lay directly beneath the bar. The steep lay of the land, as it fell away to the rivulet, created space for a cramped windowless storeroom. It was a Pandora's Box of time-warped treats and sticky energies – some good, and a lot bad. Everything was stored there: a Second World War regalia of dress parade uniforms, captured flags, swords, Sheiks

costumes, Nazi helmets and Gurkha knives, large female cabaret costumes and belly dancers' pantaloons. There was also a
Father Christmas outfit that reeked of beer, and telling wood-
en reindeer cut-outs that were attached to the sides of Father
Christmas's landy, which brought him to the MOTH Club to
meet us kids every year. The facades and charades of these human foibles were now lying limp and crumpled in cardboard
boxes, their flaying arms, legs and bodices luring us Members
of the Order of the Tin Hat children to try them on for size –
size of persona: archetypal personas that lurked somewhere
within our inherited subconscious hinterland.

The reason for the existence of this Pandora's Box was simple. Besides being a repository for everything Christmassy, every
year the men of the MOTH Club invited their wives to two grand
Saturday night dances to celebrate two important days: Armistice
Day and the Battle of El Alamein. This storeroom housed military paraphernalia for those events. The MOTH Club was decked
as a European battlefield on the one evening, and as a desert
war setting for the other. On the closest Saturday to the 11th of
November, which was Remembrance Day, the Armistice Ball was
held at the MOTH Club. It was preceded by two minutes of silence in darkness, except for the candle of remembrance, which
was placed atop a First World War tin hat. This was followed by a
toast to fallen and absent comrades, and ended with the MOTH
anthem, 'Old Soldiers Never Die'. Tears were shed; and a short
while later the festivities began – that's just how things were with
men of war. The next morning, hung-over men would visit the
cenotaph to pay their respects. I saw many a grown man and
father, overcome with post-alcoholic grief, battle to hold back
tears on those days. With ashen faces, I saw these men standing to cold attention at eleven hundred hours, as a black bugler

of the Rhodesian African Rifles played 'The Last Post' in front of a stone column dedicated to those who had given their lives in war; a different cenotaph, in a different Copperbelt town, every year. Two minutes of painful silence followed, in which these men, wearing all their medals, began to sway ever so slightly, as their women and children looked on in watery-eyed admiration. The playing of 'The Last Post' still brings tears to my eyes. When our menfolk and fathers were dismissed in military fashion, we walked to our British cars in dumbstruck silence to make our way to the local MOTH club, be it in Luanshya, Kitwe, or Ndola; for a tasty buffet lunch and a much needed beer or two, or more – the hair of the dog that bit you, my father would say.

Refractions of inner light – Prometheus

Prometheus and his brother Epimetheus were the creators of mankind. Prometheus had left a mysterious box with his brother, and told him never to open it. Pandora, Epimetheus's wife, could not resist opening the box; when she did, out flew every affliction known to man. Prometheus had purposely withheld them from mankind, whom he loved dearly. When, out of fear and guilt, Pandora slammed the lid of the box shut, she trapped hope inside. Hope was a charitable gift from Prometheus, which was meant to balance out all the human ills that Pandora had released. With hope now trapped, would perfect peace ever be restored to the world?

The imagery that these artefacts of war released upon us children marched a goose step of permanence across my awareness of *things*. What was intended to be a parade march of respect for the past, was inexplicably transformed by our psyches into a nervously confused excitement of the 'Now'. We children desired to relive every one of those archetypes of human existence represented by these mummified props of human war and history. German camouflage nets smelled of big gun oil and dust; maybe even Rommel's North African desert dust. The British Army officer, the paratrooper, the Arab potentate, the German cabaret dancer, the voluptuous belly dancer, magical Prancer – the Bambi turned sledge puller, the seven dwarfs: They all tugged at our imaginations for immediate attention. They were no longer tired props; our innocent psyches had resuscitated them. We changed from being bored children into mercurial figures of glory, fantasy and tragedy in a bunkered room below; all the while the instigators sat on bar stools above, their minds flabby with alcohol, their lost spirits morphing like injured ghosts from the crumpled paraphernalia of war and broken dreams below.

We children of the MOTHs were toying with the frayed threads of these sensually real worlds of human history. Our wants had become enmeshed in a universal story that was calling us to attention. The same spiritual 'last post' that was subconsciously driving our hopeless fathers, as spent soldiers, to drink.

My friends found it great fun, it was an in the 'Now' moment of giddy theatre. But for me, these bunkered nights left a dis-ease in my mind for days. It kept going back to dead men's epaulettes and brass buttons. Sometimes the call of the wanting unknown was too painful for my Velcro sensibilities.

4

I LOVE...
LOVING KINDNESS

WATERMELON RAIN

WATERMELON RAIN

So Hum – loving rain

*S*o Hum left the thick branches for the delicate higher ones, and *that was when the tourmaline dream rains fell. It was a good move – So Hum felt love. His dream rain was a dream come true. He was in love with life. He had scraped together his entire being and with a quiver of excitement, was attempting to offer it to someone at the top of his rain tree.*

He saw love as a gift bestowed upon him from high. It was a token of his bliss and he offered a gratitude for his existence.

In his simple dreams, his good intentions seemed to unfold effortlessly. It seemed that everything was in collusion and everything was going his way. He no longer felt the earlier needs to shy away from the dark or to look for others. All was one and one was all, and that's all there was. His love of everything was proof of this cohesive state of being.

His gratitude poured out of him, then oozed out and then became a trickle before it dried up. This was because he started to take love for granted and love's aethereal spirit departed to an imaginary distant

*shore. Was he ever a part of the eternal loving oneness that those pink
and green rains had once promised him?*

*In pain-slow time these malignant feelings migrated to the heart of
him, where they sat like leaded maggots eating away at his self-esteem,
his passions, and anything else that he valued.*

*These voluptuous watermelon rains had promised love; life should
have been good – but it wasn't. So Hum did not understand the spiritual laws of the Universe. He didn't realise that love is not a third party
issue. To get love he had to first give love and not take another's for
granted; to be loved by another he had to love himself first – which he
thought he did, but he didn't; to find love he had to be love – which sadly
he didn't think he was, and therein lay a flaw. Stupefied, he sat among
the delicate branches which seemed too fragile to support him.*

Ah hum's roots – I love

In strength Ah Hum's emotions were the ground on which he
was able to stand tall and fight in the name of love; whereas in
situations of weakness his emotions were a pitiful flight of lost
love. When his roots were nurtured, they gave him his positive
determination to continue loving; when he abused them with
spurned love, they spewed up a directionless lassitude which
turned into resentment.

> Love was a complex state of being that needed
> the support of powerful allies. Out of his alche-
> mist's calico bag he drew:

>> Hiddenite and orange blossom oil: *to-
>> kens of heartfelt gratitude.*
>> Aventurine crystals and melissa leaves:
>> *to symbolise the sweet harmony of spiritual
>> and emotional growth.*

Watermelon tourmaline and unction of nard: *symbols of loving kindness since ancient times.*

Rose quartz and rose oil*: the eternal symbols of unconditional love.*

Kunzite and palma rosa oil: *the possession of which would induce a state of inner peace within him.*

Loving kindness

> Heartfelt stirrings
> Kindness
> Conjugation and subjugation
> Manhood overboard
> Icarus
> Feminine blind faith and a hankie up her sleeve

Heartfelt stirrings

The energies, far more than fleeting emotions, which were released into my being by my Italian cameo, lead to an epiphany of self-discovery. They reduced my spirit of adventure to nothing more than the outer patina of a far more valuable object – my universal Soul. So deep were my feelings, that I knew they were not a fleeting passion, nor in the spirit of the moment.

They appeared in the urgent 'here and now' of my youth as the ultimate in perfection, and my Soul had to yank my body out of its physical and intellectual limitations to evaluate their foreign grandity. My Soul wanted to dance forever with their Souls in the fields of oblivion. It was a breathlessly exciting introduction of Souls that made me reel in giddy complicity whenever I thought about them. It was a first-hand impression of the pristine energy of love. It was an echo of a Universe that communicates through love. At Soul level, we are awareness, and awareness is love. We are love.

Refractions of inner light – an awareness of love

Love is a building block of an awareness that we 'are'. We would not build upon our conscious

awareness without the focused desire to be
'one' with someone – those are the mechanics
of attraction that we loosely call love. Without
the first grain of love to build upon, our awareness, which is a wide open facet of our Soul,
would drift quietly away from us in haphazard
detachment and indifference. In such a vague
state of existence we would not be given the
chance of physical and cognitive growth in the
swirl of universal happenings.

If our emotions are the signposts of our wants
and dis-wants and our affinities are our compass, then love is the spiritual route map of our
Soul purpose. We are love, we are joy; we are
peace.

Although my Italian cameo had played a special role in my
personal growth, I also realised that the Soul is a ruthless
iconoclast – it destroys all icons of worship. I would lose touch
with my Soul if I were to idolise my Italian family or anything
else, circus performers and anthills included. All these images
of perfection that brought me so much inner warmth and excitement needed to be put into the right perspective. All that
was required of me, was to keep my true love in my heart; it
didn't have to be a token in my pocket, a mantra on my lips or
a false emotion on my sleeve. Its sentiment could remain on a
child distant shore bathed in a warm sun of knowingness, a notion that I would one day, without set due date, dock my ship
there.

I would come across other people, places and situations in
my life that would invoke the same giddy desire within me to

absorb and meld with their energies. Sometimes the induced vertigo was so intense that it made me feel queasy. My heart would have drowned in an emotional chime if it hadn't fought its way out of these futile situations. I saw these situations as emotional signposts pointing to a hidden commonality of destiny of which I was a part – we shared something, but as a child I wasn't sure what.

There were catchy tunes on LM radio, which broadcast the latest pop music from Lourenco Marques, the coastal capital of the Portuguese colony of Mozambique. There were lots and lots of songs of love on the airwaves. I was tuning into more than LM Radio and the 12 O'clock News from the BBC. I was searching for more than popular music and conformity; I was tuning into a more important message carried on the aether. It was a message without a specific meaning, sometimes without directional intent. It was a background aethereal buzz, an open and unconditional awareness of everything that was as it was, and nothing more. In the surround vision of my 'Now' reality show, I see this awareness as the only true reality that there is. Reality is not the temporally directed object of our time-lined perception, nor is it in the ability of the perceiver to see his own truth. Reality is an interpretive 'how' quality of perception, how we go about seeing. Reality is the mechanics of perception, not the finished product. I half-felt that love was my reality.

In essence the figurative heart is a dimension of the Soul that has become entangled in the nerve web of our feeling and thinking physicality.

Unlike the brain, the figurative heart thinks outside the realms of time and space, although it stores its memories in energy bundles similar to our thoughts. Its perceptions are stored without any precondition, filtering or chronological order. It has a computing power which is more encompassing than the mind because it is free from the restrictions of time based logic.

It is difficult to describe heartfelt knowledge, of which love is a part, because of its three dimensional character. It is knowledge beyond the realms of human thought; a small part of this knowledge being what we call human intuition and animal instinct. It enables us to see closer to the truth should we so ask for it – but we often don't. The 'heart' is not a supernatural power, it simply gathers information in an unconditional way like an Internet search engine. It creates a holographic picture of everything about us and our universe as an unbiased snapshot of our virtual reality. Whether it be of flesh and blood, word and deed, thought and emotion, yesterday, today or tomorrow, it is all the same data bundles. All of life's informational imagery, be it matter, emotion or spirit, is juxtaposed and superimposed instead of being lined up in logical rows: 'animals on this side, plants on that, minerals and emotions straight ahead.'

The figurative heart is a euphemism for the working trinity of our conscious awareness, creative power and love, their script writer being the Soul. Its mechanics are not unlike a *surround time* reality show where 'Now' time has more importance than the facts that support it.

If love was an expression of my Soul, I would have to listen to it more carefully. I needed to be more familiar with my love.

207

Refractions of inner light – love

Love is not an emotion. It is a state of wellbeing in which we are resonating in harmony with the forces of our Soul and its affinities. True love is a shared oneness. A cohesive state of feeling good that puts us at peace with others in our one world. Love is a spiritual journey that we all have to make if we are to affirm our conscious awareness of our reality. It is the most important test to pass if we are to be a true citizen of the Universe.

Transient emotions are not the source of love. These emotions are the signposted unit measures, the milestones of dissonance and resonance that bring us to our destination on our spiritual journey. Large distances alert us with anxiety and worry, short distances with peace and happiness. Positive emotions empower this odyssey of the heart that we call love. Love is the journey of our Soul, a journey that should be without departure and arrival points, but often isn't. Love is also our conscious awareness of the workings of our Soul, which makes it an endearing enigma. Our Soul, as a facet of the Soul of the Universe, demands love – without love we would never be introduced to our Soul.

Kindness

Caring about something or someone is when you bring them into your awareness. Sharing is to see the commonality of Soul purpose between others and the self. Both are the spiritual attributes of love. My mother was caring and gave her life for my father to share while he was desperately trying to resuscitate his life force.

Sympathy is when you partake in the emotions, usually sad emotions, of others. Empathy is the cognitive understanding and respect for another's emotional hurt without taking any of its energy on board. Empathy calls for spiritual fortitude and wisdom. Whereas sympathy could be simple unconscious and sometimes thoughtless resonance with another's disturbed emotional energy state. My mother gave my father empathy and I believe my father in turn showed spellbound empathy for all, but his war years had taxed his spiritual strength. His awareness was faltering.

With duty-bound empathy my soft mother penetrated my father's psyche to join him on his Asian sleeping mat woven with the grass from the stained killing fields of the Sino-Japanese conflict. Her Soul knew what she was taking on. With unconditional acceptance she carried his mat behind him wherever he went.

Sadly it took many years for that mat to be replaced in spiritual texture and design; his living nightmares were too difficult to be forgotten. It is quite possible that this poignant love story of tragedy, empathy and forbearance coloured my spirit world.

Conjugation and subjugation

My shy mother made a tall call one day. Cousin Joe, my father, came back from the war as a physically emaciated and psychologically spent young man. He had been a long absent family member; lost and pronounced dead – killed in action in the Far East, they said. Now he stood before her. He had nothing to show and nothing to tell. His ill-fitting 'civvies' suit, a small metal box, a tatty photo album retrieved from friends in Singapore, and a few war medals, the Burma Star included, was all that there was to him, and there was nothing to fall back on either. Humility kept his war successes under lock and key. Besides his difficult war years, he didn't even have much of a memory of his younger years. His Lancashire youth was worth nothing more than a muttering under his breath. As a boy, he had had fun on the moors chasing rabbits, and fishing in the brook at Barrow Bridge – but his teens were hardly worth remembering. As for memories of the Shanghai heydays of his early twenties – like the mosaic mirrored balls in the dance halls, these reflections of a young lover's dreams were smashed. Jungle warfare against the Japanese, Wingate's Chindits, the Red Army, and death and destruction had all marched into his energy fields. They took possession of whole territories of his psyche; his good times had been tortured into submission.

He was demobbed and back on home turf. He still experienced route marches through nightmares of his Asian hell. He slept with his eyes open in wait of his Japanese assailants; like a paranoid Zen Buddhist mindfully waiting for nothing. He shared his world with exterminated military mates who continued against all odds and without the common decency of the dead, to fly their brave spiritual flag against an expansionist cult that showed no human remorse. There is no finality in the spiritual world and so his aethereal mates were still fighting.

Without rational thought, and in unconditional resonance with his Soul; my mother, her own Soul laid bare by the intense emotion of seeing this fragile being before her, consummated their spiritual union there and then, and later physically married her second cousin.

She knew what fear had done to him. She was a shy person who suffered as a child from the early death of her mother and the ensuing battle for religious custody. Her mother was a Catholic, her father a Protestant. Catholic nuns would hunt her down after her mother's death to get her back into the Catholic school that her father withdrew her from on the death of his wife. She was frightened of nuns, who she viewed as scavenging crows. She hardly ventured out and hid when they knocked at the door. Her elder brother, who was a devout Catholic, fought a war of words with their father. My poor mother cowered between the two, desperately trying to please both – but the decision was not hers to make. She was a meek and reticent young woman, who hardly stepped out onto the bleak Lancashire streets and had never been dated by a man. That she should take the lead, and consequently, the hand of a once strong, now broken commando, was a miracle of the Soul in itself. I was born out of this union.

My parent's conjugation was a union of love, not so much in a physical or emotional sense, but love in a spiritual sense. Neither had anything to give, and yet they gave. Neither had anything to lose and yet they were prepared for loss; such was the universal gamble they had entered into. They stepped together into an open energy field of an unequivocal acceptance called love; where they sealed their union in a barren post-war period when there wasn't much more. As part of their matrimonial life, their circumstances would change.

My Soul being was born out of fateful consequence: the spiritual status of my father, my mother's raw compassion, the ill-health of my siblings, the country's colonial status. Perhaps even the superficiality of a flutter flood of a million butterflies over an African River, and the particular phase of the moon on a summer equinox, the day I was born: Countless happenings, some serendipitously light, others grave, were the provenance of the universal spirit swirl that had touched upon my Soul. They were like spiritual spiders that spun unbreakable micro threads of attraction and aversion that would enslave my passions to particular objects and events as my 'white boy in Africa' life unfolded.

Manhood overboard

My Father was unusual in looks, with soft curly black hair and eyes set deep in their sockets. His body acknowledged past athletic prowess and his tattooed arms showed the legacy of his years in the British army. He did not look English at all. His skin had, not a southern European olive, but an unusual dark-edged pallor from which one could only surmise that he was of possible Eastern European stock or from Asia Minor. If he was of Armenian tribal decent, and that was only a wild supposition of mine, he carried even older spiritual baggage deep in the recesses of his Soul. There were swirls of an archetypal pathos that would have been present at both of our conceptions. An imprint of Eastern European history, which at the point of its own tragic emollescence was written into the genocide and the forced exile of many of its people by the Ottomans. Nobody questioned his identity except for me. All I did know, was that he was christened in St Barnabas's Church. Many years later, I read that St Barnabas's was one of the first Armenian churches in the North of England. England was a refuge for the Christian Armenians who fled their country in the early nineteen hundreds. Many of the refugees took up work in the cotton industry centred in the North of England.

My father was of male yang essence: virile, humorously warm and outgoing. Sadly he glossed over love and sensuality with light jocular humour and a varnish of bonhomie; which in essence, reflected only the wishes of others. He made it difficult for any of us to look into, and thus value, his deeper sensitivities and needs. Although in looks he was similar to my Italians, in spirit he was totally different. I never saw him moody, whereas my Roman gods could throw quite a few lightning bolts for no apparent reason – so people said. My father was short in stature, five foot two, but never short tempered. Good old Joe, placid and funny; what pain was he covering up, they could have asked if they had bothered to look into the cavernous recesses of his eyes.

My Father had grown up in the cotton industry of Lancashire in the North of England where his father was a mill manager. He was brought up by his sister Annie because his mother left home, leaving six children behind. His mother was an amateur opera singer; his father a strict religious martinet. He forced a separation upon her to her absolute detriment. Most of the adult members of his family had left England for America to become Quakers. Perhaps they were trying to shake off the sticky emotional soil that still clung to their Eastern European roots. I was never told, but I can only imagine, that the family dynamics were tempered into puritanical steel and hobnailed down with denial. All I did glean from my father was that Annie, given no option, sacrificed her youth and young adulthood to become nursemaid to her siblings. My father loved his sister so much that he never spoke of his parents. I didn't even know their names. Annie would sometimes take my father as a young boy to the market where a woman would pat him on the head. In his early teens, his sister Annie told him that the friendly person in the marketplace was his mother. He did not want to ever see her again, and he never did, such was the pain of abandonment and rejection in his heart. At sixteen he never saw his father again either; he falsified his age to board a slow boat to China from the Liverpool docks – to join the British Army in China.

What urgent calling, what spiritual hankering at such a young age beckoned him to the tropical splendour of the Colonies in the Far East? A world so alien to the cotton mills and bleak factories that were propped up by the working class of Lancashire. It was an industrial world that blighted the surrounding moorlands, clouded the horizons of the working folk and sullied the sheep with its belching smoke. To most workers, your world was what you saw around you and you asked for nothing more. The many young Englishmen who ended up in the exotic Far East did so because of the war. My father arrived there entirely on his own initiative, and before he was seventeen. What indeed was the footprint of his Soul that seemed to have such a clear prior ken? How powerful could an affinity be?

He grew up to be a dapper young man in the Shanghai of the thirties; glittering dance halls, 10cents-a-dance women, chop suey restaurants, tuxedos and big bands. He became the British Army boxing champion of South China and spoke Mandarin and Cantonese fluently. Sepia pictures from Shanghai photography studios and black and white group shots show a handsome young tanned Englishman with Eurasian and cheongsam clad Chinese beauties on his arm. He was short; they were short. He was dark; they were dark. Life moved fast.

He was in his physical prime and life was on his side for a little while.

When the Second World War broke out he was a good and brave soldier. He became one of the Wingate infamous Chindits in Burma. They operated behind Japanese lines as saboteurs, for which my father was awarded the Burma Star for bravery. He was somehow involved with Vinegar Joe Stilwell's mission into China, carrying relief supplies 'over the hump,' the Himalayas, into Nanking. At some stage he was seconded to the communist Red Army in the Western Allies' covert attempts to control the Japanese advancement in China towards Burma. He suffered greatly as a result of the Japanese megalomaniac preoccupation for domination in Asia, which incinerated the memories of his Soul and left an emotive numbness on his tongue. What an unbelievable force it was that he and his fellow soldiers were up against.

When they were captives of the Japanese, men he dearly loved were humiliated, tortured and some shot. His best boxing mate of those hazy days of Shanghai and Singapore was shot in front of him, their eyes in Soulful union as a life was snuffed out for an imperialist ideology on Christmas day. My father never told me this. It was one of his MOTH Club mates who told me as a rebuke for the disrespect I sometimes showed my father in my teens. I read later that the Chindits shot their injured fellow men with their own personal revolvers, rather than leave them to the cruel torture that they would undoubtedly receive from the Japanese. What depth of manly love did this courageous act call for?

So humble was my father's nature, so sore his sensitivities; that he never bragged about his bravery. On his return to

England after the war he underwent compulsory psychological investigation and reorientation as a result of his exposure to Japanese cruelty, as well as Chinese communist indoctrination during his sojourn in the Red Army of Mao Tse Tung. One worked; the other didn't. He definitely was not a communist, but they were unable to rehabilitate his ego. He remained a softly spoken man with bad dreams.

A cosmopolitan young man had now returned to his English home town. If his war experiences were still causing him pain, they were now joined by an intense feeling of alienation. The British way of life was incongruous with his Eurasian spirit. In his hometown the cotton mills and factories lay like derelict buses in a breaker's yard. A different kind of monsoon, an inhospitably cold one, was coming down on the soot black buildings and cobblestoned streets – he had to break free and escape. A brief stint as a gilly for a Scottish laird near Fort William in the rugged highlands, where it was even colder, didn't do the trick. Through a local newspaper advert, placed by a Northern Rhodesian copper mining company, he found himself in colonial Africa. As good a place as any to give the Soul some R&R, or so it would have seemed then. It was a good life on the Copperbelt and people's needs were simple. There was no reason that everything should not go his way, especially as his personality endeared him to everyone he met. The stage was set, the props were in place; there was no question as to why he should not return to the physical prime of his boxing youth and re-plough his fertile spirit: once again be who he was when he turned pretty oriental girls' heads. The problem was there was no Eurasian high life and he carried his darkness with him. Was Africa a mistake?

I can only synchronise the events of my father's life by joining the dots of repeated stories from his tipsy MOTH club mates, my child perceptions and emotional pictures I have of him. But I trust that I have gone over these dots like fingers sensitive to braille, and intuitively I feel the story is true. It is a story of a kind young man who was a brave soldier, who found the good life for his bride, and who unwittingly allowed the good life to hurt himself, as well as the ones he loved.

On deeper reflection, it seems that my father's fresh start was marred by a few demonic stowaways lurking in the bilges of his psyche. What was it like to be creeping up to an adversary in the jungle behind enemy lines, who was in turn creeping up to you with your destruction on his mind? What was it like to see simple people of a forest clearing destroyed by both sides in a war? What was it like to face humiliation and death? What was it like to join a Red Army representing communist values, the opposite of what you were reared and fed on? What was it like to finally return to the homeland that you fought a war for, only to be viewed with suspicion as either a psycho or a communist; of which your subjugation was not even of your own making? What was it like at Soul level, to feel permanently alienated from your tribe? To not have a clearing of your own, both inner and outer? His first clearing was squeezed out of its perfect roundness by the forced departure of his mother, the second to be destroyed in war. To survive it all and then be given false hope back in Good Old England; and now to be offered salvation on a new continent with a new dark side. This earthly baggage of consequence was overloading his Soul purpose.

It was on a new day in 1947 that he had first stood on the edge of a fresh clearing on a new continent. He knew it had a dark side – the darker side of life was well known to him. It was

the side he had penetrated many times in his Burmese skir-
mishes. His sensitivities told him not to even contemplate going
anywhere near it, no matter how much fascination and intrigue
might have pulled at his Soul. It could only lead to no good,
this time African no good. His Soul might have erred, but it
was a scarred Soul. It was now erring on the side of caution.
He chose to work his way to an off-centre point of the clearing,
somewhere near to his point of arrival, where his toes could feel
the warm African sun in safety. In short time he was pushed
and lifted by the reactive consequences of his compassion and
loving kindness to be closer to the centre of the clearing – the
centre of attention. Things were good, and people adored him,
called him a little Greek god, but at the same time, squandered
his love. In so doing, they destroyed him as they slowly melted
his true worth to a trickle.

His name was Joe, and everyone knew him. Everyone loved
Little Joe in the black and white TV cowboy series 'Bonanza' and
everyone loved Little Joe in Luanshya too. My father was the life
and Soul of a very large circle of friends. He was unassuming,
he was kind; he had fresh jokes at his fingertips and colonial Far
Eastern mannerisms that charmed and endeared him to everyone. He was a special sort of person. He had a magnetism that
no one could resist. He was also greatly admired, respected and
befriended at the MOTH Club for his outstanding contribution to the war effort. He worked tirelessly for MOTH charities,
helping the families of not so fortunate ex-servicemen, black
and white – a black regiment of the Rhodesian African Rifles
also fought in the Burma Campaign. No one realised that in his
current fight for the war veteran cause, he was hiding from his
own wounded Soul – a survival trick he had learnt while serving
in the Chindits.

I would pore over the few photographs that told the story of my father's life prior to my mother's arrival in Northern Rhodesia. I was curious about his early days on the Copperbelt. With a spiritual eye I searched for meanings in these small black and white portrayals of his new life. The way he stood, wore his clothes, smiled at the photographer and what company he kept, was under close scrutiny. He often had his picture taken standing on anthills in the bush that had their vegetation macheted and mown down to make way for levelling and development. Whenever I looked at these pictures my heart felt the soft sadness that accompanies the deepest forms of nostalgia: whose nostalgia – his or mine – and a nostalgia for what? I was looking for the same spirit 'thing' that first drew him to the Far East, and had now brought him to Africa. He was looking for his purpose and I resonated with his search. His deep set eyes seemed to be looking right through the camera, scouring an unknown horizon for a distant shoreline lost. If war hadn't broken out in Asia, he would have lived a life of accomplished glory and satisfaction as a good father to a large family of Eurasian kids. I might have been half Chinese, curly hair and oriental eyes. Now he was bravely looking for his purpose in Africa, but I did spot a hint of resignation. His new African shoes didn't fit that well. I got the feeling from these black and white photographs that he was not happy about feeling sad – he wanted to be happy, but it seemed to be out of his reach. His Promethean curse was that he loved everyone and he used it as a crutch. He leaned heavily on it: he wanted them to be happy; he didn't want to hurt them with his inner sadness. He smothered them with his unique kindness. He vainly hoped that other people's happiness would be a sufficient veneer for his own battered Soul. It wasn't, but only my mother and I saw that.

The pictures showed a limp hope, the last remaining item in Pandora's Box after the escape of the Asian devils. It was wearing the coat of a willing spirit, daunted but brave, but like a Chindit mission, more than likely destined for failure; and my father had experienced too many of them. It was a sad hope because it had an inkling that somewhere along a winding African strip road a strange flock of Soul pilferers, Harpies, mythological vultures, Soul scavengers of the ancient world, would again feed off a part of his everything, test his metal, and steal his purpose.

His spirit was supported by a lean frame in those early photographs in Northern Rhodesia. That was before his voluntary submission to the deceptive ways of an easy colonial life. I cannot describe the disappointment that suffocates my heart whenever I contemplate his life. It is not that I wanted him to repeat himself as a hero with fresh exploits under his belt and ardent feminine admirers at his arm. I would have wanted him to grow in a self-awareness of his own Soul: selfishly I too wanted to know his Soul better. In my wildest dreams I would want to parley as facets of one Soul. But nothing seemed quite so simple in the Luanshya he got sucked into; the one my mother and I were spiritually drowning in, and so was he.

After I was conceived, my parents left the mine and moved to Salisbury, the capital of Southern Rhodesia, to be under professional medical care. They returned to Luanshya when I was one. They were grateful for my safe arrival. My intuition tells me that my parents had invested too many hopes and material assets into the arrival of my deceased siblings: life insurance policies, clothes and names. This time around they preferred to live in the 'Now' of gratitude without too many material affirmations of my existence. There are few pictures of my babyhood.

Not at all in keeping with his warm personality, when I started junior school my father moved a short spiritual distance from us. As the years moved on, he proffered little guidance and gave only veiled acknowledgements of our worth. It could have been a gesture of pending farewell, yet it was full of love – such are the emotionally complicated ways of the spiritual world. It wasn't a quest for change that drew him away from us, and there wasn't a particular third party, a lover to bring it down to a base level – his passion was too grandiose for that. Below the surface of his MOTH Club ways, he was driven by mysterious micro-threads of wanting that pulled and twisted upon his Soul. Now I can understand that; we were both consciously aware of the same pull. It was a mythological siren whose call echoed uncannily in the recesses of our sensuality. It was as if we were both chasing galactic storm clouds of an immensity that completely overshadowed the lawned village pond that was our lives. At best, we tried to catch the fizzled sparks of half-familiar fallen stars that occasionally appeared in our skies. At worst, with empty hands, we gazed around as the Universe continued to host its complex extravaganza without us. We were uncomfortable observers of our own search for the truth. It seemed a confirmed arrival was never to be given to our yearning eyes.

My father had one bit of shrapnel above the tattoo of an anchor on his right arm; he would let me wriggle it around under his skin. He would never have it removed. Perhaps it was a touchstone of his reality; a crude token of his self-worth constantly being measured in spiritual pain.

My father continued to be under pressure from wartime allegiances at the MOTH Club. It seemed normal for men to distance themselves from 'the wife and kids'. Conjugal relationships seemed least of all on their 'man's world' minds. My father showed love for us – unfortunately even that was sullied. He was always in debt through bar bills, which made life difficult. He was well known for his generosity in buying everyone a round, no matter the size of the crowd of heavy beer drinkers standing at the bar. To add to his debt, there were those who swopped from drinking cheap local beer to double shots of imported Scotch whisky because Good Old Joe was buying a round – war seemed to have severed the nerve endings of their scruples. It was not the Japanese who pushed the dagger deep into my father's heart. It was his 'good friends'.

Icarus

Daedalus was the Greek Leonardo da Vinci of the classical world. He was a knowledge seeker, a mathematician, an inventor and an architect; but, as an Athenian, he paid heavily for his talents in both guilt and sadness. He had been contracted by King Minos of Crete to build an inescapable labyrinth to both house and hide a dreadful flesh-eating creature who was half-man, half-bull. Poseidon the Sea God had been greatly displeased with King Minos for not sacrificing his gift of the Cretan bull. As a revenge, Poseidon effected the conception of this dreadful creature, called the Minotaur, between Minos' wife and the sacrificial bull. To show his supreme power over Athens, King Minos demanded that each year, the finest seven young Athenian men, and seven of the most beautiful young women, be sent to the island of Crete to be devoured by the Minotaur within the labyrinth. This filled Daedalus with deep remorse. King Minos, so as to keep the intricacies of the laby-rinth's paths secret, imprisoned Daedalus and his young son Icarus in a high tower, denying them the possibility of ever re-turning to their beloved Athens. These circumstances were the first dominos of guilt and sadness to fall against Daedalus.

Daedalus, spurred by a deep longing for Greece, made fantastic wings out of bird feathers and beeswax which he strapped to himself and his son Icarus in an attempt to flee the island of Crete. Like Leonardo da Vinci, he had studied birds in flight, but it was Daedalus who pushed his studies too far by taking to the air like a bird, with Icarus flying pre-cariously behind him. Before they launched themselves into angelic flight, Daedalus explained to Icarus the dangers of flying too high and too close to a sun that would melt his wings, or too low to a treacherous sea. As they broke through the clouds, and took to the Mediterranean air, the peasants on the ground saw them; not as flying men, not even as an-gels, but as Gods. That was an unforgivable travesty, seen and condemned by the Gods: for which father and son would pay dearly. Another domino in the relationship between Daedalus and the Fate sisters had fallen.

As Greek pathos would have it, both the Sun and the sea got their evil ways. Icarus, infatuated by the freedom that his father's creativity had given him – in what could be perceived as blasphemy against the Gods – flew too hard, too high, and too close to the Sun. His wings melted, and he plummeted, without any divine intervention, into the deathly embrace of what is now the Icarian Sea. As kindly water nymphs recovered his broken body and Soul from the cruel waves; the Muse of Tragedy, Melpomene, looked on in theatrical compassion for a Soul whose predilection was that it should lose its way.

The Muses were the daughters of Jupiter, the sun god, and Mnemosyne, the goddess of memory. They nurtured all the memories of mankind in remembrance of his happinesses, sadnesses, tragedies and loves; which it is said, they dished out as intricate theatrical scripts for lives of mortal Souls such as Daedalus and Icarus to follow; as if they were footprints of their own Souls. It appeared that the Muses had purposely let the dominos fall against Icarus' favour. Was it perhaps a case of poetic justice in which a crime, the egotistical rise of man, was being punished by the tragic downfall of a hapless young man? Would innocence and virtue not be rewarded through the salvation of Icarus' Soul from the oceanic depths of destruction? Who knows what melodrama the Muses had in mind?

Icarus was drawn with such conviction and foolhardiness towards the Sun, where the almighty sun god of the Universe reigned in full glory. Maybe that was his Soul purpose; that's how things were meant to be. Or was it that he had foolishly confused the deep sensual feelings that the Sun had stirred within his heart, for spiritual aspiration. The important point in his story was that it was not a human premeditated act: His story unfolded without any manipulative intent from his or his father's side. The Instruction to fly higher was issued from another quarter; so profound, that it was like a footprint on his Soul. He really couldn't have saved himself.

He was a mortal, and mortals easily lost control of their senses, not to mention their reasoned purpose: Was it then surprising that he should cast caution to the wind, and fly with his passions well beyond the boundaries of moderation; to where a mortal death and not divine acclamation was to be his lot.

Of this tragic but insightful story of a young man: The Soul of Icarus, in an act of divine grace, had been thrown into the fate of a youth who can't be condemned just because he wanted to fly higher than the angels and dance with the Gods; begrudged because he was bravely chasing after his Soul purpose; ridiculed because he was under the narcissistic spell of his own glorious sensuality; mocked for his failure to follow convention, and judged by his apparent failure to succeed. Perhaps he did succeed!

Of Icarus' downfall, his plummet into a heartless sea: was he not also paying dearly for his heady affinities? After all, his excruciating conscious awareness of a beauty so far beyond the boundaries of earth and the common man, could and should only lie within the aethereal realm of the Gods themselves, and not be his mortal right to behold. The subject of his fancy was well beyond his earthly right, and well out of his mortal reach. He was thus left deeply in love with its remaining threads of aethereal consequence – an overly sensitive mind and body, and a dolefully searching Soul. That is why some writers on Greek mythology saw him as having been softly narcissist in his apparent self-assured need to have union with the sun god as his glorious equal.

The truth, which is very hard for grown-ups to find – in a story that could be seen as an example of an impulsive youth with an inappropriate appetite for adventure; who was overly led into temptation by his untamed senses, and who was addicted to his imagination – is that Icarus did fly high. He flew so spiritually high; higher than any mortal before him. Human timelines, and the set roles and events that punctuate them, have no meaning for the divine, nor do they have any relevance with little children. With no reasons or ending required, the story of Icarus is a powerfully simple one.

Whether he reached Athens to kiss the sod of his motherland, or plunged into a sea of despair, is materially immaterial. All of Crete, and the Gods on high, witnessed the intriguing sight of a flesh and blood youth on the wings of full flight. It is a timeless story because it hovers between how it should have, would have, and could have been; an imponderable story without end. How it did end, if it did end, is of no importance in how everyone saw it in the 'Now' moment of their timeless sight. It was a Soul in full flight, for everyone to observe as the all-encompassing testimony of their own Soul purpose. On the surface, it is the story of a tragic young man; but in essence, it is soft swan down caught in the spiritual thermals of the ever-expanding Soul of the Universe as it spreads its wings out into eternity.

Was my father's story at all in tandem with Icarus' spontaneous rise to heroism of a tragic kind? It could have been that he had committed a travesty against the Gods: He had innocently flown too hard, and too high, in both glory and war – he had spent all his chips in an Asian casino of luckless hope. Perhaps it was my mother, as one of the gentle sea nymphs, who had gathered up the broken wings of his battered self-esteem. Melpomene could have written his story right from when as a youth, he had boarded a slow boat to China: and still she had more to write.

Misconstruing colonial good life for a spiritual path, he searched for his Soul through an urgent and altruistic desire to help others, but his spirit was hoodwinked by false admirers in the clearing. He would never see the truth, no matter how high he flew towards its centre. He couldn't be blamed for his bacchanalian desire to live as a free spirit among reckless satyrs. To be taken for granted as a warrior who throws himself between the wheels of his Soul purpose – to love others more than himself. Was this all a predilection written on his Soul, my Soul; our one Soul? Melpomene had certainly woven an intricate storyline into the emotional fabric of his earth journey.

Prometheus loved mankind. Perhaps my father and Icarus were disciples of Prometheus. Prometheus, against Jupiter's orders, had travelled to the Sun to bring back fire to warm the hearts and lives of men and their families. Jupiter punished Prometheus for this charitable act by delivering Pandora, who caused the release of one too many social addictions from a box of human vices: Was there ever any real hope for Icarus; would there be any hope left for my father?

My father, with a soulful uncertainty from within, hovered in the aether space between earthly reality and the heavens. He chased illusive silver linings on the drifting clouds of war memories blown in on bacchanalian summer winds. Summer winds never stay long enough, and nostalgia's allure gradually faded in the chill light of reality. Little Joe, the Dionysus of Luanshya, like Prometheus, was being eternally punished by the almighty Jupiter for being the friend of all mankind. He found himself chained, like Prometheus, to a hard rock, where he had his vitality pecked out of him by war-torn vultures every night, only to rekindle his love for his fellow man the next day anew.

Prometheus is famous as a symbol of humble perseverance and hope in the light of unmerited suffering. That was my father. An Icarus who found glory in his downfall.

Feminine blind faith and a hankie up her sleeve

The first mine rule was that newlyweds did not travel out to the Northern Rhodesian Copperbelt as matrimonial couples. All the new young brides followed their men at least a couple of months or so after their husbands had made the journey out to Africa. From their single quarters the young men would have to borrow or buy a set of spoons and cups here and a knife and fork there, mostly thirdhand. Old established colonials would take pity on them and help them out wherever they could. My father's bonhomie engendered kindness from the well-established couples and he was thus able to pull together 'enough' for my mother's arrival in Northern Rhodesia.

An eclectic collection of bric-a-brac-ed people and objects and a loving and faithful, and hopefully not drunk, husband would welcome the trepid young English lady off the boat train. In those days most white people walked or rode bicycles in the town. My father caught a lift to the Ndola railway station twenty miles from Luanshya with a good-humoured older couple who owned a car. With this nodding twosome in tow, he welcomed my mother onto the terra firma of the Ndola railway platform and into their new life.

That my mother was capable of such a long journey would have appeared an act of spiritual determination if it hadn't been for a matronly colonial Soul who tracked her down like an elephant cow who had lost its calf at a busy waterhole. Before the ship had even left the South Hampton dock on the English coast, she rapped on the door of the cabin shared by six lasses about to leave for matrimonial life on the Copperbelt. That's how friendships were forged in a colonial mining world; they were of formal consequence, not of a selective Soul: maybe husbands were chosen in the same way after the war. This imposing lady introduced herself as Mrs. Worthington Brown from Luanshya. She had been visiting family in England and now would be my mother's and all the other gals', as she put it, chaperone all the way to Northern Rhodesia and Luanshya. Do not fear my dears. It is a long journey but the rewards will more than exceed any hardships along on the way, she probably said with bosom booming certainty. I never met the good lady, but I can imagine she wore a tweed two piece suit and sensible brogues, all topped with one of those trilbies that Ingrid Bergman wore in *Casablanca*. She had been instructed by telegram from the Roan Antelope Mine and other mines to take good care of all the young women on the boat who were on their way to their new husbands and lives on the Copperbelt.

At the end of a long sea journey down the west coast of Africa, Cape Town and the backdrop of Table Mountain welcomed a simple Lancashire lass, my mother, to the vast continent of Africa. The boat train awaited them on the dock only a gang plank's distance away from their ship, The Carnarvon Castle, one of the passenger liners that ploughed between Great Britain and South Africa. The boat train inched its way through the Swartberg Mountains, and then the Langeberg Mountains, through the Hex River Mountain tunnels and into the mini scrub deserts of the Klein Karoo and the Groot Karoo. They chugged through the dusts of De Aar and past the famous diamond town of Kimberly, and then up into the British protectorate of Bechuanaland; where these, by now slightly debonair, young English women bought their first African artefacts. Curio sellers at the Mahalapye siding clamoured around the carriages to sell their softwood and goat skin drums, tribal dolls, and bead necklaces. Lovely people the Bechaunas, boomed Mrs. Worthington Brown. 'Don't over pay them too much darlings, they hardly understand the meaning of money,' so my mother told me.

On arrival in Bulawayo in Southern Rhodesia – Lobengula's 'House of Bulls' and site of the Matabele rebellion against the British in 1893 and 1894, they were escorted to the Grand Hotel, where high tea awaited them while the train was cleaned and new staff boarded. When the train departed from the Bulawayo station, it had grown in size. Heavy freight wagons had joined the bevy of beauties all going up to the prosperous Copperbelt. Bulawayo was an industrial town and it had lots of things to sell to the copper mines in the north. Meals were served in the dining carriage by white waiters on white china plates with silvered teapots and milk jugs 'for one', all with the Rhodesian Railways insignia stamped onto them. The boat train – it was still the boat train, even though it had left the coast a long time before, and had traversed the scrub lands of Bechuanaland and South West Matabeleland – was now entering the magnificent teak forests of Matabeleland North. At one point the train stopped because there were elephant on the line. My mother and the other young brides 'oohed and ahhed' at an elephant bull as he trumpeted and mock charged. The train gave an equally pompous warning call, and soon they were on their way again to the Victoria Falls. There they disembarked to walk the short distance from the train between low privet box hedges, to the Victoria Falls Hotel: a grand railway hotel opened in 1904 and rebuilt in South European Renaissance style in 1917, where steaming hot baths and fresh towels awaited them. This was followed by high tea on the lawns, graced by the view of the spray of the mighty Victoria Falls. The Zambezi River created a raincloud of spray as it threw itself three hundred feet out of the dry riverine surroundings to the thunderous applause from the Nyami-Nyami River God.

As if not to be outdone by the backdrop of Cape Town's Table Mountain, the Rhodesias put on a spectacular show as the boat train chugged through a microcosmic rain forest permanently buffeted by the clouds of rain and hot air that were forced out of the bowels of the Zambezi River. Palms, remnants of early Arab explorer's provisions of dates they said, glistened and thick mosses and ferns carpeted the buttress roots of ancient riverine trees. It was a strange oasis sitting in the middle of a leafless grey African bush, suffering yet again from a taxing dry season. The surrounding bush was home to elephants, buffalo and even the odd opportunist lion. The river upstream was dotted with flotillas of hippo that raucously called to each other and the sand banks were scarred with crocodiles. Small animals took refuge in the rainforest. One could see secretive bushbuck and indiscrete vervet monkeys; while baboons attempted to board the slow train for a free ride and a bit of pilfering. It was a utopian world perched on the edge of basalt cliffs and ravines that hurtled your senses down into the waters of an angry river below.

Palm groves and waterlogged mini vleis were the last vistas of Southern Rhodesia as the train crossed onto the steel bridge connecting the two Rhodesias. Once on the bridge the train travellers, fresh from a bath and likely smelling of a light splash of Lily of the Valley perfume and Old Spice aftershave, in keeping with this important part of the journey, took in the Victoria Falls on their left at slow chugging speed for all to witness the power of Southern Africa unleashed. White sheets of water were being drawn into the rocky earth many tens of feet below. Evergreen forests hung suspended in permanent mist and leaves and grasses quivered in the powerful up currents of winds that were ejected from 'the boiling pot' far below. The river was in a vortex of mayhem and confusion as it frothed and swirled in gargantuan proportions, hurling its waters high into a cloudless sky to return to earth as a heavy deluge which soaked the steam locomotive and its carriages of new arrivals. It rid them of the psychological dusts of a long African train journey where coal dust engrains both skin and Soul. Every time a powerful steam locomotive billowing black smoke and steam crossed the Victoria Falls Bridge tugging at a long line of important cargoes, it was dwarfed into insignificance. Only its Soul purpose remained as a figment of Cecil John Rhodes' dream of a railway line from Cape Town to Cairo. It was a grand spectacle. It was short and had punch, and would have hopefully had a lasting impression on the travellers. They were soon to enter the town of Livingstone, to proceed on to their new homes on the Congo border. But did it have an impact and leave an everlasting impression on these neo-colonials? As a youth I used to wonder what had crossed my mother's mind at the time. Perhaps the expansive colonial mood of the 'then' made such vast natural magnificence something to be taken for granted and even to be expected as part of civilised man's taming of Africa. Perhaps she and her fellow travellers took it in their stride. Maybe humans and their manmade achievements like the Victoria Falls Bridge, built in 1905 under considerable financial speculation, were of greater importance than the wonders of nature at that time.

I believe what might have surprised her more, was that on disembarking from the train after traveling the Atlantic and half of Sub-Saharan Africa, she didn't get whisked off to be carried across the threshold of her new home. My father and the good Samaritans trundled my mother and her sea trunk off for drinks at the Ndola Hotel. For my mother, who didn't 'drink,' it was a pertinent indication of what Luanshya life was to be, very little was said or done without drinks, that's just how things were in the Colonies. Even after drinks, she wasn't carried off to her new home. My father had managed to find accommodation, a partitioned space on the built-in veranda of someone else's house. Before my mother arrived he lived quite comfortably in the single quarters provided by the mine, but on my mother's arrival they had to make do – it was a man's world.

I read a book about St George and the dragon which was given to me by the Rector of St Georges church in Luanshya. Inside it was stamped in copper plate gothic, 'This book belongs to the Sons of England.' Our life style belonged to the SOE which, on reflection, was a euphemistic statement of colonial power and control that ruled at arm's length from its command centre – 'This is the BBC calling from London'. The SOE allowed for limited self-expression and little self-discovery. It forced its minions down a narrow bush path that was soon to peter out into defunct colonial nothingness. A path that intrepid new arrivals like my parents, might not have chosen had they been offered a choice.

The SOE was a group of women furthering the pastoral wellbeing of the Queen's flock overseas. They tried to rope my mother into their well-meaning machinations. She was however a simple Lancashire girl who had worked in the cotton mills prior to the war and then in 'munitions' as part of the war effort. The SOE was propped up by older women, a lot of whom had left England in the twenties and thirties. My mother found them sanctimonious and hoity-toity. She felt they looked down on her humble origins and she withdrew to become a stay-at-home wife with a manservant who polished the floors, peeled the vegetables and did the washing and ironing. I could never understand why the frumpy women that presided over jumble sales and fêtes should be called 'The Sons of England'. In the spirit of segregation of the sexes, men were absent from their flock. The Rector told me this was only because the men were too busy working down the mine. He was inferring that women were called Sons of England because their menfolk were miners! He omitted to say that the women were avid knitters of jumble sale jerseys and made cakes, while the men were jolly good boozers. The two did not mix. Perhaps the Sons of England needed a new charter.

My mother found it difficult to socialise. There was class distinction within the white community, which was determined by which club you belonged to, and as a consequence, what you drank. Gin and tonics and John Collins were popular at the golf club. Beer and 'hard tack' was the order of the day at the MOTH Club and the mine long bar; and beer-shandies, Pims and angostura rock shandies were supped by those indecisive sorts who sat in the middle of societal segregation. I noticed that the MOTH Club members comprised mainly of non-commissioned officers and riflemen. Perhaps the Souls of commissioned officers had managed to move on in life; gardening at the Luanshya horticultural club; with light exercise and not so much drinking at the tennis club, where 'tall drinks' rather than local beers and 'shorts' were the order of the day.

My father's penchant for drinking in a men's bar limited my mother's options further.

As a young woman like my mother, if you didn't join a club you were left high and dry from society life. However, the type of clubs on offer, did not really appeal to the feminine psyche – clubs seem to be a man thing which called for the wife's support in the background: making teas and lunches. Embroidery, floristry and cake decorating were the lady thing. My mother was no gardener and couldn't arrange flowers; she could cook well, but for some quirky reason, she couldn't bake cakes. Her father's confectionery shop was famous for its meat pies – we ate a lot of meat pies, but no cakes. Because her options were narrowing down to none; because trite ladies morning tea parties were alien to her Soul, and she genuinely couldn't embroider dollies or knit jerseys; because she couldn't even hit a tennis ball, and there was no work; because she was too soft to forcefully 'man' a stand at an SOE charity fête: my mother found it hard to keep her free spirit afloat.

My brave mother accepted the early days of Northern Rhodesia, but slowly the predetermined way of Luanshya bar life and isolation sucked the spiritual pluck out of her. Love's loneliness, spawned by my father's intransigent bar ways, was clouding her vision. I remember her, often with teary eyes, as she put me to bed. She would tuck her hankie into her cardigan sleeve, or under her watch strap in a false sense of tear dabbing preparedness for the long night ahead. She would patiently await the return of my father, hopefully without the Glaswegian Minotaur on his heels. There she was alone in the African night, an insecure English lass who had suffered the loss of more than one child, sitting in a spartan mine house, before the days of television and with no phone, missing her overseas family dearly. As a child, her many lace handkerchiefs denoted sadness for me.

My parents were in a working class mining community painted in brash strokes: he coped, she felt alienated and things were unlikely to change. I believe she even confused her love for my father as humble vassalage instead of an equal partnership of give and take. Her self-worth was being eroded away by the same colonial white shadow that confined our black domestics to their 'back of our garden' houses at night – no one seemed to see or understand the restriction of it all. I did.

At night I would hold her cool Pond's Cold creamed hand for comfort. The meal that she had prepared and cooked the whole of that afternoon was drying out in an oven on low heat to await my father's beer-full return. My father had gone down the mine by the time I woke up the next morning and my mother would be sorting out the washing with Wilson the domestic. There was a tell-tale bottle of Enos fruit salts or a tube of Alka Zeltzer effervescent tablets on the shelf above the basin – 'reg-makers' or hangover cures in Afrikaans – and a few well used ladies hankies in the tribal weave washing basket.

My mother was a Lancashire rose looking for a new identity on an incorrigible continent – what chance of success did she have? Africa was a gargantuan Pandora's Box in the inept white hands of a colonial past that was losing its grip on a continent's fear based spirit. She was the true spiritual soldier in my parents' Luanshya life. My father had met his monsters before; she was meeting them now. His were well known and he was whole-heartedly supported for his brave stance. My mother's gargoyles were insidiously superficial, and nobody knew of them or cared. Her troubled voice in the night, and her loving ways during the day, showed me the complexity of the feminine Soul. Like a bramble rose that endures untold hardships, it never fails to delight all and sundry with its sweet scented bloom. Sadly the hooked thorns of her self-perceived inadequacies imprisoned her Soul. My mother showed me unconditional love, but circumstances prevented her from showing self-love. Without a self-love to call her own, without an ego to wear, she was forced to secure her self-worth in passive loneliness.

5

I CHOOSE...
EXPRESSIONS OF BEING –
GESTURES OF MEANING

AMAZONITE RAIN

AMAZONITE RAIN

So Hum – jungle rain

Nestled in self-pity, it seemed that love, which required more effort than So Hum could muster, had departed from his canopied world. He might even have thought about returning to the lower branches when another rain arrived out of the blue.

This rain was awe-inspiring, but So Hum was not in the mood for more rain. It was bold in its approach of drumming drops, thunder rumbles and lightning-pierced clouds. Should he try to stop this dream, or should he let it unfold? A flicker of delight made the decision hard to make. He tried to turn his bow saw back on this new dream rain, but its approach overtook his senses: It was like none before. A power came rolling out of the sky to fill the anticipatory void that preempts every tropical downpour. The rain was upon him.

The choice was not his to make. This dream rain quickly took possession of his harsh world. Steaming pendules of green amazonite and weighty beads of silver and turquoise: It was an equatorial deluge that housed the mechanics for unstoppable growth. Its brazen freshness tickled his cracked senses.

It was as if a universal truth that had lain limp within him for so long, was now uncurling its leaves. A turgidity of spirit urged him to express himself in harmony with nature's exuberance. Even the delicate branches seemed to grow stronger.

He could have chosen to rebuff this new rain as another emotional squall, but he didn't. Instead he embraced it for what it was – a heady miracle.

In his dream, every drop that hit the branches burst forth into greenery afresh; the aethereal sight of which sent his emotions into a state of happiness. If he had eyes, they would have cried with tears of joy, and those tears, would have turned the bark into leafy sprays.

So Hum was once again happy. He had been the victim; but now the victor was him. How could he have ever believed that there was someone out there with more: He had it all, he had always had it. All he needed to do was express his deepest intentions, which was his Soul purpose. It was a simple choice of honest being for him to make, and the world would unfurl at his feet. Luscious growth was all around him and in him: he was abundance. In his darkness, he was all the changing colours of an ever-expanding Universe through and through.

Ah Hum roots – I choose

In essence Ah Hum's choices could have told him everything about himself and his tribe: They were his collective subconscious, his tribal values. They pointed to a rich world of magic and abundance that, like a footprint, would lead him to his ultimate success. In reality, they came from his roots. Hidden from view they had dug themselves ever deeper into the all-knowing earth of his universal existence. From there they would spread out to assist him in his spiritual purpose of unbounded growth. His subconscious choices were expressions of his closest affinities and intentions.

Inner magic on a material plane

Decision making is no easy task. As a geomancer at heart, Ah Hum naturally turned to his allies:

> Amazonite and fennel seed oil: *to release mental blockages in the expression of his deepest inner truths and needs.*
>
> Sugilite and peppermint oil: *to enhance intuition and lucid dreaming.*
>
> Labradorite and myrrh: *symbols of the unavoidable synchrodestiny in his life.*

Expressions of being, gestures of meaning

> The Rosetta Stone
> Cracks in my emotional skin
> My philosophy of the Obscura
> The leopard
> Who is watching the three musketeers?
> My Soul is not mine
> The Zanzibari boy

The Rosetta Stone

The Rosetta Stone was a tablet of stone from which, using a bridging language, ancient writings were able to be translated. As children, we create our own Rosetta Stone. We gather snippets of information from our Soul, and align them with the factual building blocks and meanings of our current outside world. Teachers show our deft little fingers and minds how to put all these Lego blocks of spiritual persona and life together into a personal living code, which we place at the back of the classroom of our minds as a daily reminder of how to best behave; how to make the best choices to be successful in life, and how to add and subtract our personal issues.

In essence, we are cajoled into tempering our swashbuckling Soul to build upon a steadfast ego: as well as to oil the cogs of our materially solid purpose in life with respectable manners and diligence. I never liked or trusted junior school teachers – their motives were suspect. Mr Harrison tried hard to launch our free Souls into blue sky flight, but he had a band of brigands, Soul pilferers, as teachers. I reckoned some of them were even grave robbers.

What were they teaching me? Of the twenty-six letters of the Roman alphabet, I could choose to write a hate letter to Rosemary, who was prissy and annoying in class. Or I could choose to write her a secret BFF note. Mrs. Versaakie would condone one, and definitely not the other, no matter how grammatically correct and neatly written the poison letter might be. Spiritually speaking, both had value. Both would be recorded into the eternal scheme of things without prejudice. They were of equal importance as universal archetypes of good and bad; the one in fact, helping to define the other.

There is no right or wrong choice in a young child's inner life. A present moment choice, good or bad, is an 'in the zone' energy flow in resonance with the spirit of the moment, where there are not yet any timely consequences, such as a smacked bottom or a correction, or an achievement badge.

A child's voice is its personal choice. I want to discover the origins of my choices, those deep calls to follow my predilections, which urged me to express myself in the ways that I did. I want to consciously enter the space where the pre-emption of my choices and their application took place. That fecund 'nothing' aether space which both buffered and connected my child being to the world; the mechanics of which, made me feel oddly different. I want to go there because that's where the alchemy of my Soul unfolds; where my Soul's creative purpose precipitates out of the aether of Universal knowledge into my good intentions: where my affinities lie.

I wish to revisit the spiritual battlefield of my childhood Luanshya. I want to pay homage to those conquests, where choice was either defeated or hailed. Choices made, not by societal convention, but by my Soul itself. To be more specific, I wish to retrace the footprint of a Soul that seemed to be on a different path to the conditioned me. I still very much want to get to know my Soul better.

I want to dig up my own Rosetta Stone. I want to use the 'Now' information of my present understanding to reveal the knowledge of the spiritual past. I wish to be able to read the original cuneiform writings that tell the story of my thinking Soul in the 'then'. I want to go beyond the *au courant* pontifications of what I think I know now, to reach the origins of my truth. Using my Rosetta Stone I want a bridge to cross over to my boy-spirit past, which still exists somewhere within me in its original state. I wish to read about my love, willpower and desire in their original tongue. When they were embryonic choices of the aether – not choices seen as steadfast happenings measured in degrees of right and wrong.

It seems to be our human destiny that we should misplace this stone of spiritual importance, often forgetting about it altogether. We move on – but to where? To another empty space anchored in linear time that we find difficult to read? An even further distant shore where we hope to find a meaning to our search for love and happiness – our need for oneness; where new faiths, followings and adopted values are negligible dusts on the original.

To go forward with my purpose in life, with even the slightest scrap of spiritual security, I need to know at least something about my Soul's thoughts. Without its rationale, my physical timeline will continue to be what it has always been, and I will continue to get what I have always got. My spirit of adventure would die, and so would I. Without a recognisable Soul purpose, a chunk of informational awareness will be missing in my life and I might even believe my lot to be a long and empty one.

Of course workaholics don't worry about that. They look for a constant supply of material things to fill their empty time and space with. When, out of neglect, their non-replaceable Soul battery runs out on them, their lament is familiar. 'Oh life is so meaningless, what have I got to show for it all'. Nothing, because there was nothing to start with.

I want and need that stone. Like an alchemist's magic formula it will show my misconceived, 'peeved little sod' side in a better light. Like an African washerwoman's stone, it will lift the stains of misunderstanding and ignorance out of the colonial white linen that floats in the murky sop of my African conscious awareness. It will give spiritual value to all my past choices, deeds and shortcomings. It will tame the hyenas that haunted me as they scurried through my confused psyche, ripping at the throat of my good intentions. My childlike guilt and fear will be defunct. Fear and guilt are not parts of my Soul. They are social affectations that have soiled the sleeve of many school uniforms and put indelible black marks in my academic reports.

Maybe because I enjoyed the timeless reverie of my youth so much – which now seems to have partially fled from my greying mind – I now want to parley with my Soul full on. I want to sensually indulge in a spiritual knowledge once cataracted by my mortal view on life. Youth has no timeline; like root fear, love and joy, youth is a facet of the Soul outside of time and space. Youth is a state of unconditional being, not cellular freshness. It is the perpetual echo of our inner child. It is no slight on me that, within my mortal timeline, I thought my youth had been swept away by a gravitational wind of change called age. Serendipitously, thanks to my *surround time* reality show, I have caught sight of my youth in my present moment of inner inquiry. It is tugging at my attention – it always was, but responsibility encouraged me to ignore it. I am now old enough to know better.

Cracks in my emotional skin

My sensitivity to the African world around me was not a blessing for most of the time, as my childhood choices bear witness to. My little boy status often showed cracks out of which leaked a protoplasm that exuded further realms of heightened self-awareness from somewhere within me. Layers of feeling upon feeling, pain pressing upon pain, love calling love. Every sensation of perception layered in thumping resonance with my cupidities.

Long-time always seemed to be a problem for me; it rubbed against my wants. Children despise long-time and his prissy sister patience, both of which have no attraction or useful purpose in an eager 'Now' world. Short-time was not much better: it cut the far ends of the good times off.

I wanted every boring time to be speeded up, and every good time to be slowed down. I made pre-emptive choices as to how time should unfold as an immature expression of my need for timelessness. I had a lot of energy, and I wanted my world to resonate with it on my terms. I had strong longings, and I wanted them to be satisfied outside of time. I was a spiritual haemophiliac – I wanted to squirt my life force on everything in an instantaneous non-spatial way. I opened myself up to Luanshya in a bold offer of oneness. There was no light at the end of the tunnel – there were no walls of permanence and perspective – there was no tunnel – there was only a burning light of immediacy, and I wanted it in a blinding 'Now'. Was I wrong?

The slow times were so slow that they faltered, and then teetered backwards. 'Too late to go the vlei' Saturday afternoons were killers. We had been out somewhere for lunchtime drinks, and had returned around three o'clock to our heat-twisted house. My parents wanted an afternoon nap – lunchtime beers did that to them. Sometimes, lying on top of my bedcover in my airless room, I would read my tatty book of Somerset Maugham short stories set in the twenties and thirties where time often stood still; Somerset Maugham created time warps in which his characters became trapped. I could relate to his characters drowning in slow time. Being stationed on a lonely Malaysian rubber plantation cut off from the world by inflexible British colonial rules, torrential rains, towering jungles and resentful hill tribes seemed like heaven compared to those Saturday afternoons with nothing to do. I half understood his big words and obtuse meanings to life, but easily picked up on the mood of his characters.

On those hot and dreary Saturday afternoons I would be conscious of walls that were about to fall in on me in slow domino motion. I imagined they would start at my gauzed–in window, then move in an anticlockwise direction around the room. Everything I owned, including my flesh and blood, would be squashed into a pile of useless rubble. Then they would be sorry, I would declare. Who was 'they'? Were 'they' my dozing parents, the mine management, the Rector or the Soul pilfering junior school teachers? I wasn't sure myself – it was just that I was angry! Angry with what? I didn't know – that was the problem.

Before I was crushed by the brick and mortar; speared by splintered rafters and sliced by the sharp roofing of my imagination – I would sneak out of my room. Bare-footed, wearing my grey going out shorts hoisted high, and sporting my once-white jockey undervest, I would unlock the back door and venture into the hot afternoon sun. I would open my poop-steamy pet chicken's coop and throw myself onto the front lawn in the silent anger of absolute boredom. The sun only aggravated my odious state, but my lame mind could not think of anything else to do.

If I didn't feel up to searching for hidden worlds in the clouds, I would simply fall into a mindless funk. Sometimes my emotions were so scrambled that they had no flow. Instead their oscillating drone sent my mind and body into a numb state of anaesthesia. Cheapie, my pet hen, chasing grasshoppers, would sometimes peck at my caterpillaring eyebrows – but even that didn't cheer me up. I loved Cheapie and he would make me giggle, but everything that I had and loved could not rid me of my deep yearning for something that I didn't have. I felt a pining pain. It was as if my senses were drowning in the empty adult absence of a lover. On those days, my worth would seep out of the cracks in me and spread out onto the grass like dirty engine oil.

On futile days like these I was searching for nothing and everything: Even on my bad days when frustration had me in a half nelson, I was working towards knowing my Soul better. Only foolish mortals searched for the divine in heaven – so Madam Vlei once told me during an intense storm. 'There is no god of goodness, nor is there a god of evil – there is only one god of good and evil' – she howled as a tropical hail storm cut miombo forests' leaves to shreds. She was right about what was right or wrong in my search for the truth. I did honestly believe that my Soul hung out in the strangest of places – but that had nothing to do with the fact that I was desperate to meet it. On days like these, even a short glimpse of it, wherever it might be, would do.

My philosophy of the Obscura

The camera obscura is an old optical contrivance whereby external objects can be made to appear on a white surface in a closed box by means of a small aperture. Sometimes, if the closed curtains in a darkened room allow just the right chink of light to project on the opposite wall, an obscura effect can occur – one can see an inverted image of the outside world otherwise hidden from view by the curtains.

The light seems just right: I want to use my philosophy of the obscura to catch a fleeting image of my Soul – not with reflected rays of light of my outer world; but through a reverberated echo within the inner darkness of my own biorhythms.

I define my Soul as perfect knowledge which has coalesced into a full awareness of its own aethereal reality, and as a consequence, it holds the recipe for my continued physical existence. I was born of a Soul that only partially expresses itself within my conscious mind and body. For the rest of my time, it bestows a feeling of knowingness upon my self-awareness, which silently says everything about me. It mischievously whispers an ongoing legacy of eager self-inquiry – which one could call Soul searching.

I want to see my Soul because it is a personage of far greater worth than my cognitive physicality will ever be. It is not a passive tag along travel partner on my life's journey. It is the mover and shaker: It holds the route map of our one earth journey.

Refractions of inner light – my Soul

With my camera of the obscura in hand, the
morning mist of my early years shows promise
of lifting.

The clarity of my mid-morning years seems to
be strong.

There is the assurance of a sunny afternoon
ahead,

An afternoon brightness that will eventually
flow over into a late afternoon light.

A meditative luminescence unfolds in the satisfaction of an after-the-storm sunset.

There is a faint flicker and a familiar image
dances across my silver screen.

Is it a reflection or is it an entity?

Its glimmer is in resonance with something
bigger than itself – something of universal
proportions.

Could it possibly be my Soul – is this the real
me that I see?

I open the shutters of my heart – in the hope
of capturing more of the spiritual light that is
undressing my Soul before me.

The leopard

In reliving this child's story in *surround time*, I want to lift the
thick veil of conventionality that has veiled my vision for more
than two score and ten. I have a desperate need to unfetter
the earthy wisdom of my Soul, which like the elusive leopard
was always there: the presence of a magnificently mystical creature that was erased by societal thought patterns as if it were a

pagan dream symbol; something my child's mind was told not to play with. My psyche now wants to put a stop to this ridiculous grown-up mind game of deception, which it now declares as its own mistruth: a miscreant truth to be hunted down and devoured by the divine leopard of my Soul-driven dreams.

Behind my vlei, a couple of hundred feet back, there was the 'No Go' caved-in area. I had my back to it when I sat on top of my anthill. The caved-in area was an area of possible land collapse as a result of the early mining days, when seams of ore ran close to the surface. By the fifties the mining companies had to dig deeper to get the life force they were looking for. The prized green serpent had dived further down into the earth. Caved-in areas were the remnants of easy mining days long gone by.

The area was surrounded by a six foot high diamond mesh fence with barbed wire on top and signs saying '*Hokoyo Skelem*', beware of danger in Chilapalapa. We miners' children were always told about the danger of ever going near a caved-in area. No one ever entered. The land was unstable, and could collapse beneath your feet. If you did go in, you would never come out. I had visions of bodies lying with broken bones, half-eaten by hideous African beasts that may have never been recorded before. I could never accept that zoologists had identified and named all the animals of Africa. I could see from the London bound CAA plane, that there were vast areas of Africa that had never been penetrated, or so I thought in my child's mind. Just because scientists had never seen a particular beast, did not mean that it didn't exist. What dark secrets lay lurking in that closed off area; what strange beast could creep under the fences and into my vlei when no one was looking? Maybe it was one of these dark, secretive beings that had carved the clay seat with its beastly haunches at the top of my anthill! I felt there were lots of areas like this, especially in the jungles of the Congo, where biologists were simply too frightened to ever go and have a look.

The fence ran parallel to my vlei for a good mile, then moved away at a right angle as far as my eye could see. This caved-in area was the watershed of my decision-making for years to come. This glorious piece of bush, untouched by human penetration since before the Second World War, symbolised for me everything that the African bush stood for. It was an exuberant show of unbridled vegetative growth. The very thought of its existence sent a reverberation of excitement through my body whenever I thought about it. It abducted my senses from their propriety. Its forbidden nature made me sick with a longing that urged me to be one with it.

There was a clear emotional difference between the caved-in area and my affinities. The caved-in area stoked a strong desire for me to experience it in the physical 'here and now'. Whereas in the case of my affinities, objects and situations were reminders of a mysteriously timeless longing for something as yet unknown; a footprint of my Soul, which as an earth traveller, I was duty bound to follow.

From the little that I could see of the area, all I could imagine was that it was a very dense piece of African bush. I was sure it housed a lot of immediate African unknowns, hence my urgency to know it better. I desperately wanted to know what it was like inside, what kind of magical landscape carpeted its crumbling earth. Standing at its fenced-off edge I felt honoured to be able to peer into its secluded forests. I felt time stood still there. Africa had taken advantage of man-induced seclusion to totally undress herself. She was released from the white men who had bored into her heart to steal her serpentine blood; and the black men, who would hunt her wildlife and hoe her surface to grow sorghum and groundnuts. Her subterranean destruction and subsequent isolation was her liberation, which she showed with abandon – I felt happy about that. I could smell her luxuriant growth in the rainy season as I pressed my body against the fence. It was an olfactory potion of mosses and tree lichens; decaying leaf litter and tree orchids. Fly-pollinated flowers added to the mix with their putrid smell, which, along with the Mobola plum's cloying smell, added the right base note to this African perfumer's elixir.

More than want, I needed to enter her private domain. But I shouldn't, couldn't, and didn't. It was a hard decision to make, and it didn't happen overnight. It was normal for my sensuality to beat my logic into submission when adventure was on the cards. I came up with plans: creep in on my stomach to spread my weight over as big an area as possible; make an airborne reconnaissance by climbing through the trees – they would have secured their roots in firm ground, I told myself. I even scoured its perimeters to find game trails by which to enter; game intuitively know what is safe. Callously I even thought of bringing Kerry my dog along and sending him ahead of me each step of the way. For reasons of the Soul, all plans were aborted, and so the pain of forbiddance remained. So did the grandeur of my allurement, which wasn't a bad thing. The caved-in area kept my spirit of inquiry in fine fettle with its many unknowns.

The last suburb before the caved-in area, on the other side of town, was buffered by another no-go area, the mine dumps. People said every now and then, you could hear a dog scream in the night as it was taken. They said that domestic dogs were a delicacy for leopards from the caved-in area. 'And what about strange beasts?' I thought. 'How the hell could they say it was a leopard?' While I certainly believed there were leopards in 'my' caved-in area I felt it was morally wrong to blame such a fine beast with such a gutter-snipe crime. Deep down, however, I knew they could be right, and from then on I made it my duty to respect the leopard of the caved-in area. I knew that leopards could travel fair distances in search of food. When Kerry used to go outside at night for a piddle, I would stand guard against leopards at the back door, where my Makishi ceremonial dance mask stood guard for us both. My parents, and Wilson, who would be tending to his night fire at the bottom of our garden, never said anything untoward. Sometimes Wilson would watch us from the corner of his vegetable garden where he grew sweet potatoes. When Kerry had finished, and had kicked up enough dust to hide the evidence from leopards on the prowl, Wilson would call out, *'Ena lo mushe'* – well done! Other grown-ups might have thought I was silly; that's how ignorant they were of African *things*.

Leopards, *ingwe* in most Southern African languages, were the Gods of the African world. They stood spiritually taller than the Lion King, and looked down on ethnic chiefs and white colonial administrators. Their attendance had great aethereal importance in African bush affairs. Like Gods, their presence was rarely seen, but it was certainly felt. I had once seen a leopard, only fleetingly so, in a national park while on holiday in Southern Rhodesia. Most of my knowledge about leopards came from the old diviner who had seen a few. Going off his incredible stories of leopards, I decided to make it my humble duty to swear an allegiance to the leopard of the forbidden bush.

The leopard was like one of those elusive forms – those strange footprints that propelled me to follow my affinities and desires. He evoked an intangible force that weighed upon the behaviour of all creatures. His arrival sliced through the trivial monkey goings-on in the African bush. The leopard's presence created an impala ear-twitching silence that punctuated the African day with its taloned intent – a final warning against any further frivolity. Slow-flow turned instantly into short-lived pain, a quick death and spilt blood when an unfortunate animal submitted its fear of self-preservation to the Soul of the leopard. There is not an animal on the veld that is unaware of the leopard's ability to alter the psyche of the common herd.

The leopard of the caved-in-area crept into the recesses of my mind, where he took up permanent residence. The thought of his muscular symmetry and resolute action awed me. I wanted to be like him; not a shifty hyena child – at least not all of the time. It seemed to me that the leopard of my caved-in area dreams had reached the nirvana of all knowing perfection – he was my hero; a symbol of physical perfection and beauty. No other animal had the carnelian eyes, jet whiskers, pink rasp of tongue, alive pelt – nor the hypnotic flick of the tail as the leopard did – so the old diviner stated, and I fully believed him. This inner knowledge of my leopard and his concealed ways, hidden in his clandestine forest world, made me a happy boy in my musings.

For me, the leopard was one of those rare creatures that could access the latent energy of its Soul at will. It was an aethereal gift, an animal's equivalent of grace, which was given to tigers but not to lions. I needed that gift; it was the sharp tooth truth about everything that was. For me the leopard was the Zen of all truth – my truth.

Ardent game watchers may not extoll the beauty of a leopard's form or psyche adequately. That is because they are embarrassed to say that they have hardly ever seen one. If they had, it was a fleeting glance, or their view was obstructed by a camouflage of dappled light. Should an experienced hunter come face to face with a leopard, he will openly tell you he has seen God. A full on encounter with a leopard instantly robs the most ruthless of hunters of his identity. He becomes the morphed slave of the leopard's Soul. By the grace of the almighty God, unlike the lion, it is not the leopard's penchant to be a man-eater. The leopard imprisons the hunter's being in his psyche for a split second only – long enough to command an undying respect from his victim's Soul. He does not need human flesh to satisfy his needs. In my child's mind this explained why leopards were everywhere in Africa. If they were man-eaters, they would have been, like the lion, mostly shot out – a clever trick I thought to myself.

It was very likely that the leopard from the caved-in area had visited my vlei. I would never have seen him, or his footprints, but that didn't mean a thing. The old diviner told me that leopards can frequent a vlei or a bush clearing without leaving a pug mark, not even throwing their shadow on the ground. They are of a spirit order higher than the Makishi, infinitely higher than the hyena. That's why I never saw a Makishi costume or mask portraying the leopard.

Unseen, the leopard of the caved-in area had walked ahead of all the goings-on in my vlei and the surrounding miombo woodlands. He was too cunning to put his cards on the table – should he deal a winning card, he did so in apparent absentia – not a spoor was to be found. I could only join the dots to describe his stealthful ways. In degrees of 'felt nothingness' he cloaked the bush with his omnipresent awareness.

The leopard was the custodian of all bush knowledge. The old diviner also told me that the same informational network of all things, that took a million termites to amass, was computed just as efficiently by one leopard. I was sad that I would never meet him: But I wholly respected his penchant to be invisible. Leopards and Souls might be annoyingly illusive, but they make up for it in their ability to be everywhere at once.

The leopard is the noble savage. Leopards are not underhand like the hyena, simply cunning; sophisticatedly cunning in keeping their secret worlds to themselves. Lions have no secrets: anger, greed, boredom and domination are all rolled into one overlording persona that they wear as their royal insignia. It was misguided to call the lion 'King of the Jungle'. On an African vlei you will see lions walk in pompous processionals past impala that seem to show neither reverence nor fear of their so-called king. These goats of the savannah don't take lions too seriously. Although every now and then one of them would pay dearly for their stupid but perceptive assumption. When a half hungry, half bored lion is too lazy to go the whole hog of a zebra or a buffalo, an impala will do nicely. On the contrary, impala are the litmus proof that a leopard is in the area. Their noses and ears twitch, their tails flick nervously and their glance sharpens. They tread their hooves in agitated unison and group together in a soft snorting chorus of approaching doom. They know that one of their herd will soon succumb to the leopard's magnificence. All ungulates have a fearful respect for the leopard.

Never could you tell what a leopard was feeling or thinking; that's why hunters were so wary of them. Like cowards, hunters didn't track them down. They laid bait and shot the awesome beast from a well-secured hide. Of all the African beasts, I would have liked to share a Soul conversation with a leopard. It made me very happy to think that a human no-go area was the kingdom of the leopard world. It seemed completely logical in my child's mind that a beast of such vitality should live in such a verdantly rich forest to the exclusion of man. It occurred to me that, because no one would ever enter the leopard's kingdom, it would last into eternity.

In my musings of my leopard and the caved-in area, I came to the conclusion that the leopard was the Soul reason for the fertile 'Now' existence of this miraculous piece of untouched African bush. Without the feline piercings of his all-encompassing eye, it would not exist. His singular observer status gave it its utopian Soul. Without my feline sparring partner and mentor for my own Soul, I would probably be the same. I would collapse into obscurity. So important was the leopard to me. Without leopards and white ants the Soul of Africa would die, and so would I.

It was for a Soul-driven reason that I chose never to enter the caved-in area of the leopard. The risk of changing my perception of my leopard's Soul perfection was too great for my own Soul to bear. As the fleshed epicentre of this marvellous piece of bush, it was the leopard who had conquered my insatiable curiosity. As an extension of his Soul, I no longer needed to penetrate the bush to know it. One day his Soul would tell me everything I needed to know.

The caved-in kingdom of the leopard was a perfect spiritual world. It was not crafted or embellished; it was not honed with the fine grit of reason, nor was it safe – it just was. It was real in its honeycombed danger of disused mine shafts; it was surreal in its beckoning unknown-ness. The unknown carries far more aethereal value for the human psyche than the known. Its allure is an icon of supreme mystical power. The unknown is a secret leopard that pulls on all our needs and desires to demand our attention. I felt his pad upon my body. I felt his hot, panting breath against my Soul – he was an overpowering affinity that penetrated my sensitivities. He called to me with an urgency of oneness. I did not idolise him. I did not need his closeness, although I felt I had it – I respected his distance. He was the emissary of someone far greater, of whose identity, I was not yet sure.

Who is watching the three musketeers?

My psyche, that which dominates my thinking, is the cognitive part of me, and together with my body, we have befriended my Soul. As a congenial musketeering threesome, in telling this story, we have been trying to tell the rounded truth about us. We have included some spiritual snippets to underscore certain nuances of meaning, and as such, my story comes across as a quest to find my Soul's purpose – but my Soul shows no superiority above the rest of us. Our story is one that has appealed to all three of us. We feel it is a story with some exciting, some sensual – my body's contribution; some amusing – my mind's contribution; and some supernatural moments – my spirit's contribution: and there are some mind-bending enigmas thrown in for literary effect – for which none of us want to claim responsibility. Our *surround time* story continues to cause a pleasant pain, a flutter and a sensual throb of the unknown in our figurative heart. Egotistically, my mind wishes it were a story unique to us, but it isn't – the props might be, but the storyline belongs to the Universe. It is your story too.

If it is our common one story, what might pull you in deeper, the reader-sharer of my story, is that even as a small boy, I knew that there was an observer watching me. Perhaps watching through me, maybe even using my eyes. Whether he was a part of me, or I was a part of him, I was never quite sure. All that I do know, is that he was not my conscience, for he definitely did not flick dollops of guilt upon me. His presence was a state of non-judgemental and unconditional permanence within me.

As a small white boy growing up in a 1950s and 60s African mining town, I possessed all the knowledge to write this book. All that was required was that I served an apprenticeship to know my Soul better. Was my observer, the silversmith of my Soul - teaching me to polish my Soul in order to see his reflection better? Was he the icon of spiritual truth that I had been searching for? Perhaps I am writing this book on his behalf.

When I finally get to know my Soul better, I am going to ask it to introduce me to my silent observer. It would seem the right thing to do, given the societally-forced estrangement that has up to now, kept us apart for so long.

The Zanzibari boy

On my insistence, my parents took me on a seaside holiday to East Africa. I had been reading a small tourist book that had been lent to me. It was about Fort Jesus, Portuguese explorers, slaves and Arab traders on the East African Coast. After a visit to the Fort in Mombasa and old mosques, and a beach holiday in Malindi on the Kenyan coast, we caught an East African Airways flight to Zanzibar. My father enjoyed the flight because they served lots of ice-cold Tusker beer. My mother didn't;

the steep incline of the passenger aisle of the small aircraft, a Dakota DC3, as it squatted on the runway in Mombasa, with its bum-tail on the ground, unnerved her. The flight along the East African coast down to Zanzibar was very bumpy; the pilot seemed to be looking for air pockets. I liked it because the air hostesses, one white, and one Indian, were beautiful and friendly; the Indian lady wore a sari. In Zanzibar, an island off the coast of Tanganyika, we visited coconut plantations, a coir factory, and spice traders. We sniffed anaesthesia-inducing clove flowers, and I stuck my finger into a cocoa pod that I found on the side of the road. It didn't taste or smell like chocolate at all. Travelling around in a rickshaw, we visited small Arab shops in alleyways too narrow for cars. The local tour guide explained Zanzibar's historical connection to the Sultanate of Oman. He told us that many ancient treasures were still to be found in these Zanzibari Arab shops – at bargain prices. He said that the shops were mostly owned by Omani traders who still travelled up and down the coast between the Arabian Peninsula and islands like Zanzibar, Lamu and Pemba. They travelled on small wooden ships called dhows, taking advantage of the trade winds. My father said that our 'smarmy and over talkative' guide would be paid by the shop owners if we bought something from them. That was the reason for him being so helpful with the historical background that I found fascinating. Grown-ups could be so insensitive to the reality of *things* sometimes.

One of the shops specialised in metalware. There were copper coffee urns and charcoal burners; brass trays and engraved goblets; scimitars, swords and daggers. The floor was covered with oriental rugs, and we were invited to sit on coir futons covered with geometric patterned kilems on which we were offered small glasses of lemon grass tea. I was enraptured by it all, and in a strangely familiar way, I felt I had been there before. I wished Mr Kumar, the Indian tailor, had been with us to share the experience. There was an aroma in the shop, but it was not common agarabatti; it had a turpine menthol-sweet resin smell. Mr Kumar told me later that it was probably balsam benzoin from Sumatra. There was a small boy sitting in the middle of the room with an embroidered white skullcap. I felt I should know him; he seemed familiar. He sat quietly in a cross-legged position with his bare feet sticking out from under his djebella. He never even gave us a glance. He was totally engrossed in polishing a large copper plate with a thick fluffy cloth. In spite of his reserved demeanour, his face looked happy; busy-happy without a smile, his small body working without any effort.

The owner of the shop was an old man with a straggly betel-nut-stained beard that grew out of his jowls like Msasa bark lichen. This wily old Arab trader, with a calculated turn of a hand in a gesture of 'salaam', set about wooing my already beguiled mother into his bear-trap of finely polished oriental wares. My father, who was already wise to the ways of the East, and who had the infinite patience of Job, sat quietly taking it all in. My mother and I were fascinated by it all, including the old man's Arab gift of the gab as he offered us his wares. I could visualise the Arabian world where all these treasures came from. However, the more my father rejected his gracious offer of ancient treasures at giveaway prices, the more his initially perfect English seemed to deteriorate. It was to a point that he seemed not to understand us at all, and became visibly frustrated. How strange, I thought, and turned to my father, who gave me a knowing wink. Three times my father explained that we had arrived on the island of Zanzibar in a small Dakota DC3 aircraft with little room for luggage. There was absolutely no room for a copper coffee urn three quarters my height, and more than half my weight. Each time he gave a desolate shake of his head; then out of nowhere, his demeanour changed. 'Aah, now I understand,' he pronounced – his command of the English language had returned. He leant forward, looked around, and in a hushed voice, throwing mistrusting glances at no one in particular, he spoke: 'You my friends, you are honourable white people. Where do you come from?' Northern Rhodesia, I piped up.

'Ah, I have a brother in Ndola,' he said. My father told me afterwards that oriental shop owners had a claim to family relations in whatever town or place you came from in the world: Bulawayo, Bangkok or Dublin. At the time my mind was racing. Maybe his brother had told him about Mr Kumar, the finest Indian tailor in Luanshya – the only tailor, but he was fine in other ways too. His storyline, as he furtively looked towards the vacant doorway, went like this. 'My friends I can trust you, my white friends.' Oh no you can't, I thought. Not that drunken Glaswegian you can't.

'Listen my good friends, we all know the revolution is coming. Things will be bad, there will be bloodshed, much bloodshed, and we will have to flee our businesses, shops and homes. I cannot take all the valuable items in this shop with me on a dhow to the mainland. Even if I did, the government will still take everything off us anyway.' I was startled by these ugly words and gestures that were thrown at me on a tropical island holiday full of coconuts, spices and sandy beaches. It was so spiritually far from the steamy dark forests of the Congo, and yet it was the same African story of spilt blood and fear.

With a sharp twist of the neck, and an upwards flick of his chin, the trader beckoned to an older boy who I hadn't noticed.

He had been watching us from behind a heavy curtain in the darkness of the back of the shop. The young man brought out a finely carved wooden kist and placed it in front of the old man, who was now kneeling in front of us. With another silent flick of his head he instructed the boy to close the heavy door to his shop. A perfume escaped from the kist and cut into the muggy air that weighed upon us. I had never smelt such a strange aroma. I knew quite a lot about Eastern aromas because of my many visits to Mr Kumar's tailor's shop. I had put every type of agarabatti that Mr Kumar had to my nose: musk, patchouli, sandalwood, amber and more. I could recognise some traces of these scents, but there was a dry undernote, a turpentine sharpness of pepper and cedar wood. Later Mr Kumar told me it was probably frankincense. It cut through my reserve and went straight to my psyche. It prickled my awareness and I felt an urge to move forward to get a better sniff. I eagerly leant over and put my nose against the closed lid. For a moment the trader gave a stern and unapproving look at this odd infidel child who was wiping his snotty little nose on his kist. Then he remembered his purpose as a trader of oriental fineries, and he gave my parents an ingratiating smile and a servile bow of his hawkish head. He used my odd behaviour to his best retail advantage.

My parents had no time to admonish me because he quickly thrust open the kist and in a flash, cast a crystal necklace into my mother's hands. While the virtues of genuine crystal were being bestowed, and with my psyche inveigled by an Arabian aroma, I looked at the small boy in the middle of the room. He remained poised in total serenity as he polished away at a silver samovar that housed a rich collage of metal wares and kilems in its reflections. He never looked up, and seemed unblemished by tourist banter and the talk of a revolution.

The strange aroma that escaped from the kist affected my mind. Questions were thumped out with every beat on my temple. My curiosity was demanding the truth about this enigmatic boy. Did this boy have any toys? Did he ever play outside with his friends? Could he even hear or speak? Why wasn't he at school? Did he ever do anything naughty? He seemed to have little of what a boy of our age should have. Why not? What was it that made him so interestingly different from me? I later told my father that I was sure that he was a slave, for he seemed not to be a normal curious boy – his situation was peculiar. Yet, at the same time I felt a strong resonance with him. Something about him found a place under my emotional skin, where it danced to my pulse. My father said he was probably the shop owner's grandson. He said in Muslim culture, grown-ups were strict with the young, and that his only education would be to learn his grandfather's trade, the Koran, and to attend prayers in the mosque.

This bodily image of a boy troubled me, but not in an unpleasant way. It was almost as if his intangible presence transcended into a longing for something lost, but for a brief moment, found. Up till then, my desires had always called upon my sensuality to heed their urgent calls. This time in that attar-infused room, I was called upon to take a salaam of withdrawal from my sated senses, leaving my Soul bare for his imprint. I did not want to talk with this Zanzibari boy – I simply wanted to parley with his Soul.

'My friends, take. Take something – take anything – they are all precious. Chose something special – I beg of you. You pay me in Northern Rhodesia – you pay my brother in Ndola. I don't want the money now; the regime will rob me of it. You take now, you pay later.' I noticed his English was deteriorating again. Once again he repeated himself, 'They will rob me,' as he flicked a glance towards the closed door. 'I trust you white people, please take,' he implored as he shoved the kist with its hypnotic aroma further forward. It held a glittering filigree of jewellery; bangles, earrings, necklaces and pendants. My father now seemed interested to a point where he wanted to buy something and I was being drawn into the bartering between him and the wizened old Arab. I thought I saw a slight smirk of a smile crack above the Omani's beard. His skills were rewarded: My father's eyes were drawn to antiquity and possibly memories of Burmese ruby dealers; my mother attracted to pretty things, pieces that she said would go nicely with her gabardine suit. All the while, I kept one eye on the small boy.

We left the shop after more than one cup of lemon grass tea, small cups of coffee, more extolling on the old Arab's part, and curious confusion on mine. The Soul of this boy had reached out to me from the centre of the room. It said it wanted to tattoo my being from the inside out with its purpose. Isn't that what I had desperately wanted from the night robber on that dark and rainy night? I had wanted recognition, more than close proximity. I wanted spiritual acceptance, and the unapproachable boy seemed willing to assist.

My parents were in possession of a small sandalwood trinket box inlaid with ivory and ebony, and a fine crystal necklace; both of which my father paid for there and then. He said he didn't want anyone breathing down his neck about money back home – I think the bank manager did enough of that. I had something oddly precious, and I was rubbing it: tracing

its aethereal edges under my skin with my spirit of inquiry –
deciding what it was and what I should do with it.

What had seemed to be convoluted tradesmen's banter;
turned out to be the horrible truth. There was a bloody revolution and many Arabs and Asians in Zanzibar lost everything
they had, including their lives.

In later ruminations on my anthill, I realised that this
young Zanzibari's divine state of accomplished being was that
of my leopard too. Both made no effort to see things in a better light – they were the light. They were their own touchstone
of perfection. I was an earth traveller, a Soul seeker on a quest
to find my own. Without my searching, their reflection of the
divine would never have been seen. Without their presence, I
would never become a see-er.

> *All he had to do was express his deepest intentions,*
> *his Soul purpose, and the world would unfurl at his*
> *clawed feet: luscious green was all around him and*
> *in him, he was abundance, the rich bluey green of*
> *the Universe through and through.*

My Soul is not mine

The boldest step I had to take in putting this book together was
to totally accept my inkling that my Soul was not a possession
of mine.

It is difficult to place a finger on my Soul; and it would seem
that I have no jurisdiction over it to do so. My Soul has to be the
better part of me; it is far more than I will ever be, either cognitively or physically. If ownership had to be attributed to either
one of us, I would say the rest of me belongs to my Soul. If I were
to describe this lofty proprietor of my being, I would say that

it is the permanence and consistency that gives my day-to-day existence its relevance; but that the force it exerts, is difficult to describe; its actions equally challenging to define.

By default, the raw flesh, actions and thoughts of an English child in colonial Africa belonged to my Soul. It was my Soul that held the key to the door of my destiny, not my circumstances. The events of my childhood do not delineate who I am. They are mere chaff in the wind compared to this inner presence that continues to redefine the physical thinking me.

My Soul is like a miraculous lover that far exceeds my worthiness, who deserves far more than my utmost devotion. As a small boy, it pierced my love-aching heart with the barbs of possible desertion. I desperately did everything that I thought would satisfy its desires, but felt that it was never enough.

Refractions of inner light – my Soul

My Soul is the essence of life that pre-empts my first breath prior to breathing.
It stimulates my nerves and muscles prior to movement.
It feeds my cognition prior to thinking,
It leads my personality away from my ego.
It defines my willpower before doing, and my love before loving.
My Soul is the summative proof of all my personal attributes.
How much more will I know about it when we are finally introduced.

6

I SEE...
NOW THAT THERE IS A
CLEARING IN THE CLOUDS

INDIGO RAIN

INDIGO RAIN

So Hum – all-seeing rain

Without knowing it, So Hum had climbed higher. It was there, among the aerial branches, that the Indigo dream rain fell. It was so exquisite that, in spite of So Hum's blackened world, it demanded further sight. So Hum sensed it fall in penduline drops of the royal blues of lapis lazuli and Congolese azurite.

This marvellous rain did not only heighten the potential for real sight to his wayward eyes, but to a third eye, which started to grow above and between them. His third eye never broke the surface of his scaly skin. It didn't have to; it simply claimed ownership over his aethereal sight, that which had forever shown him his dream rains. It left the mundane job of 'real' sight to his ugly gyrating physical eyes – should they ever be given the chance to part the curtains in the darkness of his inner world.

If So Hum could have seen, his real eyes would have provided him with the baseline of physical reality; whereas his third eye took on a more sophisticated role – it hinted at the underlying truth behind all things. Intuitively he started to tie up the loose ends of his long life. Slowly he was able to wrap it up into a small bundle without a beginning or an *end. Without any importance being given to the past or the future, his destiny was rounded off – he realised that from the start, it had been synchronised from within. What he was seeking was actually seeking him. This revelation sent his sightless reptilian eyes reeling with upbeat confusion. He had moved into his sixth sense, and he felt dizzy.*

His third eye also disclosed something of great spiritual worth. All the serendipitous happenings, of coloured rains, warm feelings, and auspicious messages, even his darkness, were all part and parcel of his synchrodestiny – the fulfilment of his Soul purpose. The whole of the Universe was conspiring in one momentous altruistic move to bring him peace of mind. Peace of mind was his truth.

It was then that he realised that his peace was part of the something bigger's peace. His happiness, wherever it was, was the something bigger's happiness too.

Ah Hum's roots – I see

The Ancients of Old, who knew Ah Hum all too well, interpreted his seeking character. Through the elements of the natural world, they saw everything about him in talismans and omens, which they laid before him as serendipitous timings and predilections. They mouthed that the truth might lie in his odd ways. His Soul, who was eavesdropping, nodded approvingly; it already knew the answers to the signs. It had seen his world beyond time. As if in agreement with his Soul: 'Aah Huum' he whispered – 'I see'.

Inner magic on a material plane

As an apprentice to his Soul, Ah Hum was gaining in spiritual confidence; he was now beginning to see below the surface of his material world. He sought further confirmation of his aethereal state of being through:

> Lapis lazuli and cypress oil: *to rid the mind of the psychic blockages that hindered self-awareness, and to bring him to a higher level of conscious being.*
> Azurite and clary sage: *to enable him to intuitively see better.*

ALLAN TAYLOR

What I was seeking was also seeking me

> Elephant paths
> Water on the vlei
> Makishi
> Truth on the vlei

Elephant paths

Once on a small holiday with my parents we stayed in a small rundown hotel on the edge of a game reserve. It had a bar propped up by middle-aged locals wizened by skin cancer and hardships of the area: malaria, failed hunting trips, unrewarding prospecting and the underfunded logging of teak forests.

My father was not prone to hurrying past places of social interest – bars – and so we usually stayed a good few days in small hotels, which always suited me. My mother didn't seem to have much say in these matters. I was ever curious about the folk that frequented those 'bed and bar for the night' country hotels. The front of this particular hotel had a long veranda where one could sit in reclining Morris chairs and have a mid-morning beer, or for the ladies, a late afternoon tea. Sun bleached elephant, hippo and crocodile skulls placed on the floor and against the walls, were a relieving adornment to the red polished floors. As were a stark kudu skull and horns and the boss of a buffalo hanging from the walls, both painted into gloss enamelled obscurity. In the dining room there were fly-stained plywood flaps hanging on hinges from the water-marked ceiling. A thin rope that connected each one of them disappeared through a rough hole in the wall. On hot evenings, 'a young black lad' as the old white barman called him, was employed to slowly pull and then release the rope, which caused the flaps to sway in unison, fanning the diners with a squeaky breath of fly-soiled air. I always had time to kill in small hotels at meal tables bedecked in white damask cloths and served on by lethargic waiters. My eyes would inevitably float up to dining room ceilings and in this hotel's case; beyond the swaying flaps – oh so that's where all the flies went to at night. On the first evening, before dinner, as I was sitting in the hot dining room that smelt of roast beef, the old barman, who had an RAF handlebar moustache, mistook my distrustful interest in flies. 'It's an old British Raj invention called a *punkha*,' he said, as if he was immensely proud of something more than the just the punkha. 'And the young lad is called a *punkha wallah*.' He could see that I didn't have a clue as to what he was talking about. I moved a step away from him and looked away. I had been told to be wary of barmen because they could read people's minds; who wouldn't learn that aethereal trick in a stuffy hops and cigarette smoked room full of men becoming verbally incoherent. 'From British India you know old chap,' he proclaimed in a pompous manner. I thought it odd that he called me 'old chap', and odd that he was in Africa being proud of India. 'When I was in the RAF in Indiaah…' he continued, but I was now further away, and no longer listening. The diner gong had sounded, and the punkha had started to sway. Some of the many flies made their way to the kitchen where the air was still, and deliciously hot with gravy smells.

The next morning, an old crocodile hunter, who drank beer ever so slowly on the veranda for the better part of the day, and who never got drunk as far as I could see, took a shine to me.

Maybe this was because he saw that I was content at being a loner, and he, as hunters often are, an arch-loner himself, was drawn to share a few moments of his past bush silences with me. I was dawdling along on the dusty road kicking up stones on my way back from an old teak sawmill when he called me over for a chat. He never stopped talking, and I never stopped listening. Our chat naturally revolved around a hunter's life in the African bush. He told me many truly amazing stories. He told me that elephants have an inherited subconscious that left hunters in 'plain stupid awe', a way of knowing things from the past. Captivated, I tried to balance my bum on the slatted edge of an uncomfortable cowhide strung teak Morris chair that had no cushions. The hunter had put them on the floor for his dog, a grizzled Jack Russell terrier with fly-ravaged ears.

He talked between warm beers and slivers of his self-prepared Kudu biltong, which he shared with me and his mutt of a dog. My father knew my ways by now, and when I asked him to buy the old hunter a beer or two, he did, no questions asked, and the old hunter accepted – no questions asked. I remember it being hot in the shade of that veranda that reeked of paraffin, but I was in heaven listening to him.

With a few mused additions over the years of my growing up, this is what he might have told me: Elephant paths, never to be forgotten by the herd, cross the African landscape as if they remain outside the realms of time. Elephants have innate knowledge of these centuries old paths, which is an ongoing mystery that many an experienced hunter has never been able to fathom out. Human habitations and structures, unwittingly built on ancient elephant paths in the bush, would suffer the wrath of elephants. In spiritual cognisance of their inherited routes, they would walk through them, mock charge them, and even trash them if they could. Matters of the spirit could not be altered, burnt, crushed or wet – they were simply timeless and indestructible, the old hunter might have implied. Elephant paths that pre-dated the building of Lake Kariba were still a permanent spiritual residue in the psyche of all elephants of the herd. A strong affinity would draw them to a place on the water's edge. Whereupon they would enter the deep waters to swim the same elephant paths, now sitting many feet below the surface on the lake floor.

The old hunter left the hotel the day before we did. After he had gone, musing alone, with a flat coke and floating peanuts, I knew his story, from what I could grasp of it then, held a lot of truth. My own experiences on the Luanshya vlei, which had to do with water and timeless memories, confirmed everything that he had said. My mind tended to gravitate towards the mysterious as being the factual – with the factual being relegated to the questionable. Stories like the old hunter's and odd preconceptions like mine, seemed to dovetail into one: They vindicated my urgency to learn more about *things*.

Water on the vlei

I could substantiate the spiritual permanence of elephant paths that were seemingly engraved into the psyche of elephants. I saw the same thing happen with rainwater on the vlei at Christmas time.

The Luanshya River was never a trickle. She was always aware of its weighty importance in the scheme of all things, even though the dry season did tame her spirit. She provided needed water for the birds and animals, and housed fish, leguaans and terrapins within the safety of her meanders. The Luanshya River was very proud of her permanence, a little bit too much;

verging on arrogance, I felt. She encouraged prickly reeds to keep me away from her inviting waters. She bred bilharzia and blood sucking leeches to broadside my attempts to ford her lazy shallows. She belched from her still muds wherever I thought the fishing was best: and worst of all – every year, she forged a war of attrition with the surrounding bush. Stretching all the way up to the miombo tree line the soil was leached by her insatiable desire for water. Month by month I watched plants succumb to her riverine thirst as their leaves dried out to join the tinder pile for the next October fires. The Luanshya River claimed that all the remaining waters of the vlei were hers to suck upon: and in a conceited way, she exaggerated her watery curves and bends. That's when she would inform everyone that the powerful Kafue River was waiting for her many vleis and forests further on. She didn't have time to sit around enjoying the sun and fishing with us as she busily flowed past. Hurried time, her time, home time, my bath time, Mrs. Versaakie's test time, everyone's idea of their urgent linear time got in the way of my life. Even on the vlei I was under the vassalage of time; time didn't seem to be mine to own and do with as I pleased – I really did not need time; it was far too complicated.

The Christmas holidays were humid and wet – it was the rainy season. The ITCZ, the International Tropical Convergence Zone, which normally put its large and pendulous bum over the Congo basin, had already moved southwards to drop its rain on the dry miombo forests of Southern Congo and Northern Rhodesia. These rains changed my world. Every living plant was affected by jungle fever and grew and grew. Overnight things appeared on the vlei as if by magic; well it was magic. It was the festive season and the bush had joined in.

It was also the time when the African bush got its own back on Miss Fancy River. She hadn't seemed to have changed much as a result of her rendezvous with Mr Big Kafue, who was probably too preoccupied with his promised *tête-à-tête* with the grand lady of Africa, the great Zambezi. As the rains set in, so water appeared, and not only between the selfish banks of the Luanshya River. Nor did it just fall out of a bruised sky. It bubbled straight out of the ground: from under logs and out of gullies; it seeped out of the edge of the miombo forests; it even formed small pools on bush paths. New swells trickled out of nowhere to form their own small river courses – which in a shockingly quirky manner, flowed away from Miss Luanshya River. Water was no longer her prized possession; water was everywhere; and it was as if this virgin water knew exactly where it wanted to go – in a lucid show of awareness, like the elephants, it had been there before and knew which way to go. As if it was following a timeless path of prior knowledge, it formed mini river courses that were completely invisible in the dry season.

The vlei and the woodlands now had an abundance of water, and in a show of unconditional largess, without even thinking further, gave Miss River some of their precious water. Not all of it, as she expected. She was visibly peeved by the disrespect she was being shown by all on the vlei, and in the deep Msasa forests. Her idling eddies turned to scum-sucking whirlpools. She hurried her huffy waters and shook her quivering reeds in anger, but nobody cared; except for perhaps, her pink bellied bream – their mud nests were being swept away in her torrents.

I would get so excited about finding new pools of water and mini watercourses that led away from a river that had lost control of its resources. In no time at all, there were frogs and water beetles occupying these fledgling waters. I even saw small catfish and minnows in deeper ones that had formed far from the banks of the Luanshya River. It was as if the fallen Congolese rain was reliving a memory of long past waterways; and an aquatic life, that miraculously found itself there, was a partaker of the same reincarnate memory. These self-declared waters and their living fauna were spiritual eddies that had manifested themselves as being free from the gravitational flow of reality. They were certainly not a product of the Luanshya river goings-on. In the grand scheme of things, they more than likely preceded her, and were as such, the *raison d'être* for her existence. The thought of such temporal tiny and wayward puddles and trickles giving birth to a sizeable and permanent river with large catfish, bream, leguaans and leeches, appealed to my sense of free spirit. A riverine world sedimented out of aethereal nothingness brought a knowing smirk to my Soul.

Even Mr Harrison would have said, 'Well Sonny, it's all a consequence of gravity. The rainwater is following the shortest route to the lowest point, which will eventually be the Luanshya River. You will learn how to calculate its gravitational force in High School.'

'Well Mr Harrison,' I would be tempted to say, 'I have often seen water run the other way. It is not falling out of the sky; it comes from somewhere else, and I don't believe the bush gives all her water to the greedy river.'

And he would retort, 'I don't think so Sonny, it might look like it, but it isn't true. Run-off rain water can be very deceiving. Gravity is what it is.'

'But I have seen little rivers with fish and frogs arrive overnight,' I would've blurted out.

'Did you do know that barbel can bury themselves in co-
coons of dry mud for a year or longer; that minnows can leave
their eggs in the drying mud to hatch when conditions are
right?' would've been his repartee. All gems of biological information that normally would have enchanted me; but when
used as an argument against my heartfelt take on *things*, were
like water off a cormorant's back.

What I might have wanted to say – but due to my immature
state of spiritual logic would have only felt at the time – was that
there were aethereal frogs and fish out there waiting timelessly
in the aether for their quantum world to coalesce into reality.
A reality born out of a spiritual eternity that incorporated the
past, the present and the future, as well as the normal, and the
paranormal. Adult reasoning was skew: my grown-ups could
happily accept a quantum leap from fluid ectoplasm into the
meat of creation inside an egg or a uterus, but not outside on
the ground, or in open air. They need the closed doors of eggs
shells and female bellies to cover up for their absolute spiritual ignorance of magic and miracles. My river-alien tadpoles,
minnows and catfish had the intended existence of fledgling
waterways engraved on their incubating psyches. They were in
eager abeyance for exactly the right number of raindrops to
fall, to become a precipitate of nature themselves. They were
waiting for the right moment of habitat; a bush path, or a piece
of open vlei, known to them since the beginning of time, to
tumble into their material form. Every single drop of equatorial
rain had the same knowingness – a potential to be a rivulet,
which in turn, had the innate knowledge to eventually become
a raging African river – or to remain as a mini catfish-inhabited
puddle in the middle of nowhere. I tried many times to be present for the moment when wholesome pond life would fall out

of nothingness, but without success. I would tramp home wet, cold and with a downcast spiritual eye that had seen not a single miracle. Yet with the heartening knowledge that, in the next day or so, a living rivulet would have appeared out of nowhere. I could only surmise that it happened in the black nothingness of the night.

Mr Harrison and I were both right – it was just that I was looking at spiritual gravity, and he was looking at material gravity. That the one was inside the other all depended on where you were looking at things from at the time – from the outside in or the inside out.

Elephants, frogs, catfish, minnows, and even raindrops, all have a thumbnail sketch of their collective subconscious that tells them everything about their material and spiritual beings outside of time. What makes them different from us is that they are closer to their spiritual source; fickle emotions don't obstruct them from their purpose. They have easier access to their spiritual knowledge than humans do. Even a tadpole is closer to its spiritual core than those grown-ups on my prig list. Their eternal life spans are timeless collections of miracles to be punctuated by material births, deaths and rebirths, with vast planes of spiritual non-stuff in-between. Everything they do is a spontaneous re-enactment of being able to follow centuries old elephant paths, or sitting in mysterious pools of water. They are creatures with habits devoid of concrete provenance, but full of prior knowledge. Every wild creature has this quirk, something that we struggle to intellectually understand. At best, we call it instinct, and at worse we call it a mystery. Mystery being a word we sometimes use when we are in denial of miracles.

The intrinsic thought pattern of every bygone elephant that has walked a path is an electrochemical formula in the elephant's nervous system. In time it becomes an inherited particle of intelligence within the instinctual wisdom of the common herd, an aethereal message that ensures the beasts' future permanence. The directions are not there hanging around on an old elephant path for toe-stubbing discovery for the herd: They are within an informational thinking universe for an 'in the Now' elephant psyche to pick up.

The elephant drops a thoughtful intention into a pool of information that makes up his herd's collective subconscious. I want to get to water. It is an open-ended statement of intention that evokes the need for a solution – and a resolution is set. Answers become easier when the informational energy pattern is repeatedly accessed and reinforced by the herd over time. In such a way, the elephant is guaranteed a spontaneous answer from the annals of the common herd's psyche – it does not arrive in a sequential linear manner. Outside of time and space, its energy simply falls into entrained resonance within the collective mind of the all-time elephant herd. The answer appears as an archetypal pull on the beast's mind – not unlike an affinity. Without further ado, the elephant and his herd are on an ancient path to water, acacia forests, reed beds or whatever was on his timeless mind to begin with.

This all-knowingness is a miracle from within the non-space of the elephant, which we naively see as a mystery on a material plane.

Makishi

This man was different to all of the Africans that I knew. Besides drawing Europeans to Africa, the Copperbelt was also a melting pot of Southern and Central African races and tribes – all migrants who had sought menial work since the subterranean vaults of precious minerals had been opened in the twenties. He had none of the large-boned purple arrogance and flair of the Congolese; none of the open-armed bonhomie, albeit sometimes false, of the Shona; none of the high cheek bones and coffee skin of the Zulu, nor the rounded, sullen simplicity of the Bemba. Certainly not a grain of the Nyanja subservience.

I was sitting on the step to our front veranda when he came up the driveway to our house. I watched him come into our road and turn right into our garden, the first house in P Avenue, short for poinsettia. The man was fairly new to the town and pushed a delivery bicycle too overladen to ride. He was a vegetable seller: gem squash, beans, tomatoes, pumpkins and cabbage – anything more exotic was grown by the white *medems* in their gardens. 'Grown' being a euphemism for getting the gardener to do it for you. He started calling. His voice was a perverse falsetto shriek; a mockingbird call that cut the air to shreds. 'Vehhja taahbles,' he screeched, wringing his bicycle bell non-stop.

He had a closed dark face that forcefully kept his scorpion eyes within the tight crevices of his skull. His wiry frame accentuated his intense demeanour, and he moved in snaps of quick motion. His intonation was totally discordant to both European and Southern African ears. I found out later that when he first started his rounds, many white women didn't like to buy from him because of his churlish, almost repellent manner. They were also, however, too frightened not to buy from him: such was the intensity of his presence at their back doors. The domestic staff of P Avenue disliked him. I felt they were frightened of him. They saw through his schorl exterior quicker than we Europeans could – he was of another world, a world of witchcraft, and they were wary of him for that.

He came to our back door, which was enclosed by a porch where I hung my proud possession, a Makishi mask from the Victoria Falls Craft & Tribal Dance Village. It was a magnificent representation of a royal ancestral spirit. Partially hidden by creepers, it was a metre in height and half a metre wide. The man leaned his bicycle against the bare brick wall of our house and stepped onto the porch with his back to the mask. He was wearing elastic bands around his ankles to keep his trouser legs away from the bicycle chain. I also noticed his feet didn't like touching the ground. They were like fidgeting hands as he approached Wilson to announce that the *medem* definitely needed good vegetables. For some uncanny reason he swung round sharply, took in the mask, and broke off his sentence. His feet stopped moving and it seemed a while before his eyes cornered poor Long One. He rattled off a harsh inquiry in Chilapalapa, as to what was the meaning of this mask at a *muzungu* house. It was as if he hadn't even seen me. Long One, with an expressionless face said, '*Piccanin muzungu,*' and then allowed an enormous grin to escape from his oily countenance. I hated being called a *piccanin,* Chilapalapa for a child; *muzungu* meaning white. The strange vegetable seller spoke back with a high pitched volley: '*Ena lo naya,*' not good, he said, and left without offering to sell us a packet of gem squash, or acknowledge my presence.

He didn't come back for a long time, even though he often went up and down our avenue. I used to see him talking to Long One, who told me that he sometimes asked if I had taken the mask down. Long One would say, '*Aikona,*' an emphatic No. One day he forcefully beckoned Long One into the road whereupon he spat out his feelings. '*Lo piccanin eno lo skelem.*' He said I was up to no good. '*Eno lo skelem,*' Long One said about him on his return to our house. *Skelem* meant devil or danger – he was the one who was up to no good.

This strange man had the best vegetables that the white *medems* had ever seen or tasted. In spite of many purchases in a day, his bicycle delivery tray was always full. I heard from Long One that the rather sloth Nyanja vegetable sellers despised him.

Our dinner table was losing out, so in the end, Long One had to go into the street to buy veggies for my mother. Wilson, the house domestic, should have been in charge of this task – after all it was his job to peel vegetables – but he flatly refused to talk to this charlatan. How dare he call the *piccanin bwana* a devil! Whereas, like me, Long One rather enjoyed the intrigue.

The quality of his vegetables was not to be questioned. Where did he get his vegetables from? He didn't have time to grow them himself did he? All the white ladies asked each other over morning teas. He had become a bit of a conversation piece. One supercilious English woman got so carried away with her own self-importance that she told him that she would like to help his business by introducing a wider range of vegetables to his public. She could possibly even arrange a receipt book for him. The story that I got, via two white ladies whom I overheard, my mother, and Long One, who knew her gardener, was that his face turned to black ice, the reds of his eyelids swelled up, and he spat out three words: No. Never. Goodbye. He refused to sell her anything for a month.

When he did finally come to our back door, it had been raining all day. I was probably in my bedroom doing an impossibly hard jigsaw puzzle of a Swiss mountain scene in the snow – the type where all the pieces look the same. He asked for the *picannini muzungu*. With his face a sullen tombstone, he asked me if I knew the name of the mask. This delighted me – he had obviously been thinking of me a lot. Oh yes, I said, it is *Kateya*. Oh, he said – rather it was a high-pitched African 'aaeeeehy' of surprise rather than a European 'oh' of nonchalance. He left without saying another word, and reverted to selling my mother vegetables through Long One as a go-between on the street. Much later, I wondered if his ancestors had forced him to ask me that question – at the time I could see he was uncomfortable. The other white ladies on the street were amazed and envious as to how my mother could keep this overbearing character away from her back door, yet still receive his bounty of tasty treats.

But as Africa would have it, things continued changing. He started appearing at our back door; not often but when he did he stayed longer at our house than at any other – of that I was sure. He never demanded to see my mother, and she continued to receive her excellent vegetables via Long One. Wilson continued to avoid him, being a Matabele – an offshoot of the Zulus – he did not believe in forgiveness. This repellent vegetable seller was talking to me, and I was talking to him; we were talking about *things* together.

I never got to know his proper name, but that didn't matter. He was a member of the *Luvale* people of the Western side of Northern Rhodesia, far away on the Angolan border. The source of his outstanding vegetables was also never discussed. I was not interested in knowing anyway. In my child's wisdom I knew that the subject of fresh vegetables and personal names was not on terra firma. The most talked about vegetable seller in Luanshya became my friend. He told me about the Luvale customs, and gave me the names of other mythical figures that the compere of the tribal dance performances at the Ndola Agricultural Show hadn't mentioned.

Vegetable sellers were notorious for, every now and then, disappearing for weeks at a time. Usually it was as a result of a debilitating hangover because of an illicit *katchasu,* moonshine, brew gone wrong, which was followed by a visit to a witchdoctor *kuchana,* far away; then an imaginary state of malaria, which eventually, in long African time, and with two aspirins from the *medem,* would be cured. Disappearing was my new friend's quirk too, but unlike the other sellers, he always had a stand in: a shy young Luvale with a petroleum jellied shiny face, who never smiled and never said a word – except for giving a price – but was never impolite. He sold wooden spoons near the *Boma,* the District Offices, when my friend was back in town. His spoons were for the African market – they were big spatula spoons for stirring maize meal porridge. I mischievously imagined the 'do-gooder' suggesting he make wooden knives and forks to go with the spoons to triple his sales, and the young man giving a silent, 'No. Never. Goodbye.'

One day I described my hawkish Luvale friend and his strange ways to the old diviner. With eyebrows raised, he said he was a Likishi, a member of a Makishi dance clan; known wanderers who were often found far from their homes at certain times. Why hadn't I thought about that myself? Of course, it was so clear. 'Local Africans call them shape shifters because they can disappear and reappear in different places – like the hyena,' he said. I could not control the pulse at my temples as it started to beat a drum solo as powerful as a heralding in of the Scottish pipers at a military tattoo. This was a revelation beyond my wildest dreams – the old diviner's words explained everything about him. The old diviner said to me that next time I saw him, I should make sure that no one else could hear, and call him Likishi, and see how he reacted. If he should show no reaction whatsoever, it meant that he was a Likishi, a secret Makishi dancer.

The Makishi were bound by their ancestors to respect anyone who showed spiritual wisdom. In my heart I already knew the truth. I did, however, do as the old diviner had told me. One day, Long One, bored of my repeated questioning about the Makishi, wandered off briefly to the PK, the *picannini kaya*, the small room – the toilet. I looked into the man's face and called him Likishi. Likishi's eyes held their sting; his face remained as fearfully impassive as always, and he said nothing out of line of our normal chitchat. Wow! I had uncovered his truth. From then on Likishi and I met often at the back door – when he wasn't AWOL that is. Wilson, wearing a heavy yoke of obligation, made forced appearances, always throwing unapproving glances as he made some excuse to come out of the house. Whether it was to check on the damp clothes on the washing line, or to empty the already empty bin, or polish the shiny brasses of the nearest window – he was always around. Long One did the same. He always found some tediously long task to do in the nearest flowerbed. In African time they both gave up on trying to chaperone an odd white boy in Africa. Or perhaps they couldn't stomach the stinging glances that Likishi always threw their way. On some days you could feel the sprays of venom that his eyes ejected on others, but never towards me.

The old diviner forewarned me of one of Likishi's longer absences some time before it happened. In my child's mind, if a diviner could tell that water, unseen by anyone else, was sitting under the ground, it was logical that he should know about the movements and whereabouts of important people too. Between Likishi, the tatty tribal dance booklet and the Afrikaans water diviner, I had built up a fabric of knowledge. It was an aethereal story made up of the weft of Likishi, and the warp of the old diviner – divergent explanations of the same Makishi truth. I started to add to this complex weave with my child's imagination in an attempt to predict what was going to happen next.

The old diviner said Likishi would be making a number of 'shortish' disappearances from August up until the beginning of November, starting about a week before the Ndola show. In time Likishi indicated that the young Luvale would be selling his vegetables for a while because he had something important to do. The young Luvale couldn't be grilled as to Likishi's whereabouts because he couldn't speak English, but he appeared to be keyed up, as if something important was about to happen. It was about that time that posters in the town were announcing the opening of the Ndola show, and the old diviner asked me if Likishi had indeed disappeared. He seemed upbeat about my affirmative answer, but wouldn't comment further – except for saying 'my parents would be taking me to the Ndola show, wouldn't they?' My mind was grappling with intriguing insights that flew at me like rose beetles in the night.

As far as I could tell, everyone on the Copperbelt went to the Ndola Agricultural Show. There were army parades, air force displays; the police band, horse jumping events, agricultural displays, and lots of prize farm animals.

For me however, the best thing at the Ndola Agricultural show was the tribal dancing, and the Makishi were there every year. The old diviner had told me that their customs, masks and dress were unique to the world. The Makishi dancers' bodies were completely covered by costumes made of crotched bark twine that was dyed red, black and white. They wore huge grimaced masks with dreadlocks that completely covered their heads and shoulders. I had gotten used to seeing Likishi, and so I could easily identify his posture and his mannerisms. Yes, there he was; Chikuza, the strict dance instructor, and I was sure he saw me too – there were not many white people in the crowd, and no white children as far as I could see. I was delighted to recognise him, but he ignored me. Then Munguli, the evil hyena came on, and Likishi and the other dancers moved to the side with the fierce Utenu pretending to beat the crowds back. When the young slender Mwanapwevo had finished balancing on a high slack rope between two dangerously thin swaying poles, the original dancers moved back into the centre of the dance arena. I looked at Chikuza but something strange had happened; it was his mask, but not his body: this one had much thicker legs, larger buttocks and a paunch. No one had left the dance area – so what on earth had happened? I searched to find him among the other performers, but his body form was not there, and it certainly hadn't slipped into the crowd as far as I could tell. I spent the rest of the afternoon confused as to what I had seen, and what I had not seen. From my pillow that night my child's logic came into play. I had witnessed Makishi shape shifting; perhaps I was the only person in the uninitiated crowd who could have pinpointed such a rare happening. My knees curled up to my chest as I was carried off by a Makishi dance troupe for further subconscious musing.

The next time I saw the old diviner I told him what had happened and he gave a dry lipped smile. I did finally find out his name – Oom Geert Oberholzer – but I preferred the title of the old diviner, the name given to him by the geological prig.

All he said to me was, 'That's what they do at the *mukanda* to confuse the villagers.' '*Mukanda*, what's that?' I asked. 'Likishi might be away again at the end of October, as there might be a *mukanda* this year,' he said. 'A *mukanda* is a month long circumcision camp where young boys, your age...' I interrupted. 'My age?' Young people always think their age, no matter what it is, makes them immune to anything untoward,'... are introduced to manhood with circumcision, and given lessons in dance, culture; sexuality and family responsibilities.' My mind was flying again; all those bush paths with ragged strips of red cloth tagged to knotted elephant grass at junctions in a bush path. So that's what they were – circumcision camps. I had an inkling that they led to somewhere no good. As if he could read my thoughts – why couldn't he – the old diviner said, 'you needn't worry, the *mukanda* happens far away from Luanshya in Luvale Province five hundred miles to the west.'

'How will he get there?' – What a stupid question! – I already knew the answer. My mind was now reeling with the thought of shape shifting and hyena antics. 'Nobody knows these things. Nobody even knows who the Likishi are – except this time, maybe you and me,' he said. Gosh that made me feel so proud, so special.

Over time he told me everything he knew about the Makishi. He had worked near Balovale, a small town in the Luvale Province for a short time, water divining for a Catholic Mission station. He said that he greatly admired Catholic priests because they made the effort to speak the local language and get to know everything about the local people and their traditions – they did not just preach their own religious doctrine. Because he showed an interest in the Luvale people, the Italian priests had told him everything they knew about Makishi traditions. Some of the things he told me were awful, but he said they were important if I was to learn about Likishi. I was so lucky to know the old diviner.

Likishi was gone for the month of October, and the silent young man returned to grace our table with the best vegies in town. I now had so much respect for this young man who had obviously once been a *mukanda* initiate. He had been painfully circumcised in the bush, his wound dabbed with a witchdoctor's poultice of clay and herbs. He had slept naked tied spread-eagled to the posts of his pen at night. He had been drilled until he grasped the finer concepts of dance and culture, and educated in the intricacies of manhood and the right choice of a future wife. In a different way to the Zanzibari boy, he had also arrived at the door of his self-awareness: the young Zanzibari, through inward polishing of his Soul in a small Arab shop; this young Makishi through retracing his strong tribal roots in dance and secretive folklore in a remote forest clearing.

Now I knew what Likishi was doing, and I knew how he got back to his roots, his rural home so far away. He was a shape shifter. Like a hyena, he could bring himself to the centre of his bubble of timelessness at will. He could reintroduce himself to the world of his intentions – all outside of time and space. His Soul could have resided in Balovale, transmitting his body to Luanshya and back whenever it was needed – or it could have been the other way around. Who knows? I felt it would be inappropriate to ever ask. A bigger question that weighed upon my mind was why did he even bother to sell vegetables to white people in a small Copperbelt town so far from his home? His presence in both places was obviously needed but was there any spiritual design of importance in our relationship. Our bush paths had crossed for a short grown-up time – for an eternity in my child's time, and hopefully for a Likishi's time too. They certainly needn't have – but they did – *things* just were. In my

ponderings at the time, I decided that because his healthy roots
bore deep down into the Balovale soil, his Soul was sated without me. I was thus the sole benefactor in our relationship – he
was a 'meant to be' in my life. On further musings, much later,
I saw things differently. In true Makishi fashion, in the donning
of a bark weave persona, the dancer himself was not important.
That his shape had shifted was of no importance either. In the
theatre of the Universe, there would be many Likishi, many
Chikuza in the timeline of humanity; each one of them the
only player at the centre of his 'Now' clearing. Life and death,
shape shifting – they were the same *thing* – it was just that shape
shifting was less perceptible to a human eye that is in denial of
miracles.

I really wanted to tell Mr Kumar that I knew a proper guru
who could shift his presence, but I never did. In the spiritual
world, pointing a finger at a revelation is rude.

One myopic Saturday afternoon on the lawn, when the light
was bright, and the heat too close to my Soul, I picked up on a
break in the clouds. It was a round patch of clear blue sky that
moved like the focused sights of a telescope. The clouds continued drifting across the sky, taking the patch with: The sun appeared in the patch, and blinded my vision. I still saw the shape
of that break in the clouds on the backs of my eyelids, and in
the middle of it I saw the clearing. It was hundreds of miles
from anywhere. It was late afternoon, and the colours of the
setting sun were drunk on the mellow sounds of weary village
life at the end of a dusty day. There was the final swish of a win-
nower's basket, the explosive spit of a dollop of steaming maize

porridge falling into the fire; the slow clunk of enamel plates in preparation of an evening meal of *nshima* and pumpkin leaves. Suddenly the Makishi entered the clearing. With high-pitched voices, and feigned anger, they forewarned the mothers that they were coming back very soon to collect their boys for the *mukanda*. The scene had been set; some people had already been theatrically beaten by the Makishi on the road leading to the clearing as a warning to the village folk of the serious-ness of the upcoming *mukanda*. No one could escape involve-ment in the most important event of the year. These Makishi were taken seriously by the people of the clearing. They knew that the human contents of these masked costumes had slept in their tribal burial grounds; they had allowed the spirits of their ancestors to enter their flesh and bones – to take possession of their minds for this auspicious happening for the Makishi people. These bearers of ancestral spirits were the ceremonial dancers who had taken on the honoured task of preparing the young men of the area to embrace the timeless presence of the Makishi culture in their lives. There was tension and nervous excitement in the clearing as lots of beer and food would have to be prepared by the womenfolk; if for no other reason than to take their minds off what they knew would soon happen.

I saw the Likishi storm the terrified clearing, separating the boys from their mothers with exaggerated force. The boys in skimp loincloths were dragged off crying to the circumci-sion camp, while some Makishi remained in the village, rough-ly pushing mothers and sisters into their windowless huts in feigned anger. They screeched and shouted as they beat the mud walls of the huts with sticks so that the womenfolk couldn't hear the frightened screaming of the abducted young boys. I heard Likishi's voice.

The afternoon sun started to fall into a faraway Angolan sea, but still I saw everything; the whole scene portrayed on the membranous surround screen of my closed eyelids. I saw it on the far edge of my inner clearing. My inner darkness was dressed as the Makishi as they forcibly entered my conscious awareness. The same ghostly arms of the Msasa trees leaned out to grab me. The same hungry flames that had gobbled up an October vlei raged towards me. I saw the silent leopard as it padded the far-distant boundary of the remote clearing. The hyena lay in wait in an aethereal nothingness heavily pregnant with the sinister possibility of his re-birth. In their hearts the women and sisters sang to the boys and the boys sang back to them from their secret, maybe even imaginary, camp; hidden somewhere in the suffocating forest on the other side of the clearing. It looked like my Luanshya clearing. I thought I saw Pegasus on the tree line.

The *mukanda* was now in progress. The secret proceedings would be for Makishi eyes only – and yet how strange that I was there too. The tension ran high on my inner clearing. My fingers took grip of a stubble of lawn.

In the dead of the night, the hyena came and sniffed at the walls of a hut where a village elder was lying. There was no need for the hyena to remain; the elder's Soul had turned death away. The leopard made his silent patrol among the huts: He saw what he had to see and he left. His felt presence was received as a blessing – his all-seeing eye had sanctioned the *mukanda*. The ancestors, the bush and its people were one. The collective psyche of the tribe was now to be once again augmented and reinforced by their ancestors through the drawing of fresh blood and the sexual mutilation of their novitiates. They were ready and waiting to be inducted into the tribe through ritual, folklore and dance. This was a truly auspicious occasion in the happenings of the Makishi.

On that close Luanshya Saturday afternoon, lying on the itchy grass, the days and weeks went by. Then it was over – no more terrifying visits from Utenu and Mwendumba, who had for days after the initial abduction continued to pressurise and beat villagers for no earthly reason other than to show that the Makishi were omnipotent and above man. The tension was punctured by the lion Ndumba, who arrived at the edge of the clearing. He was the most fearsome of the Makishi. He roared as he shook his bark woven persona and blood caked dread-locks to prove his almighty power. His arrival was the harbinger of change. The next morning, the dark fear that had the bush clearing and its people in its powerful grip, finally had its back broken by a chilling dawn. The prospect of a brand new era in the lives of the Makishi was heralded in. Fear's tight hold on the people of the clearing had died. The *mukanda* was nearly over, but there was still a cautious chill in the air. In nervous anticipation of a final and necessary conclusion, a fresh and very large batch of *katchasu* and sorghum beer had been brewed in the preceding nights, and lots of food had been prepared. I saw it, smelled it and tasted it. I felt it all outside the boundaries of time and space, and all within my inner clearing. My body had allowed stagnant pools of blood to gather at the back of my calves, bum and back; the synaptic chords of my spine had been overplayed. My musculature had lost its integrity – I was numb – and I couldn't move. I had experienced a cataclysm of the mind, and my body was struggling to deal with it.

The village boys re-entered the clearing as enlightened young men. I saw Chikuza, and in him, I saw Likishi. The sight of him returned life to my limp body. For days, I watched the boys perform dance routines and express the mythology of their tribe in songs and animated stories. It was the last day of the ceremony – a collective subconscious had been borrowed and shared. It was now to be rightfully returned to its custodians, the ancestral dead who were becoming increasingly impatient in the burial grounds. The *mukanda* was over.

With my spiritual eye focused on the backdrop of my subconscious awareness, I had extended the boundaries of my inner clearing way beyond Luanshya, to as far away as Balovale in the North Western Province. I had ripped open the amniotic sack of my white subtribe of Africa: I had escaped to a clearing beyond my plausible ken and far beyond my belief. A numb feeling of reverent oneness crept over me as I lay on the lawn. I wanted for nothing. I had ingested a timeless lifeline, and I was full.

Luanshya nighttime, and the quiet hum of her magical wings no longer emanated from her alone – what I could hear in my bed was the primordial hum of a creative universe. It was an aethereal undertone that carried the creative messages of every living thing; be it a social evening at the MOTH Club, a Makishi ritual in Balovale, or the death of an animal on the vlei. The same intrinsic message was sent out to us all to interpret according to our need and call. It was a repeated message of unavoidable perfection. For a perfect universe to unfold, we all had to do what we had to do. We each had our own footprint to follow, our personal affinities to be met and nurtured. The old diviner, the Makishi, the Zanzibari boy, the Bemba fisherman, the missionary, my parents, the robber and me – a born meddler and peddler of spiritual wares. We all had a role to play, not just for our own benefit, but for the benefit of each other. My leopard could not exist without me, nor could I exist without him. We were all entangled in each others gossamer threads of purpose and perfection.

The synchronicity of our well-worn bush paths could not be ignored. I was just child lucky that my moments of serendipity did bump into each other and danced a *pas de deux*: to such a degree that they became a cross-referenced, cross-cultural, and lifelong philosophy of musings.

I had witnessed the far away *mukanda* on my suburban front lawn – I didn't have to physically travel to observe it – it came to me. Those seductive bush paths that seemingly led me into the beckoning unknown; those irresistible callings that tugged at my sensitivities – perhaps they weren't going the other way – they were coming to me. I had longingly assumed that paths and affinities were always leading away from where I was – going to somewhere exciting where I wanted and needed to be. Perhaps, they were bringing different worlds like the *mukanda* to present themselves to me. I had always felt that bush paths were urging me to follow them. Perhaps they were the all-time paths of omnipotent Titans who were making a lumbering effort to come to me? A simple white boy in Africa; to openly present themselves before my bleary spiritual eye as a humble lesson in a shared common oneness? How much clearer could their message be? After all, they had enraptured my Soul from the beginning. It was I who had assumed separateness, when they had espoused a familiar oneness. I was sweating over my out-of-reach cravings, wanting sensual finality with them, when in fact, they just were, without end – an enormous power that just was, and of which I was already a part. Our relationship did not need to be consummated if we were one. What more of them did I want to see if that was all there was? The shapes of my spiritual giants would always be tattooed on the inside of me. This was how the Zanzibari boy and the leopard saw things in their timeless worlds. Was the footprint of my Soul walking away from me or towards me?

Maybe I did not need to find my Rosetta Stone if the whole of the Universe was colluding to educate me in its ways of synchrodestiny. A perfect world was unavoidably rolling at my feet: I wanted it to, was happy for it to – it had to. My affinities were nothing more than the sensual calling cards of a Universe unfolding before me on my earth journey in material time. I had heard its undertones calling me. I mistook them to be emotional signposts pointing to another vlei, different shallow waters – a strange beast or a new 'different skinned' friend: but in fact they were inferences of a wide world within me. A world that needed my indiscriminate conscious awareness for it to briefly crystallise into reality. My sensuality was the viewfinder of my spirituality.

Of this absolute truth, of which there was no question, it seemed as if I was still not certain. I still seemed to be desperately searching for something. My affinities, like eager dogs waiting for their master to take them for a walk, continued to cavort around the heels of my sensitivities. They pulled at the leash of my self-control in an attempt to satisfy their sensuous longings for more – more in the urgent 'Now' time of my curious little white boy's wantings. Was this then not my role on the centre stage of my inner clearing?

I was to play who I was meant to be: an intemperate earth traveller on a Soul journey. Without my upbeat sensitivities how would the universe be able to reflect upon its giddy self?

Truth on the vlei

Because things were still building up, there were days when I thought that the magic of the anthill on the vlei was not getting me anywhere fast enough. The dry-throated anguish that still raked my searching would have to be quenched if I was to ever see my Soul. Spiritual freedom seemed to be on my subconscious child's mind most days, and I was too young to carve logical sense out of my existence.

I had to find a fix that took into account my ballooning differences from others. Spiritual suicide, whereby I would become an upstanding Luanshyaite, had crossed my mind on more than a few occasions. It seemed a politically correct and easy option. All the tools were at my disposal: confirmation classes at the Anglican Church, age-grouped fishing competitions at Makoma Dam, discos with tipsy parental supervision and extra cricket lessons. Run of the mill boy activities, which would culminate with English-styled boarding school in Southern Rhodesia or South Africa. Yes, that would do the trick nicely. My spirit, embalmed in Brylcreem, would be placed in a lead coffin. The eulogy would be an announcement of team members for next Tuesday's cricket match against the Hindu school in Ndola without me. The music played as they flung my coffin into Tartarus would be a rousing rendition of Elgar's Pomp and Circumstance Marches. There would be no one at the graveside. In spite of the lead-lined coffin, there would still be a sticky inhuman seepage – the spiritually contagious consequences of that could be fatal. Spiritual suicide was like slitting your wrists slowly in a warm bath as Handel's Water Music quietly strums in the background. It seems to be an easy way out, but it seldom works without a silent pain that goes on forever into eternity. I couldn't do it.

I even contemplated physical suicide, purely to spite my spirit which seemed to flaunt my physical importance in such a careless manner. In what I thought was an abuse of my physical assets, my spirit won. It announced that it needed the biological mobility of a mind and body if it was to get to reconfirm its thoughts about a world that it already knew.

Instead, I became a spiritually shackled lone ranger, a prisoner of inner circumstance where my Soul was hooked on playing hide-and-seek. There were times when all my mind really wanted to do was to be like the other boys: ever changing pop music, jokes, supposed girlfriends, and an urgent desire to climb the skills ladder of school sports teams.

I seemed to be too sensitive for normality – as if I had an extra sense of perception that was 'touchy'. The more egocentric I became in trying to contain my sensibilities, the more they increased their intensity, and the more I suffered. Both my parents and I found my behaviour hard to deal with at times.

Like Camus' character Mersault, in The Stranger; while I rebuffed my society and its values in a cold-hearted way, life was one endless landscape of emotional colour: and yet I couldn't seem to hook my feelings onto anything within the logical hierarchy and sequence of my Luanshya growing up. In fact they seemed to be determined by events of different times on different paths. It was as if they were an emotional script written for a particular scenario and I was on centre stage in the wrong production – the spotlights highlighting my error in blinding pain.

According to Peter, the psychologist to be, the African bush was a pleasantly evocative symbol that stood for no more than youthful happiness in my life. Should I not now do my homework, pass exams, go to university in the UK, relax into early manhood, drink a self-satisfied beer or two and conceitedly pat silly little boys on the head? One day you will understand sonny, I would tell them all – oh yeah sure! Grown-ups could be so insensitive to things sometimes. No, I definitely didn't want to be like that. Peter was right in one way: The vlei with its anthill citadel, and the Makoma waters were not to be idolised. They were my allies, valuable members of the spiritual confederacy – my league of affinities that flew the flag of my Soul purpose.

Words on the vlei

If I had asked the vlei to help me find my Soul purpose, my truth, she would have replied in watery gurgles, and grassy swishes. She would have announced that her role was nothing but an observer of repeated present moments of magic in an endless sea of timelessness. In what could have been seen as a contradiction in terms, she would have continued that she was a timeless state of conscious awareness that forever moved on. How could she move on if there was no time? What on earth could she have meant by that nonsense? She often talked to me in riddles.

She would have explained that besides her rough physicality, she had an aethereal presence. It was a full awareness of her each and every present moment as it appeared on her horizon. African things happened all the time on her wide open spaces, in her dark creases and muddy folds: They happened in the hurried immediacy of her flora and fauna moments – to which she purposely did not attach the labels of time. She observed them all with an aethereal eye outside of time because she was not at all interested in their urgent storylines. They only led to consequences of pointless sentiment, she would have said. Her mechanics were centred on being in a space so small that it was almost a non-space. It was the space between every one of her present 'Now' moments; not unlike the space between breaths, or the space between thoughts. It was from this free-spirited position that she could view her time bound events from a time-less point of view. That's where she would see their 'Now' truth. Her awareness was above being magic, and thus was beyond any sleight of hand tricks that I had seen in her valley. It was of a far higher realm than the dubious ways of the shifty hyena.

So what did this mean in relation to my request for the truth? I would have become impatient with her around the bushes talk. She would have once again said that her unfettered from time and space awareness was of great use in seeing things in their true light.

'So how could I get some of this aether magic then?' I would have asked her in a rather forward manner.

When the vlei laughed it was the staccato cackle of a noisy flock of francolin, which would start unexpectedly and stop just as abruptly.

'How could she help me find my truth?' she would have said with the cool air of regained composure. A gentle breeze was wistfully thinking of leaving its sodden river quarters for the dangerously hot high ground on her edge. How could she help? The air would have been sucked back, as if she needed to hold on to her cool breath. I heard the whirring clack of locust legs, and her breath would have unavoidably escaped her swampy clutches with a cormorant's hiss.

In her haughty manner she would have continued. The non-space between the endless present moments of her eternal life was both the birth place, and the resting place, of each and every one of her 'Now' moments. Where else could they come from or go back to, she would have demanded with impatience.

It housed the mechanics, of not just the last, present or the next moment – it was the spiritual backdrop for the collective unfolding of all African bush moments. Where life and death were neatly written in the symbolic scheme of things. The death of a duiker by a hunter's gun on the vlei was nothing more than the re-enactment of a spiritual story without end. That it was death by a gun, and not by a leopard's claw, was materially immaterial. Oh how she loved conundrums.

'How could she help?' she would have mused with the torpid plod of a black-headed heron wading through her shallows. 'Well it all depended on where I felt my Soul should be,' she would have said, with a sudden plop of words, as the heron speared a hapless frog. 'Should it be on the 'this side' of the Luanshya clearing, the easy side, where a pleasantly predictable mortality will fulfil its role? Where one's lifeline would be long and straight, often tediously straight, but comfortable in its guaranteed finiteness.' A mud chilled gust, a half yawn, spilled across a piece of her open ground taking an old broken tumbleweed with it. I would have thought I had heard her mumble under her lazy breath, as to how pointless our conversation was becoming.

'Or should it be' – she would have hesitated for a moment, as the heron retracted its snake-like neck, as if to attack another frog. Instead it flew off in a show of black edged wings, to roost in a eucalyptus tree on her hairline. This one, a dead one, with a couple of cormorants perched on it, was a barnacled shipwreck – white bird pooh covered the skeletal branches of its rotted mainframe. It would have looked particularly desolate far from its antipodal home on that African day.

Visibly enjoying the drama that she had managed to put into our tête-à-tête she continued, 'Or should it be on the far side of the clearing? Where death is never quite where it should be. Where mortal reason loses control, where the Soul wilfully defies both physical and spiritual gravity as it pushes all boundaries to find its purpose – all the while, pulling further away from its source.' With the whirring of an agitated guinea fowl, she would have blurted out more. 'A most exciting life of perpetual unknowns and narrow escapes – but a dangerous one. Where fear and death are your ill-fitting accomplices, and the Gods are sought after and embraced, screamed at, and rejected. A place only for the youthful warrior, whose divine perfection is tempered by either arrogance or dedication.' When she had got this out she would have been breathless, and the hot sun would have taken advantage of the still moment to further bake the clays of her embankments.

She would have then given an enormous sigh. 'Or should one be in the middle of the clearing?' A strong gust of wind, warmed by her toasted flesh, made the Msasa trees on her hairline shudder in singed memory of October bushfires. There would have been a further long sigh as her long grasses and bowing reeds were rubbed together by a wind whose wide berth took up the whole valley – 'now that is the question.' She would have seemed so satisfied to reach this point in our conversation, that she would have sat back in her armchair of surrounding miombo woodlands and mused. I would've waited patiently. I felt that there was something interesting scurrying through her mind and in her reed beds. I wanted to see what it was.

What she would have been telling me would have been in symbols and riddles that related specifically to me. I might have needed my Rosetta Stone. My fingers would have fumbled deep into my pocket. My imagination would have been there:

illusively sharp and angular in its all knowingness. I was ready for her to continue.

If I wanted my Soul to be in the middle of the clearing, she would have continued, I would have to pay dearly: if that's what I really wanted. The rewards would be great, but in her opinion at too great a cost for most mortals. It was a place where my physical being could find its true worth. It was a place where everyone would view me in the light of my perfection and power only, but I would view myself in lonely seclusion. Could that possibly be my father, I thought to myself. The high expectations of others, she said, like a swarm of bees, would sting me into submission of their wants. They would force me to follow a tortuous path of repeated successes and failures, watching me rejoice and suffer, she said. Everyone wants to see the winner they have been looking for in vain, and the loser with whom to share their pain. She also told me that it was a constant battle to keep the centre of a clearing free from the overhanging branches of confusion and self-recrimination.

A wind devil flew up and spun across the same piece of open ground. It took dry leaves and dust with it. It seemed that she was now so keen on telling me more that she had become a bit tongue tied and overexcited.

She drew on another riverine breath. As an arch dame of geomancy, or was it necromancy, she prophesied that she knew all about me – she had watched me in that non-space between my many present moments. She had followed my two sets of footprints that were leading to both my inner and outer clearings. The two journeys of your one being are so intertwined that you don't have a choice but to follow them both, do you? The footprint that leads to your outer clearing tells me about where you are coming from, and where you want to go to. The footprint that leads to your inner clearing is not interested in its origin nor its destination; it is only interested in the aethereal power of your intent, the quality of your purpose. Her words were spat out and punctuated by exploding Msasa pods as they ejected their seed. 'Most mortals find double paths difficult to follow – they are full of contradictions.' I could see she was now becoming impatient as the sun beat down upon her brow. 'Most mortals choose the path of least resistance,' she muttered. 'They forsake the needs of their Soul and tread the well-trodden earth path of the many. Whereas the Soul, given the chance, chooses a path unknown to all.'

By now there was a storm cloud on her horizon. She was irritated. Dusty sweat smears were drying on my sticky body in the accumulated heats of her afternoon – things were becoming irksome for us both. I wouldn't want to show her my growing restlessness. I wouldn't have wanted to upset her in any way; so I sat there as quietly as I could.

I crouched African style on the anthill in lazy anticipation of her next word, however long that might take. My impatience would have slipped comfortably away – grain by grain, each moment melting in the sands of African non-time.

I didn't notice a chameleon on a low hanging branch: a big one, with an armour-plated head and satyr horn bobbles growing above its swivelling eyes. Its long tongue was curled into its soft dewlap. The chameleon caught my attention because it had changed its colour and was swaying back and forward. Its one eye had spotted a kill on its doubled vision horizon as its other eye stared at me. I measured the time of execution by the bulge of its tongue as it writhed like a snake in a bag in anticipation of a release and strike. In that moment of pregnant anticipation, the vlei rashly took me into her confidence. The chameleon struck: and the vlei launched herself back into my unfolding search for the truth.

She said that my story was all about the curious unearthing of a place in the bush where the penchants of my Soul ran free. Where self-discovery and my conscious awareness of things were growing. She said that I was a high-spirited speck of self-awareness: and I was being blown about in the aethereal dusts of the clearing by fortuitous circumstances. With the heavy wing-slap of a dove from a fig tree, she launched into my story unforetold: It appeared that my journey might be speeding up – but then again, not necessarily so, she squawked. The chances of my acquainting myself with the far side before attempting to conquer the centre of the clearing were slim – in spite of my prized collection of serendipities, she said – it was a natural state of affairs – I should not take it personally: it was just how things were. She could see that the urge within me to reach out to my affinities was an irresistible addiction, but addictions meant nothing to her. Whether my affinities took me backwards or forwards didn't matter either, she said – directions were pointless when it came to happenings outside of linear time.

As if to negate her prediction, in the ponderous tone of a bush shrike, she also felt that her advice was as stale as the muds of her reed beds. She had a hunch that I might have already visited the other side without anyone noticing, which she found intriguing. Had my shape shifting to Balovale escaped her attention? She would have continued: 'Whether you want to be on the 'this side' or the 'that side' or even 'inside' is a question of your intent. When you cast your intentions into the in-between world of things, that mysterious place where your breath finds seed, your purpose becomes a matter of Soul perception – material standpoints of the self and of others are of little importance,' she said.

She reiterated that the mechanics of finding my purpose, lay not in the every moment of my curious days on the vlei. It lay in the aether space that connected each of these moments. It was in this non-space that the mechanics of my world lay – not in the materialised magic and miracles that I was revelling in. I had to hook my spiritual eye into the diaphanous threads of nothingness that bound all things. That 'in-between' space was the substrate for my reality. 'It is where your truth will unfold,' she said.

I heard the sound of disdain on her dusty breath when she said, 'For most mortals there seems no connection between random events in an ordinary day. They see no connection be- tween the death of a sparrow hawk, and a poor November rain. I do. That's because I view all time bound events in a floating sea of connected timelessness. I see the connection between you and your Soul; you and your tribe; you and your father. It is in the footprint of your one Soul that I can see it all. I see an awareness that speaks to your mind and body of worlds beyond your current experience. It communicates with you through the urgency of your affinities. In its ever-fresh permanence, it connects and furthers your relationship with everything that is. It is the safeguard that removes you from the danger of empty nothingness, and leads you to the fullness of everything.'

'The crazy thing is,' she continued, 'that the truth that you are chasing, is actually chasing you. It is hunting you down – and you don't even know it! It is wanting contact – it is closing in.

'Is it your death that I see in my timeless folds – or is it your spiritual rebirth? Oh I always get the two confused.' A loud babbler cackle burst out of the Msasa trees on her hairline. So loud and infectious was it that the miombo woodlands broke first: a leaf trembling nervous giggle, followed by a July wind guffaw, and then, abruptly, a self-conscious silence. It was a deep forest silence; perhaps the trees had realised that they had missed the point of her black humour. She was laughing no more. She was dead serious about my search for the truth.

The rest of what she had to say, as clouds hid the sun and reduced the glare, came in bittersweet truths and emotional nuances of an unravelling sadness within me, and I became entangled in threads of lingering regret. My mind, without prompt, dropped the 'I' of its avid inquiry. It picked up on the life of the man who deserved my unconditional love and attention. My father. He was the iconic seed of my Soul searching. My quest had been pushed aside, and his purpose brought into full view. Was it his Rosetta Stone that I was now rubbing in my pocket? What shifting magic had the vlei cast upon our sands?

My enquiring mind, seeking the truth about myself under the grand tutelage of Madam Vlei, had taken a leap from my story into that of my father's. In seeking my Soul's worth, I was seeking a spiritual reunion with my father's Soul, our one Soul.

On the surface it appeared that my father and I had drifted apart: but that was not possible. The vibrancy of my affinities, my frustrations, my quirks, my love and my sensuality: everything about me made sense if I wrapped them around my love for him. Our Souls were one. We were one with our ancestors of an enigmatic bygone world and we carried its print outside of time and space. In the spiritual safe haven of my mother's nurturing love, our one Soul had meiotically expanded into two, and in my familial time would split into four and so on, into an unfathomable eternity of spiritual inheritances. It seemed that although consequence had taken us on separate paths, I was still seeking affirmation of our hidden entrainment, our 'oneness'. There were many stories that our Souls shared: this one being the story of our apparent estrangement. One day, perhaps another will rest its wings to drink from our one forest pool of spiritual inquiry and love.

I truly loved my father. I now fully understood his suffering. He had found it impossible to demarcate the boundaries of both his inner and outer clearings. His Soul, overwhelmed by the accolades given by his followers, was at a loss; too weak to lay down its own terms. He was crying out for attention, but the wrong attention kept turning up. This was the worst possible state for a true spirit warrior to be in.

We shared the same penchants of a one Soul, but our time lined physicalities were the cause of our drift. I was a child doodling in the sand of my clearing. He was an adult cajoled into playing superhero with an addictive social commitment. We saw the same spiritual rainbows that arched across our one Luanshya sky. If we couldn't see our one purpose, it was because society's tall trees got in the way of our common horizon.

The final word on the vlei
I had been on the anthill on the vlei all afternoon. It was now late; I had to get back for my bath. Late afternoon light is made up of an aching familiarity that imbues your heart with kindred

oneness. All of the warm sensations of the day lazily roll themselves into a one feeling of satisfied joy. The sun doesn't cast its brash reflection on glossy leaves anymore; instead, its light shines through them to reveal three dimensional shades of beryl green. It doesn't bounce off the water in razor blitzes of white light; it reinforces the soft curve of each oiled ripple as they mirror the subdued colours of a leafy watercourse and its mudded banks. It steals the deep forest dapple and strews it as amber corn onto exhausted open ground. Homeward-bound time, edged in late afternoon light, made me happy.

I reached Cerberus' gate moments before a cool damp rose up from shadowed reed beds: I hurried away in retreat from the rapidly changing vlei. It folded its grasses, trees, river bends and murky seeps into the owlish wings of a draping dark. In a show of complicity, a little ditty fell from her reeded lips. Somewhere from within her riverine expanses came the melodious rising call of a Hueglin's robin. It's up to you, it's up-to-you, up to you; its call rose up into the evening air with a sharp final crescendo. I was smiling at her cheekiness. I knew what I had to do, and I felt Madam Vlei was smiling at me in agreement. When I turned round she was gone; Africa did not believe in sentimental twilights. I ran home as fast as I could to escape long limbed shadows that could easily outrun me.

I see further – celestial rain

So Hum – rains of truth

Cosseted in gratitude for the indigo rain that had brought him inner sight, So Hum was not surprised when a new rain showered down upon him in his dream. He had been intuitively expecting it. This jewelled rain was from the highest heavens. It was of the diaphanous blue crystals of celestite. They tasted so pure on his tongue that they cleansed it for life. No longer would he be tongue tied or tell an untruth. If he could ever talk that is.

Their crystal clarity split So Hum down his middle. They gave him the spiritual knowledge to see the two sides of all things. He could simultaneously see right and wrong, truth and untruth. The beauty of truth became his obsession. Though he might never be literate in a world where he couldn't see or hear the truth, he could feel it – his emotional literacy and intuition were sharpened. Truth was no longer a mantraed muse. He felt it as a state of being beyond beauty; it was of the highest inner wisdom, and he bowed down to it.

Ah Hum's roots – I see

At this stage of his life, Ah Hum did not need soothsayers or divination. He used the intuitive powers that swirled within him.

Inner magic on a material plane

In this state of inner knowingness choice was an unnecessary faculty of being. Should he have ever needed to, he would have instinctively reached out for:

Angelite and celestite minerals and angelica seed oil: *that would purge his being in preparation for spiritual awareness.*
Sodalite and benzoin gum: *as preparation for his spiritual journeys in prayer and meditation.*

Truth lies in that space between thoughts, words, and
deeds... Is that also where my observer stands?

> Mr Kumar's guru
> Stones from a dry riverbed
> Carnelian worry beads
> Karnataka journey

Mr Kumar's guru

Mr Kumar's tailor shop was in the second class trading area of
Luanshya town, on the other side of the railway line. I used to
go to his shop with my father when he was having fittings for
a suit; or if he was buying chappals – heavy Indian leather san-
dals; or if I was having a fitting for jodhpurs.

Mr Kumar was a kind man, and was easy to talk to. On
our arrival, he would turn down the music on his Pye radiogram. He liked listening to high-pitched singing broadcast
from India. He also liked to chat to my father and me about
the Far East. My father would stand patiently, arms akimbo, as
Mr Kumar diligently chalked, tucked and pinned the material
of his suit to the contours of his body. I would have ample time
to nosy around his shop, feeling the gilt and silver grey statues
of Hindu gods, sniffing incense, and ogling trinketry for sale
under a cracked, cello taped together, glass counter. If I arrived
in in a bad mood, which I sometimes did, his shop would inevitably cheer me up.

My attention, in particular, was drawn to a gaudy poster
on the far wall of his shop. It had an ochre background with a
scrawl of Indian writing across the bottom. On the poster was
a bald-looking man with a burnt orange cloth wrapped around

his chest and over one shoulder, leaving the other fleshy shoulder bare. There was a large daub of orange paint on his forehead and wooden beads, ending in a red tassel, hung around his neck. I felt his large bovine eyes roved the room to find me wherever I stood – he did not, however, frighten me in any way. There was a small shelf below the poster on which an agarabatti stick smouldered in a filigree incense holder. Pinned around the poster was a fresh garland of African marigolds. Another hung around the neck of a statue of Ganesh, the benevolent Hindu god with an elephant's head and many arms, which guarded the door of Mr Kumar's shop. I knew those hardy drought resistant flowers well. They had an intense bitter-green perfume. The old diviner told me how to use a related plant, the khaki bos as an insect repellent in the bush. In Mr Kumar's 'little India' they had taken on another meaning, a meaning of spiritual colour.

Above the Indian poster was a picture of President Kaunda, the newly elected first president of independent Zambia; formerly Northern Rhodesia. He was wearing a collarless Mau Tse Tung suit and a red hankie in his pocket. Next to him was a shiny copper plaque of the God Shiva, who looked femininely beautiful – but also very fierce with his trident spear. Next to them both was a wall calendar from Patel's, the Indian grocery store, and a school calendar. This eclectic placing of objects, pictures and faces always captured my interest, and I couldn't help but stare at it every time one of us went for a fitting. On each visit the flowers were fresh, and an incense stick unfurled its perfumed wisp of smoke into the small shop, which also smelled of all the different types of cloth. Suit material smelt of rich camphor and naphthalene, silk lining smelt of prawn crackers, and cheap calico of dry flour and rice.

Mr Kumar noticed my fascination for what he called his shrine. When my father left me with Mr Kumar to do errands for the MOTH Club, Mr Kumar and I would chat about things for quite a while.

Mr Kumar told me that the poster announced the visit of an Indian holy man, a guru, albeit a junior guru, who had arrived a year or two before. What was a holy man? Was he like a god? I asked. 'No. He was a simple man who had given himself to God,' he said. He told me that this holy man was a Brahman, the highest caste in India, and that he had nothing: no wife, no children, not even a pair of trousers or a shirt. He spent his life either sitting still in peace, or travelling the world to give a recipe for peace to others. In my mind he seemed very different to the Anglican rector who had a house, a car, a miserable wife, three small children, and two overweight Jack Russell terriers. When he travelled it was for himself and his family. He put his dogs in the kennels and went off to England to see his relatives, or to South Africa for beach holidays. Mr Kumar told me that some gurus went into the snow-capped Himalayas of India to sit and think for months at a time, eating only nuts and honey. I couldn't imagine the rector ever doing that, and if he ever did, his wife would surely leave him. He said that some gurus even sat cross-legged and naked in the snow and ice to find the truth.

He also told me that gurus were able to swop pain and frustration for peace and happiness. Just like the Indian fakir at the Ndola Agricultural Show that August, who had walked across burning coals with a peaceful smile. The fakir carried out this amazing feat for the shallow amusement of the white folk and to the shocked amazement of the black audience – who were blown away by an uncanny tampering with reality. Who were the civilised ones to be able to look into the depths of an event that shook my child's sense of reality? Not the white grown-ups. A dishevelled looking little Indian man was showing us how to swap pain for happiness, and it was for free! I felt that the African audience had fully understood how to walk on fire, but that their tribal roots would forbid them to ever try – that was the spiritual prerogative for the witchdoctor elite.

In showing my curiosity for the guru and the fakir, this was not the first, nor the second time, that Mr Kumar had both noticed and bolstered this white child's fascination for worlds beyond his own. He would quietly nod his head sideways whenever we met, as if he was pondering what to do next with my overly inquisitive, albeit, sometimes peeved presence of arrival. Gradually these nods became a pre-emption of stories to come; new spiritual anecdotes about Indian people and their customs. I was enraptured in the sensual exotics of it all. Ivory and silver filigreed palanquins for princesses, Maharaja sandstone palaces, festivals of a million oil lamps, tattooed albino elephants, sandalwood funeral pyres, fierce Rajput warriors in rhinoceros skin armour, wretched untouchables and frail Himalayan gurus. Like a trace of patchouli incense that strokes the senses, his stories egged my curiosity into wanting to experience more of everything heady and unknown.

One day my father left me with Mr Kumar for a good while. Unbeknown to me, he was making final plans for the building of my yellow canoe. Mr Kumar told me he had noticed that I was sometimes in an unhappy mood when I first arrived, and asked why that could be. This pleasantly surprised me, as although I always thought he was kind, this direct question about my persona meant that he was interested in me. On that particular occasion I arrived in a particularly bad mood. He took great pains to explain 'tings' which could be useful to me. Because of his interest in me, my mood softened, and I listened in respect and full attention; although he had made me feel a tad uncomfortable to start with. I also felt that the guru's Brahman eyes were now fixed on every surface of my being. The spiritual truths that he handed to me on that day, and other days afterwards – when I arrived as a peeved little sod, and left as guru's novitiate: as far as a silly little white boy was capable of – became engrained in my subconscious awareness forever. Although to be truthful, after our first chat about 'tings', by dinner and bedtime my easily bewitched mind was back to thinking about heavy night rains and the release of their macabre jetsam on anthills.

Mr Kumar said how I was feeling and what emotions I was expressing on a particular day, was a measure of how far my mind was from the workings of my Soul. He told me that my Soul, which was housed in my heart, was to be treated like a priceless gem. In a serious tone, he said 'To see its true beauty, you have to polish it like a precious stone.'

Mr Kumar had hit a soft spot in my psyche. I had a strong passion for stones, and searched for them wherever I went. When adults thought I was being moody with my head down at outdoor events, I was often looking for stones – sometimes being moody too. When I was disrespectfully kicking up dust, I was breaking the surface to find new mineral riches below, possibly a tad peeved. Amenity departments all over Africa would bring in river sand to level foundations of buildings and roads. Often amazing pebbles of river tumbled jasper, chalcedony, agate and more, could be found lying around in the oddest, and most ordinary of places. I once found a deep purple amethyst crystal in the dusts of the Gymkhana Club car park.

Mr Kumar told me that the way I behaved today, the simple actions of my 'Now' world would affect my future forevers. 'When you are kind to others, you will give off a beautiful light which will light up your tomorrow. Gurus call this polishing the Soul to reflect the divine. We all give off a light because we are made of light,' he said, all the while talking with tailor's pins held between his lips. He said that the most dangerous thing that people had inside them, worse than bacterial infections and parasites like bilharzia, were uncaring thoughts. You will not find happiness in their murky light, he said. His head did a slight sideways bob as he said, 'Loving kindness has power and beauty, but its importance is overlooked when we are too busy to care about each other. Humans who show loving kindness to others are in a state of grace. They give off the light of love.' Mr Kumar's words seemed to surprise him, as if they weren't his. For a moment or two he fell silent; his eyes seemed larger than normal, and they began to water. A faint smile came to his soft purple lips, he gave a long sigh, and his gaze crossed to the maize meal wholesalers on the other side the street. He took a long breath, and with careful words, he said, 'I see grace in your father's eyes. If you want to find happiness, look into your father's eyes and introduce yourself to his Soul. It wants to share its light with you.'

Many years later I was given a book before boarding a London bound plane. I was making the journey to console my father on the death of my mother. It was *The Seven Spiritual Laws of Success* by Deepak Chopra. I read it through the night: I read about my affinities, about grace; I read about life and love. I read the truth about my father. When I buckled up for the final descent, and the plane took on its shuddering change of circumstances in time and space – so did mine. I saw them all: Mr Kumar, the old diviner and Likishi, the night robber and the missionary, the Zanzibari boy and the leopard – in those few moments before touchdown, they might have told me, without words, that we were all on a spiritual journey of the senses: On my earth bound journey, the pain that I was feeling, was actually my conscious awareness cautiously finding its way in love. 'Get over yourself boy,' the vlei might have said – 'It's no big deal!'

Refractions of inner light – conscious awareness

Conscious awareness is a state of grace, a spiritual wisdom that prevents us from falling into unthinking self-centred behaviour and ignorance.

Conscious awareness requires that we look at every situation with equanimity, and with a high degree of empathy for all.

Conscious awareness colours our world with beauty and love.

Conscious awareness is seeing the light, the light of mankind of which we are only one refracted ray with a Soul purpose.

Conscious awareness is the sensual recognition in a material world that we are all one – we are all the spirit of love.

Stones from a dry riverbed

My growing conscious-awareness, with a nudge from Mr Kumar, compelled me to sand and polish my affinities as a lapidarist does to a rough agate pebble from a dry riverbed. He intends to look beyond the diffracted light of its opaque and pitted crust. He wants to release the primordial swirls of the earth's creative energies, and with refractions of light he exposes its bands of crystalline colour. When polishing my child persona, there was always the remote possibility that, in a flash of conscious aware-ness, I might catch a fleeting glance of my truth.

At that same bar, bed and breakfast hotel for wizened old white men, where I had met the wise crocodile hunter, I also met an old prospector who took me down to the riverbed one day to search for agates and other semi-precious stones. Among the basalt rocks we found a small sandbank with more pebbles than sand, and I returned to the hotel with my pockets bulging and my floppy sun hat loaded with promised treasures; prom-ised because they looked like nothing more than lumps of hard earth: but my mind was pummelled by the impatient thoughts of what rainbow colours these little dull brown beasts would release with a grind and a polish.

Back in Luanshya my father took them to a geologist friend on the mine who tumbled them for me, and what a collection of bonbons it was when they came back wrapped up in pink toilet paper in a Bata shoebox. Much later my father told me that he thought the man had added more than one or two specialties himself. There were agates, feldspars, chalcedonies and more, with every permutation of coloured pattern possible: banded caramel with dollops of clotted cream, curdled milk puddings with smudge lines of treacle, raspberry fools with burnt sugar edgings. I was very lucky to be in an area full of minerals and kind geologists who parted with their special stones so freely.

I was especially fascinated by translucent stones: iolite water sapphires, carnelians and beryls. I could see into them, but they made sure never to reveal their deepest light secrets to me. My favourite stones were the carnelians. They took on more of a polish than all the other stones. With my eyes closed, I could pick out my carnelians by touch because they had a smooth tactile depth to them. The geologist told me that this was because they were made up of millions of microcrystals that lay like the fibres of rich silk. They created a three dimensional translucence of fine crystalline pathways that crossed their centres with endless rays of reflected light. Although their surfaces shone like glass they led my gaze deeper: past speckled impurities of iron, through orange rainbows to where I was mesmerised by shimmers of trapped light at their core. Because of their boundless depths of refraction, I felt carnelians possessed timelessness. Like amber, the petrified resins of the dinosaur era, they held on to history more than the other stones in my prized collection. They stored snapshots of bygone worlds that endlessly bounced off the walls of their silica labyrinths to give them their translucence. Like stars, they gave off a light outside the boundaries of time.

Carnelian worry beads

I was surprised when one day Mr Kumar took out what looked like a very small necklace with overly large beads. He was troubled by one of the sleeves of my father's suit which was not hanging right. As he took a step back, he was fiddling with the necklace in his left hand, rubbing the beads with his pin-nimble

fingers. He saw me staring at the necklace. 'Vorry beads,' nodding his head sideways with coy embarrassment. 'I am vorried
about this arm you see,' he said in his inimitable Bombay Welsh
accent. 'Carnelians,' I said.

'Vhot?' he said. Those beads are carnelian stones, I said,
and after that, he let me rub them every time we went for fittings. They were not new; they had seen and housed an awful
lot of historical imagery – after all, what is new to a stone taken
out of an aboriginal earth? In human terms, they had, however,
been owned by someone else before him, and before them, and
before them – so Mr Kumar said. They housed the memories in
hidden light images of ancient Indian epics and deities – I was
sure of that.

I enjoyed talking to Mr Kumar so much, listening to his
stories and rubbing these wonderful orange stones during our
fittings. He told me he had bought them from a Parsi devo-
tee of Zarathustra in Bombay during the Second World War.
Parsis, he told me, were not true Indians. They were a lost race
of Persians who had possibly arrived in India around the 8th
century. He told me that they worshipped light, and one sect
in Bombay carried little lights down deep wells into the earth,
leaving them on narrow ledges all the way down. He also told
me that they didn't bury their dead. They had a special place in
Bombay where vultures came to strip the bones of their flesh.
I was enchanted by it all. I wished I had been born a Parsi in
India. Mr Kumar's story reminded me of an occasion during
our holiday in Zanzibar. I had seen an Indian man with eyes
like murky moonstones. I found it strange, and when I asked
my father about it, he said he was probably a Parsi who may
have inherited his eye colour from Alexander the Great. Mr

Kumar said that he might have been right about the man being a Parsi – but for the rest he was 'spinning a yarn.' I liked Mr Kumar because used funny English expressions.

As a budding novitiate of sentience in a material world, I had the strong desire to imbibe everything that was exotically different, and not of my own, nor of my tribe's making. I was searching for the sensual truth. I wanted to be in sensory harmony with the objects and ideas of my immediate attention in a 'like attracts like' energetic resonance. I wanted to osmotically suck up anything and everything that was attractive to my boy-child imagination. I needed to hurl the heated magma of my emotional being on 'like' objects and situations of my world as if we were both in search of a reunion of a one Soul. I was a driven addict of my affinities. The vlei and its anthill wanted me, the Makoma waters called me – I was not the instigator of my affinities nor of my sensuality. My desires were not a child-ish game of shallow connivance. My affinities and their circumstances threw themselves upon me, and I welcomed them. They were the dance master of my Soul. It was all a lot deeper than sweet and casual serendipity.

The Universe had spewed up a dollop of spiritual larva – that was me. All it wanted to do was resonate in repetitive harmony with energies of the same spiritual stuff: be it the vlei, the first rains, Mr Kumar's India, the anthill, an invisible leopard, a semi-precious stone, or a particular person. The uncanny thing was that my emotional state would oscillate with a 'like' synchronicity so intensely familiar, that it enflamed my heart and Soul with sweet remembrance. So powerful was this remembrance that it blurred my reality like the October heat waves off the asphalt road to Ndola. So powerful was it, that my body and its five senses were disrupted, dismissed, and replaced by a sixth sense of perception – a fresh state of conscious awareness; a knowingness that hurt in a sensually pleasant way.

'I like to rub my vorry beads because they help me see tings clearer,' Mr Kumar said.

Karnataka journey

I was twenty, alone and a part-time spiritual bounty hunter in a crowded public bus when it was brought to a halt in the Indian state of Karnataka. A rambunctious religious procession had blocked the road with its heady fervour. The inherited subconscious of the devotees that I saw at my window, and the common aether informational field that had birthed them over centuries, had today been pierced, and access had been granted. Like gate-crashers at a Bollywood movie wedding, these high-spirited folk stormed into their inherited subconscious. Vivid colours, incense, amulets, mantras, loud music, and garish pictures of Hindu deities bore witness to their ancient roots. They could expect no peace of mind in the 'Now'; they were captivated. It wasn't just tradition handed down that caused them to behave with such passion. They were like exiles catching sight of their fatherland after having been banished for an eternity. They behaved recklessly odd, oblivious to the traffic, bystanders, holy cows and each other. They were revelling in a life throb outside of the time frame of their current living.

I could see bliss in their eyes and I could smell their humanity as they pressed their attar-scented bodies against my window. I felt their intensity and at the same time a swell of familiarity tugged, then surged at my temples – the novelty of it was gone, and I found myself in breathless compliance with these overexcited devotees. My logic lost its balance and my senses began to hyperventilate in a surreal world of Asian worship. A déjà vu 'ness spread over my being like a lover's perfume and I felt deeply moved. As a sensual being in search of my Soul, my senses had been abducted by the kinetic energy of these Hindu zealots. They beckoned, and my spirit had willingly followed: In that crowded bus I became impassioned; I was one with their chant.

My sense of comportment seemed narcotically adrift when I was snatched out of my religious experience. Stripped naked of my time and place, I was dumped into the confused childhood of my African past. My fellow devotees were banished from view; my senses were no longer attached to the overloaded Tata bus. A trepid creature of frail awareness appeared from the back of my conscious being. It settled itself down in front of me within the image of a sodden witchdoctor's hut. It was the same hut near Luanshya that had proffered a portent of both dread and excitement to my childhood senses. Suddenly, like an offended apparition at a séance, it was gone.

The fearful trimmings of witchcraft in the African bush had my respect. It was not something taught to me: something else far greater had been my informant. Now the same unrehearsed emotional experience and its nuances of fear were repeating themselves on this Mumbai bound bus.

I felt queasy as my mind tripped and fell over the two psychic experiences. The one a religious extemporisation; the other a macabre exhumation of childhood fear. They were emotionally discordant and yet I felt they were somehow connected. It was as if they were two pieces of well-worn furniture, of a different use, but of the same house, now incongruously thrown together without any sense of common decency.

My reality had jumped its rails – my 'everything' was out of place. I spent the next hour on that journey struggling to deal with what had happened. My cold reality of a post-colonial young white man, who had recently completed both boarding school, and a stint of national service in an African bush war, had been blown out of the water by two seemingly unconnected but connected psychic events. The one was of needy uninhibited bliss, the other of addictively lewd repulsion. What had tipped the scales of my awareness of reality on that bus?

Refractions of inner light – A quantum leap

Quantum: 'In physics, the theory that energy transferences take place not continuously, but in bursts of a minimum quantity or quantum.'

Collins New English Dictionary. 1956 Edition.
(Happy birthday to Joe, with love Annie)

How much of a quantum was required for a conversion, a gathering of enough psychic material to generate not one, but two leaps of the spirit across the boundaries of time: devotional Indian time and fear-locked African time. How much of a quantum was required to throw me into the surrealism of different inner worlds?

When my mind came back to sit on the chivda oil stained seat of the bus it had received a snippet of directional information from my Soul. It was a scribble on my spiritual route map for me to follow.

The answers that I had been chasing on the Luanshya vlei were still hunting me down. Now they had caught up to me on an Indian bus: they were breathlessly telling me that what I was looking for – wasn't there...

The immensity of star light is not out there, it is in here.

Looking at the spirit-willing fellow passengers in the hulla-baloo, I was reminded of the mothers and daughters of the mukanda who saw beyond the inflicted terror of the Makishi. I smiled to the bus conductor, who was renting his lungs in Malayalam and English, telling people to get off in Poona 'NOW' even though the bus hadn't yet halted in a cloud of dust. He had been kind to me on the journey, and found me a non-existent seat. He gave me a Long One smile with his black coffee eyes. It was as if he, a stranger to me, knew my truth better than I, and I gave him a smile back. As a present moment speck of humanity he had played his part in the gestalt of my all-time conscious awareness, as did the Bemba fisherman and the night robber; all of whom I never held a conversation with, but were just as important as each other in explaining the circumferential truth about my timeline. The impression they each left on my Soul was a comfortable know-ingness that I was a small part of something bigger, and that like the quirky affinities that pressed themselves against my ever-curious being, they were proof of my 'oneness'. In one-ness I would never be lost or alone. A necessary attribute for an earth traveller to have.

Refractions of inner light – oneness

My Soul is not an insular bundle of energy,
It is one of countless oscillating waves that make
up the aethereal sea of humanity.

It is my spiritual destiny to unconditionally resonate within these spiritual waters.

When I hear them wash up against the shoreline of my being,

The familiar lapping sound that I can hear, is my homecoming.

7

I AM THAT I AM...
GOD CONSCIOUSNESS

AMETHYST MIST

AMETHYST MIST

So Hum – the seventh rain

Just when So Hum thought that he had climbed to the highest source of all truth, another rain-like substance percolated out of yet another dream. This time it didn't percolate down in resonance with the gravitational laws of the physical world. Instead it percolated up and outwards, in resonance with the spiritual laws of the Universe. In his dream, a heavenly mist arose from around and within him. It was an ever-expanding cloud of minute droplets of aether. They had no meniscal edges; they were simply shimmering effusions of rising lights. As they ascended into the sky, they shone with diamantine clarity, casting an amethyst penumbra upon him as they eclipsed the sun. They filled the air with the essences of frankincense and sandalwood. So Hum could neither slurp nor gobble up this scented mist. His jaws fell apart, and his long held breath left his body with the first sound his keloid lips had ever released: 'So haaaum'. It was a strange and haunting sound that reverberated endlessly around and through him. Its resonance found its way into and out of Ah Hum, his host's body; who found it so soothing, that he made a conscious decision to repeat *it to himself time and time again. 'So Hum,' his heart called from deep within him.*

Because of eons of slow chameleon growth, So Hum's host was not his original host, but that didn't matter. The same devotional words still echo in synchronised unison in mind and body throughout humanity in a universe without end. So Hum, Ah Hum… Amen.

So Hum had reached his seventh sense, full conscious awareness. He was in a state of selflessness knowingness without knowing why or for what. It was an unconditional devotion to a divinity that demanded nothing, and in return offered him nothing more than faith and trust.

It was then, from deep inside, that So Hum fully recognised the someone watching him, and he bowed his head in recognition, and never said another word – not just because he couldn't, or wouldn't; but because there was nothing further to say.

Ah Hum's roots – I am that I am

It was his Soul that spoke of the truth in his ear and said 'I am that I am'. He was in a state of knowing oneness with everything that was. His self-observance was his sixth sense; full awareness of the Observer at the edge of the clearing was his seventh sense. He was now in seventh heaven, the seventh faculty of perception, God consciousness.

> ### Inner magic on a material plane
> At this stage of his mortal life, Ah Hum wanted to silently rejoice in the presence of God. He turned to these stones and aromas for an acceptance of the divine:

Charoite and sandalwood: *to reinforce spiritual awareness through humble devotion and compassion.*

Amethyst and frankincense: symbols of divine union; *a realisation of the divine connection between the material and spiritual worlds.*

I see the observer watching me watching him watching me at the edge of my clearing.

> I am that I am
> A flood of stink bugs
> Dandelion spiders

I am that I am

There is someone beyond the edge of the Luanshya clearing. He is watching. He is always there, always watching. I can't say he is always watching me; maybe he is. Maybe his focus is narrowed in on me, as if I were the centre of his attention... but maybe I am not. Perhaps he is looking at the world through me.

This Someone and I have a straightforward symbiotic relationship. He doesn't exist if I don't, and I don't exist if he doesn't. I don't do anything for him and he doesn't do anything for me. We love each other dearly, but there is no fluxing human emotions of want or rejection to sully our heartfelt and unconditional love for each other.

Refractions of inner light – unconditional love

Unconditional: the state of cause and effect whereby a happening is neither affected by the past nor the future. It has escaped the threads of time-bound reasons for its being. Anything unconditional is in the state of the 'Now', a free zone in time, the only place where magic and miracles take place.

Unconditional love is a heartfelt expression of the miracle of oneness, a reunification of the mind and the body with the Soul. It is God's

greatest gift to man. It is his greatest miracle,
the only miracle – the rest are repeated reflections of the original light of true love.

He is an adjunct of my physical reality because although he is
of nowhere in particular, he is in my every present moment.
Without the abstract non-space that we create and share between us, there would be no magnetic power in our relationship. Our shared space is as powerful as that between protons
and electrons. Our distant but close relationship is our potential for being.

Whether he is or isn't watching me, or watching through
me, doesn't change his status. He is the Observer in my life. I
am conscious of his presence, therefore, in an abstract way, I
am also observing him. He is not only in the 'here and now'
of my mind, his presence is felt in the in-between non-space of
everything that is. I experience him through my subtle senses
of perception where ever I am.

If I were not a consciously aware being, I wouldn't see him,
or myself, or anything else. I would be a bag of unconsciously
selfish thought patterns. His non-space defined presence opens
up a subtle yet powerful all-enquiring, all-knowing facet of my
being. He is the only constant in my existence within an ever-
changing material reality.

Besides offering me the surrogacy of spiritual watchman,
he doesn't make me do anything, and I don't want him to do
anything for me – no favours. Conditional love would sour our
relationship. It is his silent presence alone that defines my conscious awareness, and sets my desires and intentions on a high.

Everything about me is consciously being observed, every
word and deed of mine is a noticed happening recorded by
me for him as a measure of our reality. What I call inner-me is

literally created out of him, watching me, watching him, watch me. My life, and my everyday world, as I see it, are the material consecration of the intimate relationship between the Observer and my Soul – a facet of which, is my conscious awareness of him and the aethereal reality that houses him.

If I were in my material world without taste, touch, sight, hearing and smell; my inner world would be divorced from my outer world. It is the same in the relationship that I have with my observer. Without him, I would not be a conscious witness to my existence. I would be a mere mortal without spiritual reflection. My subtle parts would not exist, and my physical and cognitive beings would be seriously maimed.

One could say he was my conscience – but he is not some icon of internal moral rhetoric trying to prove my guilt, reinforce my pride or defend my ego. He never judges me. He has no ulterior moral motive other than to be an unconditional presence – an omnipresence for my Soul.

I wish to keep space for him between my deeds and words. I want my Soul to keep up and be in harmony with him. If he is of the same space stuff of my Soul, which I am sure he is, by consequence of his observer status, I want to find the real truth behind my thoughts and actions. I want him to show me the footprint of my Soul. By observing on his behalf, I wish to align my purpose with the intra-cellular non-space that I call my being, that which I call the observed.

Refractions of inner light – the observer

It is he: the Observer
Without him, I would be unable to measure my
true worth.

His omnipotence is the catalytic spark that births the creative force that I am.

He is the aethereal power whose presence coalesces my spirit into the physical being that is me.

It is I: the Observed

I am not a singular linear self-contained happening. I am like a mote of dust in a swirling desert sandstorm, a minuscule reflection of a multi-faceted field of existence and creative expression.

I am a microcosm that unwittingly mirrors the vastness of the universal whole as my own small reality.

As small as I am, I am an integral part of an intense, non-localised field of creativity that is here, there and everywhere, all of the time.

When my small seeing eye observes the patterns of this quantum sandstorm of which I am part, I localise into my 'time and place' frame. The dust settles and my life takes form, but I am still of the non-stuff of a creative universe.

That is when my Soul energy will birth my kind: be it a rebirth of my own being or a new birth of a child, or an act of loving kindness unconditionally given.

My 'I am' is not limited by the physical boundary of my skin. The results of my thoughts and actions are far flung across time and space and he is there too. The phenomena and actions of others are not limited to their boundaries either. They affect my being, and he is there too.

The observed that I now muse upon is my life experience; out of which come my thoughts, words and deeds: these are the distillate of my hard-working Soul, who has worked tirelessly for him.

As an observer on his behalf, I am looking for the moment when my actions fully reflect the thoughts and feelings of my Soul, an emissary of this omnipresence in my life. The Observer.

A flood of stink bugs

It was one of those slow Saturday afternoons whose weekend excitement had been gagged by grown-up lassitude. I was flopped on the cool cement floor of our veranda listlessly polishing my Katanga cross. It was too hot, and the light too bright, to go to the vlei, or to even lie on the lawn and gaze up into the black magic of the clouds. They were brewing up a stinking hot November storm. It was a pity, because those were the skies that I loved, bruised clouds that continually changed their billowing shapes. A southerly air flow from Bechuanaland had buffeted their heavy-footed arrival from the North. It was a clash of the elements whose oppression had chased me indoors: There would be an electric storm that night. My lazy body sensed something in the thick air – a mucus floater in my left eye, followed by a cooling sensation on the eyelid, a twitch and then a blink – it was telling me that more than a storm was brewing. Something rustled past the poinsettias – there was a strong gust of wind. SWISH – it pressed itself against the mosquito gauze of our closed-in veranda.

There was another even stronger swish; a solid bank of air forced itself through the fine mesh of the gauze. PING, the first bug flew hard against the copper mosquito screen. Ping, and another, and another, then countless pings. On tiptoes, I pressed against the dusty mesh. Light green bugs the size of finger nails flew against the gauze in ever-increasing numbers, all with great speed and force. I stood there with my flattened nose against the gauze as this hail storm of insects got heavier and heavier. My senses were confused; the staccato pings were a continuous pulsating clamour; like an ill wind, they forced themselves through our slothful house. It rattled the psychological steel of our front door, our inept gauze windows, and our corrugated iron roof. My parents, disorientated from their afternoon nap, joined me. We stood there three as one in amazed silence. Our senses hovered between awe and fear. At its onset the bizarreness of it tickled my boy-curious senses, but soon the sheer immensity of it all unnerved me. In both sight and sound there seemed no end. If we looked past our immediate aggressors hurtling themselves against the copper mesh, which was difficult in itself, we could hardly see across the road. If we looked up into the sky, there was a thick mist of insects – all in northerly flight, flying as high as we could see. Every one of them had an internal compass and a command; a footprint that they had to follow.

The bugs came in opaline waves of sound that broke against our ill-prepared defences. Our Saturday afternoon had been stripped to its core – all forms of understanding and ordered sense had been erased by an alien presence. It was a rare phenomenon which, in spite of its surrealness, was demanding immediate recognition from the permanence of all things.

With their free flight thwarted by our house, the lower flying individuals, powered by Herculean effort, crawled through every crack and cranny available to them. They squeezed into the cracks in our ill-fitting window frames, swarmed through holes in the gauze, under the front door, and fell down our chimney. Watching countless iridescent scarabees moving though our house, all in the same direction, with a singular purpose, was unnerving. Their presence gave a high-pitched screech – a razor blade scoring on glass sound that severed our nerves and mutilated our structured awareness of the afternoon. When we recovered from our initial shock, we ran for brooms and dustpans to sweep up the invaders; we stuffed towels, tea cloths, and socks into every vulnerable crack and crevice to stem the ever-advancing flood of assailants.

We might have been repulsed if they had scurried around in a loosely opportunistic manner like scavenging cockroaches running up and down our legs and arms, but they didn't. Instead we were overcome by their militant need to head north. It was their intent that was so frightening.

When I thought they would never stop bombarding our house, the wind stopped and the flood faltered. Within five minutes, operations had completely ceased. As in the case of the flying ants, there were no stragglers, no soft waves of second thoughts.

If the sonic piercings of the actual attack were discomforting, then the deafening silence that followed was worse. Kerry, my terrier, lay in a corner of the darkest room, with his paws against his ears, whimpering – there was terror in his eyes. If vacuums can make noise then this was of the lowest decibel. The overpowering smell given off by these invaders, edged with the nauseating silence that enveloped us, issued foreboding within our senses. My mother left for the bathroom to be sick. Wilson said his *mwana*, his child, was crying and he had to go. My father and I stood there – we both just stood there.

We couldn't talk above the deafening silence. My father stared straight into my eyes. Never before had our psyches been as intertwined as they were in that uncanny present moment of the unknown. I heard him without words. We were communicating in the ancient hieroglyphic symbols of our one Soul. I did not need my Rosetta Stone – nor did he need his.

He seemed to have lost his way. His eyes were searching for our one truth in my eyes. They said that the silence was the same non-sound that follows the death of comrades in bloody battle; that envelopes the cruel execution of a prisoner of war; that witnesses the stillbirth of a child. His face was a limp piece of muslin, behind which irised shadow puppets played out a universal tragedy, of which his being was a small facet. A tragedy where youthful innocence, his, is hypnotised by its own exquisite glory and joie de vivre. A gossamer fine thread of bold existence to be severed in a brutal manner, never to be fully mended by the promises of a new beginning. Had the spirit of universal love deserted one of its most ardent and worthy devotees? For how long would Melpomene, the Muse of Tragedy, continue to twist events to suit her ultimate desire for a fateful outcome? Perhaps he saw this theatre of the Soul to be my spiritual inheritance. Perhaps it was this sad thought which had caused him to behave the way he did. This was not the first time I had seen fear in his eyes. It was his fear, but it was tired. Tired because he had been looking for all over Luanshya for his truth: all the while it was curled up inside him, a chrysalis pining for change. A flood of stink bugs had pushed him over the edge: pulled his focus off its fatal course, and pointed to a facet of our one Soul for an urgent answer.

No matter how purposeless it all seemed, it was not a story of blighted worth. My father's story was a rare sighting of a Soul in glorious full flight. He was truly loved by all. Perhaps my father was not seeing it that way – he had been too busy falling. Now trapped in the wreckage of an old soldier's body, his Soul was crying out; his mind and body were in need of help – would any kindred Soul answer his call? Like Echo the forest nymph, who had been fated to repeat Narcissus' every last word in un-fulfilled love, my father seemed destined to repeat his Asian pain in duty-bound soldiery love. The unconditional love of a free Soul seemed out of his reach.

Although we were of a one Soul outside of time and space: If I were a father, and he were my boy; I would have hugged him through the darkest Luanshya night, shown him the evening star, and given him the first ray of light of a hopeful new dawn.

In the aftermath of this auditory mayhem we picked up the pieces. The physical debris of crushed thorax, legs and stinky beetle juice were dealt with by my parents and I. Wilson's *mwana* was still crying uncontrollably, and we couldn't get the God-fearing Long One to leave his house. I really wanted his take on the event, but that would have to wait. I later got on my bicycle with no shoes, and Cheapie in my carrier basket. I cycled up and down the street for a quick post-event inspection. I felt the strong need to collect some of the spiritual bits and bobs that were strewn across our clearing. These identical looking, thinking, doing creatures had died in drifts along the edges of everything that they had crashed into: hedges, car wheels, tree trunks and houses. There wasn't a house in the street that hadn't been under their attack. It seemed that they were blind to objects in their way, but once grounded, had become small-minded creepy crawlies again, although still with a short-lived urge to head north.

I came across Long One in a street further up. His feedback was crucial in understanding what had happened. His bush telegraph of gardener to gardener information told me, us, that this wave of bugs had covered the town, but to all accounts, we were in the eye of the storm. Everyone had been frightened by the intense noise of their pinging arrival, but few had heard their post-departure silence. I imagined that every white grown-up was too busy tut-tutting about the mess with feigned indignation as they ordered their domestics around; the black folk too busy Bantu clicking in the wake of black magic. In one of my later musings, I realised that every race has a way of preventing their sensitivities from picking up on aethereal messages. In one way or another they filled their inner silences with noise – curses, orders, and chit chat. Mr Kumar once told me that a novitiate might tell God his life story, ask questions about it, and get no answer; whereas a guru will tell of nothing, ask for nothing, and get everything.

I was Mr Kumar's novitiate: Where had they come from? How long had they been traveling for? Where were they going to? How long would it take for them to get there? How many would finally get to where they were going, and what would they do when they got there? The answers were hard to find. Some might have said that this hexapod cataclysm was balancing out a deficient food chain, but it wasn't. This event was the opposite of a flying ant food fest – nothing seemed to want to eat them. There were a couple of decrepit Abdim's storks in funereal plod on Mrs. Gouws' front lawn. They looked down their long beaks of disdain at the whole affair with a vague and watery eye of slow disinterest. If anyone in the African bush could eat these distasteful beetles, it would have been these moth-eaten birds of cadaveric disrepute.

In later musings of my youth, I realised that the stink bugs, unlike the white ants, had no superior authority, no king or queen who would have had orchestrated everything from an earthen throne. A physical wave of a million African stink bugs was not magic on a material plane either. The stink bugs were driven purely by a common weighty intention. It was an archetypal collective purpose that their one mind had turned into their cognitive reality. Their physical journey was a coalescence of their intent. Their truth was more than individual eggs in a cocoon, or grubs in the soil – their collective truth was pointing to something 'greater' and their psyche wanted oneness with it. Individual existence was no longer an option. Outside of their 'Now' time and space, it had happened before and would happened again, and again.

The next day was an empty Sunday that offered no promises with its dripping gutters. The solid night rain had washed the town of scattered stinkbug carcasses, causing drains to choke in disgust, and had turned our gardens into a thick mud that was busy digesting the rest of the beetle bodies. Because of the soft rain that followed, I was only able to make a brief pedalled reconnaissance between showers, before I was whisked off to the MOTH Club for lunchtime drinks. For some unknown reason, my subtribe decided to sit in a large group in the hall, and not in the bar, and so we 'just-kids' milled aimlessly around them and their conversations. I overheard one of my father's know it all friends, still on the fringes of a hangover, say that hostilities had broken out to the north of us in the Kolwezi province of the Congo. 'It happened only last night. It was a nightmare. Innocent people raped and butchered, houses and shops looted – bloody dogs, Jesus they make you sick,' he said. I was reminded of the refugee Sunday; the grown-ups nodded in numb stoicism – the Congo rebellion was never far from our troubled thoughts. The table fell silent. What was there to say when fear was edging its way across the clearing in your direction? 'Not at all expected,' the man pontificated with a cold Castle lager beer in his tremulous hand. Droplets of heavy condensation were rolling in rivulets down the beer bottles and glasses; rain snaked down the gray window panes in a same miserable manner.

Of course it could be expected, you foolish man, I thought to myself. The simplest of things like a bug's wing can be caught up in the unfurling of the most important of things – Madam Vlei had taught me that. The same primordial swirl that had pulled on a nation of stink bugs, could have released venom in the dark hearts of African revolutionists. I had already been left in awe of a one God of good and evil. A God who blessed both crocodiles and bats, hyenas and termites: but I was unable to process a single thought as to why God had blessed stink bugs and Congolese murderers. I went to bed that night with the uncomfortable words 'Jesus, they make you sick' stuck in my jaundiced mind.

Dandelion spiders

A year or so later, I was cloud gazing and enjoying a Friday's promise of the weekend to come. The late afternoon light was playing games with fanciful reflections and shadows when it caught a silvered thread floating through the air. The sun was in my eyes, so I moved under the eaves of the house to see what it was. I could see countless strands of what appeared to be threads of spider webs that glistened and twirled above me. In synchronised uniformity they hung down with a gentle curve, like spinnakers on tiny airborne sailing boats. It was a brief sighting for as soon as the sun went behind a cloud, their reflection was gone, and they were no more. Long One was watering the canna bed with his usual Friday disinterest. He dropped the hose pipe, letting water gush away the top soil, and came up to me. *Kangera lo baas*, look at this, he said. He shoved out his large gardener's hand: he had a fine thread wrapped round his mud cracked fingers and in the middle of his calloused palm was a minute insect. He pointed upwards. *Naya baas, Eno lo sikelem ku denga!* – Loosely interpreted, something untoward has come out of the sky. Tiny spiders were floating invisibly on the Luanshya air above us. It was as if somewhere, an enormous mama arachnid dandelion had released her cargo of progeny to the wind, and was intent on having them blown above the town. It was a fleeting sight for few to see – perhaps this aerial flotilla was noticed by no one else but us.

Maiwe, Mother of God, Long One muttered, as he staggered off back to the bed of red and yellow cannas, his wet heals making rude noises as they plunged up and down in his rubber gumboots. His was the only comment of any significance on that lazy afternoon. The regatta, in keeping with the dignity of the sport, quietly sailed high over our heads, houses and hibiscus hedges and was gone, leaving nothing but wisps of faint curiosity in my mind; and one lonely commodore left to its fate in Long One's hands.

If Long One and I hadn't have seen the dandelion spiders, they wouldn't have existed. A million little spinnakered spiders sailing through the air. 'Never' – everyone would have said. That's how important we were in the bigger scheme of things. I also thought that Long One's penchant for weekend *dagga*, marijuana, was part of the bigger picture. By the next day he had forgotten all about what we had seen, and I selfishly never reminded him. I became the sole agent of coalescence in the life of a million arachnid sky pilots in 'my' sky. I really liked the idea of that.

It was almost as if a serene apparition had crossed my sight; and in so doing, it had placed a comfortable knowingness upon my chest – it was as if I had been expecting their arrival, and now I could relax. I had no inclination whatsoever to ask the usual 'who, what, why and when' questions: I did not see the need to resort to the gardener information network. I never told any other person about the dandelion spiders – not even the old diviner. I was content to let things be. The word and the world was mum. There was nothing more I wanted to know or tell. All the answers were inside me, should I ever need them – but probably never would. Unconditional knowingness, conscious awareness, love and peace – God consciousness.

LUANSHYA MUSINGS

After years of absence, I revisited my anthill on the Luanshya vlei. It wasn't there.

THE END

AH HUM

APPENDIX

Selected reading

A New Earth, Eckhart Tolle, Penguin Books; ISBN-13: 978-0-141-02759-3; ISBN-10: 0-141-02759-2.

Collected Poems and Plays of Rabindranath Tagore, Rupa & Co., New Delhi, ISBN 10: 8171677029; ISBN: 9788171677023.

L'Étranger, Albert Camus, Folioplus Classiques, ISBN -13: 978-2070306022; ISBN-10: 9782070306022.

Myths of Greece and Rome, Thomas Bullfinch, Penguin Books, ISBN 0-14-005643-2.

Power, Freedom and Grace, Deepak Chopra, Amber-Allen Publishing, ISBN-13: 978-1-878424-81-5; ISBN-10: 1-878424-81-5.

Rumi, compiled by Juliet Mabey, One world, ISBN 1-85168-215-5.

Synchrodestiny, Deepak Chopra, Random House, ISBN 1-8441-3221-8.

The Alchemist, Paulo Coelho, Harper Collins, ISBN 0-7225-3293-8.

The Power of Now, Eckhart Tolle, Namaste Publishing, ISBN 13: 9780968236406; ISBN: 0968236405.

The Seven Spiritual Laws of Success, Deepak Chopra, Transworld Publishers, ISBN 0-593-04083-x.

The Way of the Wizard, Deepak Chopra, Random House, ISBN 0-7126-0878-8.

Printed in Great Britain
by Amazon